Tracks to Exile

by Peter G. Williams

Magnum Press

This edition published in Australia in 2012 & 2014 by Magnum Press
PO Box 1477, West Leederville, Western Australia 6901.
www.pgwilliams.com.au

First published in Australia in 2006 by Bedouin Brothers Publishing.

Order this book from Amazon.com
Join Peter G Williams' Friends of Billy Peters Facebook page.

Tracks to Exile

ISBN: 978-0-9871485-0-6

Fiction

Managing editor: Christine Nagel, Christine Nagel Literary Services
Original cover artwork: Mike E. Unique Tattoos
Cover design: Sue Grey-Smith
Cover photo of author: Sanya Aksamja

Chapter 1

It's Been a Hard Day's Night

Old Blue Eyes crooned softly from the bedroom stereo telling a tale of few regrets, the lyrics merging with the rain tapping across the window on the cold Sydney night. Detective Sergeant Bill Peters heard but didn't register the intertwining melodies of Sinatra and nature. He was deep into his own experience, which involved being not quite so deep into the New South Wales Police Commissioner's wife, as she moaned and whispered under, and moistly around, him.

Shit! How did this happen? Too late now mate, concentrate, boy, concentrate. "Ahh, but I've got to admit," Yin commented to Yang, "for an old tart, Mrs Italiano is a beautiful lover. She must be what, 55? Italiano's near 60, the lucky old bastard," he thought. "Now wait on let's do the sums, so she's what? Shit, when I was in nappies she was 29! Help me, I'm in the clutches of a Peters-phile!"

Id to ego: "Jesus, what a policeman. What a man you are, Peters. Tasked with security at the Commissioner's house, and now going well below and beyond the call of duty". Oh well, it was she who asked him in from the cold night as he greeted her arrival back at the mansion. The dutiful wife back from seeing old Franky off at Mascot on his way to a Police Commanders' conference in Melbourne. He had spoken to her often, but only ever briefly over the past 18 months. She was always the lady. A slightly sad class act.

He on his permanent night shift. Sometimes on the warmer Sydney nights, late, she would walk to the edge of the garden, and stand there looking across the dark harbour toward the bridge. Theirs was an elite Mosman address that housed the Commissioner and his lovely, lonely, tipsy wife. Bill would sometimes ask her if she was alright. She would thank him, want to talk to him, ask him if he was alright. Bold with liquor, she would hint that she knew about him, that the Commissioner had told her about "what had happened in New Zealand".

Tonight he had met her limo when it arrived at the end of the red gravel drive that swept up to the mansion's front entrance. He had opened the rear door for her, and nodded to the police driver, Hughes, in friendly recognition. He caught the warm whiff of musky French perfume and vodka as she breathed a soft greeting and thank you to him. As the car pulled away, he instinctively took her arm to steady her as her heels skidded on the drive. She asked him to join her for a coffee so that she wouldn't have to be alone. Inside, she told the butler, old Gerald, to "go to bed. It's after eleven". Gerald had partaken of the usual two to half-a-dozen tawny ports he allowed himself on the colder nights, and with a nod to Bill and a formal goodnight to "Madam", he swayed off to his quarters. They talked in the informal lounge while she made him a pungent espresso in a solid mug with "The Boss" on it. "One of Frank's," she said.

She decided against a coffee. As she sat him down in the lounge by the open fire, she helped herself to a small brandy from the bar, then sat across from him on the dark green velvet sofa. She asked him if he were lonely. The events of New Zealand only one-and-a-half years ago had resulted in his 'secondment' to the NSW Police until further notice, and the cushy number working permanent night shifts at the Commissioner's mansion. He didn't want to go into it with her. Not like this. He knew she meant well, and he was soft with her in his response. Embarrassed, she apologised for intruding.

"No," he said, "it's ok, I just don't like to think about it."
He noticed her beauty. Long lush dark hair to her shoulders, naturally streaked with grey. He noticed the darkest eyes, her

lusciously full lips, as she softly told him that she was lonely. He sympathised,"Well, the boss will be back tomorrow."

"No," she breathed, "I'm lonely even when he is here." She paused. "Especially when he is here. I shouldn't be bothering you with my problems."

"Oh no, it's fine," he said, and lied: "I didn't know." Others had told him the marriage was a sham. None of his concern, but he did like her and felt for her. After a few moments he stood and said, "I had better get back out there and earn my money." She stood to take the mug. Only petite, 5'4", he 6' plus, she came close in the dimmed light, took the mug, took his arm, hugged him, arms around him tight. Naturally he enclosed her into him in a comforting embrace, and then she lifted her face to him, and then goddamn it, she kissed him.

Those soft lips, the aroma of the brandy heated by her mouth. The tentative tongue flicking his lips, shyly exploring, then more boldly as the passion hit and mutual heartbeats accelerated. He realised the feeling of her body against his. The soft cushioning of her breasts against his chest as she lifted up into him, on her tiptoes, tilting into, against, his maleness. She held him, pulled away, but held his hand. Dropped the "boss" onto the carpet with a muffled thunk, and without resistance led him up the stairs to the bedroom. "Don't worry, Bill, he doesn't sleep in here," she whispered, as that mouth again covered his and he felt the solid Police buckle surrender. He felt the shirt being lifted out and buttons hurriedly near torn open, those elegant hands electrically inside his shirt, up his chest to the nipples, as she moaned into him.

Another fine mess you've got yourself into Costello. His hands slid up the flesh-warmed fabric of her dress to pull down the zip. Fingers spread inside the parted garment followed the goose-dimpling curve of her back down over the lacy bra strap. Down onto, under, into the lace of her panties, cupping in each hand each flesh-warm globe of her buttocks, and stroking, squeezing as she pulled him down on to the bed and lay over him. Raising herself into an anxious impatient feline crouch she peeled back the blue uniform trousers, flung the shoes off the bed, pulling down, tugging

3

off, his Donald Duck boxers. Standing then haloed in the pale moonlight from the window, she elegantly slipped out of her dress, bra off, heavy breasts swayed free. Panties silkily down and flicked away, then back into his impatient embrace with all her passionate softness. Those magic hands encircled, teased, pulled, and he with heart racing stroked, kissed, tongued as he tipped her off, over onto her back. Legs pushed gently apart by his as he, with forced patience, took over. Not the aggressor, but in control, and slowly teased and treated her with hand and soft swirling tongue until she moaned a deep and contented release.

And while she lay sighing, he arched and entered her silky grip, and slowed himself to allow her to recover, while he marvelled at the ever-amazing sensations, and tried hard not to come. She, revived, got back into it; she worked that smooth muscle to roll up and down in a fleshy squeeze that almost undid him. Oh shit … think Billy Boy, think, Mr Prime Minister, Mr Prime Minister, shit just in time, oh, wait on, not too much of the little fella, or I'll lose my little fella altogether.

She picked up the pace, she in control now, he helpless. Sinatra irritated from the left, her soft moans and wet tongue confused him from the right, flicking into his ear as her hands swept down his back and dug into the muscled knots of his arse, the pile driver, yee hah!

And then he felt it and didn't know how she did it.

A leathery embrace around his bag. "God that's good," he encouraged into her ear. Then a feeling of coldness like steel just above the tightening grip. "Not too hard darling, not too hard," he groaned as he felt her hands claw again up his back as she felt some tide rising within her. Wait just one fucking minute! Both her hands were digging into his back. Whose hand is that down at the docking bay?

He looked over his shoulder, suddenly oblivious to her grunted encouragement.

Oh shit!

There, standing at the end of the bed, was his boss, Mr Frank Italiano, NSW Commissioner of Police, and husband of very current

4

sexual partner. But also, crouched there at the bed's end, leaning
in toward him with one NSW Police-issue leather-gloved hand
encircling Bill's scrotum and contents, and the other holding and
forcing a cold circle of steel handcuff roughly around the back of
his thighs to capture the wayward nuts, was the boss's right hand
man, Detective Inspector Barney Hill. The most feared cop in
Sydney."Ok arsehole, put her in neutral, I'm going to tow ya out,"
gravel-growled the hulking, menacing figure of Hill, pulling the
cuffs backward.

"Oh fuck!" Bill grunted, shocked, totally vulnerable. Fight or
flight instincts kicked in, naked, nutted, back to the enemy and still
held tight by his oblivious lover as she moaned his name in her
orgasmic release.

Prick-o-deflato, sans orgasm, the survival reality abruptly
replaced the sexual urge, and his cock plopped from the lovely Mrs
Italiano. She, confused, unaware of the audience, assumed that her
energetic young lover was heading south to repeat the dose of tasting
and teasing, and kept her eyes closed and sighed appreciatively. But
then her husband spoke.

"*Slut.*"

She opened her eyes and, stifling a scream of horror, she clawed
in panic for the sheet.

"Listen, Boss, let me " His knees were now on the plush carpeted
pile and his body was bent over the end of the bed. "Shut the fuck
up, Peters!" snarled Hill, as the cold oil smell of the issue Glock
9 millimetre slid up along his right temple. "Both hands back,
behind!"

"Hey, wait on, this is a bit over the top," he protested. The pistol
butt slammed into the side of his face. Shocked, both hands back, he
said, "Ok, ok, I'll play your stupid game." Hill reached down behind
the bed and pulled free Bill's own set of handcuffs from the belt of
his discarded pants. In a more conventional police-type handcuffing
technique he then snapped that set around Bill's wrists. But then
Hill took the free open cuff of his own scrotally-engaged bangles,
pulled it back and up between Bill's thighs toward the cuffed wrists
like a steel g-string, and cruelly joined it to the chromed links of the

5

other set, in a icy metallic sado-masochistic daisy-chain connection. Mmmm, wrists to nuts: not one taught at the Police Academy, Bill thinks.

"Ok, out!" grunts Hill.

"What about some clothes, Sir?"

"Just get him the fuck out of here!" grated the Commissioner, and Hill pushed him forward and out, yanking enthusiastically at the cuffs to encourage forward movement. "Please Sir…" he says as he exits stage left, "it was all my fault," and then as Hill kicked the door closed behind he heard the first heavy slaps and muted desperate cries.

"Ok sir, I'm in the shit obviously," he said to Hill as, naked, he is forced down the dark stairwell. "But what's this all about? Am I under arrest? What for?" Silence. Thinking quickly, trying to reason, he says, "Listen. How about we start again, Sir. What's say you get this crap off me?"

"Shut up Peters," Hill just grunted. He marched him across the cold slate formal entrance into the side-door access to the large garage. There, Bill saw the Boss's official black LTD still tick-ticking cool after its return trip from the airport.

"We wait here." Hill sat him down on a chair at the pine workbench. Bare bum on cold wood. Bill carefully adjusted so that the cuffs didn't emasculate him. Hill reached into the mechanic's locker, took out a set of grey overalls, "Get these on." Pistol out again, one cuff off right wrist, disconnected from the second set, Bill got the overalls on, grateful. Hill re-locked the wrist cuff to the chair.

"Hey, Sir, what about these other cuffs?"

"Shut it, we wait."

Then heavy steps came down the stairwell into the garage. Commissioner Italiano. Not a big man 5'10. Slight build, almost elegant, a finely featured man. Roman face accentuated by a hooked nose and dark eagle eyes. Angry? No, fucking furious. Oh well, looks like maybe a bit of a bashing, Bill thinks. I'll cop it sweet.

"Well, Sir, what can I say? I am sorry," he offered. No reaction. Italiano nodded at Hill and the two men walked away, stood close by the door with heads together. Bill watched across the dark garage, Hill nodding, agreeing. Italiano glanced at him across the garage. They returned.

"Detective Sergeant Peters." Strangely calm.

"Sir?" Casually shitting himself.

"How long has this been going on with my wife?"

"Sir, I am sorry. This was the first time, the only time, Sir."

"Fuckin bullshit, Peters!" from Hill.

"No Sir. Just this one time, a mistake."

"What has my wife talked about to you Peters?"

A pause from all participants, Italiano encouraging, suspiciously friendly. "Listen man, all will be ok. I will get you back home to New Zealand, no black mark. Let's just all forget that this ever happened."

Talked about? Bill thought. Where was this leading? Where was Italiano coming from he wondered? "Sir, ah, only about herself. Nothing about you, Sir." The two again turned together to walk away, then Italiano stopped, swivelled back, "Wait here Detective Sergeant. Soon as we have cleared this up you will be released." The two left, the garage door slammed.

Time for quiet calm reflection.

Fuck! fuck! fuck! What's the time? A glance to the oval face of the garage wall clock, after 2am, damn it. The Commissioner's flight must have been cancelled, dirty weather the Melbourne end, maybe. Of all the dirty, stinking, rotten luck. "Ooh well, Billy Boy," he muttered aloud to the dark garage, "you play with fire my boy, you get burnt." Jesus! But ain't this equivalent to a raging bush fire and third-degree burns. Still, what could they do? He shifted uncomfortably with a clank from within the overalls. An internal Police charge? *Almost worth the charge I got going internal on the boss's wife, ha ha, what a fuckin comedian!* Probably shoot me back to good old NZ. His mind was racing as he settled down to wait. What are they doing, for fuck's sake? Must be organising his OC, Detective Inspector Charles, the officer in overall charge of security at the NSW Police facilities to come and get him. Shit, old Charley will give me a growling, that's for sure. But he's a good old sort, really. Looked after me this last 18 months after the transfer from the undercover operations in New Zealand.

Now there's another story.

Chapter 2

Memories

He was born an Army brat, right smack-bang in the middle of the North Island of New Zealand, tussock high country. His father, a career soldier, was based at the Waiorou Army Camp, not far from the pristine snow-chilled waters of the mighty aquatic heart of the island, Lake Taupo. A more isolated place within the tiny nation did not exist. The majestic volcanic peaks of the three ash-black mountains Ruapehu, Ngauruhoe and Tongariro crouched like silent sentinels in the barren landscape of the tundra, tipped white with snow in winter, exuding a foreboding presence, the periodic black breath of Ruapehue's volcanic sigh adding to the tension.

His father had fought for his country in the wars of other nations, in Asia, Africa, eastern Europe, as the young men of the proud but distant South Pacific colonial outpost valiantly supported far distant allies with a vague, often unrewarded loyalty, owed from those earlier days of dominion and the big wars. At the time of his birth, his father was a captain within the intelligence section of the country's elite Special Air Service regiment. He had led a secretive existence, often disappearing for weeks and months to far-flung never-mentioned theatres and returning distracted and silent.

His mother, much younger, was an artistic, academic soul, and suffered the restrictions and politics of the Army camp life poorly.

Her health suffered, and she compensated for the lack of fellow travellers by pouring her affections and energies into her small son. He was the only child she and his father were ever to produce.

The first five years of his life were spent in that bleak place. His memories, though, were sweet: days filled with love and warmth, the constant stimulus of the gifted young mother teaching and loving him, and him alone. The walks on crisp snow-carpeted mornings with his tiny gumboots crunching through layers of ice-cold crystals, as he staggered around the manicured plot, snug in handcrafted woollen beanie, tiny knitted mittens and lamb's wool jacket.

Then at five a wrench, as his father was transferred at the request of the Minister of Defence himself into the Diplomatic Corps. A reward, they told him, for his long and dedicated service and for wounds suffered both from bomb and bullet, and the incremental stress of survival and danger. He was asked to further serve the nation in a series of overseas postings as the officer-in-charge of the security of the tiny country's embassies in the outposts of the dangerous world.

A mish-mash of memories. Kampala Uganda from six to ten years, a life within the whitewashed walls of the diplomatic compound; his friends Americans, Swiss, French and the jet-black offspring of the Embassy's local employees.

Washington from ten to 14, just as the hormones began to rage. School days spent at an international junior college for diplomats' children, secure and guarded to protect them from the growing threat of international terrorism. His mother was much happier here, with access to art and music, and her enrolment at Washington University to complete her long-neglected Master of History degree. Again, he was buffered from the outside world by his father's membership of the diplomatic community. Teenage memories were of fleeting stolen kisses and tentative gropings of the budding breasts of precocious and well-developed American girls in his class. Memories also of awkward teenage exploration and lust/love of perfect young girls/women in steel-grid braces, and a seemingly permanent throbbing hard-on to distract from the monotony of academia.

Then, at 14, he was torn again from his peers, from normality, as his father was posted to Seoul, South Korea. Back into the bleak, the cold, the snow of that grey city, back into tension with the communist heavy to the north, hulking like the fuming silent volcanoes of his birthplace.

Again his mother suffered, yearning for her Washington friends. She sickened and after two unhappy years was sent back to Washington by his father to recover with those esoteric companions whom his father had tolerated but had never understood. She did not come back; she could not. She moved on to New York, to a job lecturing at NYU, and settled in that city. She spoke to him by phone, he 16, needing her, missing her. She told him she loved him, that it was not him, it was not even his father, it was *her* she needed back: her time stolen first by Army life, then by the service. Now he must be a good boy, he must stay with his father for the time being. She would arrange her life and then send for him. He must be patient. She needed to get well first. He must be patient. His father organised a local housekeeper, offered to send him back to a boarding college in New Zealand. He told his father no, he was happy enough, considering. He enjoyed school; he wanted to complete his university entrance exams with no further disruption. He had several close friends, he was old enough to look after and amuse himself. His father agreed to trial it for six months until the end of the school year and promised no decision would be taken without consultation.

He could cope. As an only child, he had developed a shell that protected him when torn from one place, torn from peer groups, from homes, from familiarity and thrown into new alien situations. Always the new kid, he had adapted before, he would adapt now, older than his years.

He was kept busy by parents of friends within the close-knit diplomatic community in the city. The sympathetic mothers clucking over him and loving him vicariously, shaking their heads and wondering how she could have left him, abandoned him.

There was his best mate, Geoffrey Bing, and his older sister Massie Bing, English diplomats' kids. She was a peach-skinned, blonde pommy princess. At 19, she was the assigned baby-sitter when he stayed with Geoff. She, naturally maternal in her affection, proffered feminine comforting hugs and sighs of "poor boy". He fell in love with this magical creature. The sweet smells and softness and cuddly woollen warmth was taken full advantage of by him. Shy but sly, he acted with testosterone-induced courage when Geoff fell asleep late one video session. Lying with her on the soft cushions of the sofa watching a video, she spooned into him lazy, sleepy, his arms around her comradely, like a brother. But then slowly, terrified, his heart so loud she must have heard it. Rubbing her shoulders, arms, back in a soft massage, she purring and writhing back into him, as cock guiltily stiffened and he thought she must feel the fleshy stab into her soft track-suited buttocks. She, stretching like a pussycat, sighing, he trying to pull his groin away while wanting desperately to grind the hardness into her soft cushion. He, shifting his arm, placing it around her just under the heavy softness of her breasts, holding her into him firm. Wanting more than life itself just to tell her then that he loved her, more than anything in the world. She apparently asleep, eyes closed, breathing heavy, deep, slow, but still her soft arse pushing back, he was sure of it, pushing gently back, his cock now slotted between the gorgeous cheeks of her firm butt. Separated from heaven by only the thin barrier of tracksuit pants. No going back. He shifted slowly, softly, his hand lightly onto her belly on soft woollen jersey, minutely, slowly, up around the feminine curve of ribs, up up under her breasts, dare he? Dare he? Light strokes under each soft mound, no bra just warm soft flesh, no resistance, is she asleep? Agonisingly up and over the curve of beautiful young breast until the light stroke connects to erect nipple jutting proud under the wool. An almost electric jolt of emotion. A moan, almost inaudible. From him or her? Then soft stroke, soft now deliberate cupping and squeeze as his cock leaked and throbbed against that softly tortuously gyrating butt. A full fearful heart-thumping exploration of her breasts. Now emboldened, he slips his hand up under her jumper onto the satin warmth of her hip, then belly, marvelling at the texture, the sensual sensations, the

12

difference. Then again tracking up the ribs and on to the gorgeous mounds. Her eyes still closed. But now deliberate, excited rotations of her sweet arse into him, as he slips his other hand under her cooperative body to possess each breast in each hand, and lovingly squeeze the globes in triumph and temporary ownership, rolling the crinkle stiff nipples between each thumb and forefinger. Her hands now reaching back, pulling down in the soft pulsating light thrown by the video, her loose track-pants, baring the twin downy hemispheres of her bum. Then to his drawstring pants, pulling pushing down, he lifting hips, unwilling to release his twin prizes, allowing her to release his sopping member, marvelling at her soft but insistent touch as she holds him firm, lifts and parts her rear, holding him at the base as she reverses her heat and guides his cock into her blood-hot cunt.

"Oh Billy," she sighs and turns her blonde head to wetly kiss him, pumping that soft arse backwards. Young Billy lost, out of this world somewhere deep, deep in space.

"I love you, Massie, I love you," he whispers in desperate teenage intensity, and then as she murmurs her feminine assent, he empties, explodes, self-destructs, and she moans sweetly as she feels his viscous virginity pour into her. "Oh Massie, oh Massie," he weeps now quietly, confused, emotions raw, still clutching her breasts, and she still cunt-clutching him, pushing back and holding him into her. "Shh, Billy, shhh," she comforts, and they lie that way, he in the newfound haze of post-orgasmic bliss, until he again hardens with the vivacity of his youth, and she rides him gently to her release.

Massie then took his clumsy hand and showed him her needs, teaching him the soft circular touches in the mysterious silky folds, while his mate Geoff snored and farted wetly on the other sofa. They lay as lovers for hours, and then she reluctantly disengaged and dressed, kissed him deep and long, kneeling before him.

"Mummy and Daddy will be here soon love. This night will be our special secret."

"But Massie, I love you," he offered hopelessly.

"I know, Billy, and I love you too, my dear. But I'm away back to UK soon to uni," and then he drifted off and remembered Massie covering him with blanket and a soft kiss.

He woke in the morning with Geoffrey body-slamming him with a leap from the end of the sofa. He was not sure at first if it all had been a dream until he tumbled out to counter attack, and his mate burst into laughter and pointed at the impressive crusty stain on the front of his black trackies. Geoffrey, in hilarious delight, accused him of being "a right wanker", that was, until a headlock and a knee drop to the solar plexus took all the piss and wind out of his mate and as he lay gasping like a beached fish, and Bill escaped into the guest bathroom to change before Massie or Geoff's parents spotted the evidential spot.

Two weeks later his beautiful Massie flew back to university in London. He waited his turn and hugged her farewell at the airport, and told her again in anguished desperate whisper that he loved her. And she patted him in maternal sympathy, hushing him while his young heart broke. Meanwhile Massie's parents nodded in parental appreciation of their oldest child's sisterly warmth toward "our Geoff's poor young New Zealand friend". Massie, with tears in her eyes, waved him goodbye at the customs gate, then turned and disappeared from his life forever.

Gone. His first love, an older woman.

His father did his best to keep him occupied but did not have much time to be with him. That was ok. He knew his father was a good man and did not doubt his love. Despite the infrequency of parental contact his father seemed to notice a change in his son. He put it down to maturity and commented that he seemed more relaxed, more settled.

"It's the exams," he explained to his dad. "I'm keen to do well."

He discovered the martial art of Korea the ancient science of *tae kwon do* first practiced by warrior monks some 2000 years before to fight against the series of Asian invaders. Over the generations, techniques were developed and refined by that fiercely proud people as an ethical, mental, and physical discipline and the only one of the martial arts to be recognised as both a sport and a traditional art form. He attended the bare-board Dojong, the training hall of the Kwanjangnim or Master Kim Jung, in the wooden village across the highway from the steel-bollard gates of the diplomatic compound. Here he found that the rhythm and beauty of the discipline took all other thought away. He toiled willingly to proficiency until at 18 he achieved, under the watchful and proud eye of the master, the treasured black belt.

He was a man now, his father said, he must visit his mother after the two-year absence, his schooling successfully completed. University beckoned, but where? He must take the time to decide. His father said, "Go to New York, stay with your mother, or travel if you want." Soon his father would once again move on, he was welcome to accompany him, probably Thailand he thought, there was an international university in Bangkok he could attend. "Or why not take some time off, Bill, and travel? Hasn't your old school mate from Seoul, the English boy, Bing, hasn't he returned with his family to a posting in London? Why not take up the invitation and visit England, Europe? Mate go, go, and have some adventures."

Bill decided though, after a phone call from his mother, after her tender entreaties that she wanted him to come and live with her in New York for as long as he wanted. "Please, son. Please, Billy. Please think about it."

Yes, he would go to her. He needed to get to know her again. He had never resented what she had done; he didn't consider that she had abandoned him. He understood, he thought, her needs, and had spoken about this with his dad. She had loved him and did love him. They had talked by phone religiously and happily and affectionately once a week for the entire two years since she had left.

His Mum was an American citizen now, she had completed the master's degree, and then a PhD. She now lectured at the university in ancient Asian history to the fresh-faced children of the USA. As a citizen and as a Professor at NYU she had been told that he could attend the prestigious university and complete his three-year degree there.

"Please come, Billy." She had a university-provided apartment deep in trendy Greenwich Village. She had an attic room set aside for him in the beautiful old brownstone that housed the elite of academia and the arts. She entranced him with the magical possibilities of living in that city, the café life, the parties, the exposure to the conglomerate of the world's dreamers and thinkers, the poets, the writers, the artists, the actors. And after the clinical reality of his college years in the harsh greyness of Seoul, the invitation excited him.

He hugged his father farewell at the airport and told him that he loved him and would miss him. He would write and he would call, and he would take care of himself and he would give mum a big kiss for him.

Touchdown, New York. What a city, what a view he had as the Boeing circled down and down in the queue and onto the tarmac of JFK. He was tired but buzzing with excitement and anticipation even after the long flight across the massive expanse of northern Asia. He disembarked onto the massive concourse feeling tiny, insignificant, amongst the rush of multi-coloured, multi-accented mass of humanity. Coming through the Customs Hall he felt the visual shock of spilling out the auto door, the waiting faces scanning his in expectation and then discarding him, not recognised, not theirs. Emerging into the Arrivals Hall where is she? he was finally engulfed by her, the familial familiarity, his mother in a rush to him, "Billy, oh son, oh Billy."

She was smaller than he could believe tiny, shrunken, and older he now a man, only a child when she had left. She, dressed like a hippy, with flowing red velvet dress, and crying, laughing, desperately clinging, chanting *sorry, sorry* as she reclaimed him as her child. He, happy, so happy, towering over her and hugging her back, "Oh, and this is from Dad," he said, kissing her on the cheek. Leaning down to do it and tasting the salt of her tears, then just holding her tight; comforting, protecting her now, as the tidal surges of unknown travellers and their greeters swept around them, mother and son reunited, a tiny island in a flood.

His mother finally led him out into the massive car park. She has a friend ("Say hi to Maggie") waiting in an old purple Chevy van. They load in, bags and bodies, and mother and son talk non-stop on the 45-minute ride into the city and to the apartment block on 22nd street in the village. Bill carries the backpack with all his worldly possessions from the van, still holding hands with her. She can't let him go, and up the old-style clanking lift to the top floor and the apartment where she settles him into the tiny attic room that is to become his home for the next three years.

Chapter 3

Love Hurts

He is woken from his dreamy recollections by the sound of a vehicle crunching to a halt outside. Shit, I hope it's Old Charley, Bill thinks.

One, two, then three car doors slam shut, unseen. He hears the steps of the new arrivals fade in the gravel as they move toward the front door. He hears heavy-booted steps as they enter the slate entranceway behind the closed internal access door and then out of his hearing into the depths of the building. A long ten minutes pass and it's Hill who appears through the opening side door. An unseen assistant holds the door ajar. Hill enters the gloomy garage with a tray, a mug of steaming coffee and a sandwich in a plastic bag.

"Listen Hill, if you don't get these fuckin cuffs off me then I'm straight to a fuckin' lawyer with a wrongful arrest suit against you, the boss, the entire fucking New South Wales Police Force!"

"Relax, man," Hill grunts, but friendlier now. "You will be released ASAP, that is once everything has been checked out."

"What do mean 'checked out'?"

"Well you see, Mr Peters," Hill lectured with a grin, "You may have raped Mrs Italiano for all we know! You have been formally and lawfully arrested on that suspicion. So just a little word of advice. Play the game son."

"Come on Barney, that's bullshit and you know it." What the fuck are they up to? he thought, suddenly scared. Rape! Jesus, would she say that just to get out of the shit? A brief flare of panic, his immediate future flashing before him. No way would she say that, he knew it instinctively. Still, Hill had a point. He had better play the game and see what develops.

"Here son, have this coffee and eat the sandwich. Remember, I'm on your side."

Oh fuck yeah.

"Just relax boy," Hill said, smarmy now, "I'm working things through with the Commissioner in regard to your immediate and your long-term future. It won't be long, but just cooperate and I will get you out of here."

Ok, self-preservation, he thought. But to trust Barney Hill was like trusting a heroin addict to water your poppies while you're away on your summer hols. Still, what choice did he have? "Thanks, Sir. Yeah, ok, I do see your point. But any chance I could perhaps just get these cuffs off my nuts?"

"Soon, Bill, soon. Just relax. I'll be back shortly and we will get you home, son." Hill placed the tray down on the bench in front of him. Then he left. The door closed.

Bill was alone again and mighty worried now. Might as well have the coffee and the sandwich looks ok, white bread and thick slice of ham off the bone. Yum, looks too good to resist for a hungry gutted bastard such as me. He removed the food from the plastic bag, tricky with just the one hand, and chewed slowly, thoughtfully, washing it down with hot gulps of the strong coffee. The coffee reminded him of the start to this adventure, the cup of coffee with Mrs Italiano. Oh shit, what a night.

Ten minutes, and Hill was back in the door. "How was that, son?"

"Yeah, pretty good thanks." Play it cool, play it cool. Hill picked up the tray, empty mug and crumpled plastic bag. "Be a few minutes son, the Boss has something to say to you boy and then you're away. It's sorted."

Thank Christ, he thought, the nightmare's nearly over; can't wait to get to home for a shower and a sleep. He lived in the Sydney beachside suburb of Manly across the harbour from the city's CBD. The NSW Police had owned the safe house for years. They had placed him there 18 months ago when the deal had been done between the two police services to get him out of New Zealand urgently after the shit hit the fan. The safe house was a secure, fully duress-alarmed, two-bedroom upstairs apartment, renovated from the original 100 year-old red brick and tile villa at 177 The Esplanade. From the living room through armoured, double-glazed window was a view across to the picturesque white sands to the world-renowned surf break of Manly beach. From the back window of the apartment, standing in the modern kitchenette, Bill could look back toward the obscured skyline of the city and surely one of the most beautiful harbours in the world. The occupants of the three other apartments in the building were all retired coppers and wives who were paid a small stipend to keep an eye on whoever was resident in the safe house. He had enjoyed the lifestyle of Manly. Working nights at the Commissioner's residence kept him out of public view. He had treasured his healing time there, recovering after the tragic events that had unfolded in Auckland at the completion of the undercover operation so long ago now.

The door again swung open. This time three men accompanied Hill.

Hello, here we go, he thought, tensing. All three were big men, muscular, fit. TRG Tactical Response Group the heavies; a specialist squad set up to deal with dangerous offenders, dangerous situations. He didn't know them. But he recognised the uniform: black overalls, heavy belt cuffs, Glock pistols, black combat boots. All three wore baseball Police caps, peaks over eyes, hard to see their faces in the gloom, standing behind Hill, backing him up. Why?

Hill spoke. "Well, Detective Sergeant Peters, thanks for waiting. We have now searched your flat at Unit 3, 177 The Esplanade, Manly, with a duly authorised and signed search warrant under the Misuse of Drugs Act." Why so formal? Bill thought, confused, and then he saw the dicta-phone.

"Searched my place? Why? Misuse of Drugs Act…?"

"If you will please let me finish, Mr Peters. That search located hidden in the roof-space a plastic bag containing what we suspect to be a Class-A prohibited drug. Forensic testing has now established that powder to be heroin."

"Bullshit! …hey! Wait on Barney! What the fuck…?"

"… Heroin in a trafficable quantity…"

"This is crap!"

"Further, your fingerprints have been found on the plastic bag holding the heroin."

"What?!" The fucking sandwich bag!

"I must caution you that you are not obliged to say "

"Fuck you Hill! This is a set-up. I want a lawyer now."

The dicta-phone clicked off. "He's yours, boys." The three big men moved forward. He tried to stand, to fight, to resist, but the handcuff held him down as the first boot smashed into his side. Down he went, crumpled, as the fists hammered head, back, ribs, one arm helpless the other desperately covering up as the three helped themselves to a defenceless target. Thudding blows target to disable, to hurt, kidneys, the backs of legs, until the crash of a size 12 combat boot into the side of his head mercifully faded him into the black.

Bill was very unconscious when Detective Inspector Hill, one of New South Wales' finest, escorted the three heavies outside. He walked them to the TRG sedan parked in the shadows of the ancient fig tree spreading high, wide and handsome on the harbour side of the red tuck-bricked mansion. Hill leant into the driver's window with muffled appreciation of their muscular assistance, and then the car fired into life and eased away, lights off, until the sedan turned away onto Mosman Avenue. Barney Hill paced in front of the roller door of the garage muttering into his mobile phone and then waved impatiently toward the gatehouse in a come hither, and quickly! action. With the gate barrier raised, an innocuous white Ford Econovan turned into the driveway and crunched up the gravel, lights off, navigating in the soft yellow glow thrown from the mansion's security lighting. At Hill's waved command the van parked with its snub nose just inside the roller door to the garage.

The driver and sole occupant of the van was a clearly nervous young man of Italian descent. Carlo Cossatta's father was from the same harsh hilly feudal regions of Calabria and the same small stone village that one Señor Francisco Italiano-Senior, the Police Commissioner's own father, had also originated and emigrated from, some 50 years before.

Carlo and Barney Hill needed no introduction. "Do it, he's over there," Hill grunted. Carlo approached the slumped man who lay awkwardly, breaths rasping, on the oil-stained concrete floor where the beating has left him. Anxiously, as he was no Roman hero no macho-Mediterranean warrior Carlo skulked closer, tapped the broken man once, then more bravely twice in the ribs with his pointy toe boots. Bill Peters did not stir, just moaned at the patent leather speared contusion. Hill reversed his Police Holden into the garage. Carlo quickly knelt beside the man and pulled one sleeve up. Carlo followed precisely now the earlier clear and exact instructions given him in that harsh pidgin English that still characterised his father's speech despite the old man's five decades as an Australian citizen.

Only 90 minutes earlier the old man had shaken the son awake. He needed Carlo "to do sometheeng". "Go to cousin Lou, Carlo. Tell Lou to make up one hotshot of shit from the stock. Ok? Boy youa fucken listen me?"

"Yes Pop," scared as always of the cruel old man.

"Ok, you get that from Lou, you take it to Frank's place, ok. You know Barney, Frank's man?"

"Yes Pop."

"He a waiting for you. You give it thata shot where Barney show you, ok?"

"Ok Pop."

So he went, dressed quickly, took the van. The goods vehicle ran imported Italian salamis, cheeses and fine hams around in the daytime routine of his father's legitimate business. The same van transported drugs and drug-money around in the night-time routines of his father's and his extended family's much more rewarding

illicit businesses. He drove through the moist darkness of the early
morning from the family home in the affluent suburb of Vaucluse
to Lou's high-rise security apartment in Dee Why. Carlo woke Lou,
and with the authority only of his father's word commanded from
his cousin the hot shot of horse. The gritty off-white derivative of
the poppy had been warmly carried through the customs borders
of several sovereign nations wrapped in five condoms up the arse
of a desperate junkie. From the Golden Triangle via the chocolate
starfish lovely! The aptly-named mule was just another of society's
casualties, prepared to risk the sudden brutal snapping of her neck at
the end of an Asian rope for the promise of a small percentage of the
booty to which she was so fatally addicted.

Lou had prepared the shot in his apartment, heating the powder
in a blackened spoon held over a plastic Bic lighter, until it bubbled
and merged as a solution and he drew that thirstily up into the small
hypodermic. Carlo took the needle from his cousin. Neither spoke.

This was now the needle that he placed carefully on the ground
next to where he knelt in the garage. The garage of his cousin.
Francisco's little boy, Frank. Carlo was in a hurry. He quickly
wound the short length of rubber tourniquet around Bill's upper arm.
Slowly the veins visibly expanded and rose like dark blue ribbons
from the pale flesh of the inner forearm. Carlo jumped, startled at
Barney's gruff, "Hurry up boy!" behind him. Then, nervously, he
stabbed that poison arrow into the unconscious man's arm.

Three things saved Bill Peters that night from the fatal smash of a
heroin hotshot.

The first was Carlo's technique. In his nervousness, the stab in
the dark grazed and cut, but in the main, missed the vein, and the
toxic juice was injected into the forearm muscle of the victim. This
was nowhere near as effective as an intravenous hot-shot that would
have taken the opiate straight to the heart.

Then there was the purity of the heroin.

Up the mule's backside the rock was 100% pure. When Lou
received the rock on behalf of the family business and before he put
it into stock, he deducted his commission. Lou took what he had

been taking from his kin over the past several years without anyone ever finding out so far.

Lou cut 20% from the rock, and then mixed back in an inert pharmaceutical powder. This was Lou's superannuation scheme, his nest egg. It was growing nicely. It was a bonus for the additional risk he bore by directly handling the product, while pussies like the boss's son, Carlo, lived in fucking luxury at his expense.

One other thing saved Bill Peters that night.

Carlo was a heroin addict. Carlo's father scared him, but nowhere as much as did the demons of his addiction. "Just a little," he convinced himself, "just a little won't matter," and before he got to Cousin Frank's, Carlo had pumped half of the shot into his own arm.

Carlo pulled the needle free of Bill's flesh and retrieved the rubber cord. Later that day, all going well, he would wrap that same cord around his own arm, pulled tight at one end held in his teeth, as he topped up with his drug of desperate choice. But here and now he had done it, he was out of there.

Before he could go though, Barney Hill had Carlo help to lift the heavy man. By the shallow slowness of his breathing, he was dying. As Carlo pulled the man upright off the floor, sitting, head hanging, Hill unlocked the handcuffs from the chair and from Bill's now clammy wrist. Hill put the cuffs back onto his belt. Then they clumsily dragged him across the garage floor. With effort, they slumped the body into the back seat of Hill's Holden, along slippery black plastic garbage bags laid down by Hill as protection against the blood and tears of the dead man. Then Hill found a spade in the gardener's tool racks of the garage, and clunked it into the boot. No space in there for a body, not with the fitted LPG gas cylinder of the dual-fuel system, one Police-issue racked double-barrel shotgun, orange plastic traffic cones, portable hazard lights, and other useful police stuff. Barney Hill then waved Carlo away with a grunted, "Give my respects to your father." The younger man made no reply but ran to the van, reversed it wide, and then rolled away down the long driveway toward the road.

Barney turned to close the back door of the car. He jumped, startled to find his employer now dressed elegantly in a crimson dressing gown, slippers, standing quietly beside the dying man. Frank Italiano, with the bloodlines of a Calabrian peasant, hawked loudly. He spat the sticky mucus upon his defeated rival, and slammed shut the sedan's heavy door. The Commissioner shook Hill's hand, slipping his bad lieutenant an envelope, bulky, heavy. "Thank you, my friend," he said.

"The pleasure is all mine, Boss. Catch you at the office," Hill replied, and then with a last wave of farewell he drove from the mansion to tidy up the last loose end.

That loose end awoke, groggy, sore.

I'm in the back seat of a car, silent fuzzy deduction.

A black interior, a Police V8 Holden, engine purring through smooth automatic shifts. Moving on wet sounding roads, the radio buzzed and chattered quietly from the front. A TRG command vehicle, he thought. Bill realised that he was no longer cuffed. At least not by the wrists. The night sky is still black through the windows. How long have I been out? he thinks. The steel grip of the cuffs around his aching balls reminds him of how he got here, but why? What the fuck is going on?

He was dreamy, confused, like he's drugged, slow. Must focus, must focus. No one else in the car except the driver and him. The shape of the back of a head, Hill's head, in the front driver's seat. The prick's whistling to the song on the radio, he realised, Oh lovely, Englebert's "Please Release Me", he recognised. He moved with the car's motion and stifled a groan from the bashing. Through slit eyes he saw Hill twist back to look at him, he played possum, doggo, dead.

"Hey Peters!" Hill screamed over the seat.

Bill stayed still, stilled his breathing.

Hill turned back, announced, "Elvis has left the building," and then laughed and whistled the sombre chords of the Funeral March.

Ten minutes pass.

Bill noted that the car is slowing, stopping. The indicator tick-tick-ticking, and then shaky back tyre acceleration and onto a different surface, no longer the smooth moist hiss of highway asphalt, now a clunking, sticky splatter. Maybe a dirt road, not gravel. No patter of stone chip thrown up on to underbody. Bill worked his mind to focus through the diminishing opiate cloud. He was beginning to achieve a clarity. And in the air-conditioned warmth of the Holden and with the comforting patter of rain on the windows, the slap slap rhythm of the wipers, he realised with cold certainty that they wished him dead. He recalled the set up, explained to him by Hill in the garage. The "arrest" for "the possession for sale or supply of a class-A drug, namely heroin". Hill had paused for dramatic effect when he told him they had his "prints all over the drug bag". The suggestion that he had raped the woman, Mrs Italiano. He could imagine how they would explain his disappearance to the world. That is if the world cared. But yes. He could just imagine the marketing plan, the tactics. They would notify the media of his history in New Zealand, his fragile mental state. The NZ Police will be advised of the actions of their damaged goods. They would destroy his character. A drug dealer, a rapist. What will Mum think? Kingi?

Hill obviously believed that his back seat passenger was dead, Bill thought. Surely not just from the beating. No, the fog that was clearing from his head must be a drug, he reasoned. If they think I'm dead … then my life can't be a factor for them. Hill was dumping his dead body. That cold reality hit him. They had tried to murder him with a drug. Scattered thoughts. Rape? No, that is why they doubled up on him with the drug set-up. Not rape, he just knew she would not attest to that. Bill was confused. What the fuck did they think she had said to him?

The car was slowing. He had no idea where he was, just knew from what little he could see outside that they were in the bush. Clearly Inspector Barney Hill was not taking him anywhere good, anywhere safe. Hill thought he was dead and Bill decided then that unless he acted he may well be dead very soon.

Barney pulled off the dirt road and Bill could see dark trees close in on the car, shrubs scratching, bumping, rocks scraping underneath. With the disguising noise of the car's final approach into a stand of scraggly bush Bill moved carefully on the seat. He curled his legs up against his chest, rolling gently up onto the rear bench

26

seat, his head farthermost away from Hill's left side. The driver was now visible between the front two buckets seats. Then, with as much force and venom as he could muster, Bill struck out. His body uncoiled from his shoulders to release the double axe-blow of both his bare feet, a technique acquired at tae kwon do sessions. The weapons of callused flesh and bone then smashed onto the left side of Inspector Hill's unsuspecting face.

The stupefying force of the kick was enough in itself to knock Hill completely out. The bonus was that the Inspector's head continued to the right with neck muscle shearing and tearing. But for every action there is a reaction. So with the force applied to the left side of his head, the right side of his head hit the unforgiving driver's side window at mach speed. Barney Hill used to prefer his right side profile. "Quite handsome really," he would preen, but that was before Bill's kick mushed the fragile cheek and jawbones into a jigsaw. Very fucking sore.

Just at the moment that Barney Hill dropped off into lala land, the big car had slowed down to about ten kilometres an hour. Barney had just clicked off his seat belt. He was thinking ahead of himself. Getting ready to dig a little hole in the bush. When his lights went dim the powerful Holden became pilot-free and Barney's accelerator foot convulsively stamped down and the V8 roared. The back wheels spun wildly on the slippery grasslands and the car smashed straight, head first, into a solid, unforgiving, mature silver gum tree trunk. This time Barney's head went forward. And it smashed into the heavy-duty, double-laminated, impact-proofed windscreen, starring both the glass and Barney Hill's frontal cranium into many little fractures. Then a millisecond too late, the driver's air bag exploded from the dash. And Barney's head went back, his body too close to the bag, unrestrained as it was from the seat belt. Again delicate muscles in his neck whip-lashed.

He would never be the same, poor Mr Hill. The damage would see a rigid plastic neck brace required by his floppiness for several months to come. Bill, meanwhile, simply rolled with the sudden start-stop of the car, down into the cushioned space between the front and back seats. The car's engine died in an angry clatter as the fan moved back several centimetres and chewed a coppery crater in the radiator. And all became very quiet.

With the blind panic of the instinct of self-preservation, Bill scrambled desperately from the car, rolling and crawling blindly away from the crash, uncertain, uncaring of Hill's state. He stopped ten metres away, cringing into the dank soil. He forced himself to stop, freeze, wait, listen. No-one was pursuing him from the car.

Bill lay there for a moment to catch his breath. He had no shoes, was dressed in overalls, had handcuffs around his testicles, was battered, bruised but alive. He had to take stock, take some precious time to think clearly. He waited, panting, looking back to the black hulk of the silent car. He had to know if Hill was alive. He had to be certain that Hill could not call others on the car radio, on his mobile phone, others who would hunt him down. He crawled back towards the car, slowly, terrified, forcing himself to approach it. He heard ragged breathing. Hill was alive, but battered. Moaning. Bill reached over him and took the sinister black pistol off the belt. He threw it under the car. Then he pulled the radio microphone from the receiver set, broke wires, and threw the handpiece behind into the bush. He found Hill's mobile phone, clicked off the battery, threw it into the dark. He stood then at the driver's door, relaxing, heart beat slowing. He considered this man who had meant to kill him. Hill was injured, badly injured. But the neck pulse was good, strong. He walked to the other side, pulled the door open, reached in and pulled Hill down across the two front seats, awkwardly into the recovery position.

Bill knew that some of the operational command vehicles were fitted with EPIRB type emergency beacons, similar to the marine versions that saved so many lives when trouble hit on cold waters. Beacons that, when activated, beamed out an identifying electronic signal to a guardian satellite in space. He saw that this vehicle had such a beacon, and if activated that signal would make its atmospheric way into the eerily lit Police operations room at Sydney Central. The green heartbeat would then allow the operator to identify the source vehicle, and to plot on the computer's screen the signal's exact geographical location. And then the Police Service, or if necessary the state's other emergency services, would physically seek and find the vehicle to discover the nature of the emergency that had caused that activation. He knew that if he left Hill here, he would probably die, slowly. The man's injuries were severe. With hesitant regret Bill Peters then saved Barney Hill's life. He clicked the switch to activate the EPIRB distress signal that would lead to Hill's rescue, but in the same moment would further endanger his own liberty, and he was sure, his own life.

Bill ran then, ran from the car into the black. He ran for an eternity until in the dark, in the rain, and the confusion of the mass of vegetation, he tripped, and grunting, fell into the moist trap of an irrigation drain. He forced control and he sat up in the earthy smell of the clammy wet soil in the drain. He adopted the meditation stance of the lotus from yoga lessons he had enjoyed at NYU in his futile attempts to impress the American girls that he was a new-age type of bloke.

With eyes closed he then called upon the seven years of training and discipline of tae kwon do.

He cleared his mind of physical influences, of dangerous distraction.

Pain from the beating, from bruise from scratch be gone.

Cold, wet, discomfort be gone.

Fear, panic, shock be gone.

With concentration and breathing deliberately controlled, he regained the power of focus and slowly, logically ran the cold hard facts of the problem through his mind.

The simple equation was that he had been set up for some reason.

It could not just be the act of sexual infidelity with Italiano's wife. Not even a hot- blooded man of Italian origin would take things this far for that, surely. Both the Commissioner and Hill had asked, and asked again, what she had said to him. Why? That had to be the key. They suspected that she had told him something, a secret, but what? He had no way of knowing. But whatever she knew and they suspected she may have told him, it had to be bad, very bad. Clearly it had to be illegal. The Police Commissioner of NSW must therefore be crooked, he judged. Look at what they had done to *him*! The corruption must be of the worst type because they had tried to kill him. He put himself into their patent leather shoes, into the mind of the enemy. If the secret that the lovely Mrs Italiano held was not that of the most extreme corruption, then they could have just set him up on the drug charges alone. Surely?

A drug set-up where the witnesses were Commissioner Italiano and Detective Inspector Hill. That would have been impossible to defend. What with the dangerous mentally unstable rogue ex-Kiwi copper scenario he would have had no credibility. They could have tied him up pretty good. If he had tried to tell the world that they were rotten, corrupt, or just really annoyed because he had bonked Mrs Italiano, the world would have pissed itself laughing. The old "disgruntled employee" defence. He laughed despite himself. They didn't have to kill him. They would have had him by the balls.

Shit, that reminds me, they do have me by the balls. He opened the front zipper of the overalls and looked sympathetically down at his landing gear, shrivelled, sad and as sorry looking as a trapped one-eyed possum. Bruised and held coldly by Messrs Smith & Wesson please be careful guys. This is one thing he had to sort out and soon.

"Ah, fuck!" he cursed elegantly, suddenly realising that he hadn't searched Hill for the handcuff key when he'd had the chance.

Ok. First move is to start moving. Taking the loose end of the cuffs he forced the serrated edge through the right pocket of the overalls at groin level. This held the cuffs in a position that wouldn't weigh so heavily on his mind. That done, he stood and looked around. He was in the drain and could see the dirt track, close, over to his right. The dead Police car was back to the east. That must be back toward civilisation. He could hear the distant murmur of the sea to the north, he must be near the coast, or the inner harbour. How long had he been unconscious? No way of knowing, had to get moving. How long before the cavalry arrived to answer the EPIRB's silent scream for help?

And how long then before they could talk to Hill? What would he say? Bill had no doubt there would be some concoction, some fantasy of assault, abduction, violent escape, to add to the trumped-up drugs allegation. But that all depended on Hill's condition when they found him. What then would they do? Helicopters with intense spotlights scouring from above, or maybe heat-imaging scanners? Tracker dogs on his fresh scent, mounted police, horse and motorcycle? All armed and dangerous. Orders, he was certain, would be shoot to kill. If he avoided that early police attention, then of course there would inevitably be a general public alert. A release to the media, photographs all over the papers, sombre interviews to the TV, radio shit, that will surprise the folks back home "local boy does maybe not so good".

He took a deep breath and climbed out of the drain. Toward the sea, he thought, then decide which way along the coast. He jogged awkwardly, sore from the beating, still slightly disorientated from the heroin. Jogging along the side of the soft dirt track, there were no recent tyre marks, he noted; a quiet area. Within ten minutes he rounded a bend and the coast was ahead, the sea in sight. But gradually he realised that in fact he was still within the confines of the mighty harbour. Off on the far right horizon he thought he could just see the Sydney skyline. He was west of the city, probably near Concord, he estimated, a coastal suburb 20 minutes from the city centre. In the dark morning light it looked to him like Canada Bay. He could see the trendy pole houses dotted within the native bush of the steep hills that rear off the water.

He needed cover until dark, but he needed to get far enough away from the dirt road in case they came with tracker dogs, helicopters. It started to rain. Sydney in winter, cold, as a front swung in from the Heads. Clouds, grey and laden with icy wetness rolled inland off the dark Tasman Ocean outside the sheltered harbour. The rain suited him; heavy enough would wash away tracks, wash away scent from the dogs. Also heavy enough for long enough and it looked like that now would keep the locals inside. No reports of a bruised and bloodied man in grey overalls running bow-legged. Now it pelted down. He needed shelter through the growing daylight until it was dark again. So he ran. Ignoring the pain from the damaged and dented parts of his body, he knew each of those parts, and as he ran, he counted, identified the damage. He ran along the waterfront just within the overhang of the bush and trees at the water's edge, toward the bridge and the city.

Manly was across the harbour and off to the northeast. He knew Manly, he knew people there. Who would help him? Fuck! Who *could* help him? He had to make his way toward that possibility of haven, of safety. He knew that to run or walk to Manly would take hours and hours, maybe the whole of the next day. But he had no other choice he ran. As he went, the sharp rocks and gnarly tree roots cut and bruised his bare feet and he pushed his mind into the zone that athletes and warriors rely on, where pain becomes pleasure, where cold becomes warm. Hours became minutes. And it was an hour later that he stumbled around another rocky headland. He saw a small boat shed back off the water, old and weather-worn, back inside the tree-line, above the high tide mark. "Keep Out, Private Property, Trespassers Trespassed Upon," the weather-faded, rusting old sign warned. An old-style heavy brass padlock barred entry. With a shivering yank at the door the hasp pulled away from its rotten base and he fell into the dark mustiness and lay frozen on the reeking floorboards. His body rapidly becoming hypothermic, he forced his aching, cramping, seizing self up. He pulled closed the creaking old door, timbers swollen from the wetness. It jammed back into the square and stuck closed against the storm battering and whistling against the ancient structure. In the blackness, using groping, frozen-fingered touch, he shakily dressed himself in old stinking oilskins on hooks hung after some long ago fishing trip. Three of them he put on, one over the other, all full-length Man from Snowy River stuff.

Poppa bears, mumma bears and baby bears, he giggled nonsensically. Someone's been wearing my raincoat Poppa and he's still here. Oh look it's Goldilocks, and he's fucked!

Sleep, need sleep, and finally wrapped, warming and exhausted from the events of the night, he crawled into a sail cupboard, pulled shut the plywood door and fell into the deepest slumber.

Chapter 4

Knowing Me, Knowing You

The Big Apple, New York: what an adventure, what a city! From the secure base of his mother's apartment he dived headfirst into the lifestyle of that huge melting pot of the world's citizens 'just doing it' in the cradle of the free world. His mother showed him proudly around the picturesque campus of NYU and signed him up into the Bachelor of Science degree programme, majoring in human movement. She also showed him what she did, how she worked, and he sat in on her lectures, fascinated by her competence, her intelligence, her knowledge and the ease and style with which she shared it with the students of her classes.

He slowly got to know this woman again. He could see how happy she was. He accepted that Maggie was more than just a friend; that his mother had found her soul-mate in another woman in the later years of her life. He soon knew that for her this was right and natural, and he understood even more clearly now why she had needed to move away from that decent, good man she had taken as her husband so long ago in a different time and circumstance. Her happiness was complete now her son had come back into her life, the only piece that had been missing from her emotional jigsaw. She was so proud of him; he had done well in the final year exams at the college in Seoul, had easily qualified for entry into NYU. She marvelled at his physical prowess during a tae kwon do display. He joined the Dojong of Master Sun Li four blocks from the apartment in the small Korean quarter, and then became an instructor or *Sabomnim* under the Master Kwanjangnim as he progressed through the Dan gradings of his black belt status.

He enjoyed the strange new experiences, the interactions, sensations, tastes and sounds of her world. The large circle of talented friends and associates, the parties each weekend at the apartments of incredibly diverse and gifted people. His amusement that his mother smoked pot, so passé to him now, as if she had rediscovered and captured as her own the missed hippy days of the sixties when she had been an army wife in the depths of conservative New Zealand.

He had immediately loved the lifestyle, his tiny attic bedroom accessed from the main body of the apartment by a narrow spiralling wrought-iron stairwell. With a view from the bed out across parkland, this was where he spent his time studying (on the bed, books on bent knees, papers spread haphazardly about). His home life had him revolving like a small comet around a sun of warmth and love from the partnership of his Mum and Maggie. They shared funny, three-way conversations over meals in the small warm kitchen. Once a week, when Mrs Hernandez, his mother's attractive Puerto Rican maid, came to clean, he would shyly flirt with her, and, to her ongoing amusement, awkwardly offer to help her clean.

He made friends his age from the student body of NYU and from tae kwon do and rugby union. He had played the primary sport of his home country through his life. Each collection of New Zealand diplomatic or embassy personnel always included the fanatic followers of the 'religion' that placed the nation's All Black Rugby Union team above mere mortals in the NZ psyche. The entire nation's mood seemed to depend upon how the team was going at any given time, with important losses plunging the parochial and unforgiving rugby-mad population into mass depression and recrimination.

He had been pleasantly surprised to find that the university had a rugby union team the NYU Ungulates, a messy mob of

rugby ex-pats. The team was comprised of lecturers and students
from England; Welshmen who loved to sing at the drop of a hat;
hard men from Scotland; hilarious happy-go-lucky Irishmen; mad
beer-sculling Aussies; the guttural serious South Africans; a united
nations of quicksilver Kenyans, Zimbabweans, and Ugandans; slight
but lithe Singaporeans, Thais, Chinese, and one or two locals who
couldn't resist the craziness of both the game and the players and
then never left. The two other Kiwis in the team welcomed him
in like a long-lost brother, more so when they found out he was
one of that rare breed a front-rower, a loose-head prop. The team
played through the winter against other university teams throughout
the state and at carnivals in neighbouring states, which entailed
infamous bus trips during which he risked permanent brain damage
from the amount of beer he was compelled to consume. They won
some, they lost some but he enjoyed that special camaraderie of
groups of men who engaged together in sporting combat. Outsiders
who had never experienced it would never understand. The bond
of the like-minded glued them on and off the field no matter their
background, their physique or skill, even their intelligence, wealth
or social standing. Once accepted into the team, into the club, each
was a "bro" for life. The togetherness allowed, some would say
encouraged, outrageous behaviour such as the special party trick of
Rexy the coach.

At the end of that first season at the restaurant night for the
wives and girlfriends (and to which Bill foolishly took his Mum)
just before the dessert was to be served, the lights suddenly went
off in the restaurant. Eerily through the gloom the very large, very
white and very naked body of the coach came leaping over from
the direction of the rest rooms. Up the huge ghostly figure leapt,
stepping off a chair onto the long table above the shocked gaze
of the partners and guests, and a large group of stunned Chinese
tourists at the next table. The unknowing spectators then sighted the
burning wick, a meter-long length of lovingly twisted toilet paper,
plugged securely into his backside as Rexy gyrated in a terrifying
example of that rugby classic the "Dance of the Flaming Arsehole."
The Chinese tour-group escaped in a mess of tipped chairs and

35

spilt food from what they later decided by communal discussion and decree must have been a capitalist American sex club. The pyrotechnic ballet almost ended in tragedy when Rexy stood in the custard bowl and fell off the table. Sadly, this happened before he had a chance to put out the shortening fuse by his usual flourish of squatting into a jug of beer. So, as he lay, dazed like a massive deflated party balloon on the floor, Rex then suffered an involuntary cauterisation of his haemorrhoids before the awed audience.

His mother laughed for days after that, breaking into giggles during lectures, at breakfast, late at night.

During this time of study and sport he dated only occasionally, mainly just friends from shared classes at university; beautiful, healthy, virginal specimens of womanhood who retained a healthy suspicion about his motives. They liked him for his difference, for his politeness and humour. But these girls had clear goals in mind either a carefully selected marriage, or a career. And that did not include casual sex with a bloke with an interesting accent, who happily confessed that he had no idea what the hell he wanted to do after university, and whose Mum was a lesbian lecturer in Ancient Asian Studies who he still lived with.

He found anyway that really he did not have the time to court them nor did he have the money to treat and spoil these women in the manner to which they were definitely accustomed. His membership of the rugby team also added to their suspicion and acted in itself as an effective contraceptive. So out of necessity he developed and perfected the act of masturbation into an urban art form as night after night of failed attempts to convince any one of the flaxen, auburn or raven-haired beauties that his declarations of love and respect deserved a physical response. And his groin ached in blue protest.

It was whilst in the act of self-satisfaction that he embarrassingly solved his immediate problem of celibacy. The night before, on the Friday, he had a date with one of the ice-princesses at the university's summer season outdoor cinema. They had lain together on a blanket with a cane picnic basket under the spreading branches of a 100-year-old oak tree. Bill had gone to some trouble to prepare the basket. The fare purchased from various fantastically pungent continental delis in the village included plump, cold chicken and door-stops of fine ham, crusty French bread stick, salted butter, a mixed green salad with balsamic dressing, a nice bottle of Californian oaken chardonnay. Very classy, he thought as she cuddled up to him on the tie-dye beanbag he had borrowed from his mother's sitting room.

At the interval he tried to kiss her and she had avoided the attempt, but remained in the embrace.

All through the second half as the wine kicked in for him she expertly halted every advance he made by hand or mouth. Patiently and gently she moved his hands from too near a breast or hip, turned her face from him with perfect timing leaving him kissing air, instead of ear, but all that time she stayed happily in his embrace, frustratingly gorgeous, warm and sexy. Halfway through the second half he had really given up, it was just too ball-breaking, so he accepted the inevitable and held her warm and cosy. Later he took her to the steps of her fraternity house after a chatty, friendly cup of coffee in the village where they dissected the art movie they had watched. Then, as he bade her a brotherly farewell in the darkened doorway she came into his arms, placing a hot mouth over his and he tasted that sweet tongue between his lips. To add insult to injury, her elegant fingers then slid down the outside of his jeans and she found and gently squeezed his pulsating cock in a rhythmical and surprisingly expert fashion. Then in her husky American twang she whispered into his ear that she had had a "great taame" and they must do it "agayin" before spinning out of his grasping hands and swishing through the door out of sight, though by no means out of mind.

He staggered home that night hugging the beanbag and dreamt of sticky, sexy, soft female all night.

It was on the Saturday morning when his mother called up to him that she was going out to the markets with Maggie that he decided to take matters in hand. Fuck it, he thought, time to visit Mrs Palmer and family. He found his mother's massage oil in the bathroom. Back in bed he stripped back the sheets and lay naked with the warm summer sunshine pouring in through the small attic window. On with the stereo headphones, a CD of the latest Top 40 hits mainly the melodious sexy rhythms of the sensual black American girl groups that he enjoyed so much. On with the black eye patch he had kept from the American Airways flight from Korea. Now by touch, off with the top of the oil. The musky scent of sandalwood clouded into the small room. The music, the eye patch, the hot sensual sun across his body, the oil on his hand and spreading it onto erect and throbbing cock. Now, to remember the ice maiden in all her teasing sexuality. "Take it slowly big boy, enjoy, enjoy," he muttered in selfish anticipation.

And then as he slowly rotated his fist, cunt-like, up and slowly down, a hot wet mouth descended over the point of his problem and a suction was fiercely applied.

What the!? Bill jumped near off the bed with shock but a hand on his chest kept him flat on the bed, the busy mouth never straying from its task. With free hand he ripped off the mask and there holding his naked body down and sucking for all she was worth was Mrs Hernandez. The 30-something widow was stronger than he could believe, she kept him pinned as he briefly struggled but then the sensations of the mouth and twirling tongue decided the matter and she felt him relax into the experience and enjoy the unexpected treat. The tension that had led to the event anyway, and then the adrenaline-charged exhilaration of the ambush by Mrs Hernadez soon had him panting and thrusting deep into that talented mouth, and when she combined hand-stroke with mouth-stroke he exploded into her, apologising weakly, but quietened by her free hand as she licked him almost dry. When he recovered, he took her into his arms onto the bed, and she explained in halting English her loneliness since her husband had died two years past. A good man, a security guard, shot during a bungled robbery of the small city bank branch he guarded. He made love to her that day, enjoying her passion and urgent need and then that relationship became for each of them the physical release both needed through the remaining two years he was in New York.

The time passed way too quickly. He studied hard and well and each year passed the requirements of his degree despite the distractions. He and his mother enjoyed and prospered in each other's company.

He spoke to his father once each week by phone, first in Seoul and then in Bangkok, Thailand. His father was happy that he was doing well, and happy that he had renewed the bond with his mother. He told Bill that Thailand was his last posting before retirement and that he intended to finally buy that block of land on the beautiful Hokianga Harbour near the top of the North Island of New Zealand and retire there. "Come and visit me boy why don't you come visit your old man after your final exams?" "Sounds good to me Dad," he responded, immediately keen. "Ok, Bill, let's do it, eh? Before you decide seriously what you want to do with that degree." Bill agreed, and promised to see his father in the homeland in his 23rd year.

Chapter 5

Take a Chance on Me

He is being hit, smashed. Three men, and big, dark, fragments of sound. He can't fight back, he is helpless. "No! No! Fuck off. No!" Bolt upright, bang, he hits his head on the top of the sail cupboard, pitch-blackness. Where in hell is he? What the fuck? Panic he's trapped, can't move arms, legs. He kicks out with bare feet, kicks the cupboard open, moonlight glinting through dirty windows.

Shit, that's right. The old boat shed.

"Jesus, a nightmare. But, fuck, it is a nightmare," he mutters. He forces his heart beat to slow, controls breathing, lies back against the musty sail folded in the cupboard that had acted as his cradle. The oilskins with their stinking crackly embrace have saved him; he is warm, even hot.

How long have I slept? He gets up, walks to the small wood-framed, salt-grimed window. It's late at night. The moon's mid-sky, near midnight. The storm has passed. Shit, must be about ten hours I've been tucked away.

Ok, time to take stock to plan.

SMEAC: Situation, Mission, Execution ahh, ok, what do the A and C stand for? The old Police training, a handy way to compartmentalise a situation if only he could remember all the acronym. Oh well, three out of five ain't bad.

Ok. *Situation*. First, himself. Right, the beating by Hill's apes had not disabled, only bruised and damaged; no bones broken, no real wounds to infect, to bleed. The grazes to the face and head, and the cuts to lips, were already closing, scabbing, healing. The drug that he believed must have been used on him by the way he had felt, and by the clumsy puncture tear to his inner right arm, had faded and now gone as a result of both time and his exertions.

All in all, he thought, although rooted he was really ok physically.

Hungry? Yes but not a real problem for another 12 hours or so, the last food, the damn ham sandwich from which they had gotten his fingerprints.

Thirsty? Yes but it had poured with rain, there would be ground-water puddles, water caught in vegetation, so thirst would soon be quenched.

Mentally, ok, the long sleep had freshened him, his powers of focus sharpened, he needed to think clearly, plan for probabilities, allow for the possibilities. By now the entire NSW force would surely be on the lookout for him. He wondered if Hill had been found, felt certain that he had. By now surely he had spoken. If not then no doubt Mr Fucking Italiano would have contributed to the falsity of the dangerous drug abusing, dope-dealing rapist-escapee-Kiwi-bastard fantifuckasee. Worse, the public interest would be intense, the media in a feeding frenzy to track this rogue copper down. Shit. He knew the story would be hot for days, weeks even. Quotes from local sources, stories of his exploits in New Zealand to prove what a dangerous, unpredictable bastard he was. This was not going to be easy.

Mission: he had to get out of NSW, but how?

If they cornered him in this state he knew the scenario the TRG would be called in to talk him out.

Yeah right, he thought.

Execution. He lay back on the sails and worked his way through the possibilities.

Who would help? Who could help? He hadn't made many friends in the 18 months he had been in hiding in Sydney because, fuck it, he had been in hiding. The night shifts at the mansion had kept him off the streets at night, he had mostly slept during the day, and his life, except for the periodic secret trips back to Auckland for the court cases in the first months, was deliberately, intentionally quiet. It was not even so much out of fear, on his part at least, that they would find him over here. He would welcome that chance; he had lived solely for that day. That day of payback, revenge, *Utu* in the Maori language. No, it was more by official decree, on the recommendation of the New Zealand police psychologist. And then the personal request, and when that was ignored, an order from the NZ Police Commissioner. But even then he had needed to be told by his mentor, the old Maori warrior, Kingi Potiki, before he agreed. Take the time, they said, to recover. To heal mentally from the two years deep undercover in their world, and from the trauma of the dramatic conclusion. The tragic loss by violent murder of those two precious souls 18 months ago fuck, only 18 months!

No time for this he thought, keep the focus, no distractions, weaknesses. Assess the facts and plan the escape.

Who can I trust? he thought. I need clothes, food, money and transport. He could not call upon any of the friends he had made in the NSW Police, it was too dangerous for them and for him. Inspector Charles, his immediate boss, "Old Charley", was a great guy but they would be watching him, surely.

Gerald, the butler at the mansion? The two had become friends during his time there, as close as that regular contact could make two very different men, shared meals and long healthy, humorous discussions over the respective merits of the All Blacks and the Wallabies. Then, more in Gerald's interest, the fortunes of both nations' rugby league teams, the mighty all-conquering Kangaroos of Australia against the not-so-powerful New Zealand national team in the less popular code of his motherland. But no, not Gerald.

What about Mr Sung? He had been able to keep up his tae kwon do. That disciplined world the training, the focus had helped him especially in the early days. He had found a Dojong near to the apartment, a 20-minute jog down into Manly's commercial precinct. Here, late at night, after the regular classes had finished, he joined

the Master behind locked doors for private sessions of breathtaking athleticism. Full combat. Both men were padded, protected, both enjoying the freedom rarely experienced of two black belts in balletic battle, no quarter asked and none given. But no, he could not impose upon the quiet and humble Mr Sung. By day a polite greengrocer, by night a Korean warrior.   But wait on …
Of course! Jack Waratini, the big man, the bro. He had met Jack on the nightly trip from Manly to Circular Quay on the old, throbbing, green-painted Sydney ferries that plied their busy trade back and forth across the inner harbour. Jack was of the Ngapui tribe from Auckland but that was 25 years ago. He had followed the course of so many of his country men since the war: "Go to Aussie bro, go for the big money in the mines, work hard for a couple of years and bring it all home, man. Enough to get set up, buy a house." And he had worked hard and saved the money. Years in the remote mines of Western Australia, in the red dirt country of the Pilbara and the Kimberley, digging iron ore out of huge man-made holes in the ground. It then was sent across the world by massive ship to Japan where the industries of that island nation turned it into the steel that built modern cities. Years had been spent in Kalgoorlie in the semi-desert lands where hard men went underground to search for the yellow traces of the metal which drove the nation's economy. Where those men pissed huge amounts of that blood- and sweat-earned cash against the dirty steel urinals of the dozens of pubs; delivered it in sheafs of fresh printed paper to pretty maidens for one hour at a time of their precious soft feminine sweetly-scented attention. But Jack was smart, he mixed with anyone, with everyone. Big Jack always ready with a song, get out the gat bro, "I have a band of men" and "sad movies" late into the night. Through it all, Jack saved his dollars. "Got to look after the missus and kids, bro." Based the family in Sydney, "with the cook's relies in Bondi bro" and during the 15 years he toiled and saved enough to buy his home in Manly freehold and sired nine kids on his brief holidays home.

When Bill met him on the ferry, Jack picked him straight away. "Kiaora, bro, where you from?" with eyebrows raised in the facial sign language of his people. Bill felt immediately comfortable sitting near the huge man on the green wood slats seats of the ferry as they chugged into Circular Quay. Big Jack was about 6'2" but he had to be 130kg of not-so-rippling muscle.

"From Auckland, mate," Bill responded, and then the two talked rugby.

"How long since you been back? What did you think of the place, cold eh?"

Then Jack talked of his life and loves; mainly food, then his wife and kids, "But really bro, first is the missus, then the kids, then food, no, really, bro! And he punctuated each paragraph's end with his rolling high-pitched giggle.

Jack had finished with the mines and Bill could see from the black pants, white shirt under the fading swandri that he was in security. "Just my town job, bro," Jack told him. "I drive interstate, got my own prime-mover, a big Kenny," he said. "I pull refrigerated 16-wheeler trailers through to Melbourne each Friday. It's my superannuation bro, that truck, bought it with the money I sweated for in the mines." Then into the quay and the big callused mitt swallows his in meaty bro-shake, thumb upright, two men bonding. They met this way, two, sometimes, three times a week, then Jack asked him around for a boil-up and Bill went and he was transported back home. The boil-up smells of the pork bones and watercress sweet-potato, the stolid, fried Maori-bread, the belly-rippling laugh of his mate, the lovely Polynesian warmth and beauty of Jack's wife, Maude, and the immaculate politeness of Jack's brood of nine as they brought him by insistent turn another beer and to keep them all happy he drank all nine. He felt relaxed for the first time for a long time, and Jack asked nothing of him only the company of the like-minded, happy to be here but still in another land. Someone who knew rugby so that the two of them could sit and watch the tests, kick the missus and kids out of the room until it was finished, moan about the refs, pick on the Aussies, sweat on the All Blacks doing well whilst in that sanctuary pouring down beer after cold beer.

Yes, Jack would help and Jack had a truck and it was Thursday night. Jack would leave at 6am tomorrow for the run to Melbourne in the Kenworth. Bill had to get to Manly and he had six hours or less to do so. Six hours to travel say, 20kms as the crow flies, straight across the lower lobe of the harbour. If only he were a crow.

Right, what are the options? By road? The highway was back up the hills off the bay, he estimated, say five kilometres back over the first ridge of the wooded coastal range. He could be there in 45 minutes to one hour depending on the ground, but with houses spotted through the hills along the coast, there will be roads or tracks leading back up to the asphalt artery. He could already hear in the still air of the early morning the steady, distant rumble of traffic, the low growl of engine compression brakes, the blipping of gear changes as the big machines grumbled up and down gradients toward and away from Sydney. They were mainly hauling the vital supplies the fresh produce that fed the big city, milk from the farmlands of the Hunter region, fruit and vegetables for the early markets and fresh warm bread from the bakeries. The opposing flow of huge vehicles pulled freight away from the port, heading north to provision and supply the satellite cities and towns up the east coast and on toward Newcastle.

If he tried the road he might flag down one of the speeding behemoths or thumb a lift from someone if he was lucky, but the news would be out by now he was sure. His (very handsome) face would be splashed over TV news and in the early edition papers. Then of course the police would have to be patrolling, searching for him. Marked cars and plain cars, uniformed and plain-clothed coppers from the big, bad, blue gang. Seeking vengeance for their damaged goods as coppers always did, anywhere in the world, when one of their own was hurt. No, the road was not an option.

The shoreline? Along the rocky beach? No. The idea was immediately discarded, it would take too long, and be too difficult around the rugged bays and then there were problems of people and dogs as he got closer to the city.

By water? That was it, but how? Well I am in a frigging boat shed. He turned and searched back into the gloom, back where the shed leaned away from the door and angled down into the hill. There in the dark was the upturned, ribbed shape of a small wooden dinghy. He quickly investigated, suddenly excited; it was possible, he thought, but shit it would take some effort. The dinghy was heavy-tarred, wooden-planked and snub-nosed. The wooden oars lay along the sidewall of the shed. Must have been used to access a larger vessel maybe. Or to fish just offshore, the wide beam and shallow draught not conducive to the deeper, choppier waters of the outer reaches of the harbour.

Too slow, too hard, he thought, and turned away. Wait on. There, further back, set on a wooden rail/rack off the back wall of the shed, was the shark shape of a kayak. Eu-fucking-reka! Yes, that's it. He was forced by the sloping roof to crouch and duck-walk on bruised, stiff legs to get to it. It was old but perfect a solid, strong sea kayak, canvas skirt still enclosing the cockpit and when he unzipped, there inside was the paddle and even a plastic water bottle.

"Baby, you is the real-deal! Almost a pity to steal you no, sorry borrow you. Ok, this is the way." He had paddled kayaks before in the rough waters of Auckland harbour, and then in the big rolling seas of the west coast of the North Island. He had overcome the beginner's disbelief as to how the thing could even be designed that way, so low in the water, so goddamn tippy. He had mastered the urge to fall to one side or the other, had learnt that forward motion gave stability, control and the placement and attitude of the body became part of the craft. He knew and loved the sleekness, the speed. This was the way he could get to Manly before light, follow the coast weaving in and out of the thousands of parked, anchored pleasure craft that fringed the great harbour. The varied mass of fizz boats and graceful yachts, playthings of the populous that frolicked within the aquatic theatre that geology and nature had gifted to Sydney.

Bill cradled the fibreglass body of the craft in his two widespread arms and lifted her gently off her resting place. He then slowly duck-walked backward until the angle of the roof allowed him to rise with his booty, almost like a bride to be carried to the marital bed. He placed the kayak down softly by the door, stripped off the two outer oilskins and hung them back on the bronze hook where he had found them the night before. He took off the innermost coat and squashed it behind the seat in the tiny storage area. Then softly, carefully wincing at the creak squeak of the wet timbers against the jamb, Bill pushed open the door of the boat shed to start his journey.

First a recce. He crept down from the shed, tucked like a squat brown head looking out into the bay. He panned left, right: nothing, all clear. Back into the open door, picked her up and carried her out, down to the water's edge on rocky shore. He unzipped fully the skirt and taking the water bottle returned to the shed and from shallow fresh-filled puddles beneath the corrugated roof he filled it, then drank it dry in earthy fulfilment and filled it again for the trip.

He closed the door of the shed, pushed the rusted screws of the hasp back into the soft, wet fibres of the wall timber until there was no sign that entry had been gained. Then back down quickly in the soft gleam of the half-moon to the craft and slipped, legs stretched long into her shape, onto the seat, rudder pedals found by bare feet in the bullet bow. He tested the left then right pedal and found the wires tight and responsive, as he manoeuvred her deeper off the shoreline with rotations of the double scoop-ended paddle.

Hesitantly at first and then, as old skills returned and forward motion gave confidence, he was off, slicing away from the dark shore and turning east in the direction of the heads and toward the Harbour Bridge and the Opera House to angle north past those landmarks toward Manly. He stayed at most 50 to 100 metres off the curving shoreline and he negotiated each gentle bay of the south side of the great harbour.

Where possible he moved in between and through the great civilian fleet that sat and rocked at anchor in the gentle conditions that had followed the sudden winter squall of the night. The city still slept and so did the waters. Way across the water mass toward the heads and the rolling ocean outside the navigation lights of bigger craft, huge steel-plated foreign flagged ships with the orange pilot boats like remora to shark accompanied each other out from Sydney port to release the big ships on great trade journeys.

He had been paddling now for about two hours. He had the city in sight, on the southern shore. The famous bridge was a fluorescent archway toward which he aimed the tiny bow. He saw through the darkness the majestic, gleaming curves of the Opera House off to his right. His level of alertness, of fear, rose again. He was getting close to the CBD, to well-lit areas, where police patrols as a matter of routine periodically crisscrossed the wharf areas, the city's streets, the waterways and even the airways, with regular sweeps of the Airwings white liveried choppers. Bill crossed then, powering across the fast-flowing tide-chopped channel, away from the city toward the darker north shore coast. He speared the tiny craft toward the bluff from which Mrs Italiano had sadly stared toward the skyline a lifetime ago, from the grounds of the mansion. As the night moved inexorably toward the day he saw the rolling greyness of incoming foul weather and he realised that he should be off the water sooner than later. Under the massive span of the Harbour Bridge he aimed her back mid-channel. He was paddling strongly, warmed muscles powerful and working in the rhythm, all easing the stiffness of the bashing, and repairing bruised muscles.

Then he saw her. Powerful searchlights switching a hot beam of daylight from front then port side back to starboard, the NSW Police launch MV *Justice* slowly appeared, her bow sharp as she purred toward him from the Circular Quay wharf complex. She eased her imposing but graceful length into the channel and turned and steered directly at him, a small white 'v' flicking up from the bow knife where she slickly kissed the harbour waters.

Shit! This had to be it! It was all over rover. A breath-catching, bowel-loosening flare of panic reared in him. In moments he would be in that hot beam like a startled aquatic rabbit. A bruised and battered kayaker in Police-issue overalls. What would they do? What could he do? Sweet f-all, he breathed. How the fuck would he explain himself if they just stopped to enquire? But as the possibilities, and the much scarier probabilities, came to mind, suddenly, from behind, in friendly, deliberate ambush came a pack of kayaks. Early morning trainers out for their regular daily paddle; young and not-so-young athletic men and women. The lettering on their fluoro yellow rashies said *Darling Harbour Kayak Club*. And with the goodwill and disgusting vigour of the fit, they shouted friendly "giddays" and "how is its" and he recognised the opportunity and powered up behind and into the loose-knit bunch at the back of the fleet and made friendly responses. He asked if they minded the company and was happily accepted into the pack as they swept past the *Justice* and she greeted in familiar "toot toot" of the siren and friendly waves from the crew and then continued on her patrol.

Breathing easy now, he hung at the back of the pack as they led him past the city, made small talk, glancing backward. They invited him to train with them and "come on back to the clubhouse for a spot of brekkie after." He, tiring now and aching from the unfamiliar exercise, was polite and non-committal, but appreciative of their company, and he responded briefly as possible in a clumsy attempt at a German accent which made him sound like a drunken Pakistani.

He toiled through another hour of paddling, bunched at the rear with the less competitive of the pack, having watched the elite spear ahead and later come back past them with cheeky insults on the return. Just as the morning sun started its slow rise from the east they reached Manly. The friendly pack circled like joyous dolphins and he waved a relieved farewell. The first of the early ferries was just warming up, diesel fumes pulsing from her stack awaiting the 5am commuter service to the city. The big wharf clock confirmed the time was 4.50am. He had just over an hour to get up to Jack's house, only 1km up the hill from the waterfront. He slid the kayak's fibreglass derriere up onto the rocky beach on the darkened side of the wharf. Just then the rain started. It was slow at first then gathered drizzling force as the cloud he'd seen earlier rolled in and over the coast.

His legs were stiff and he stretched to ease a tight lower back. He pulled the vessel right up under the wharf above the high tide mark and tucked her safely away with the paddle inside and her skirt modestly zipped up. Bill patted her sturdy fibreglass body and thanked the graceful lady for a good time. The old oilskin pulled crackly out from the tiny storage hold, and he put it on. With the hood up and over his head providing both smelly protection from the rain and disguise, he emerged from under the wharf by a rusted steel ladder fixed to the rock.

He was barefoot and still he had nearly forgotten! intimately
encircled by the steel cold of the handcuff. It was still dark at 5am
on the cold, wet winter's morning. Cars and buses were starting to
swish past on the slick asphalt, streetlights still on were throwing
down yellow cones of light with the rain glistening through the
illumination.

He needed to get moving and did so with a determined stiff-
legged walk away from the shoreline. He knew this area; 177 the
Esplanade was three short kilometres away along the waterfront.
Not even tempted to go there, to check it, it was too dangerous, they
must be watching, a surveillance team would be assigned for sure.
He quickly entered the narrow street system away from traffic both
vehicle and pedestrian, although periodically he met and passed
early risers on the way to the wharf, and grunt answered grunt
of greeting. It didn't take him long. In 20 minutes he was there,
Beaconsfield Road, Manly, and there across the road from number
10, the home of Jack and Maude Waratini and tribe, sat the huge
dark shape of the Kenworth prime mover.

Now what? He was not worried about the police being here,
no one knew about Jack. But he didn't want to drag Maude and
the kids into this so he had no intention of knocking on the door.
He remembered then that day when Jack had shown him over his
'baby' the first time he had been there. He recalled that Jack, proud
as a lover but beer-fuddled, had left the key to the Kenworth in the
house. Rather than stagger back in to get it he had scrabbled for a
spare he had tucked into a welded case in the beast's chassis ("Never
know when I might need a fast getaway bro jealous husbands eh?"
he had laughed).

The street was only modestly lit by well-spaced jaundice-yellow
streetlights. Bill crept up to the big truck, tentatively searching as
he had seen Jack do until cold fingers found the welded slot and
retrieved the key. With bare iceblocks of feet, he climbed up onto
the shiny chromed running board to the passenger door and, praying
the thing was not alarmed, he inserted the key and pulled open
the heavy door. No alarm, thank Christ. Into the leathery-scented
dryness he climbed, then up behind the seats and into the sleeper

50

unit behind the cabin. Bloody luxury, he breathed, teeth chattering staccato. He awkwardly stripped off the oilskin in the confined space, and then climbed into the immaculate white-sheeted bunk that Jack had had especially modified at the factory as a condition of purchase, to cater for his 130kg, 6'2" body in comfort.

He was safe, for the moment. And all he had to do was convince a huge Maori of warrior ancestry that to hide a wanted man and to risk his liberty, his family's security and future, his truck and his livelihood, was a good idea.

Chapter 6

Green, Green Grass of Home

This time it was his mother he farewelled. He told her that he loved her, would miss her, yes he would ring, yes, take good care of himself, yes, he would give dad a big hug from her. She tried to be brave, she had had him for three whole happy years, and at least this time it was like he had grown up and was leaving the nest; normal stuff. And he hugged her and then Maggie who burst into tears, and told him in her sweet southern drawl that she loved him also. And when he pulled the two, a mother and a mother-figure together into a bear-hug of goodbye and turned waved tear in his eye, and disappeared out of sight through the customs gate, she lost control and sobbed as Maggie comforted her with gentle tones. Then the two matronly figures, arms around each other, turned and left JFK for what each privately suspected was to be a somewhat emptier life in the small apartment in the village.

Although sad to leave his mother, he was excited as he boarded the Air New Zealand Boeing 747, with its pristine white and green curling Koru design on huge tail, through the sloping claustrophobic tunnel of the motorised finger. He was shown to his seat by the attractive, immaculate Polynesian hostie, and settled into the window seat for the 18-hour flight to Auckland.

The big bird tracked down from the east coast of the USA over the white-tipped Pacific 20,000 feet below, over the eastern edge of Australia toward the shaky isles, his homeland that he had left 18 years before. And then, after his sixth plastic meal and seventh in-flight movie (American action flicks, all car chases and granite-jawed heroes, and the others light English romantic pap) the Captain announced that the tip of the North Island of their destination was in sight: Cape Reianga. And when he looked forward and down through the distortion of the double plexi-glassed porthole, all he could see was the fluffy white cloud bank that gave the islands the Maori name, translating poetically as "The Land of the Long White Cloud". Within the hour the plane began its long gentle descent through the cotton wool, softly shuddering as the whirring and alarming clunking sounds of the mechanical preparations for landing the massive machine heralded the proximity of touchdown. They broke into the clear blue sky again under the cloud and the green patchwork of pasture and agricultural endeavour. Too quickly then with abrupt sensation of the captain's minute corrections from side to side, up and down, power on, power off, the 747 gently adjusted from flight to tarmac and she settled her massive weight and precious cargo down.

He was tired now and crawled out of the plane to face the interminable snail-like progress through the customs gates. Passport presented, followed by friendly comparison of photo against photographed, and a warm "Kiaora" in broad kiwi accent. Then a uniformed arm directed them into the luggage recovery area to collect his backpack from the ever-rotating conveyor. Again the déjà-vu of the experience of coming out of the artificially controlled static environment on one side of the luggage hall as the auto doors suddenly and silently slid open to expose him to the harsh reality of the un-met masses in the arrivals hall. Then a sudden cacophony of sound and colourful sea of sight and faces eagerly checking him out, until he sees his father waving and waiting in the mass for him. His dad looked the three years older, he thought, greyer, smaller, like a childhood house revisited. He had grown of course and his father commented on how fit he looked, how big he was. Proudly, the old bull admired the progeny, and felt suddenly old.

"Come on, son, let's hit the road, it's a three hour drive home."

Then he led his boy out and into the humidity of an Auckland summer afternoon and Bill broke into an immediate clammy sweat and felt the fatigue of the flight and time lag. He was happy then to enter the air-conditioned leathery comfort of his father's gutsy Landcruiser. They caught up on the journey as his father pointed the comfortable vehicle north toward home. Up the inevitable freeway through suburban South Auckland, through the bustling harbour city and over the steel-grey of the Auckland Harbour bridge.

He brought his father up to date, with the health and happiness of his mother, with the result of his exams, the satisfaction of the honours awarded with the degree, the progress of his tae kwon do and current ranking of 7 dan black belt.

He recalled with pride the tournaments he fought in and won to achieve his rise.

He reminisced and enjoyed again the hilarity and fun of his rugby. The huge, drunken, unforgettable farewell party the boys held for him. His father laughed at the images he drew of Rexy and the "smallest penis in the world" contest in the bar at the team's favourite watering hole the last thing he could clearly remember. Rex won several healthy bets after loudly, commandingly, proudly announcing that he and he alone possessed the world's smallest member, only to be taken to the cleaners by a Singaporean winger who, once the bets were placed, revealed a wrinkled brown acorn. Then Rex won back his money and more when he tortured his stub by sitting it into a jug of iced water for ten minutes until it developed a countersunk attitude above his shrivelled gonads, and the Singaporean conceded defeat.

His father brought him up to date with the important things like the immediate past performances of the All Blacks, and the promising new players emerging from the professional restructure of the game. They talked for an hour comparing past heroes to the modern versions.

Then, with the state of the nation dealt with, his father told him what he wanted to do. "Mate, I have a plan depending, of course, on what you want."

"No, Dad, I'm at your mercy."

"Ok, boy. I want to take you, just the two of us, on a tiki-tour of God's Own. What do you say we do the breadth and length of the nation?" His dad looked over at him, uncertain. "Both major islands, east and west coasts, top to bottom and maybe even a visit down to Stewart Island?" Stewart Island was the tiny, rugged full-stop off the end of the South Island.

"Dad, I could not think of anything that I would like to do more."

"Excellent, mate, that's decided then."

So it was agreed they would leave in one week, towing the small runabout and with the fishing rods, hunting rifles for pig, deer and goat in the forests along the way but most importantly, that they would take their time.

After two hours of talk, Bill slept, as the vehicle cruised smoothly, effortlessly north through the picturesque harbour city of Whangerei then through the mighty pine forest at Wairoa. The forest was planted during the not so great depression of the thirties when thousands of men were out of work and the government of the day created huge labour-intensive projects, anything they could to give those men the dignity of paid work, no matter how demeaning or pointless at the time. The result was now a magnificent towering forest of prime timber, harvested and milled for the local and export markets. They rose up to the coastal range with its beautiful rolling green farmland, cleared in back-breaking toil in the forties with the return of the tired and battle-weary battalions from World War Two. A grateful nation rewarding the servicemen with cheap defence force loans to farm the land.

Bill woke bleary and stale, and just as they crested the summit of the coastal range. The sudden view of the white sand on the opposite shore of the sheltered Hokianga harbour took him back years. His father steered the cruiser down as the road followed the contours of the hill and curved along the shoreline and into the village of Opononi. The small settlement was famously the home of Opo, a bottlenose dolphin who had gained worldwide fame and affection in the 1960s with her friendly trusting visits.

"I'll just stop at the Four Square." His Dad pointed to the small cluster of shops next to the pub. "We need milk and bread." The Landcruiser whined to a halt outside the old weatherboard shop with its advertising hoardings now faded from the harbour breezes and the sun and salt.

Bill eased out of the car wearily but was immediately refreshed by the pure perfumed sea air off the harbour. He bent to find and then skip a rounded pebble off the beach watching it *pitt-pitt-pitt* across the water. Then they were back into the vehicle as his father placed the groceries on the back seat. The glass-bottled milk had a clear tidal mark of yellow butterfat, and the warm smell of fresh-baked bread, wrapped in wax paper, flooded the vehicle's interior and had both men breathing in hungry anticipation of feasting on the heavy crusted staple. With windows down, Bill's father drove slowly through to the northern side of town and turned off the narrow winding asphalt road onto a black dirt driveway.

"Here we are, mate," and he pointed out the patches of native bush bordering pastures on which fat, young, black-Angus beef cattle grazed and mooched, trusting and contented. Bill admired the raw beauty of the location to the proud satisfaction of the owner. The ten-acre block was set up on a slight hill at the far end of the small harbour, prime waterfront land. At the highest point of the lot sat the comfortable modern villa that his father had built with his retirement fund. It had all the mod-cons, with no expense spared. His dad showed him to his room. "This, mate, is the guestroom although I rarely have such creatures." It was on the second floor, with light pink stucco walls and a huge feature window with a small balcony providing a spectacular vista from the harbour-facing bed. "Bill, get showered and changed, take your time and I'll see you downstairs when you're ready," his dad said and impulsively hugged his son before leaving him. Bill stripped off his travel clothes and showered, spoiling himself with the lava-hot stream from the tap, heated, his father had told him, by large solar panels on the flat roof of the house. He felt exhilarated after the long and tiring crossing of time

and datelines. Then, renewed, refreshed, dressed in jeans and a
t-shirt, he joined his father for a light dinner and a couple of cold
beers.

"All ready, boy, come on and sit down," his father welcomed.
He had fired up the charcoal grill and plump, finely-marbled scotch
fillets ("from the last beast we killed," he boasted proudly) were
soon sizzling on the hot steel. Bill had tasted his father's cooking
before. It was a task they had shared when his mother had left for
the USA, and both enjoyed the creativity and satisfaction of the
preparation, presentation and most of all the consumption of the
food. His dad stood at the grill and handed him tongs. "Remember,
boy, a perfect steak? Flip only once," and Bill laughed in
recollection. It was not long before the succulent grilled meat joined
buttery baked potatoes and a fresh garden salad on the plate and they
ate. They downed their first beer and it was soon followed by one
then two more as they talked about the past.

They reminisced about mainly the good times, in Uganda, and
Korea. Fond discussions about his mother. Bill shared a somewhat
abridged version of his adventures in NY and his father told stories
from Thailand. That first night Bill was fading by 8pm and with
an affectionate hug and a warm goodnight the two men reluctantly
parted. Bill climbed the stairs to his bedroom for a deep, dream-
filled sleep. His last thoughts were of a fishing trip on the harbour in
the morning.

That first week was a happy time for both father and son as
they revived and renewed their bond, recognised and remembered
the goodness in each other, enjoyed the comfort and respect of the
other's company. They fished and they talked and they cooked for
each other. Each tried to out-do the other, striving for the ultimate
culinary compliment. They played darts and 8-ball together at the
local hotel where his father proudly introduced Bill to the friends he
had made in the town, men and women. Bill had quietly looked in
his father's house for any sign of a woman, but had found no such
evidence, and he didn't ask. In the friendly warmth of the small
pub, Bill, after proud paternal introduction, shook the calloused
hands of fishermen, the strong grips of the foresters and farmers and

suffered and delighted at the soft-scented welcoming kisses of warm
Polynesian matrons. He enjoyed the earthy humour of the locals
as, inevitably later in the evenings as the fuel intake increased, they
sang with guitars into the dark and smoky night. The melodious
voices of the land and water's traditional tribal owners, the Maori,
joined in easy harmony with their more recently arrived colonising
brothers.

So after the too-short week they loaded the landrover and hitched
up the boat. With the bush-fridge loaded with steamed fat crayfish
tails, succulent salty rock oysters, orange tainted smoked snapper
and a supply of ice-cold lager, Bill's dad pointed her south and
they began the journey. It was a journey that was to culminate in
the meeting that would change the course of Bill Peter's young life
forever.

Chapter 7

Pig's Arse!

Bang!

Jack slammed shut the front door and cursed loudly at the rain
as he moved at a cautious, heavy work-booted trot from the porch
across the wet road to the driver's door of the Kenworth. There were
more gentle "fucks" as he fumbled for the keys while juggling his
oversized tartan thermos and the near suitcase-sized lunchbox that
Maude had packed for him that morning. She had risen early to feed
Jack a cholesterol mountain of fried thick bacon, four eggs over
easy, cheese-grilled tomatoes and butter-fried mushrooms, with a
high rise of thick white toast and mugs of sugar-sweet milky tea to
wash it all down. "Got to start my big man off right on his trip to
Melbourne, eh?"

Then Maude kissed him a fond farewell. "Take care my love,
don't forget to ring me so I know you got there ok," and she ushered
him out the door and set to the task of preparing nine breakfasts and
nine school lunches for her awakening brood.

Key scrabbled into door-lock finally and there was a big exhaled
grunt like a breaching whale as Jack rose up on the steps and
thumped down into the cab, the hydraulic driver's seat squealing
softly in rude adjustment. Jack whistled happily, a sweet melancholy
country and western tune ("the only two types of music I like, bro,)

and he fired the big machine into growling life. He blipped the
accelerator once, twice to warm the massive turbo-injected diesel.
She's a 600 horsepower Caterpillar, a powerful machine to pull the
big 16-wheel refrigerated freight trailer with smooth mechanical
ease through 18 gears over the 1000km haul to Melbourne. Jack
sat there watching gauges waiting for his baby to warm herself
("foreplay", he calls this time; "make her hot and loose for easy
running into the freight yard at Liverpool"). There he will hitch up
to the 16-wheeler already loaded with prime young pig carcasses
having sat overnight connected to the depot's mains power.

Bill hesitated. Does he say something now and risk giving Jack a
heart attack from the shock of his voice or does he wait until they hit
the depot? But his dilemma was quickly solved.

"So, Billy my man, how the fuck are you, bro?"

"How the fuck did you know I was here, mate?"

"Hey come on, bro, you're a fucking media star boy, TV news,
news-flash, papers, you the man, Billy! You aaaare the man!!
Anyway I knew that if you could you would get to me. I'd have
been mighty pissed off if you hadn't, mate. And no offence, my
pakeha friend, but you whitefellas stink. As soon as I opened the
door knew I had a visitor. Either that or a cat had pissed in my
sleeper, eh?"

"Hey, it's not true Jack. What they say: it's not the truth."

"Fuck, bro, I think I know you by now! I know you don't
do drugs. When that came out Maude and I knew straightaway
something was not kosher. Listen, Bill, you lay back there and let
me get this thing on the road. We can talk as I drive. You hungry,
bro?" "Shit yeah," and then Jack handed back into the sleeper the
mega lunchbox, the thermos of steaming sweet coffee, and after
a firm and meaningful bro-shake through the black curtain, Jack
drove and Bill greedily ate, perched on the bed. He helped himself
to the unusual but tasty cheese and curried egg sandwiches, cold
baked spuds and fatty, cold, deep-fried pieces of chicken, and drank
the sickly sweet coffee. Shit, this will be good for my cholesterol
count. Then with hunger and thirst sated at last he sat back against

the padded sleeper and through the black curtain told his friend the whole story of the night before.

Jack laughed uproariously with that distinctive bubbling giggle while effortlessly negotiating the big prime mover as it cruised through the Sydney rush hour. They were travelling away from the city centre and soon were within the street network of the industrial suburbs toward the freight yards.

Jack especially enjoyed the vision of the handcuffs snapping around Bill's "bag of tricks" as he called it. "That'll fucking teach you, bro," and Jack giggled on until he became angry at the story of the beating that the TRG thugs had dealt out. "Fuckin coward wankers," the big man growled. He went past anger when Bill told him of the drug the puncture hole that still gaped, the way he felt when he woke in the car, the fog. He went quiet when Bill told him they meant him dead. And he roared once again in laughter when Bill explained the damage he'd done to Hill. "You fuckin beauty, Billy boy," he said, smashing his huge fist onto the armrest. "That guy Hill. He's a fucking hero, according to himself. By the way, mate, his version is that you took him hostage then beat the crap out of a defenceless Officer of the Law, and stole his fuckin gun. I got to tell you Billy," Jack warned, "they are very very hot on you, the local gendarmes."

Bill was quiet for some minutes, troubled. But then for the sake of completion he rounded off the tale with his escape to Manly in the kayak.

"Jesus, little bro, you have had quite a night, eh?"

Bill then explained the set-up, the prints on the plastic sandwich bag, the insistent and unbelieving questioning about what Mrs Italiano had told him. The certainty that the Commissioner was corrupt, very corrupt. Then he fell finally quiet, still amazed at the turn of events and the way his reality had so radically changed in such a short time.

Jack spoke. "Ok, Billy my boy, so now what do we do with you?"

"I've thought about the options. I have got to get out of New South Wales. If they track me down I reckon I'm brown bread. No offence."

"None taken, man."

"Mate, they will have the goons out there looking and they won't want me talking if they get me."

Jack agreed with a grunt. They talked about options: places and people Jack knew, where he could hide out. Bill spoke of his homeland, New Zealand. "Mate, there is no way known that I can get there. Not yet anyway. My passport, everything, is at the flat. Anyway there is no doubt that in the western world Interpol shit Customs, Army, Navy, Airforce fuck the Bondi dog ranger and the Manly Brownie Pack Ahkayla would have my photo by now. I am going to have to lay low for a very long time I would say."

But they both agreed. Bill had to get out of New South Wales now before they had time to really organise, to search, to plug gaps. He had to get out in Jack's truck to Melbourne.

The truck growled into Kelly's Interstate Freight yard, where Jack spun it around in a semi-circle, crunching through blue-metal and then smoothly reversing with delicate precision to mate the prime mover to the waiting trailer. "Give us a few moments, bro, I have to get her hitched up and then I'll be in the office getting the paperwork sussed, ok? Hang tight."

Bill, by this time, was lulled sleepy by the heat rising from the cabin's warm, circulating air. Jack left the big motor idling as he married the truck to trailer. With the exertions of the night before and despite the omnipresent sense of danger, for the moment, in the gentle care of his friend, Bill felt secure. He lay down and tucked himself between the fresh Rinso-scented sheets, regretting his stench and the stains and marks he knew that Maude would fuss over. He found that he was falling and did then fade into a fitful sleep. He was woken briefly when Jack climbed back into the cabin and fired the big engine's revs up to towing torque.

Jack, realised that Bill was weary, insisted that he sleep first, talk later and they slowly made their way out of the huge metropolis of Sydney and onto the highway system, steadily moving west toward Victoria. Bill gained desperately-needed rest and slept as the truck purred west, chewing up the miles, with Jack singing along to his *Top 40 C&W Hits by Australian Stars* CD. Male and female true-blues warbled the sweet tragedies of the genre in mock American accents telling those simple rhyming tales of heartbreak and the heart-broken. Jack called it "white-man's soul" and his own Polynesian heritage of song and melody drew him to the simple tunes.

It took two hours just to wind forty kilometres away from the heart of the city and onto the main route west. Jack heard the first warnings from the brotherhood of truckers crackling over the citizen band radio. New South Wales' finest had set up roadblocks at the city limits and were searching all vehicles with police dogs.

Bill woke to a big mitt reaching back into the sleeper and shaking him out of the fog. "We got a problem, bro, the bears have blocked the highway ten ks up."

"Shit. What now?" Groggy with sleep, confused.

"Ok, here's the plan, Stan. We put you in the fridge and hope like fuck they don't search it."

"The fridge? You reckon, Jack?"

"We got half a chance, man, because the hygiene regulations won't allow no cops or fucking dogs walking amongst export hogs, now, can we? What do you say, bro?"

Bill considered his options. "You know, big-man, you're not just a pretty face. In fact, let's face it, mate, you are not even a pretty face. Let's do it."

Jack pulled her off the highway at the first opportunity, whining sweetly down through the gears into a truck stop. He parked her hard up against the bush. The depot was a staging point just outside the city where the big machines picked up and dropped off trailers and refuelled for the run to Melbourne.

"Ok bro out the side door and around the back of the trailer. Give me two minutes. Stay out of sight, man, there's eyes around."

Jack nodded to the NSW Police Heavy Transport Patrol Landcruiser parked in the forecourt of the pump area 100 metres away. No sign of the occupants must be inside the roadhouse. Bill's nerves were suddenly as raw as his aching body.

"Jack," he stopped the big man as he went to exit the cab. "If they find me, you didn't know. Ok?"

"Calm down cowboy, they won't find you," and Jack smiled that piano-key smile, even one or two black keys further back in the jaw, Bill noted stupidly. Then he was gone, door slammed. Heart pumping as the adrenalin kicked again into the tired body, Bill counting to two minutes, "one potato, two potato."

Jack vaguely heard whistling innocently down the back of the rig.

"Shit, Kenny Rogers again, "The Gambler", how appropriate," and he couldn't help but chuckle at his friend's sense of humour. Sliding low across the seat, Bill cautiously opened and slid out the heavy passenger door, closed it softly, brushed down along between the side of the big rig and the scrubby bush to the back of the massive trailer. Jack, busy at the rear door, talked softly to the crouched ashen-faced fugitive. "Ok, Billy boy, I'll swing her just open and you're in. It's going to be fucken cold man but it won't be for long."

The refrigerated seal gasped open. Bill stepped into the clinical cold of the fridge unit. He quickly shouldered through the swinging porcine carcasses as Jack slammed shut and secured the rear door. Bill's world was suddenly cold and black and smelt of frigid death.

Mercifully, Jack was back into the prime mover quickly, firing her up with hissing of air brakes and slow roll of forward motion. Bill steadied himself at the cab end of the fridge unit, hugging the nearest gutted pig.

He swayed in a desperate dance as if to an unheard waltz as the rig manoeuvred out again onto the highway toward the police roadblock and his immediate fate.

Shit it's cold.

He had on Jack's knee-high woollen ugg boots that he'd found in the sleeper. He still wore the overalls from the Commisioner's garage and over them still the oilskin from the boatshed. But the pervasive circulated chill of the fridge began to sink into him and he willed Jack on at all speed. To add to the tension, he realised that the steel cuffs were attracting the cold. The thought of an icy castration by frostbite focused the mind like nothing else. "Go, bro, go" he squealed in a newfound Bee Gees falsetto.

It took 15 interminable minutes to reach the roadblock. He felt the big truck decelerating smoothly to a hissing standstill, all engine and airbrakes as she eased softly down to a halt. In the frigid blackness he pondered his fate. Would they search the fridge unit? And if they did he was dead meat ... so to speak.

Suddenly, the big back door squeaked ajar and Jack's booming argumentative tones made it plain he was not a happy traveller. Just before the full light of the day chased down into the 20-metre length of the fridge unit, Bill squeezed fully back into the cab-end corner and swung himself up off the floor. Legs up and around and squeezing in intimate embrace the arse-end of a fat pig carcass and arms similarly encircling his immediate neighbour in a desperate hug. Hanging helplessly in the porky menage-a-trois Bill could only listen as Jack Waratini, infamous Maori orator, convincingly debated his case with the Canine Squad Officer at the door of the trailer. Meanwhile, the officer's highly trained attack dog barked madly with canine orgasmic delight at the olfactory assault on his snout as the scent of 200 dead pigs drowned him in a vapour-fall that he would have paw twitchy dreams of for many years to come.

Jack's baritone argued that for man or animal to enter the fridge would irretrievably contaminate the export meat and would cost the police the value of the freight, which Jack slightly exaggerated to be "a million bloody bucks, mate!"

Jack's aggressive eloquence appeared to work. After a careful but long-distance examination by powerful torch, the police officer was either apparently satisfied and/or intimidated by Jack's reasoning and he allowed the big door to be eased shut. Soon the rig once again purred away and was at speed, heading westward. And as the truck picked up momentum Bill lost his grip, dulled and weakened by the cold and simply fell off his perch, sliding slowly down his bristly companions' chilled bodies to crash awkwardly to the icy steel floor. He lay face up under a sea of grins of dead pigs with their dulled eyes and floppy ears above him.

That's where Jack found him when he finally stopped in an off-road parking bay outside a quiet country town ten minutes later. Bill, moaning, stuck icily to the floor and curled into a shaking shivering hypothermic ball of misery.

Jack noted with exaggerated chagrin only that, "Hey, bro, you got my bloody slippers on eh?" and Bill mumbled a dopey apology for the ugg boots and smiled his thanks for the escape. Satisfied, Jack dragged his carcass down and out the length of the trailer by the scruff of his stiffly frozen oilskin. The big man bumped him out of the tail onto shaky legs. Then he propped and half-carried the smaller man like a wounded soldier along the side of the trailer and into the warmth of the cab and sleeper and Jack tucked Bill away into the bunk.

"Next stop Melbourne, my friend."

Chapter 8

Funny, Familiar, Forgotten Feelings

South they headed, father and son, the boat on the trailer skipping
along behind. His father, to his delight, was a surprising human
encyclopaedia of local historical and geographical information
as they purred down Highway 1. One hour to Whangarei, the big
city of the northlands set on a narrow isthmus, the Tasman Sea and
unseen Australia to the west; the Pacific Ocean and far distant South
America to the east. They went straight through on this occasion,
but his Dad filled him with tales of the port city's colourful past.
Stories of whaling stations with wooden ships, and hard men out
of Nantucket, Marseille, Bristol and other exotic ports. There
were stories of the Kauri gum diggers in the late 1800s. Men from
Dalmatia, from London, Dublin, Sydney and New York, armed with
long steel poles, sturdy shovels and sinewed, muscled arms. They
sought the amber lumps of ancient gum from prehistoric forests for
export to the markets of Europe.

He told of the Maori, the warlike tribes of the Northlands led
by warrior chiefs like Hone Heke. They were fierce warlords who
led immaculately trained and ruthless raiding battalions south to
terrorise and conquer. Their aim was to kidnap to provide slaves
and breeding stock or, incredibly, to take simply as protein the more
peaceful tribes of the Bay of Plenty and Taranaki to the south.

His father told him of the madness of the gold rush of the 1920s and of the hoards of the desperate, the adventurous, the entrepreneurs, the soldiers of fortune and even the criminals lured by gold fever. Very few striking it rich beyond their wildest dreams, most labouring for nought, some stayed to populate, farm the land and build the young colonial outpost.

They cruised through rolling pasturelands and into the sprawling metropolis of Auckland, the nation's biggest city. It was a multi-coloured, multi-cultured mixing pot. The heart of the city was surrounded like a wagon wheel by sprawling suburbs to house the Pacific Island population, encouraged to emigrate in the 60s and 70s. The people were needed to power the factories that drove the budding economy as the small nation cast aside colonial dependency and found its feet. It was a difficult climate as international markets faded for the country's traditional wool, lamb and dairy exports. Again, his father deliberately by-passed the city, saying it was, "another we can stop at on the way back up".

"By the way if you're a local boy," his father commented, "they reckon you're an Aucklander first, and then a North Islander, and only then a Kiwi. The rest of the country call them Rangitoto yanks," he laughed alluding both to the tiny beautiful wooded island of Rangitoto that sits as an ancient volcanic peak in the harbour, and to the perceived superiority complex of the inhabitants of Auckland city.

And so, Bill and his tutor rolled on that first day. They ate a roadside lunch fit for royalty of scallops, fresh crayfish tails the sweet aquatic meat almost too rich washed down with a lager.

And so the next six weeks were among the best so far in Bill's life. Father and son undertook a tour of the heart and the heartland. They were getting to know each other as blood first, and then as men. Bill came to the pleasant realisation that he liked his father as a man, and that this was different from his instinctive love as a son. He was also getting to know the country from where he came but had spent so little of his life.

They played the tourist game. They took an all-day visit to the historical steamy working Maori village of Whakarewarewa at Rotorua. It was a precious glimpse into the past of a cultured people who based themselves around the thermal wonderland and implemented the warmth and power of the steam and hot sulphurous waters for village life. They stayed a week, soaking in the natural beauty of the area's forest and lakes. Each night they soaked their tired bodies in blood-hot natural spring waters of the thermal network diverted into a spa pool. The sulphurous mineral soup lulled the body and relaxed the mind.

Then it was off to the pristine aquatic heart of the North Island, the huge Lake Taupo. Its snow-fed fresh water reached 40kms from pebble shore to pebble shore. They stopped in luxurious accommodation and took the dinghy from the trailer, and launched her for days of fishing for rainbow and brown trout. They enjoyed the shivering strikes of the mighty fish and the inevitable conclusion of the uneven fight between man and beast.

His father surprised him by chartering a helicopter to fly them deep over the forested Urewera mountain range. The chopper put them down into the mysterious world of a misty landscape. On these lands, long before Captain Cook, lived the proud tribe of the Tuhoe, a musical and artistic people, known as the Children of the Mist. It was here that his Dad first mentioned his friend, Kingi Potiki, as these were his tribal lands. With backpacks and rifles slung they trekked by survey map deep into the enveloping native bush. Under dripping canopy they found the forestry hut and soon had a crackling fire going and a billy of tea steaming the small bunkroom.

For five days they hunted pig and deer. Bill discovered in himself the contradiction of a primal satisfaction of the stalk and then the terrifying screaming violence of the kill. His father was more used to death than Bill, who was uncomfortable that the power to destroy life was his.

Bill shot one pig on the second morning. He and his father hid in ambush beside the spoored trail where the pigs descended down off a high ridge. They came in a single huffing grunting file into a sweet fern-fronded gully to root with snout and ivory tusk into the soft undergrowth. His father, by nod of head, invited him to experience the kill, and unknowing but excited, he aimed the World War Two vintage Lee Enfield .303 carbine on his prey. A young male boar, his bristles were black wire, his tiny eyes red.

Bill fired. Foresight just behind the leading shoulder. The copper-tipped bullet exploded the red muscle of the heart and smashed bone and tissue in its gory entry and exit. The pig screamed that near-human peal of anguish and pain that only pigs can. And Bill knew instantly that this was his last kill. He would spend the rest of the week assisting his father to hunt, to skin, gut and carry. But he didn't want to get used to death. His father understood. He had been in theatres of war in distant lands where men younger than Bill had killed others by gun and knife at his command.

That first night they sat together outside the hut in the soft yellow light of a gas lantern. They sat companionably, upwind of the crackling fire. The sap-engorged pine burned hot and noisy in the river stone pit outside the hut. Both men, hungry from the day's exertions, salivated at the smells of fresh fat pork chops grilling, fat spitting and hissing onto the glow of the embers under the wire grill. Boiled sweet potato and heavy syruped baked beans simmered in blackened iron pots on the fire's edge.

Frank Peters sat back and spoke for the first time of his military past to his son. They quaffed in white enamel mugs generous measures of the sweet green ginger wine that his father preferred when playing or working in the elements. The tangy root wine was perfect for such a night under the clear black sky with distant stars sparkling. "Ah, my boy, very moreish, what?" his Dad inquired and Bill sighed his agreement. Maybe it was the magic of the drug in the wine. Or more probably just the moment where a father felt he could, or maybe should, share with his progeny the secrets, the terrible wonders of a past. Times long gone when he was young, younger even than Bill was now. Times where he had witnessed or even caused the violent death of an enemy. He spoke to his son. "I saw today at the hunt, mate you did not enjoy the kill."

"Well yeah …" Bill paused for another sip of the honeyed liquor. "I loved being out there with you I loved the hunt for the pigs…. but it's true… As soon as that bullet hit the pig I just felt sick," he paused. "It wasn't because of the blood and guts. Not even the

70

bloody horrible baby scream of the poor thing." Bill struggled to enunciate his emotion. "I guess it was just that power ... having that power, that ability to destroy, you know? To take away a life ... I'm not explaining it that well," he said, taking another pause. Both men stared into the ever-changing campfire. "God knows how a man could shoot another man!" Bill declared honestly.

"Well, you've got that in one, mate," his father spoke. "The various gods of the world must know why ... because I certainly have never worked it out ... In fact, the older I get the less clarity I have on why man kills other men." He reached over with the heavy green bottle to top up Bill's enamel mug. Bill leaned toward the embers to turn the chops.

"You know, my boy, I have fought in many battles as a soldier, and I have killed other men," his father revealed to him. Immediately Bill recalled his childhood. The memories of his father in the combat uniform of a soldier. Late night departures, the long absences, his mother's tension, the somewhat distracted man who returned and took time to slowly unwind back to the gentle father he knew. He recalled the tiny treasures his father brought back to him from some noisy marketplace, some in Asia, some from the Middle East and some from Africa. His father waited, hovering over the cooking, the chops nearing crisp perfection.

"Dad, I don't need to know, but I would like to know about the things you have seen; the things you have done."

"In the service of our country, son, I have fought in war and secret actions against men of other nations. Most of the time, and more so looking back now, I have no real idea why a Kiwi soldier would be shooting at men in Cambodia, Malaya, Ghana, Indonesia, Bosnia, wherever. But we did go. And we did fight." There was another pause, another sip. "It was always in support, of course, of the UK, and then later, the USA. Basically, mate, we fought for the values or, more properly, the financial interests of the big Christian Anglo-Saxon societies. I can tell you, son, that I killed other men. I shot some at a distance, some close up ... I fought some hand-to-hand ... I killed some by bayonet and knife."

Bill looked across to his dad and reached over to touch his arm in affection, in support. "I can tell you, my boy, that every single one of those men I can see right now. I will never forget those men. What they looked like, the place where each man died, the trees, the time of day or night, something about the dying place…" He paused. "And yet, son, I had that legal authority of combat, my society's permission a religious right to kill those men. Damn it, mate, I was even rewarded, honoured with medals, for being good at what I did, for doing what I did. You see, boy, they were enemy … now what the bloody hell does that mean?"

The question was rhetorical but Bill thought about it. He imagined the torments that his father had dealt with over the years that now still needed dealing with. "You know, son, that is why very young men are sent to war. Young men don't question. They are distracted by the adventure and convinced of the destiny … they are bullet-proof, mate. Just like you, son, it's all ahead of you, and I am so happy that you won't have to do what I did."

"Maybe it's because of the things you and your generation did, Dad," Bill spoke thoughtfully, "that I have the choice now, the freedoms."

His father thought about that. "Well I hope so boy, but there is still evil in the world. My dream is that you never have to deal with evil." Bill considered how untouched he was by fate's destructive forces. What a pleasant and easy and lucky path he had trodden so far in his life against the harsh realities of his father before him. And then his father decided enough had been said that night. He stood to retrieve the perfectly cooked golden chops and move them across to the tree stump table where large enamel plates awaited., "Hey, mate, this is all a bit heavy, must be the wine," he joked. "Time to eat." And Bill took a cloth and picked up the fire-hot pots that held the steaming kumara and the baked beans and they served the food and ate in quiet reflection.

Back from the hunt, they continued down the North Island. A visit to his birthplace. The tiny immaculate army camp huddled beneath the shadows of three volcanic peaks. It was long ago. The house vaguely familiar, now tenanted by some other army family the small issue of which played in the tiny front yard as Bill and his Dad sat back down the road and watched silently. Again it was his father who chose the moment. "Son … how do you? … Do you ever resent the break up of your Mum and me? … The way it worked out, you know, your childhood?" he asked quietly.

"No, Dad. I have thought about it, but really the way it happened was not the typical bitter divorce type thing anyway. When Mum went back to the States to rest she sort of just ended up staying there. So there was no sort of dramatic split. It just grew on me I suppose that she wasn't coming back."

"Yeah," his Dad grunted in agreement. Bill continued as if he needed to reassure his father, "And you were both … and are, both such great people and great parents anyway. So by the time I worked out that you had in fact broken up, I was pretty much a stable person thanks to that … thanks to you and to Mum."

His father looked at him, "You know mate that we are still married, just never got divorced, it didn't seem necessary, really." Bill nodded. "So you can't claim you're from a broken home, just a slightly dented one," and they laughed comfortably together. Bill wondered then if his dad knew about Maggie, was trying to think how, or if, he should bring the matter of his mother's sexuality up. And decided not to, it was not important.

"Bill," his dad continued, "my only regrets about your Mum and I are that you in some way missed out ... or were hurt ... or, I suppose, damaged in some way." Bill cheekily looked cross-eyed at his father and began an exaggerated facial twitch, "Naa pops, me grewed up fine," and his father roared and clipped his boy affectionately around his ears in response. It was then a very quiet, thoughtful and inwardly-focused day. Little more was said about what had been what might have been.

After two weeks of casual southward meandering and east-west zig-zagging they reached the capital city of the nation Wellington, at the southern base of the North Island. The picturesque wind-buffeted city hugged the hilly amphitheatre of the deep-water harbour.

"We won't stop this way, Bill," his father advised, "but on the way back up to home we will spend a few days. I want you to meet my best friend, Kingi Potiki. Kingi is a senior copper now based at Wellington HQ. But he was in my SAS platoon in those good-old, bad-old army days I was telling you about."

They boarded the inter-island ferry in the late afternoon sunlight to make the crossing of the notoriously unpredictable waters of the Cook Strait. Once parked, with the busy deck-hands axle-chaining the vehicles to the ship, they caught the lift and headed for the comfortable ship's bar. His father, always the amateur historian, told him that the strait was named after the intrepid Captain James Cook. "Listen up, boy," he ordered, all school-teacherly, "Cook was an English mariner and explorer who raised the English flag in New Zealand in October of 1769." His dad read from a booklet in the warm wood-grained bar area of the modern craft. "Cook arrived after a heroic journey on the tiny converted collier, *The Endeavour*," he continued. "You know, boy, this guy was a real hero. The Endeavour was a tiny three-masted bark only about a quarter of the size of this ferry."

The crossing proved calm and some four hours of effortless steaming later, ensconced in the bar aboard the MV Moana-Tane of the NZ Federated Line, they arrived at the South Island into the picture-postcard port of Picton.

Bill and his father spent three weeks touring the major southern island and were awestruck by the physical beauty and majesty of the land. The rugged wave-smashed west coast, the mountain range significant enough for the early settlers to compare it to the mighty European range and call the granite spine the Southern Alps. On their boys-own adventure they drove along the sheer-sided cliffs of the island's infamous west coast on precarious slippery blue metalled ribbons rudely gouged from rock with the ever-constant danger of slips from above and floods from below. This coast of the early gold rush fame boasts local legend that the west-coast men are really men, the beer is colder, the crayfish bigger, and the women prettier. "Prettier than what? The crayfish?" the northerners would ask. Then down to the far south of the south and to find the deep glacial-gouged majesty of the Fiordlands. The bleak drive then in cold grey rain around the tussock country to the rugged fishing village of Bluff at the bottom of the island. They stood on that day beside the cruiser stamping their frozen feet and feeling their ears and noses begin to painfully numb. They drank cups of hot thick seafood bisque bought from the small café on the dock. They watched from the tiny wharf as the trawlers chugged back in the bleak afternoon. Sturdy, deep-hulled boats returned to the tiny port from the oyster beds delivering a succulent booty, the deep water treasure of the Bluff Oyster and black water fish for the markets in the north.

That night, after the drive to the mountain village of Queenstown, they sat in the luxury of the ski-lodge sipping hot brandy toddies in front of an open fire and his father told him it was time to head slowly back. Bill said, "Dad, this time with you, this trip, has just been bloody fantastic. And I want to thank you for the amateur history and geography lessons."

"Amateur! Cheeky bugger!" his dad laughed, delighted at his son's appreciation.

"You know, this trip has made me think," said Bill. "I guess it's no one thing, but I have realised that it's time I made a decision on my future. What to do? I do want to do something ... I suppose something worthwhile ... knowing what you did ... as a soldier. And in the diplomatic corps ... that was something, you know, something to be proud of."

"Well I'm proud of what you have done already with your life, mate," his father said, leaning toward his boy. "You have so much opportunity with your education, your degree ... you can do whatever you want in the big, bright world. Whatever you do I will support you in any way I can and I know your Mum will too."

"Yea, thanks Dad," he replied. "You know I've got to admit, after we talked at the forestry hut that night I even considered the Army. Now I know you wouldn't be happy with that."

"You got that right," his father straightened up suddenly.

"Don't worry, Dad, it was only a fleeting thought. Anyway, a peace-time army doesn't really appeal," he declared as he paused to tip the last of the drink into his mouth. "But, you know, I reckon I might just enquire about the Police. That sort of interests me. Not really the old style Bobby thing but maybe to be a detective investigate murders, robberies, rapes, that sort of thing. Just I suppose to do something worthwhile," Bill said, "but also with a bit of a challenge, you know, an adventure."

His father just nodded and thought about it. He liked that idea. He would have his son in the country then if he did join up. And what's more he could discuss the possibilities with his old mate Detective Superintendent Kingi Potiki when they stopped in Wellington on the way back home. "Yes, son, I reckon that's well worth a look at," his father agreed and rose to ask the pretty blonde waitress to refill the toddies at the wood-panelled bar.

Chapter 9

Rangi Lash

Bill woke to the melodious sounds of the truck-driving Maori Elvis as mothers cried and children died in the ghettooooos, with Jack squeezing the last possible quaver out of the poetic tale of despair. Tucked warmly in the sleeper bunk, Bill stretched stiff and aching muscles in a languid cat flex. The sounds of his awakening saw the big brown fist of his friend sweep through and part the heavy curtain separating them. Bill leaned through into the cab to meet the big man's, "How's it, bro?"

"Great, thanks, mate. Jeez, what a sleep! Where are we?"

"Well, my friend, you slept for eight hours solid, thanks to my beautiful sounds. We made it: we are in the fair city of Melbourne in the choice state of Victoria in the proud young nation and Commonwealth of Australia, Gondwanaland bro, terra nullius, cuzz, land of the long lunch, a wide red land, home of the brave."

"Yeah, yea, mate, I get the picture," Bill laughed, marvelling at the big man's stamina after the 1000 kilometre drive through the night.

"I've been keeping an ear on the news, Bill," Jack said, suddenly more serious. "The local gendarmes are keeping an eye out for you, my friend. But mate, the broadcasts say the main search is still in old Sydney town. They are still pretty hot for you, boy. The Government is talking a reward for your head, and, how's this mate: a bravery medal for Mr Barney fucking Hill … fucked, eh?"

Bill laughed at Jack's disgust. Jack continued. "They are talking about how they think you might make for home, good old New Zealand. Good thing we went the other way."

"Right," Bill was wide awake now. "What to do, mate? That is the question."

"Ok," Jack said. "While you snoozed, Snow Offwhite, old Grumpy here got to thinking. First, we get your appearance changed, and get the bracelets off the crown jewels. I got a cousin here, in Melbourne. My cuzzy Rangi. A lovely Maori maiden who runs a fine establishment which stocks handcuff keys and turns boys into men. What I say is let's drop this trailer, then head off to Rangi's. Then I will make some calls to some old mates and call in a few favours."

Bill grunted his assent in the absence of any better ideas.

"What would you think about going bush to Kalgoorlie in the Wild West my friend?" Jack asked. "Amongst all the desperados in that town mate, you could be invisible for as long as you need to be."

"Jack, you're a fuckin genius thanks mate." For the first time Bill started to see a plan, consider a future, even if only for the short-term.

"Ok young fulla, leave it to Uncle," said big Jack, proud of his efforts. "First things first: drop the trailer off." With that, Jack burst back into the final verse of the Presley hit ending with a shoot out with the police, the demise of a child and more tears from mum. Meanwhile he wound the big rig down dark streets of the early Melbourne morning with gasps and blasts of air brakes, finally pulling in to the freight yards of the smallgoods factory where the inhabitants of the trailer were to be pumped, pickled and smoked.

Two hours later in the wee small hours, the prime mover, freed of the burden of the trailer, squealed to a halt outside the rear entry of the "House of Lash" in Little Colin Street in the city. Then, furtively in the darkened back lane, one huge Maori, one fugitive friend of huge Maori and one borrowed pig carcass carried by huge Maori, quietly disembarked and slunk to the red door. With secret knock all three were admitted by a middle-aged strongly-built woman of Aotearoa, now the Madam of the establishment that profited from pain.

Chapter 10

Undercover Angel

"Son, meet my friend, Kingi Potiki. Kingi, this is my boy, Bill. The subject of those thousands of photos you have suffered over the years," and Frank Peters laughed as he proudly introduced his friend to his son. Bill's hand, not a small hand, sunk into and was surrounded by the huge and callused mitt of his father's compatriot. They had arrived back in Wellington the previous night and his father had booked them into a luxurious hotel where they had spent a restful evening. His father had spoken over dinner about the man they were to meet the next afternoon. Respectful references in the abridged stories told of his friend: his Mana, the Maori term that describes an extraordinary almost spiritual charisma; his warrior attributes. Kingi was now a detective superintendent in the New Zealand Police, where he had gone after a distinguished and legendary career in the New Zealand Army Special Forces. His career involved notoriously dangerous adventures behind enemy lines, usually under the command of Frank Peters, his father. That brotherhood of bloody combat in obscure Asian, African and eastern European villages had bound forever two very different men.

Bill examined this man, not tall 5'8 at the most strong, heavily boned and muscled frame. Deadly power through chest, arm and shoulder but compact and lithe, graceful almost. He was nearly

60 years old but Bill felt awed and immediately respectful. It was funny, Bill mused to himself, he had never thought of his father in that light. But watching the two old friends interact in the muted light of Kingi's high-rise apartment he saw now the mutual respect held by each man. And he realised that there must be many secrets held by each about the other.

Kingi had left the army shortly after his father's transfer into the Diplomatic Corps but his path had been different. For the last 20 years he had created and developed the anti-terrorist, and then the undercover, agent squads of the NZ Police. His system of selection and training of those chosen had placed agents deep into the criminal and anti-social gangs and organisations throughout New Zealand. The success of his meticulously planned deep-cover operations were now the envy of other law enforcement agencies throughout the world. As a result of his success he found, much to his disgust, that he was often required to travel overseas to advise and lecture about his secrets.

Once trained, Kingi's agents would follow him into the jaws of death. He sent them into that vicinity, into strange and often evil lives for periods of up to two years. They lived and loved with criminal or radical peer groups. As covert Judases they witnessed and recorded and sometimes participated in unlawful and anti-social acts as they ingratiated themselves into the lives of their target group. The agents were run and counselled secretly by handlers. Through planned and intricate communication they slowly pieced together the jigsaw of evidence that, at the operations end, would effectively gut the group through arrests and prosecution.

Kingi loved his agents. He had never lost one to discovery by the target group or from psychological trauma. He'd never lost one during the giving of evidence against those he or she had become close to, or through the stress recognised as a hazard in any deep-cover operation. He had never lost the loyalty and commitment of the agent when the agent risked the transfer of his loyalties and affections through the deliberate process of becoming, in almost every way, part of that target group.

The three men sat down to eat a lamb roast prepared by Kingi. He was a bachelor; no woman had been prepared to live with him although two had tried. They had found he was never at home and when he was, he was only there physically. His mind was always out there with his "kids", as he called them, the agents in the field.

Agents were typically young and lived with rebel and ethnic gangs in compounds where illicit drugs were part of daily life, and where violent group sexual assault is almost a party piece at drugged and drunken gang gatherings. Others were placed in radical cells. These were groups where the politics of the far left or the extreme right were preached and attacks on mainstream society planned by frighteningly unpredictable hard-liners. When his kids were in the field he thought about them one by one each day, even dreamt about them at night. Although his women had loved him for his qualities, to live with him was just not worth it. And when they left him he really barely noticed they had gone. His life was his work and his work was his wife.

Bill sat entranced by the two elders. He enjoyed the tender pink lamb, the sweet mushiness of the purple-streaked kumara and green peas in mint-sauced slush. Bill just listened as they spoke of others from their past and laughed at shared memories. The modern apartment looked out over the picturesque harbour. The city lights played across the placid waters on the mild summer's night as the three men finished the meal. Then, cold lagers in hand, they moved out onto the small balcony where Kingi, apologising for the indulgence, lit up the small Cuban cigar, "my only real vice." Again, Bill happily excluded himself from the conversation but felt a certain privilege in just being there. Both his father and Kingi from time to time made small effort by word or glance to include him, to acknowledge his courtesy. And both appreciated his silence and even enjoyed his silent participation. Then the two men turned to the present. Bill's father reminded Kingi of the joys and pleasures of his retirement at Opononi and renewed his invitation for his friend to come and stay as long and as often as he could. Bill learned that Kingi had been there several times when in the north but always before or after operations. Still, his short stays with Bill's father had been his only holidays as such for many years and both men had enjoyed the companionship and a spot of fishing. And Kingi always promised he'd be back.

Then Kingi talked of his current operation in Auckland. Without it being said Bill knew that he was listening to information that he could not, and would not, ever repeat. And he appreciated the trust that the two men placed in him as Kingi sought advice from his old mentor Frank Peters.

He spoke of a problem.

"We placed an operative in deep cover just on two years ago. On the fringe of the most criminal of the criminal gangs in the nation, the Te Kuri Gang". Kingi intoned in his deep voice, "*Te Kuri* is the Maori phrase for dog. A well-meaning children's court magistrate christened them when they were mere boys growing up in South Auckland. The wise man likened them to a pack of feral dogs, Te Kuri, and that name and its abbreviation, the TKs, has stuck since. They are a mixed ethnic grouping of the worst of Maori, Anglo and Polynesian men and women. They are lawless fringe-dwellers. Over the years they have become an organised crime family. They are led by strong and brutal leadership of a family of brothers, the Whetu brothers," Kingi told them, and Bill found himself entranced by the tale and by the telling of the natural orator. "Three brothers," Kingi continued, "Matu, Louis and Pedro Whetu. From a mixed Portuguese/Maori ancestry, they have a beautiful younger sister, Mere. The gang is based in a fortress-like compound which they own freehold, bought from the proceeds of their crimes, on a small island named Puketutu. Do you know it?" Frank shook his head in the negative. "It's a tiny island, only ten or so acres, separated from the mainland of the Manakau Harbour. It's on the western side of the Auckland isthmus; right by the city's sewerage plant and pond facility, which quite fittingly processes the shit and waste from the entire Auckland city. The only access to the fort is either across that stinking lake along a bare causeway, or on the other side of the island via the treacherous tidal flats of the harbour itself," Kingi explained. "At the fort there are sentry posts with a razor wire outer boundary fence and inner fence of a solid steel barrier. The gang can see any approach, be it by police or other enemy gangs, by line of sight and by CCTV video monitors and alarms."

With frustration evident, Kingi told them that no raid, lawful or otherwise, had ever succeeded in the prosecution or discovery of drugs or a weapons cache or other evidence of the gang's criminal existence. "It's got so bad," he complained, "that the local police now, after several fruitless raids, are restrained by a Supreme Court order from breaching the gang's boundaries. That's unless they can convince a judge of that court of the strength of the evidence of a specific crime."

"What's this gang all about?" his father asked.

"The gang's made its real money from production of the latest designer drugs in secret laboratories away from the fort," Kingi replied. "Gang members and associates then organise and oversee the distribution of the drugs to kids in nightclubs and on city streets." He paused then and they sat for a minute as he gathered his line of thought. "I believed, and I convinced the Commissioner back then, that the gang had, and still has an Achilles' Heel."

"Oh yeah?" Peters senior said, interested as ever in a tactical analysis of an enemy's weakness.

Kingi continued, "Yes mate. You see, over the years the Te Kuri has developed teams of teenagers that it controls. They operate in the suburbs of the greater Auckland region doing burglaries. So when I was tasked three years ago by the boss to evolve and implement an operation to terminate the criminal activity of the TKs, I finally decided on the approach of putting in place an undercover operative who would become the 'fence' for the purchase of the burgled goods from the gang. And that is now my problem." Kingi paused only to drink a long draught of the cool beer.

"The operation has worked. In fact it's worked spectacularly well. We found an agent of Anglo-Irish heritage and an ex-Special Air Service soldier through my old boys' network. I don't know if you know him: Tom Burns?" Bill's father thought quietly and then replied, "No, Kingi, I don't know him. May have been after my time?"

"Yes, I think you're right," Kingi answered. "Anyway, Tom had not lived here for over 20 years. He trained with our SAS but after the Falklands was seconded to the Brits and worked from the UK. So Tom became available. I flew to London and after assessment we brought him back to our training facility. We trained him and then placed him in deep cover in the suburbs of South Auckland as a buyer of stolen goods."

"And he went well?" Bill's dad asked. "Oh yes," Kingi nodded. "Initially he was on the fringes, then he slowly ingratiated himself as a trusted and generous fence until the Te Kuri themselves sought him out. You see, their usual avenues suddenly disappeared. Strangely the opposition was targeted by repeated Police raids." The two men laughed. "Tom's acceptance by the gang," Kingi continued, "was a carefully controlled process by both the Te Kuri and, unbeknown to them, by us. Eventually, after months of testing him with sale of goods by expendable mules of the gang, Tom was invited to attend the Island. They sent masked soldiers to his home at midnight to offer the invitation. Once there in the clubhouse the tattoos and the muscle surrounded him. He was given the once-over questioned, threatened and bluffed. Then one of them tried it on with him. Foolishly, of course. But using the skills of his past life Tom quietly broke his opponent's knee." They all laughed at the thought. "Only then did the Whetu brothers accept him into the fold. As Tom himself described the scene: with their man writhing on the floor in agony, the others stepped over him to welcome him with pats on back and bro shakes all round."

"The problem is," Kingi said, "this good man has been diagnosed with an inoperable cancerous tumour. The cancer is parasitically attached to and growing through his lower spine." They went quiet again. "He's going to die," Kingi said, "and he will die within the next three weeks or so … It looks like the entire two-year operation is destined to fail."

Bill's father nodded, sipping his beer and focusing on the drama of the discussion. "What to do?" Kingi expounded. "Write it off and grieve for the loss of a good man and a good operation? Or replace him and carry on the operation, somehow using the trust in place until the evidence can be gathered again to destroy the cancer that is the Te Kuri?"

It was then, as the two older men sat in quiet contemplation, that Bill took the first step of the process that would change his life. It was one of those significant decisions that once made could never be retreated from.

He volunteered for the job.

Chapter 11

Please Release Me

"Kiaora, Jack."

"Kiaora, my cuzz. How are you, darling?" The big man shouldered his gift of the pig into the dark and funky corridor of the club. Jack kissed his female cousin warmly on the cheek and then turned toward Bill.

"Cuzz, this is my mate Bill I told you about, and Bill, this is my most spunky cousin Rangi, the chief whip of the House of Lash."

"Jeez you talk shit, Jack," Rangi giggled melodiously and leaned toward Bill with a warm brushing of her ample brown cheek against his. "Hello, young Bill, very nice to meet you. Come in now you two, and relax," she said, leading them through a side door and into an apartment, clearly her home. "Jack, you can place your other closer relation there into the kitchen. I have some tucker cooking for you two."

Bill realised then that Jack had made some arrangements by phone on the journey across from Sydney. Rangi must know about him and why he was here; on the run, bruised, battered, reeking of the sour ammoniac body odour, still dressed in NSW Police issue overalls and complete with a set of steel handcuffs around his balls.

"First things first, love," Rangi spoke to Bill. "Let's get you two big men washed and freed up shall we, darling?" with a cheeky wink at Bill. With that Rangi pushed a small buzzer and into the apartment came a beautiful young blonde apparition in skimpy negligee. Bill's heart picked up a notch in sudden anticipation.

"Jack, gorgeous man."

"Amber, my precious little darling," the big man smiled as the tiny blonde launched herself up onto Jack's knee. Then, as she cuddled into his massive frame in a most familiar way, Jack looked across to the surprised gaze of his mate and winked a slow wink. His petite admirer pulled him up and led him out from the apartment and Jack, in *sotto voce*, whispered to Bill, "What happens on boys' own adventures stays on boys' own adventures." Then Jack boomed out his rolling laugh as he disappeared from view.

Rangi, giggling at Bill's surprise, took his hand and pulled him up from the armchair. "I like my meat white, darling. Follow aunty now and I'll get you cleaned up before dinner." And with that, Rangi led her confused catch out of the apartment, down the dark corridor to the murky far end and stood before a door labelled "The Dungeon". Bill was now suddenly open-eyed and anxious as he followed his hostess into the room and noted the stocks and cats of nine tails, the thumb-screws and other items whose use he could not imagine decorating the dark red velvet-lined interior.

"Fear not, little one," his hostess comforted. "This is the room with the spa," and she pushed aside heavy velvet curtains to reveal a steaming hot tub as if from a Roman time. Although he noted the chains and wrist restraints fixed into the surrounds of the pool, he started to relax with Rangi's giggles at his discomfort.

"Ok, spunky, get that gear off and I'll burn it for you," and he stripped the smelly overalls off gladly under the appreciative and rather close examination of his matronly companion. "Now let me check out those cuffs, darling," Rangi ordered as he had shyly turned away from her. She gently turned him back around toward her and then prised his hands from their protective cupping of his genitals. "Mmm, nice model," she muttered as she leaned down toward the cuffs and their strangled prey, as if to read the stamped imprint on the steel. Reddening with embarrassment, Bill didn't know where the hell to look. Then the unavoidable sensation of a woman gently touching, as she turned the steel bracelet, and even though he was not attracted in any way to this solid female specimen, he cursed inwardly as his damn cock began to stiffen despite his attempts to tell it not to. "Ok, honey, I think the best thing is to get you into the spa while I work out how to get that off you," she instructed, smiling widely.

Relieved, Bill quickly escaped her teasing clutches and climbed into the heated soothing water and peeking a look down at the offending member as it ducked its clearly embarrassed head under the water. Admonishing it with a muttered "jeez and you wonder why they call you a prick?" he sighed with the magic of the sensations he laid back and closed his eyes. Rangi ruffled away behind him. Must be looking for a handcuff key, he guessed, only to be proven wrong as a large, brown, naked female body the female equivalent of Jack Waratini slipped seductively into the spa beside him and the water surged up over the sides as mass displaced mass.

"Just relax, my little man, close your eyes for aunty," she murmured, "and let me get you out of these into something more comfortable." Her hands gently encircled his scrotum. Then, by touch, Rangi measured and tested the diameter of the cuffs against the roundness of his testicles, one by one, as the hot water allowed stretch and movement. Despite himself, Rangi's experienced touch and stroke and prod caused his cock to harden and throb painfully. Then, in the blood heat of the water she began deliberate manipulation, soft encircling and upward downward rotation of his tumescence, combined with the gentle positioning of his balls one above the other at the circle of the cuffs like eggs at the mouth of a bottle. With the tension of the past few days, the unusual engorging effect of the restraint of his balls by the steel cuffs, and the sensual movements of Rangi's ministrations, within minutes he felt that surge of his release excruciatingly pump from his body. And in rhythm with the natural physical contracting of his balls, Rangi expertly popped him, one by one, free of the cuffs.

Chapter 12

Does Your Mother Know?

Total silence on the balcony. Only the whooshing gusts of the Wellington night as the wind picked up off the Cook Strait, suddenly cooler. Bill's father looked at his son in the soft light thrown out from the apartment in silent assessment. Kingi looked at him with a surprised but then contemplative expression and then glanced across at his old friend.

"Before you say anything, Dad, think about it. I am 23 years old, healthy, single with no ties except for you and Mum; I am a black belt in tae kwon do; and I have not lived in New Zealand for 18 years, no one knows me here. I could be your agent's overseas son, nephew whatever."

Still nothing was said. The two old warriors just stared at the young man.

Bill, nervous now, added, "Also I am from excellent stock, Dad, and I am available."

Nothing from the elders.

"And, Mr Potiki who else do you have at short notice?"

Frank Peters looked at Kingi, and the two men, without actually talking by raise of eyebrow and minute nod of head considered the possibility. "Look Dad," Bill was excited now, keen, sensing the adventure, "after this holiday I am basically at a loose end. I've had enough of uni for the moment, I don't want to travel. I really want to get to know my country and be close to you. Also Sir, as I have mentioned to Dad, the idea of law enforcement really interests me. I was going to talk to you about perhaps joining the Police anyway." Another pause. "What do you say, will you think about it?"

The two older men looked to each other and Bill fell silent also. Bill's father was the first to break the silence. "Mate, I know this type of thing sounds exciting, glamorous, even but, Bill, these people are very dangerous. You are talking about living that life for probably two years," looking to Kingi for nod of confirmation.

"I know, Dad. All I am saying is that I want to do this. Not for you, not for Mr Potiki, it's not that. I want to do this for me."

Frank Peters, secretly pleased with his son's entreaty, turned to his old comrade at arms. "Well, Kingi what do you think?" Kingi, used to the rapid analysis of any situation, urgent compartmentalisation of each factor, each cause and effect, had already quickly examined in his mind the pros and cons of the offer by this young man. He had already decided that if the offer was genuine and if he passed through the intensive selection criteria of psychological and physiological testing, and, most importantly, if his old friend agreed, then he would seriously consider the possibility.

"First, thank you Bill for your courage and for your offer. I say to you both as a friend and as the officer in charge of the Te Kuri operation, what do you say we all sleep on this and meet tomorrow at my office? And then, if, and only if, Bill, you still want to consider this … well, I only ask you to think long and hard about the type of life you will have to live both during and, more importantly, after the operation."

"Think about living and mixing with these people, who, in every way are outlaws, for at least at the very least two *years* of your life. Think about being in danger of discovery and of death for that entire time. Think about the physical threat. These gangs are like packs of wolves, like wild animals. They have a pecking order that will include testing you against their best to place you in that order. Then think about if the operation runs as planned. That, for at least one year and probably two after you have been pulled out, you will have to face these people in court and giving detailed evidence under all sorts of cross-examination. You will be accused by their lawyers of all sorts of criminal actions."

"Think about the stress of putting behind bars some of those who you will become very close to during the operation; some of whom you will like very much, maybe even love. Think about never really being safe ever again in your life. Think about your future wife and kids always being under threat from these people years down the track."

"Young man, I have huge respect for your father. He is my friend my brother. I ask you to think about him and your mother. Do you realise that for two years you can have very little, if any, contact with them? Are you prepared to put your life on hold for that long? Because once you're in there is no getting out. That's what I ask, Bill. And if after a night's sleep you have changed your mind, believe me, son, I will respect you even more."

Bill nodded in assent. The mood was as cold as the outside air. Kingi continued, "The only other thing I ask is that your father also agrees with whatever action you take. Now let's leave it at that and have our dessert."

With that, they moved inside and Kingi served up generous dollops of Hokey Pokey ice cream melting on heavy fruity steamed pudding that "one of my nieces kindly made for the occasion." The conversation continued till midnight without reference again to the Te Kuri or to Bill's offer.

Chapter 13

Train Whistle Blowing

"Well, my dear, we did come to a sticky end, didn't we, though," Rangi murmured into his ear. Bill was too embarrassed to open his eyes. But he must admit he was sort of enjoying the warm embrace of his large spa companion, more a sisterly hug really, he tried to convince himself. "Ok, precious, time to spoil you rotten," she whispered and he panicked with thoughts of further sexual assault. But then as he heard her pull the plug and then felt the hot waters descending down his torso and spiral noisily down the drain, he cooperated as she pulled his totally relaxed body from the bath.

He meekly followed her powerless really to a massage table where she folded him face down and rubbed him dry with a warm coarse towel. Hot scented oil was applied by the strong healing hands of a woman who instinctively and wholly loved her job, loved men in fact. This woman lived for her job. Although her establishment was called The House of Lash, it was in actuality a place where Rangi and her carefully selected girls pampered her clients and attended their every taste and fetish in a non-harming fashion.

Her clients were men with a taste for spanking, a taste for bondage, sadomasochism, pseudo-slavery and ritual humiliation. Professional business men in charge of large corporations, men from academia, from politics, from the law and law enforcement and ordinary 'Neville's' from the suburbs, who found at Rangi's house, safety in the expression of their particular weirdness.

Bill had no fetishes, no weird desires. He had known since puberty that he was simply, and probably boringly, he now thought, a heterosexual male with a keen interest in the post-pubescent female. But as his large companion massaged him, probing deep into tight-knotted muscle and excruciatingly finding pressure points with strong fingers, he talked to her. And Rangi told him stories from her professional past of other men's foibles and exotic tastes and as they laughed together he lost his embarrassment and relaxed. An hour later with muscles of jelly his Aunty, as he was now calling her, finally rubbed his chest, stomach, and then teasingly his groin, dry of the sweet Sandalwood scent of oil. He stood and comfortably hugged her square-built, sarong-wrapped figure, kissed her on her warm brown cheek and thanked her.

Rangi, happy to have served and serviced, then led him to a closet where he chose from a wide range of men's clothes, dressing into blue jeans and warm, long-sleeved shirt and heavy black cowboy boots that he didn't dare ask the origin or the most recent use of. She then led him back to her apartment down the smoky passage. Upon entry, with Rangi holding the trophy of the handcuffs aloft in triumph behind his unsuspecting back, Jack noisily applauded Bill. The big man was lolling back in a suspiciously relaxed fashion with his tiny companion, who was seated behind and lovingly massaging that huge cranium, like an albino toy monkey grooming a silverback gorilla.

As the grey Melbourne day began outside, the next few hours were spent as the ladies of the house finished their night's business, ushering the final sated clients from the premises. The ladies then joined Rangi and her two visitors in the apartment for food and conversation before they returned to their real lives.

Husbands, boyfriends and families awaited them, some of whom knew the real nature of the ladies' employment, others who thought their partner or mother worked in various fantasy occupations on permanent night shifts. Bill noted the amazing normality of the

94

women, the common thread of warmth and empathy, and reminded himself that they were chosen and trained by Rangi and reflected her approach to life. He worried momentarily about the girls maybe recognising him from the media splash, but Rangi saw his initial apprehension and quietly spoke to him. "Don't fret, my boy, what happens on a boy's own adventure stays on a boy's own adventure," and she laughed an infectious, feminine duplicate of big Jack's giggle. And in the humour and good-will of the gathering, Bill was delighted to be the source of the main joke of the day, which was that Rangi owned some 50 sets of handcuffs. Hilariously to the gathering at the breakfast table she demonstrated that several of the keys fitted the steel bracelets that had so inconveniently ensconced Bill's testicles until released by what Jack referred to as "Rangi's rhythm method". They all fell about giggling at Bill's stoic discomfort until, breakfast over, Rangi led Bill to a spare bedroom, and with weary goodnight to Jack and the ladies, he fell into a deep and dream-filled sleep.

Only seconds later it seemed, but actually after several hours of sleep, Rangi softly shook Bill awake. Big Jack Waratini boomed from the kitchen for him to "get out of the scratcher" as they had "things to do, people to see, or is that people to do and things to see?" the big man joked. Rangi led him to the shower. She had him call her after the refreshing cascade and sat him down on a stool to exhibit yet another talent by expertly reshaping his hair with scissors and razor. Then she dyed it from the natural light brown to a much darker lustre and in a similar fashion did the same to his eyebrows. And even Bill was pleasantly surprised as to how little effort had quite markedly changed his appearance. His new favourite Aunty then fed Bill and Jack again with sizzling T-bone steaks, fried eggs on mashed potato with cheesy Brussels sprouts as Jack explained what he had been up to while his friend had slept.

"It's Kalgoorlie, Billy Boy. All arranged. I have called in some favours from years gone past." Bill listened intently. "My old mate, Nick the Greek, is driving the Indian Pacific train nowadays. Nick and I worked together out of Port Hedland where he drove the locos that pull the iron-ore trains. We looked after each other back then in some great old union stoushes with management and their fuckin security scabs. Anyway, suffice to say you will be on the choo choo train to Kalgoorlie at midnight tonight, on your merry way Westward-ho."

Bill, mouth full, grunted his thanks as Jack proudly carried on with his master plan. "When you hit Kalgoorlie on Wednesday night, get off the train and find a white Ford ute which will have the signage 'McLean's Contractors' on the side and will be parked at the northern end of the station car park. In the ute will be my good mate Stanislav, a Croatian gentleman, about 55 now. One of a kind; I worked with Stan the Man for five years in Kalgoorlie, underground, digging for gold. Stan will put you up in the single men's quarters on the mine site. And Stan will give you a night-shift job for as long as you need. Cash in hand. So what do ya reckon?"

"Jack, you are a legend mate." Bill thanked him as he wiped up the juice of the meat and egg with a thick doorstop of white heavy-crusted bread and washed it all down with the hot mug of sweet tea.

All too soon it was time to go.

Rangi kissed him warmly and told him to take care of himself and that he was welcome back anytime. She handed him a heavy-packed khaki canvas sailor's kitbag. "Full of clothes and food, sweetie," and she then held him in motherly hug. He kissed both her cheeks and thanked her and told her he would make it up to her, all she had done.

"Well, maybe not all."

And Rangi said, "Just shut up and go," and then kissed her huge cousin.

The two men slunk out again into the Melbourne evening to the cab of the Kenworth. By just on midnight Jack had the Kenworth down at the Flinders Street Station.

He steered the big prime mover into the dark freight-yard through the open wire mesh gate. The Indian Pacific train had arrived from the first leg of its classic journey earlier that night from Sydney and now rested patiently, diesels from the three locomotives purring. Soon they would pull ten carriages of comfortable passenger accommodation and 20 freight and flat-top rail stock into the brightly-lit passenger terminal for the human cargo to load.

This was one of the last great train journeys of the world. It did not have the spectacular history and romance of the trans-Siberian or the trans-American but enjoyed its own special antipodean attractions as the train traversed the bottom of the huge and mainly barren continent. A journey of some 5000 kilometres from the eastern seaboard city of Sydney to the western city of Perth.

As Jack flashed the Kenworth's lights once, then twice, a torch near the rear of the last carriage flashed back once, twice. Jack drove slowly down the gravel of the freight yard and stopped beside the burly figure of Nick Pianopolous, his friend from the iron ore days, now skipper of the Indian Pacific train. Jack jumped from the cab into the vigorous bear hug of his old mate, "Jack, my big Kiwi friend, how fat you have got!" Nick's shouted greeting almost drowned out by the operations behind him. "Nick, my old Greek bro, how ancient and weak you have got!" Jack returned, lifting the other up off the ground as the two wrestled for advantage like mismatched Sumo. With greetings exchanged, the two bent in earnest conversation and Jack beckoned the waiting Bill from the cab. Hidden between the Kenworth and the flat-decked carriage near the back of the train, Jack made quick introduction and Bill felt the hard but warm handshake of Nick.

"I look after you, mate. If you a friend of Jack you a friend of mine," said Nick. He then led Jack and Bill to the last flat deck before the signalman's carriage at the back of the train. "You travel in style," said Nick. And Bill saw the large white vehicle chained securely to the flat steel deck of the carriage for the delivery trip to the west.

"What the …"

He saw the familiar white and blue chequered livery and red and blue hazard light configuration. Laughing at the reaction, Nick told him that his journey was to be in a brand new "parleeze booze buzz". A custom-made vehicle designed as a roadside alcohol testing unit and constructed at the Geelong plant of the Ford Motor

Company to the specifications of the WA Police Service. The booze bus was on its way by train to Perth for delivery.

As Bill and Jack laughed at the irony, Nick took a bunch of keys from his grey loco driver's overalls and the three men clambered up the steel ladder on the front of the heavy rail wagon. Nick opened the smart white side door and ushered both men into the cavernous body of the big vehicle. "Two minutes, Jack," Nick warned and then stepped out with a "don't forget to lock the door". Jack and Bill faced each other in the dim light thrown from the freight yard outside. Jack said, "Old Nick said the coppers have already been right through the train at AlburyWodonga." Bill knew they were the twin cities that straddle the border of New South Wales and Victoria. "So mate, I can't see that they will search again, but be aware, eh? Be on the lookout won't you, bro?" and Bill held out his hand for the bro shake but was pulled into a bear hug by his huge friend. "Mate, thank you. I owe you big-time," Bill muttered, muffled by the big man's heavy truckie's jacket. "Fuck off, hairy legs. Just stay safe and get it all sorted, will you, bro," the big man replied.

"I want to see you again at the house with Maude and the kids; I need you there to drink beers and talk shit about the All Blacks, eh?"

"Thanks, mate, I'll be seeing you," Bill spoke, sudden quaver in his voice. Just before Jack closed the door and jumped from the train he threw an envelope to Bill.

As the train shuddered and squealed, steel against steel, into rolling motion, Bill counted $1000 in crisp new $100 notes and softly cursed his big mate.

Chapter 14

Fools Rush In

Bill didn't sleep. No, not quite true. He dozed, but fitfully, with
his mind going over and over all the possible angles. Why had he
volunteered? Until he had met Kingi the previous night he had not
even come close to considering a career as an undercover agent.
It was only a few days ago that he had even thought about being
a police officer. Shit, face it, he had been a uni bum, a rugby lout,
not a care in the world, his future not even considered; just a vague
concept of a life which should include at some indeterminate hazy
futuristic time: a job, wife, mortgage, family. Was it just the thought
of adventure, of testing himself, the need to face the dragon? Was
it the need to impress his father? His father's impressive friend?
As he tossed and turned in the wide hotel bed he considered all
the implications of his actions. He had no obligation. Kingi, at the
apartment, and then his father on the taxi trip back to the hotel, had
reminded him that he should think seriously about what he had
volunteered himself for. Two years of danger, of stress. Why do it?
And if he did, if Kingi accepted him, and if he passed the testing and
the training and then survived whatever challenges the operation
threw at him, why should he give up two years of his life, three,
maybe four, if the operation resulted in prosecutions?

But then in the wakening hours he knew why he had volunteered. Easy, really he was his father's son. He was of the ancient warrior races of the Anglo, the Saxon with a dash of Celt. That mongrel mix was the most aggressive, the most persistent of the dominant conquerors of the modern age. A hardy breed that had outlasted and out-bred the more primitive expansionists. Killing by force and disease and then controlling by economic and population pressure until the so-called western world was theirs.

And then there was the fact that he had nothing better to do. So on that basis, after a restless night, Bill Peters took his unknown future into his own hands and at breakfast told his father he wanted to do it. And his father was secretly pleased.

By 9.00am Bill was in the office of the New Zealand Police Superintendent, Kingi Potiki. It was a small, unimpressive, windowless room in a nondescript grey building adjacent to the Parliamentary House of Representatives. That concrete beehive-shaped construction was the seat of the New Zealand Government. Bill's father had dropped him there, delivered his son to his friend and to an uncertain future. By 9.30am Bill was undergoing the battery of physiological and psychological tests designed by Kingi in consultation with Police and Special Forces psychology experts over many years. These were tests to identify character and personality traits, to grade intelligence and the ability to think logically and laterally, to respond to crisis, to deceive others convincingly and to cope with stress and pressure. No test over a few hours could ever provide the perfect answer but these initial probings of the potential undercover agent were tried and true basic filters, and by 5.00pm Kingi felt he had a potential agent in Bill.

By 7.30pm Kingi and Bill were back at Kingi's apartment waiting for Frank to arrive for dinner. Bill answered the knock at Kingi's nodded request while he retrieved three frosted brown lagers from the fridge. As Peters senior entered the apartment with a paternal arm onto his son's shoulder he knew by inquiring glance at Kingi that his boy had measured up as he suspected he would. By a simple affirmative nod of his friend's head he realised that his son was off to war as surely as if the young man had signed up, taken the King's shilling in earlier troubled times. He felt that same range of raw emotions that any father felt when his progeny moved inexorably away from the elder's ability to care for and to protect a son. It was, he knew, as much an evolution through time, age, maturity to manhood, as it was a hunger for independence. In the animal kingdom, young males were chased from the herd as a threat to the Alpha males. In humans, the old males welcomed the rise of the younger, comforted by the often-disappointed promise of protection in the twilight years.

They sat again on the balcony around a wrought-iron table and each clinked the chilled brown glass bottles together in unison, and with a cheers, almost ceremoniously, each man drank the bitter, sweet beer. And then Kingi said to Frank, "Well, my friend, he is in if he wants it and if you want it." Bill looked to his father, who nodded his head. "You know, son, it's your call, whatever you do, you have my blessing." Bill didn't hesitate. "I'm in, Dad." And that was that, they shook hands to seal it. Father and son, Bill and Kingi, Kingi and his old friend. And then they ate.

That evening, over a Chinese takeaway meal, Kingi explained the process. Because of the rapid progress of the agent's cancer they did not have the luxury of delay, of time to properly train, to indoctrinate, to test and test and test Bill on systems, on memory and on his cover story. Against all the policies set in place by Kingi himself, he was to be Bill's handler. Bill was very happy with that and so was Bill's father and he thanked his friend. "At the most," Kingi advised, "we have only about two weeks to prepare you for the operation." There was a pause while each of them considered that time frame from their own perspective. "And that two weeks is not a guarantee, of course," Kingi continued. "We will monitor Tom on a daily basis and according to medical advice on his health." He paused thoughtfully, "Or, more accurately, advice of his death."

"Ok, first briefing, son," Kingi said, falling naturally into the role of the Agent's handler. "First thing tomorrow, 5.00am lift-off. You and I will fly by chopper to our Undercover Training Unit. The unit is a secret, son, a national secret. Its Police-talk acronym is UTU." While Bill nodded, trying to take it all in, his father leaned back out of the direct line of communication between the participants, becoming an observer only. "The unit is situated on an isolated high country farm property. It's near a small west coast hamlet called Hari Hari in the South Island. Heard of it?"

"No," and "No," came the replies. "It's set on a 400 acre cattle farming property 20 miles from the nearest neighbour. About 15 years ago now, we built into the granite hillside a multi-level training and accommodation facility known by its graduates as 'The Lair'." Bill nodded, excitement building. "The entire 5000 square meters is on three levels. Explosives and rock-breaking machinery deep in the strata of the underlying rock gouged it out. The engineers, army actually, who were sworn to secrecy under the Official Secrets Act, then constructed a steel and concrete camouflage to disguise the building so it looked like the side of the hill. Then we had a small farmhouse constructed over it at ground level. The deception was complete," Kingi declared. "No casual examination would ever detect its size or function. It is a credit to the spirit and loyalty of all the carefully selected personnel who had ever visited The Lair that it's remained a secret, but so far, touch wood," and to Bill's delight Kingi leaned across and rapped his knuckles on his head. "Not the criminal underworld, nor the media, has an inkling of The Lair's existence, let alone its function. Not bad, eh? Especially considering how aggressive and intrusive those varied organisations can be when it comes to the Police."

So this was the place Bill Peters was going to by chopper at 5am the next day. At the early close of dinner Bill thanked Kingi and, with his father, they left for the hotel to pack, and to grab a few restless hours' sleep.

Bill was up with the radio alarm and showering at 3.45am. When he answered the quiet knock at his door his father was dressed and held a steaming cup of coffee for him. The two men sat on the bed and sipped their drinks in comfortable contemplation. At 4.15 there was a soft knock on the door. Father and son stood. But before he went to open the door, Bill held his father in a hug, "Try not to worry now, Dad, take it easy won't you?" comforting the older man. "You know that I love you? Tell Mum I love her," and his Dad nodded and smiled at him. "You just take care my boy, I love you too, so does your Mum. I will tell her what you're doing without worrying her."

"Thanks Dad," and Bill stood back to pick up his suitcase. Then with his father's hand on his back they both walked to open the hotel door. Kingi stood there, dressed in black jeans and dark blue windbreaker and shook first his and then his father's hand in silent greeting, and turned to lead them to the lift. Bill saw that his father was emotional but contained, and as the lift hissed open in the lobby, the older man insisted, against mild protest, in walking both of them to the Falcon sedan parked outside the hotel. Then they hugged again as Kingi lifted the luggage into the boot. And his father whispered into his ear, "I'm very proud of you, boy," and with a final round of handshakes he watched as they climbed into the vehicle. Kingi pulled her away from the kerb and headed down darkened rain-swept streets toward Wellington Airport. Bill twisted in the front passenger seat of the car and looked back at the dark, lonely figure of his father. He suddenly wondered if he would ever see him again.

Chapter 15

Westward Ho

The massive engines of the Indian Pacific effortlessly pulled the human and inanimate cargo away from Melbourne that first night. Bill inspected the interior of the booze bus and he was pleasantly surprised to locate a bed in the first-aid section of the unit. He surmised that the bed was probably for the future reluctant clients of the bus, when blood testing was needed to confirm the alcohol content of the driver's blood.

He discovered the note cellotaped to the cabin table adjacent to the bed and found that Nick had left him some instructions. The first instruction was that he put on the pair of rubber surgical gloves and, recognising the sense of that precaution, he quickly did so and then tried to remember what he had touched so far with his bare hands. Just in case, he then took from Rangi's kit bag a soft T-shirt and meticulously rubbed down all the surfaces in the bus to remove any print that he or Jack may have left. When satisfied, he returned to the table and read Nick's note in full.

Nick advised that there was food and drink in the bus's battery powered fridge. Bill found sandwiches, chicken and fruit all wrapped separately by Mrs P, he suspected, into meal-size servings. There were also several bottles of fruit juice and soft drink cooling nicely in the blood sample racks of the purpose-built fridge. Nick's note also offered the use of the unit's chemical toilet and assured Bill that Nick would "take care of the shit at Kalgoorlie". Nick's postscript then told him that it would take "three days to get to Kalgoorlie." They would be there "Wednesday night at midnight and the train would stop for 20 minutes only." Nick said he should take care and he wished him well and he had then signed the note, "Nick P."

Educated now, and with food and drink and a timetable, Bill lay down on the fresh-sheeted bunk, courtesy of Nick, and soon, despite himself and his determination to analyse his situation, he fell asleep to the gentle movement and the rhythmical sounds of the train journey west.

The next two days passed in a similar fashion. He took to sitting in the cab of the booze bus in the plush driver's seat as the train purred west along the steel tracks. Sitting high in the comfort of the cushioned vantage allowed him a 180-degree panorama of the journey around the southern coast of the continent. His view was without risk of discovery from the passenger carriages ahead though any rear view was blocked by the first of the goods wagons.

They passed incident-free through Adelaide and surrounding vineyards and rolling pasture.

They then crossed the border into the huge barren expanse of Western Australia, almost as big in size as the entire eastern states combined, but home only to 1.5 million people, clustered mainly around the city of Perth. That metropolis hugged the pristine beaches and the banks of the ancient Swan river.

The rail tracks ran low along the southern coast around the Great Australian Bight and into the sandy bush and scrub of the Nullarbor Plain. Bill enjoyed the ride into the West with the train clicking along. He had found that the bus allowed access to an observation deck on the roof through a hatchway with a spiral steel ladder. As the long train conga-snaked through the rural expanses he took advantage of the cooler mornings to climb naked, except for pink surgical gloves, onto the observation deck. Here he sunbathed carefully and enjoy the blue vista of the clear sky above and the feeling of the cool breeze across his body. Bill figured that as long as he didn't leave fingerprints all they would find was arse prints and he giggled as he visualised such a police identification line-up, "number five touch your toes". High on the broad white convex roof of the bus above the heavy planks of the goods wagon below, and higher still from the ground rushing past at 100kms per hour, he would do some exercise. There he took advantage of nature's air-conditioning and engaged in a dramatic naked practice session of his martial art. A butt-naked, white-arsed, adult male with pink gloves blocking and bashing imaginary foes whilst train-bus-surfing westward at speed had him chuckling at the ridiculous view he must have offered.

Then later, when he had sweatily sunbaked dry he kept a cautious lookout for the big western eagles that floated effortlessly above the train and appeared to be eyeing him up. When he saw one he would nervously cup his hands over his edible bits as the majestic predators swooped downward for a closer look.

At night he lay on the bunk and thought long and hard about his situation. As soon as he was able he had to make contact again with his mentor, his old boss from the undercover days. Kingi Potiki.

Kingi had been summarily sacked from the New Zealand Police as a result of the aftermath of Operation Te Kuri. The operation that had gone so right, and then so very wrong. "Through no fault of Kingi's," Bill had so passionately argued to the Commissioner, "It was me, boss. My fault, my fuck up, not Kingi's." But under the philosophy of executive responsibility, the culture of vicarious liability for the actions and the consequences of those actions of a subordinate, Kingi had spoken, quietened Bill with soft words, and had accepted the blame.

Bill trusted no-one else. Kingi, an exemplary career in tatters, had resigned and was now somewhere deep in his tribelands. But before he left he gave to only a very few one of who was his young protégé, Bill Peters a method of contacting him: the listening post, the letter drop. The old warrior had felt as his own the full responsibility of Bill's loss. He told Bill that he would always be there, when and if ever he was needed. And so before he went into a lonely, self-imposed exile, he took Bill down to the water's edge of the Hokianga Harbour. On the soft white sand, Kingi gave to Bill, and had him memorise, a phone number.

"This code leads to a tiny pine-slabbed cottage in a central North Island hamlet. Tuhoe tribal country my country, Bill. It goes to a forestry service jumble of five dwellings, 50 kilometres from Ruatoria, the closest town. The occupants of one of the cottages are my widowed Great Aunt, Great Aunt Ruby, and her grand-daughter, my young cousin, Donna." Kingi told him, "Bill, I am going deep into the bush where there are no phones, no PO Boxes, no mail service. Where I am going, son, there are no comforts of civilisation. No shops, piped water, power lines or even roads." Kingi grew even more darkly serious, "But I promise you, Bill, on my own life, I promise you that I will find him. He who took from you and took from me." The old warrior placed his hands on Bill's shoulders and looked him in the eye and swore that oath in sombre truth to the devastated young man. And from his culture and tradition he pressed his nose in the hongi against the tear-streaked face of this son of his life friend, the son of his brother-in-arms, as the gentle Hokianga rains swept and wet them both that cold morning.

By Kingi's explanation, each could pass coded messages to the other. Every communication was faithfully recorded in beautiful copperplate hand by the majestic old Maori woman in the tiny hamlet where she had lived her entire life.

And Bill had kept in touch, dictating over the fading phone lines from public phone boxes in Sydney from time to time, short messages of respect and affection. And he received the same back from Ruby, or on the odd occasion from the sweet, rounded vowel tones of her adult grand-daughter, Donna. Words from the warrior who, in the dark of the darkest nights, would appear at Ruby's doorstep at the hamlet. She would be waiting, have ready for him that sweet cup of tea, the warm buttered scones, and Kingi would gratefully receive and give his communications. And then he would rise from the table in the small kitchen warmed by the wood stove, he would pick up his sacks of supplies and tie them onto his pack-horse, shifting heavily by the back door. He would kiss Great Aunt Ruby farewell, and the pretty Donna, who cared for the old lady.

And the two women would watch him from the porch as he led the old horse towards the bush and faded again into the black.

Kingi's old boys' network of the world's special forces serving and retired, spread from Zanzibar to Washington had not yet sniffed out the prey that both men so eagerly sought. And now, Bill thought as he lay on the bunk in the bus, he had another crisis to deal with. Now he had to seek his own exile. A haven, a sanctuary to hide from the very forces for which he had served.

He knew that all he had on his side right now was time. On the other hand, with Jack's generous help and the $1000 he had a chance now to avoid detection in the huge state of Western Australia. The police system in the nation was by geography and by structure disjointed and this was his best chance to avoid arrest on the bullshit charges. He presumed that the immediate heat of public interest at least had probably died down a little now. The public's interest in the rogue copper story would have faded as the focus on sport or the latest political scandal would have knocked him from the front pages. But he was certain that the nation's police forces would have an interest in him that was still white hot.

He knew that Hill's lies would have sparked that cultural police quirk to avenge an attack on one of their own. He knew that this would require of him the highest state of alertness to avoid capture. He needed time to figure out what to do and he had to stay free to do it.

He decided that he must stay and work in Kalgoorlie for the foreseeable future. Then, somehow, he had to get back across the Tasman to his homeland, and to Kingi. With immediate future decided, he slept.

On the third night of the train trip west he was ready. He had packed in the early evening sunset, the soft orange light infusing the cabin of his 'home'. He had felt the train several hours before swing gently north-west as the line curled lazily up into the goldfield region of the state, toward the major historical twin cities of Kalgoorlie and Boulder.

This area had been the scene of the mighty gold-rush of the late 1890s when the fossicking Irishman Paddy Hannan and his mates first found the nuggets of the precious yellow metal just out of Kalgoorlie. Since that time, due to improved generational, innovative and intensive mining methods, every tiny speck of gold was now minutely recovered from the bedrock. Gold, the commodity to which the major trading nations always returned for national security and wealth in uncertain times as the standard of financial stability and power. Over 100 years later, the town still prospered. The gold was gouged from ever-deepening man-made holes in the ground around the town, like huge bunkers around a golf course. Other metals and minerals such as copper, initially discovered but temporarily ignored in the hunger for gold, then also took their place in the cycle of prosperity of the mining industry. Even now, Kalgoorlie continued its contribution to the state and nation's coffers and confirmed Western Australia's description as Australia's quarry.

Just before midnight Bill felt the long train slowing and he climbed again into the driver's seat of the bus where he could see the train entering the environs of Kalgoorlie Boulder. A sign announced: "Population 26,340."

"Three hundred and forty one," he muttered as the train swept past. Ten minutes later the train slowed and squealed to a shuddering halt in the small but modern passenger terminal. Already the bright headlights of the WA Rail forklifts were starting to buzz about to unload inward freight and load Perth-bound freight.

With kit bag on shoulder Bill peered out the bus windows and saw that the activity was well forward of the middle carriages. With a last look into the cabin and last mental checklist as to the cleanliness of the unit he took the rubbish and remaining food and drink and wrapped it clumsily in the sweat-stained sheets and then quietly opened the door. He stepped out onto the rough-cut wooden deck and in the dark heat of the Kalgoorlie night he jumped lightly down off the train onto giving gravel and darted away into the blackness. Slowly, he circled around the back of the yard and behind the huge corrugated freight sheds until he was behind the railway station car park.

He took the opportunity to throw his sheet-wrapped rubbish into a stinking green garbage trolley, taking care to cover it with cardboard boxes already in the bin. Then, with kit bag on shoulder, Bill walked boldly into the lights of the car park and directly toward the white Ford ute, parked, as promised by Jack, at the far northern end of the carpark. As he crunched up to the vehicle, trusting in his friend's arrangements, the driver leaned across and opened the passenger door and Bill slipped into the air-conditioned cab. Stanislav Petrovich held out a callused hand and greeted him. "Velcum to Kalgoorlie, Beel."

Chapter 16

The Name of the Game

Whup-whup-whup! With gut-surging effect the Bell Ranger chopper descended, spiralling, almost auto-rotating through the foggy South Island morning. The pilot focused on his descent to the yet-invisible destination. Bill looked down anxiously from the back seat through the darkened convex perspex of the chopper porthole and was suddenly relieved when, at 200 feet, they broke through the cloud band. He saw then the lush green paddocks and contrast of plump black Angus beef cattle that so successfully assisted in the disguise of the Undercover Training Unit of the NZ Police Service. Then as they ground-metal skidded on the asphalt tarmac of the helipad, Kingi slid out from the front seat and pulled opened the chopper door, summoning his young charge.

Bill, head bent, scrambled forward and out, instinctively crouching to avoid the impending sensation of decapitation from above. As he trotted away from the circle of the rotating blades, he noted the stocky figure of the custodian of the Lair, one Shorty Dean, lugging the bags from the storage hatch at the rear of the chopper to the edge of the helipad. Shorty then ran to stand in view well to the front of the chopper before signalling with practised expertise the thumbs up to the pilot.

The three men stood then in the dawn and watched as the mat-black ranger screamed up and away. The machine disappeared in angled northward flight into the convolutions of the cold front sweeping in from the Antarctic across the great Southern Ocean. As the chopper faded and the silence once again enveloped the green hills, there was an introduction from Kingi. "Shorty, this is Frank's boy, Bill." His handshake like gripping a steel callused claw, the tough little man looked directly into Bill's eyes. Bill held the gaze.

"I know your Dad," he said, gruff, but warm. "An excellent man."

"Thank you, Sir." Respect came automatically for an elder. They followed him in. He carried all the bags, ignoring Bill's polite attempt to relieve him of them and with short quickstep they were led into the small farmhouse. "Cup of tea first." Shorty was obviously not one for wasted chitter-chatter, Bill thought to himself as they walked into the large kitchen. Kingi nodded to the offer of the beverage, and then moved forward to hug and kiss the matronly figure of Shorty's wife. She, with apron on and in a cloud of the warm sweet smells of home cooking, had turned from the wood-fired oven with affectionate greeting.

"Bill, meet Christine, Shorty's better half," Kingi said, and Bill moved forward to shake her flour-dusted hand. But instead, he was enveloped into a soft welcoming hug.

"And how's your Dad?" she inquired as she held him with both hands on his shoulders and taking a motherly appraisal of him. "And your Mum? I knew her many years ago before you were born, Bill," she said. And he felt suddenly in good care with these two people who clearly knew of him. They sat at the classic Kauri farmhouse table. Christine served up sweet mugs of tea splashed with warm oily-fat milk that had been harvested that morning from their small milking herd of ginger and white Friesians. And Bill, surprisingly ravenous, enjoyed several white fluffed scones, oven hot, with chewy black dates interspersed. Then, while Christine fussed over all of the men but mainly over Bill, Kingi and Shorty, in rapid professional shorthand, laid the groundwork and discussed the schedule for the preparation of their prize recruit. Bill was trying to listen to the men but was distracted by his hostess as he was required to explain to her in ten paraphrased minutes his last 23 years. With a final gulp of the tea and a warm "thank you Chris," from Kingi, Bill was again enveloped with a hug and they left.

The three men entered the den at the rear of the house, where to Bill's astonishment Shorty slid back a false wall panel sporting deceased deer, goat and mountain thar trophy heads. Behind the panel was a steel door that Shorty manipulated until, with air-conditioned sigh, the cooler air of the training unit was released. Bill followed his mentors down a spiralling steel stairwell into The Lair. They entered through the top floor. This was the third level the accommodation unit that slept up to 12 guests. Shorty showed him into one of the single bedrooms and he plumped his suitcase onto a comfortable bed.

Kingi took his leave then, heading down the stairwell deeper into the Lair. Before he went he told them, "Bill, Mr Dean will give you the tiki tour; get yourself familiar with everything. I don't need you till midday. Shorty will show you the video room on the second floor and I'll see you there. We'll have some lunch there while we watch some videos. Ok?"

"Yes, Sir, fine," Bill responded, uncertain now how to address his superior officer, now that he was a junior employee of the New Zealand Police Service. "It's ok Bill, no sirs between us. Call me Kingi." And Shorty added, "And you can call me Shorty. Now stash your kit and I'll show you around."

Bill emptied his suitcase and then joined his host for the induction tour. Shorty was a precise and no-nonsense tour guide, walking briskly, keeping Bill hurrying to keep up with him.

Bill saw that he was the only current tenant. He saw that there were about a dozen rooms such as his that all led off a spacious common lounge with large soft sofas, a television that clearly had a satellite feed, and games tables with cards and board games stacked neatly. Shorty showed him the kitchen leading off the lounge and said, "You help yourself to the food. Any time, whatever you want or need, ok?"

"Ok, thanks," Bill nodded.

Kingi had told him in the chopper about the luxury of the spa rooms on the top level. As Shorty marched him through he knew from Kingi that the engineers had designed skylights that both lit and ventilated the spas. "I'm warning you Bill," Kingi had said laughing, "and this is from my own experience: the spas you will find are necessary for aching bodies after the physical regime designed by Shorty." The Lair's custodian was, as Bill was told, a steel-hard, 58 year-old retired martinet sergeant from the SAS and prior to that had been a government deer culler. He had been sought out by Kingi after his retirement from the army and installed happily as the unit's physical education instructor some eight years past. Shorty and Christine lived contentedly as the apparent owners of the farm and occupiers of the farmhouse. They made a point of grandly cruising the 20 miles into the small village of Hari Hari for shopping and a beer at the pub once a week in the old Landrover that the government had assigned to the operation through a special police budget. The Minister of Police in secret collusion with the head of the nation's treasury had personally approved that budget. All the major stores for the unit were trucked in innocently by cattle truck each quarter and stockpiled to avoid any indicators of more significant activity. The occasional appearance of helicopters onto the helipad adjacent to the farmhouse, if the question ever arose, was explained by Shorty Dean as a small tourist venture that he was involved in a venture that catered for rich Japanese folk to visit a working beef cattle farm. Such an initiative was not unusual for the hardy and entrepreneurial folk of the area. And really, with helicopters a common sight along the rugged west coast for tourism and for such activities as live deer capture, goat shooting or accessing the nearby glaciers, such questions had rarely been asked of Shorty.

Shorty, the top floor tour completed with barked commentary, led his visitor down the spiral stairwell in the eastern corner of the structure. "The second floor," he said, "houses the training unit, the classrooms, both blackboard and film room, the library, and the computer rooms." Bill was now used to his pace and kept up at a half-trot. "This floor is where all the head work is done, always before, sometimes during, and always after, operations."

On the second floor the psychs had their clinics, Bill learnt. The comfortable dens had leather-bound volumes and pseudo wood fires and deep, soft sofas, creating an atmosphere that he soon was to learn belied the intensity and purpose of the examinations that took place. Kingi had already warned him that such examinations were conducted to test and predict, and sometimes to heal, the behaviours of the agents.

The medico's clinics were also based on this floor. In the sterile steel and plastic environment, highly specialist doctors tested agents before and after operations. The physicians meticulously charted the body's functions to detect, prevent or treat the stress-related illnesses and diseases picked up from the lifestyles in which some of the agents existed during their operations. Diseases and conditions recorded were the varied strains of hepatitis, the complete range of sexually transmitted ailments, narcotic and chemical dependencies, substances that the agents sometimes unavoidably and with the authority of the handler exposed themselves to, to gain and maintain credibility with the target group.

Although Kingi had never lost an agent to date, many had showed the physical and physiological scars of the battle, and the one thing that terrified him was the very real danger of HIV AIDS.

With a quick recce of the second floor complete, Shorty was again at the stairwell and Bill rotated down the spiral after him. "This, Bill, is the first level of the Lair," he said as he strode down the narrow corridor. "This is where the physical activity takes place. And this is where the firing range is located." They entered through a sound- deadened door into a long, dark room where exhaust fans dissipated cordite fumes. The agents, under the tutoring of Shorty Dean, fired countless pistol, shotgun and high-powered rifle rounds into charging Nazi-shaped targets. In darkened studios with ever-changing scenarios the agents achieved a level of performance that satisfied Shorty before they were allowed to graduate from the training facility. Shorty took pride that even the most gun-wary and target-shy pupils had never failed to pass.

Then Shorty pushed open a high door and clicked on banks of fluorescent lights that progressively flickered into life to reveal a modern and spacious gymnasium. This was, Bill knew from Kingi, the real domain of Shorty, where over the usual 12-week training period he hammered into shape the men and women delivered to him. Each took away from the unit an appreciation of the "healthy body, healthy mind" mantra of their tutor. As well as designing personalised weight and aerobic programs for the various body shapes and sizes and levels of fitness, he also introduced the agents to the science of a basic martial art.

Bill recalled Kingi's words in the chopper earlier as he explained that Shorty had studied the Japanese martial art of Karate for many years. He had graduated 30 years before, after spending two years of disciplined and bleak study at the stable of the Japanese master, Koto, outside of Nagasaki, graduating with the Seventh Dan of the treasured black belt. In the service of his country, on a terrifying night of man-to-man battle behind enemy lines in a cold desert, Shorty Dean had made his mark in the annals of SAS history. He had taken the lives of two Iraqi Republican Guard commandoes when his patrol was ambushed. In the chaotic darkness, while other men screamed with pain and terror, Shorty's training enforced discipline upon his mind. Trembling with fear and adrenalin, he stood to fight, and in a dream-like sequence he saw his targets in the moonlight and danced a fatal karate ballet. He broke one man's neck by deadly strike of fist and booted kick, and crushed in gristle-crunch the other's windpipe. As that unknown man fell, drowning in his own hot sweet blood, Shorty and his men escaped intact. They disappeared into the darkness to meet a combat-darkened chopper at the designated emergency coordinates. The pilot was a soft-drawling southerner from the good old USA who Shorty kissed in gratitude when they put down safely across the border in Saudi.

Shorty was one of very few modern warriors who had implemented the science of his martial art alone to destroy the life of others. As such, he totally respected its potential and he religiously attempted to impart upon his pupils the beauty of the discipline.

Tour completed, Shorty led him back up to the video room to await Kingi. Bill looked forward to the gym sessions, keen to try his own expertise against the older man's.

Those first days he slept only four hours each 24. There was too much to get through, too much to remember. It was for his own safety for the security of the entire operation and out of respect for the two-year effort of the dying agent, Tom Burns.

The first session with Kingi was a history lesson on the origins of the Te Kuri who, how, when, where, and why the gang was a gang the perspective compiled from an amalgam of fact and rumour collected from friend and foe. Information was gathered from the local police in the South Auckland home of the gang. It was collected from the casual or deliberate comments of members, core and fringe, when arrested and interviewed over the years. Or it was provided unknowingly on the kilometres of surveillance and audio tapes collected through Police operations in the past and through the life of Operation Te Kuri.

Kingi introduced his topic by way of a chronology of the life of the gang from the time that the Whetu family started its criminal development. It began with the three brothers' reign of terror in Mangere, a suburb of Auckland.

"The Maori father, Joe, is long dead now," Kingi began, as Shorty delivered a tray of sandwiches and strong black coffee to them. "Joe Whetu was a deep-sea fisherman. He fished for rich reward in the treacherous waters of Kaikoura, off the north-eastern coast of the southern island," Kingi told in his descriptive prose, a trait of his genealogy. The skill had developed through the generations as the Te Maori people passed on legends and history orally. "By all accounts Joe was a tough but honest man whose fatal error was that he eloped with the young Portuguese daughter of the boat owner, one Pedro D'Amato. This man, D'Amato, was a first-generation Portuguese from a family of hard men out of the coastal fishing port of Mondego," he said. "Mondego was a small village in those days, located on the rocky coast of Portugal, a nation which had bred hard men over the centuries. These men were natural mariners and roamed the world as early explorers and conquerors. As a young man, D'Amato was forced to flee his homeland after falling foul of a feudal crime lord. He escaped with nothing but a young wife to the farthest nation he could find where he could ply his trade as a mariner and fisherman." Kingi briefly halted his discourse to gulp down the hot bitter coffee. "D'Amato worked ceaselessly, first as crew, fishing lonely months in cold dangerous waters off the harsh coast and deep waters of the South Pacific. Then, finally, after two decades of labour with hard-earned and frugally-saved cash, he bought first one, then two, then five increasingly modern vessels to establish the D'Amato fishing fleet." Kingi was in full flow now. "He was in his sixties when his youngest and most cherished child, Tina, 16, fell in love with the shy 20 year-old, Joe Whetu. Joe was a man whom he trusted with his most modern trawler and in battle would have trusted with his life. But Joe Whetu proved to be his Judas." Kingi told how this man, whom the old man had loved like a son, had stolen from him in his twilight his most precious belonging, "the sweet virgin daughter an act of terrible, unforgivable treachery".

Kingi told how the desperate young couple fled to the north. "They hid from the threat of discovery by the father and his revenge, and worked in the factories of the sprawling South Auckland suburbs." They had quietly secreted themselves away in the ticky-tack state housing developments, invisible amongst the polyglot of Pacifica, as the Government imported labour from Samoa, Tonga, Rarotonga, and the myriad of smaller island nations in the region. "The young couple soon consummated their lonely and frightened togetherness. After five years," Kingi explained, "Tina, now 21, was the mother of three robust sons and a lovely baby girl. It was then that her father found them. For five years he had looked, had paid others to look, had called in favours amongst his network of those who existed on the fringe or in that dark underbelly of crime. He had looked as far afield as Australia where, in the far north-western waters of that continent, uncles and cousins from the D'Amato clan plied similar trades in the prawn fishing waters of the Indian Ocean and Timor and Arafura Seas. All to no avail. Those first angry, soul-destroying years the old man grew by the year more bitter. But then came the break. From what we know now it appears that he then received word back from friends of friends that Joe Whetu was in Mangere, South Auckland."

Even Kingi could not know what had happened although he was generally aware of the tragic conclusion. It was one winter night that Joe, weary from long hours on the concrete floors of the foundry, woke and faced the terror he had been expecting for five long years. There at the bed in the early hours after midnight were four men torchlight, baseball bats big men, holding him flat. Not a word was said; they simply broke both his knees with heavy crunching blows, stifled his hopeless screams of pain with wide silver gaffer-tape. Tina watched in disbelief as the man she loved was dragged from their bed, from their home, twitching in muted agony, from her life.

By the rising of the sun Joe was once again on a deep-sea trawler, lying face down on cold steel deck with arms pinned behind by heavy chain and legs similarly bound. As the trawler chugged on rising seas 30 kilometres off the coast from Auckland, Joe was rolled over to face the sky. As he lay terrified, into his vision came the face he had seen in nightmare each night for five years. The old man had aged beyond the missing years: his eyes were old-man watery, but merciless. He said not a word. He simply took the leg chains and pulled the silently screaming captive down the rolling deck to the rear transom of the trawler where the sea gates had been opened.

"May God bless your soul," croaked the old avenger into Joe's ear and then awkwardly rolled his victim into the icy embrace of the sea. As the bubble trail was washed away by the chop, the old man stood, satisfied. He made the sign of the cross and the trawler kicked into gear and turned to head back to port.

Later the old man joined the two men left at the tiny suburban nest. He spoke quietly to his daughter alone as she sobbed, broken-hearted, in the clammy cold of the piss-wet bed. He met his grandchildren, secretly admired the strong handsome issue, the three boys even as youngsters dark eyed and mischievous, the grand-daughter Mere only a baby, not eight months old, but a rare beauty. It was Mere that melted the old man's reserve, changed his intent.

119

He finally told his daughter that he would give her enough money to survive; that although he no longer considered her his daughter he would not abandon his grandchildren, as she had done to him. Her life would be hard and she would be alone, he told her, but she would not starve. Then the dreadful old man and his henchmen left the house and the young mother began her sad life alone.

Kingi continued, "Within ten years of the disappearance of Joe Whetu, the three males of the four siblings had carved a niche for themselves in local folklore as trouble with a capital T. Car theft, burglary and senseless, violent assault and robbery were the trademark of the three young Whetu brothers. By their late teens these young men were the tattooed muscular examples of how dangerous it could be for strong-willed, close-knit young brothers to grow up without an adult male influence to guide and provide discipline," he said. "With a mother who cherished and protected her brood against all evidence, and who herself depended totally on their unconditional love to survive her own memories, the gang of three were an irresistible evil force amongst the youth of the area. Inevitably, their ruthless influence attracted, often for reason of survival, the less forceful or intelligent and even as teenagers the rough structure of the Te Kuri could, in hindsight, be seen."

Kingi then spoke of the evolution of the loose groupings of youth into a gang as the young men grew into their twenties and refined their culture of violence for criminal reward. With native and natural entrepreneurial variations they developed their troops into tight-knit units with common goals and defined lines of authority and responsibility. Teams of pre-teenage youth were recruited and trained in burglary. If apprehended by law enforcers they were treated as children by the police and the courts, who slapped on the hand.

More often than not they succeeded, and the combined efforts of the pillage of suburbia then funded other more sophisticated and much more profitable criminal endeavours, mainly drug factories dotted in remote bush locations.

As the gang grew, the brothers' unrelenting attention to detail ensured they avoided the inter-gang violence typical of other less sophisticated groups. With early negotiation with the leaders of the rival gangs, the Te Kuri became the conduits to those feral groups of discounted drugs or an avenue to dispose of stolen property.

The Te Kuri, or more specifically the three brothers, however, were not to be taken as fools by rivals or those who might momentarily consider themselves as equals. The violent deaths or simply the disappearance of those who would not negotiate for peace, although never directly laid by law or other proof at the feet of the brothers, were soon blamed in folklore as the brothers' work.

"And yet," Kingi went on, "despite two decades of suspicion, the three brothers have never been convicted for any one of their criminal acts. Each brother has been arrested and put before the courts for acts of deceit and violence that should have incarcerated them for years. Yet on each occasion the jury had failed to convict. Strangely, witnesses who, when in the care and custody of enthusiastic and persuasive detectives had sworn to certain facts and positive identifications, then suffered amnesiac retractions with the passing of time. Time and time again, the Whetus walk free and laughing from the dock." Bill listened intently, enjoying Kingi's natural story-telling inflections and dramatic recreations. He knew the stories by heart, although he had never personally met the participants. Kingi spoke to Bill of the purchase by the gang of the island known as Puketutu off the city's sewerage works and of the building of the fortress. He spoke of the sporadic, fruitless, frustrating police raids that found nothing, with the only result being the civil action taken by the gang's high powered legal advocates that found the police guilty of harassment.

Bill sat through the first of many long surveillance videos where he met his targets for the first time. From that first session with Kingi he was tested again and again on names, traits, personalities, predilections, and relationship trails and webs of each of the 120 members.

He learnt the hierarchical structure of the Te Kuri; who was who, who knew what, weaknesses, addictions, who was fucking who, who didn't know what, names names names, then nicknames 'Grunge',

'Animal', 'Cuzzie', 'Kaka', 'Meathead', 'Chopper', 'Ganga boy', 'Hoha' 120 names; 120 nicknames.

Testing by Kingi and by Shorty was by photograph flashed in front of him: "Who is this? Name? Nickname? Brother's name? Father's name? Role in gang? Girlfriend?"

He was taught quick systems of memory recall techniques and methods evolved by academia with practical application refined by the unit over a decade. He was tested at breakfast, lunch, dinner. Tested when in the gym with Shorty Bill's favourite time.

Shorty delighted at Bill's expertise at tae kwon do. The two enjoyed sparring sessions twice a day for one hour to revitalise the body and refresh the weary mind. Shorty, the old karate warrior, had the advantage of experience, of decades of practice. He had the ruthlessness and the knowledge of the killing moves, though also the disadvantage of age and forced physical limitations on flexibility, strength, stamina. Bill had the advantage of youth with energy, flexibility, and daring to try the unorthodox. Against that was the disadvantage of his inexperience.

Then again he was sent into the classroom to be lectured on law, the collection of evidence, and "systems, systems, systems," by Kingi.

And then to his surprise, at the end of week began the periodic arrival of guests to the unit. These were Kingi's agents: men and women previously in the field on unrelated operations. And in intense valuable sessions they imparted to Bill not only knowledge, not only exposure to criminal behaviours, but slowly the self-confidence as he was assured, and came to accept within himself, that he could pull this off. Handy little tips from these "bloody heroes", as Shorty insisted on calling them. Kingi introduced them to Bill in late night sessions just before he crawled into the bed for his four hours' slumber.

Soon after, one of the nation's premier male actors, who had the lead role in the country's top-rating television police drama, visited the Lair. Over an intense five-hour session, the actor took Bill through techniques of the art of deception and role-play. The skills and systems that allowed an actor to convince its audience that a performance was authentic were explained, demonstrated, and then practiced by Bill.

After ten days Kingi woke Bill at 4am. "Tom's bad, mate; we have at the most two days. We leave in one hour for Auckland." With that, and now buzzing with excitement, Bill was up, showered, shaved and sitting at the farmhouse table for tea and porridge by 4.30am. At 5am he left with a warm teary hug from Christine in the kitchen and hearty fist crush from Shorty Dean outside, with a gruff, "Good luck, son. You will do well." Bill and Kingi ran for the helipad as the big black bird again settled momentarily onto terra firma. As the two men dived into her warm interior, out of the driving sleet of another cold west coast morning the chopper lifted, clutching back into the sky. Bill waved farewell to his hosts who stood together, small and smaller figures in the farmhouse door. He felt a sudden grab of pride and raw emotion as Shorty Dean, with faded scarlet SAS beret on grey head, snapped to attention and saluted the rising chopper and the bloody hero inside.

Chapter 17

Wild Wild West

The first weeks hiding in Kalgoorlie passed as a red dusty haze.

Stan proved to be a champion of a man and that first night took Bill directly out of Kalgoorlie to the mine, some 20 kilometres to the east of the town-site. As they drove through the old town's picturesque commercial centre, away from the fluoro bustle of the railway station and down toward Hannan Street, Bill felt as if he had gone back in time to some wild-west scene. After all, it was Sunday night well, actually the early hours of Monday morning the start of the working week in any other civilised place. But through the ute's windscreen Bill saw that the town itself was alive, with staggering, drunken men pouring out onto the footpaths from the numerous pubs that were just closing their doors. Big, sober-looking, cross-armed bouncers in the uniform of white shirt and black pants saw the patrons off into the night. He didn't notice too many women about. Just tough-looking young males yahooing and singing in groups, wandering the main street. And down one or two darkened alleys or in front of garishly lit takeaway bars he saw in passing, clumsy drunks fighting in slow motion pantomime. Then, as Stan silently traversed Hay Street, he saw the women of the town's infamous brothels. Built like stables with fillies on show, the ladies of the night posed provocatively in semi-darkness and lacy garments, waving with teasing promise at passing vehicles and pedestrians. At the closing of the watering holes there was a weaving migration from pub to brothel on a well-worn track. These were men who worked hard, drank hard and played hard. And urgently lonely, suddenly sick of the company of other males. As the alcohol released inhibition and prudence they made their drunken negotiations with the madams and paid their sweat-earned dollars for half an hour of ribbed-rubber-encased thrusting.

Stan wasn't a talker but as they left the outskirts of the town he asked how his old mate Jack was keeping. Bill gave an affectionate report on Jack, Maude and the kids as the ute travelled away from the bright city lights and into the pitch black of the desert night, with Stan grunting acknowledgment from time to time.

As they drove, the moonlit countryside looked like a lunar landscape, with huge craters and mounds of graded earth and rock, on an otherwise flat panorama. Then, periodically, Bill saw strings of distant lights on steel structures and long conveyors as huge crushing plants chomped their way through the stockpiled ore. Over the rough diesel whine of the ute, Bill could hear a constant low growl of machinery and steel against rock grumbling through the night air.

During the 20-minute drive south, the only distraction was the kangaroo that bounced headfirst into the path of the ute in that weird long hop, like a moth to a flame. The sudden, violent destruction of the national icon drew no reaction from Stan, although Bill cringed and instinctively pumped his foot uselessly for a brake pedal. Then, after turning west again off the main highway on to a crushed red rock track, they arrived at the single men's quarters of the Kalgoorlie Super Pit Gold Mine. Stan stopped at the most distant of the small white prefabricated rooms that looked for all the world like a row of freezer units. As the red-dusted vehicle wheezed to a stop Stan handed Bill a silver key and said, "My friend, this is you hut. You get sleep, don't leave hut, answer only me when I knock. I will see you tonight for work. Be dressed in the gear I have left for you. Be ready 6pm. Good night, mate."

With that, Bill got out of the ute, picking his kit bag up out of the tray, and let himself into the hut through the cloying heat of the humid night. He was pleasantly surprised to find that Stan had set up the hut for him. The small insulated freezer was an air-conditioned, self-contained living unit, and the air-con was noisily blasting cool relief from the hot, sticky conditions outside. Stan had also left soft drinks and chicken salad in the small fridge and after a feed and a refreshing shower in the en-suite Bill flopped naked onto the white-sheeted bunk and passed out in blissful release.

That first night Bill slept until midday. He had no sense of time but when he awoke he switched on the small television and caught up with national and international news. He was relieved to note that he no longer featured as a story, the short attention span of the national media feeding off more immediate and more sensational happenings.

True to his word, just before 6pm Stan knocked and announced himself and Bill, dressed in grey overalls, steel-capped work boots, white safety helmet and goggles, followed his protector out into the evening. Without discussion or explanation, Stan drove them along a confusing maze of dirt roads then descended 600 meters in huge circular rotations around the wall-hugging access road of the mine. On their descent, Stan told him the story of the super-pit, his workplace and life now for the last 15 years. "This beeg hole," Stan explained, "she was before a combination of ten holes, not together, separate understand? The first hole, she was dug by the old miners in 1893. In those time the old diggings they were the old shafts and cross-cuts of the old country, you know, the traditional underground mining. Those men brought to the desert their expertise from other lands."

Bill was surprised by how eloquent the silent, gruff man was on his favourite topic. Stan told him how the miners' early primitive efforts had rewarded some of them with the extraction of the high-grade ore bodies, but left huge quantities of low-grade ore haloes in the area. He said that each tonne of rock gouged from the reserves of the pit released on average only 2.3 grams of the precious metal. "Ve verk the mine seven days a week, 24 hours a day for 365 days each year," he said. "And it is all for a strange soft yellow metal that eez the world's financial standard, because men long ago decided that that it vould be."

Across that vast expanse of the pit floor Bill watched with wide-eyed wonder at a monster excavator working. Gaping T-Rex jaws scooped 58 tonne at a bite from the bank of shattered rock from the previous night's blasting. On the far side of the pit floor 1000 metres distant, under portable, generator-powered lighting stands, small yellow drill rigs crawled and hunched in robot-dance as they drilled the exact lines of the night's drill pattern. The rigs ground the perfect holes into which the shot-hole blasters would later set a blasting mix. Then the blast sequence would follow, in the engineered destruction of solid rock formation into the fracture of ore on the pit floor. That broken strata was gouged up by the excavators and dumped into one of the fleet of haulpack dump trucks. "All ve need to make profit eez one matchbox of gold flecks each haulpak load," Stan told him.

As he sat in the ute and took in all this information, Bill watched as Stan pointed toward the huge behemoth of an ore carrying haulpak. This huge dinky toy was a massive diesel-generated electric truck that lurched in rolling motion on five meter diameter tyres.

"Dat's your job drive truck. She cost near three million bucks herself."

"Jesus … three million bucks!" Bill whistled.

"Don't worry, mate," Stan reassured, "Piece of piss even girls drive." And for the first time, Stan laughed at the worried look on his young charge's face. Stan barked a short indistinguishable sentence into the two-way handpiece and, with that, the huge yellow beast turned from its original track toward the exit road and rumbled toward them, increasingly dwarfing the ute as it approached. Bill saw, then, the driver's cockpit a tiny ladder-accessed haven tucked out of harm's way under the huge steel lip of the ore bucket. It was three meters off the ground. Stan opened the driver's door and motioned him out.

The big haulpak hummed away remarkably quietly and Bill saw the cab door open and the dark silhouette of the driver as he crawled onto the access ladder. The lithe figure then worked down the steel ladder in a glide as he jumped several steps at a time and used the handrail to control his descent.

Then, at a trot, the helmeted driver approached Stan with a high five and the two leaned heads together to hear each other against the roar and rumble of the busy machinery. Stan turned to Bill and brought him in close to the third figure. "Bill, meet your teacher, Maria, she teach you drive the haulpak. Ok? You go."

Only then did Bill realise that the grey overalls of the driver covered one of those girls Stan had mentioned. Bill's teacher reached out to shake and he took the tiny but strong grip and followed her to the haulpak. As he followed her up the ladder, his initial innocent upward gaze confirmed that she was indeed a woman and one with a very attractive and beautifully-rounded rear end. Suddenly struck with Catholic guilt, he consciously looked downward and managed to smash his helmeted head against the bottom of the cab door, much to his companion's delight as she sat in the drivers seat awaiting his arrival. Eyes watering, he pulled himself up and into the cab, groggily apologising as she leaned around him in the confined space and yanked the door closed, shutting out the grumble of the activity of the pit. "Sit down, fool," his teacher giggled and off came her helmet with long auburn hair tumbling down to shoulder. Bill, still disorientated, sat in what appeared to be a co-pilot's seat and then turned to face her as she plopped herself into the comfort of the lambs-wool encased operator's seat.

So Bill met Maria, Stan's 23 year-old daughter. She was, he soon learned, a strong willed and ambitious young woman, the apple of her father's eye and a veteran of the super-pit, having worked under her father's close supervision since she was 15 years old. Maria was in the final year of her geology and mine engineering degree at the University of Western Australia in Perth, 600kms to the west. Her exposure to the world of mining from that young age, combined with her intelligence and practical experience under her father's guiding hand meant that Maria had consistently topped her class.

Already her father's employer had promised her a position in that massive and international conglomerate when she graduated at the end of the year. With projects spread from the steppes of Siberia to the Amazonian jungle, they selected their key personnel well to maintain competitive advantage in a shrinking world of geological possibilities. With a month left of the university holidays, Stan had chosen his daughter to train Jack's fugitive friend.

Immediately the two discovered a mutual appreciation of the ridiculous; a shared humorous perception of the world, and that first night of work from 6pm to 6am in Maria's company passed way too quickly, Bill thought. Within a few hours she taught him how to operate the big machine. With a diesel generator powering the four individual electric motors to drive the four wheels, Bill soon came to appreciate how amazingly simple the massive haulpaks were to drive. From the hydraulically-cushioned and sound-deadened comfort of the cab, he soon came to enjoy the sensation of powering the big Cat around the wide mine roads. He would grind down into the pit and onto the back of the line of other paks nudging up to the excavator for loading of over 200 tonne of ore at a time, the big machines rolling and sinking with each bucket load. Then, after the slow whining grind up the haul roads to the crushing plant, the ore was dumped off the tray as the huge bucket tipped backward at the flick of a lever. "This is definitely a big boy's toy," Bill laughed, his mind going back to distant childhood memories of toy trucks and sandpits.

In the close company of a pretty, young and intelligent woman, Bill didn't want his first shift to end. But it did after 12 hours and meals taken in the cab on the job, with Maria presenting two of everything, including big stainless steel thermoses of thick black Slav coffee for his thirsty pleasure. Then, at the rising of the hot summer sun over the distant red horizon, the shift ended and Maria parked the haulpak back in the line of identical dusty monsters sitting at the depot for the waiting day shift. She directed Bill to her ute with engine warming and air-con cooling while she signed them both off at the office transportable.

And so went the first week. His new friend dropped him off each morning and picked him up each night for the first seven days of the 13 day shift 12 hours each day. Each night they got to know a little more about each other; she refreshingly, innocently, telling this stranger all about her life, past and present, and her hopes for her future. Bill was, by necessity, reserved and evasive although her father had warned her not to pry. She knew that he was in some sort of trouble. In that town she had met many men and women who came to work quietly at the mine, escaping demons. She had learnt not to venture into areas where specific answers were required, but with this man she was curious.

Bill just enjoyed her; she was a bubbly, funny extrovert. She was also bloody good looking, but strangely, he thought, he wasn't that sexually attracted to her. I mean, if she begged for it, he pondered, I might just weaken, but he was more comfortable developing a friendship without the complication of sex. That first week, however, he did become aware that under the grey linen of the overalls Maria wore nothing but a g-string. He enjoyed that sneaky treat at the start of each shift when he followed her up the ladder to the cab. As he looked up, his face only a metre from her, he could see a clear impression of the tiny garment pressed against the perfectly symmetrical swell of her buttocks.

And then, when she led him down the ladder at the end of shift, his downward gaze was occasionally rewarded with a vista of the partially unzipped neck of the overalls of two modest, but beautifully constructed, dark pink-tipped breasts, unfettered by bra. Or as a special treat on very hot nights, he was an uninvited witness via a more unbuttoned overall to an extended view down a flat, muscular, tanned tummy.

When, at the end of the first seven days, Maria advised him that he was on his own, he put on his best puppy-dog face and told her he would miss her company. Then they laughed together as she teased him and told him she would still pick him up and drop him off and make his lunch "like a good Slav wife." So each morning and each

130

night of the 13-night shift, he saw her and only her. Occasionally Stan checked on him, but he was effectively kept separate from the rest of the workforce. Stan had given him a call sign and he did speak by radio to the other drivers and radio controllers on the mine. His call sign was "Cat 7" but two-way conversations were business only and otherwise he kept to himself Stan and Maria were the only human contact he had.

With the 12-hour shifts for 13 nights straight and then only one day off, he found that he slept most of the days anyway and had no need for other company. To keep himself fit he had Maria drop him five kilometres from the units each morning. Much to her amusement he would trudge off, fully dressed in boots and overalls, in a weary dust-spurting jog into the scraggy bush and run back to the units. He would take time out on the way to engage in a solo tree-bashing tae kwon do routine before a furtive sweaty approach to the rear of the unit to avoid being seen by the other camp-dwellers.

He had always been somewhat self-sufficient. "A bit of a loner," various teachers had described him as a child and youth, and so the enforced isolation did not concern him at first. Maria kept him supplied with reading material, with the daily newspapers of the state and the nation and the various current affairs magazine, which he consumed hungrily. When he began to get paid in cash from Stan's petty cash budget he had Maria buy him all the latest fiction and non-fiction novels on sale at the town's book-stores.

He was pleasantly surprised by the amount of money he was paid. Stan was scrupulously fair, detailing in hand-written text the breakdown of his wages. Although he wasn't able to show the wage through the mine books he paid Bill the going rate for an operator and Bill found that at the end of each shift he was paid around $1500 cash for a week's work. Bill progressively stashed the crisp bills away behind a wall panel that he loosened behind the bunk in the unit. With no need for Jack's money he had Maria post it back to Sydney, with interest. He tucked away the crisp notes in a greeting card with cryptic, "Hey, bro, just going with the flow, wish you were here" type message and added, "this is to buy some decent sounds and for my share of gas, food and board".

It was through his hunger to read, to be informed, that Maria discovered his secret and the identity of the man she was helping to hide from society. *The Bulletin* used it as its lead story that month, featuring a front-page photograph of the dangerous runaway with the caption: "Wanted, dead or alive", like an old-time western outlaw poster. A none-too flattering photograph, he felt, as Maria handed him the magazine one morning the photo face up and an exaggerated questioning look on her pretty face. "It's not me, it's not me," he joked desperately, "that's my evil cloned twin Dolly Peters I'm always getting blamed for his stuff."

"Got you, you kiwi bastard," Maria giggled back at him, "I can make some money out of you; make a nice dowry, that," and she pointed to the reward that the New South Wales' Government had offered for his capture. "Shit, $250,000! I might turn the prick in myself," he joked and the two laughed together. But his blood had frozen as he was reminded of his vulnerability the reality of his total reliance on her and Stan.

"Come on, sunshine, grab some bathers, I'm taking you for a swim," she commanded, and Bill found some shorts and joined his friend in the ute. As they drove, she told him that her father had spoken to Jack Waratini and he knew that the drugs and escape allegations were all "bull-sheet". Stan had told her that he trusted Jack with his life and if Jack vouched for Bill, that was good enough. Maria turned to him as she drove, and said, "So, you just relax, young man. I trust my instincts."

"Do you, now?" he smiled. "And what do your instincts tell you?"

She grinned at him, "My female intuition tells me that despite your many obvious faults, you are a good man. Now there's an oxymoron," she teased.

"Where? Where?" he teased back looking frantically out the ute's windows as if to catch a glimpse of that mythical being running through the bush. Maria slapped his leg and grew serious. "Bill, I'm here to talk to if you ever want to, but if you don't want to you don't have to, ok?"

"Ok, Mama," he said, and got another slap for his trouble.

They arrived after a 20-minute bush track drive at a secluded billabong. It was a clean, fresh, spring-fed oasis where native parrots and kangaroos sipped the sweet waters; where a sandalwood and tea-tree halo fringed and shaded the flat black rocks. Maria had Bill carry the picnic esky while she fetched a rug. At her direction they set up camp under the spread of the beautiful sandalwood, a tree whose fragrance had doomed the extensive stands of the area to cruel harvest from the 1840s to supply the incense markets of Asia. They had a swim. Maria stripped gracefully out of the khaki shirt and shorts, revealing a lithe, tanned body and lime green bikini, to Bill's appreciative wolf whistle, while he hid behind a stand of bush and got into his swim shorts. He heard her splash softly into the water, and then with Tarzan yell and clumsy dash across the warm rocks he ambushed her with a massive bombie that nearly lifted her out onto the rocks in the crashing wave he caused. "Wanker!" she cursed and attacked, and with her petite frame, she fought a brave but useless battle in trying to force his head under the water. The two laughed and wrestled, coughing and spluttering, until, by an unspoken mutual agreement, they floated apart and lay each spreadeagled, feet touching feet like two very badly matched synchronised swimmers. They lay like that in total peace for what to Bill seemed like hours. Bodies cradled by the cool fluid in a sensual embrace. Feet connected, heads half-submerged, faces in the warm air, looking up in to the intensity of the blue Goldfields' sky, arms outstretched with hands slowly rotating to keep floating. Neither wanted to break the moment. Finally, Maria disconnected, stood and took his feet and turned his floating body until she held his head.

She felt suddenly protective and maternal. She was worried about him although really, she hardly knew him. She sat, waist-deep on the ledge of rocks near the edge, and cradled his seal-slicked head in her lap with his legs extending out into the billabong.

He felt her warm arms around his head, hands on shoulders and chest, fingers gentle, water-washed massage, brushing of nipple. He felt the satin of each inner thigh, the bone hardness of bent knee either side of his trunk, felt that soft spring of her breasts against the back of his head. From time to timeless time he felt her soft breath and lips as she gently brushed them to his forehead. Despite himself, as he fell deeper into hypnotic trance and without intent, his body reacted to her femaleness and his cock arched in obvious sensual reaction, tenting the cotton shorts, but he ignored the possibilities and fell asleep in her arms.

He woke minutes later to her growling like a demented feral cat and chewing on his ear. "Wake up, boof-head, it's tucker time," she informed. And with that rude interruption he twisted around in her grip, stood on the rocks to pick up her slippery giggling form and threw his tiny catch into the middle of the billabong with a splash. With a bigger splash he dived in to grab her and pulled her gently out of the water and up onto the picnic rock. "About time I served you, Madam," he teased as she towelled her long auburn locks dry and shook them, flicking droplets about. She then sat on the rug in the warmth of the shaded day, the lime green bikini a beautiful contrast to her light mocha skin. Bill opened the esky and found within a veritable feast. There were frosty bottles of wine from Margaret River, the state's grape-growing region. Three bottles, he noted, as he corkscrewed the first with a "pop!" and poured the scented verdhello juices into the glasses she had packed. "Thank you, kind sir," Maria accepted her glass and they clinked the fragile vessels together and sighed in unison at the cold liquid shock of the wine. And then Bill served her from the cool treasures of the esky. There were oysters in half shell flown in that morning from Albany. There was crusty French bread baked by a Vietnamese bakery for Australian consumers in strange example of multicultural diversity. Packed away were also succulent cheeses from the south west's dairy herds and cheese-makers, whose ancestors learnt their secrets in the fields of France or Belgium. Bill found pink-fleshed smoked chicken and fragrant smoked ham sliced thick off the bone, and boiled free-range orange-yolked eggs, which he cracked and peeled and placed onto glass serving dishes between the two of them. They ate and Bill was pleased to see that his friend maintained her gorgeous body with healthy portions of the gourmet delights. He felt somewhat embarrassed by his own hunger but she encouraged him and he feasted, and they drank, and by the end of the main meal

134

they were on to the second bottle of wine, each going glass for glass. "A break between courses, my big fat friend," she sighed and he cleaned away and they lay down. "Bloody luxury," he moaned and she moved behind him and again cradled his head in her lap with her back up against the smooth trunk of the sandalwood, and then as they relaxed he began to talk about his life.

He left nothing out; told it all. When he got to the sad and desperate parts she cried, not out loud, but he felt her salty tears splash onto his forehead. She just let him release it all, let him talk, filling his glass occasionally. And then to his amazement, with the headiness of the wine, and Maria's emotions, for the second time in his adult life he wept. Softly at first, and then from somewhere deeper. Sobs of loss came from him, and Maria slid down alongside him and tried with her tiny body to encircle him, envelop him. They lay like that for a long time. Eventually, she fell asleep, and he just marvelled at the day, refreshed in body and spirit. He looked at her as she lay in his arms like a child. He looked at her pretty face, sweet lips loose in sleep. Her hair, glossy with good health, and perfect womanly body pressed into him, tiny lime green bikini barely covering those soft pert breasts and bikini bottoms accentuating strength of hip, of thigh, of buttock, and again he hardened against her through the cotton of his shorts. Determined not to offend, he pulled back, but that was enough to wake the sleeping princess. And she lay, sleepy languid eyes looking deep into his, she gently kissed him and lazily ran soft tongue across his lips. But even as he responded and stroked the fine muscles of her back down and onto the soft firm swell of her buttocks, she suddenly stiffened and awoke both physically, and to the intent of his increasing enthusiasm, and she pushed him gently back. "Ok, boofhead, listen up and listen good. You have your big ape arms around a pure Slav virgin. And, my big fat friend, I am going to remain a virgin until married."

"Can't we marr " he started playfully. "No! just listen," she laughed, and as they lay side by side, a respectable six inches apart now, and she explained the battle that she had had to remain a virgin for 23 years in a tough man's town like Kalgoorlie. She also told him that she had a man. A boyfriend, a fiancé, "TJ", she called him. "He is at uni with me in Perth. I love him and he loves me," she insisted proudly. "So, despite what just about happened here, I am faithful to my man. We are to marry," she grew serious, almost apologetic, "Bill, it is just something in me. When I give myself to a cause, any cause, I give it all," she said.

"But, I give you due credit, I don't how you did it, mister I almost weakened."

He put on his evil fairy voice. "Vell, my fair sweet wirgin, I plied your beautiful young body with evil alcohol, and told you my sad story just to get into those bikini bottoms " Slap! against his face as she laughed softly and then kissed him where she had slapped. "Idiot, there's no way they would fit your fat butt" she giggled. "Hey, come on," he protested, "it takes a heavy hammer to drive a long nail."

The tension gone, they lay together, neither wanting to break their closeness now that the boundaries were defined. Then Maria told him that she was going back to Perth the next day, back to university, and would be gone until mid-year. "How will you survive without me, Boofhead?" He pretended to cry, mock sobbing, and began tearing his hair, moaning, "Pleeza lady, don't leava me lone, you bloody cold hard Slav girl," until again she softly slapped him and kissed him, sisterly, on his forehead. She teased, "When I come back I'm bringing him."

"Him?"

"Yes, boofhead, him: TJ."

"Oh him."

And she explained that her man and his rough footy mates were planning a trip to Kalgoorlie mid-year during the next uni holidays. "We are all coming to Kalgoorlie on a bus. Young man, you are going to have to do without me until then. In fact, you are going to have to do without me even then," and Maria giggled at his puppy-dog expression.

By now the sun was setting, throwing soft shadows over the billabong. Still comfortably entwined, they watched wary kangaroos on the far shore slip cautiously down to drink before the night feeding. Slowly, reluctantly, they disentangled and Bill

136

slyly adjusted his unrelieved turgidity as he stood and felt that special male primitive ache of unrequited lust from his groin. As Maria fussed about packing, he walked to the edge of the water. He stretched his arms high and gave a Tarzan yell to the darkening sky. Then he felt her small body behind him, and as he gasped in surprise, she held her tiny left hand over his mouth from behind to quieten him, and then with her right tugged his shorts down his thighs, springing his cock free to salute the early evening sky.

"I can't leave you this way," she sang and giggled. And he shuddered in delight as her tiny hand somewhat roughly, he thought, encircled him. Bill looked down in happy amazement. She was wearing a canvas mine glove. She laughed from behind him, "I'm wearing protection, so this ain't really cheating. Is it mister?"

"Who am I to argue?" he moaned. And with the yellow desert sun setting to a chorus of pink and grey cockatoos, his friend rhythmically pumped him until, with a sticky splash and grunted, knee-shaking fulfilment and her perfectly-timed feminine rendition of the Tarzan yell his tension erupted onto the still, black waters of the billabong.

Chapter 18

Thank You For the Music

The chopper flew them high and fast through the threatening black cloud band, heading west, away from the troubled roiling air as the front smashed against the ridge of the Southern Alp mountain chain. Above the cloud they then headed north with the island invisible beneath until the wave-chopped waters of the Cook Strait were seen in brief grabs beneath. In two hours they were descending sharply down through dark cloud onto the wet black tarmac of the Royal New Zealand Airforce base outside Wellington. They flared down beside a dark grey squatting Hercules, the big craft warming its engines, props hypnotically rotating in the drizzle, waiting at the end of a runway.

Bill followed Kingi out of the chopper with thank you wave to the anonymous pilot. They hit the windy rain-lashed black tarmac and crossed through the sudden moist warmth of the kero-scented exhaust, then up the short stepladder extruding from the body of the Herc. This aeroplane, retired from active service after 40 years, had proved itself as the reliable and sturdy avionics workhorse of the nation's small airforce of the 60s. She had been used in coastal surveillance to search for robber nations' stealthy trawlers the thieves illegally working dark, dangerous waters far from their home ports as their own traditional fish stocks failed to meet the protein-hungry needs of their populace. The Hercs were also used more properly as rapid-deployment troop carriers when the tiny South Pacific nation went to the assistance of its larger allies, lumping troops to theatres of war or unrest in regions generally unrelated to New Zealand's own security. The Hercules fleet had recently been replaced by more modern versions but the government had retained one of the old Hercs for promotional and special project use.

Bill followed Kingi into the cavernous cylinder of the Herc's interior. The dark blue-suited load master beckoned them into the noisy vibrating tunnel, lit by dull yellow ceiling and floor lighting along the length of the empty cargo bay. Bill saw that this bird was combat-rigged. There was fabric mesh seating strung along each side of the cargo bay and from the mid-cabin, two more seat sections were slung on sturdy aluminium- tubed meccano structures. The load master, with black head-set, directed them both forward as the flight sergeant secured the double-skinned rear door, swinging it shut and significantly muffling the outside din.

As he followed his mentor up toward the sharp end, Bill saw that four commercial airline seats had been installed immediately behind the cockpit. He could look forward into the cockpit through the gap between black curtains where the two pilots waited, seated behind the green glow of the control panels. With Kingi and Bill seated and belted into the plush seats, the flight master gave an inaudible confirmation of readiness into the mouthpiece of the headset. Immediately the big engines were kicked up to flight revs and Bill felt the squat bird lunge and strain against the brakes as last checks were done. Then, with thumbs up from the pilot, the Herc jumped forward and rapidly built up the ground speed necessary to lift the 50 tonne machine up and away in a combat take-off that the pilots so enjoyed.

Bill had always loved the sensation of the take-off and landing of the huge passenger jets. So he simply marvelled at the gut-wrenching adrenalin buzz from the G-force of the short mad dash down the runway and jolt of sudden and steep ascent as the pilots pushed the sturdy machine up away from Wellington and set a direct course for Auckland, 700 kilometres north. And as they took off

Bill suddenly realised that his father and Kingi in their military past as young men his age may even have been in this actual aircraft in foreign lands, taking off to face uncertain consequences from certain dangers.

As they settled in they were served an airforce breakfast by the flight crew and Kingi brought Bill up to date with developments. Tom was very near death, he learnt. The aggressive cell divisions of the cancer were just days or only hours away from breaking through the final protective tissues of the spine and invading that precious fluid network that allowed Tom's body to function, to live. "There is no reprieve possible, just time to live," Kingi declared. "Tom has been taken to a hospice attached to Middlemoore Hospital at Otahuhu," he advised and Bill knew that the big South Auckland training hospital was in the middle of the area of influence of the Te Kuri. "Members of the gang, those who have dealt with Tom most closely over the two years, are visiting each day," Kingi said. "Up to today the Whetu brothers have not visited, it's been mainly Tama, Joe Tama, the lieutenant I have told you about."

Bill knew from the briefings that Tom had never become close to the Whetu brothers on a personal level. Once his place had been confirmed in the structure of the Gang's operations as the fence the man to whom the gang directed its ill-gotten gains the lines of command set in place by the brothers necessarily protected them from that mundane day-to-day dealing. Bill had learnt that the higher echelons of the gang deliberately did not deal with the tradesmen such as Tom. There were buffer levels within the gang whereby disposable gang members dealt directly with outsiders. Usually, early in the relationships between the parties, there was no stated, obvious, or traceable, connection to the next level. This structure had been a deliberate design by the brothers who were students of criminal societies around the world. From the Italian Cosa Nostra to Asian triads and the drug cartels of black America, from the ruthless Colombians to the western outlaw rebel organisations such as the Hell's Angels, the two older brothers had studied all available material: journalistic text and documentary, law enforcement reports and court precedents. From the available

140

histories of various crime structures, the Whetu brothers had taken the features and practices of the most successful, and adapted and implemented those to the local scene.

Kingi's focus with Tom had been to build the wall around the Whetus by a coordinated approach of establishing water-tight evidence of criminality against as many of the gang individuals as possible. Over the two years of Operation Te Kuri each criminal act by any member of the gang was documented and attested to by Tom on video tape. The operation's unprecedented powers and activities were legally defined and authorised by the government under the yet-to-be publicly disclosed *Te Kuri Act of State*. The Act and the actions were modelled on the USA law enforcement agencies' response to the difficulty of breaking down the protective barriers around the top Mafia, triad and other crime organisations. The theory and the practical application then targeted the organisation in joint tactical attack by the police, social services, customs and inland revenue. Even if the hierarchy escaped direct detection of a criminal act, the effect of the integrated approach to destroying the organisation was by force of society's regulators. These agencies would act together to dissemble the gang at the completion of the operation, Kingi had told his agent. With civil and criminal repercussions against as many of the gang individuals as possible, the intent was to destroy the structure by a legal war of attrition that would take the gang years to recover from.

Kingi told Bill that each night of the life of the operation, where practicable, he would be debriefed covertly. Every time Bill witnessed or participated in a criminal act committed by any of the targets, he would commit each minute detail to sworn statement and to video-taped description. He would do this until a library of evidence was built around the activities of the Te Kuri to supplement the hundreds of hours and thousands of pages compiled by the dying Tom.

On the plane after take-off, Kingi left Bill to his own thoughts. He went forward into the cockpit where he obviously knew the flight crew and only returned to his seat as the big Herc began its descent into the Whenuepai Royal New Zealand airforce base out of Auckland, 80 minutes later. Fifteen minutes after touchdown, Bill and Kingi were seated in the back of a military ambulance and making quick time through early afternoon traffic; south on the highway up and over the Auckland Harbour Bridge toward the hospice. One hour after touchdown, Bill was lying covered on a stretcher, a colourful hand-knitted beanie disguising his head and face as he was wheeled from the ambulance into the quiet pastel world of the hospice. At the head of the trolley, dressed in the pale green orderly uniform, Kingi manoeuvred Bill through the corridors and into the private room immediately next door to where Tom was counting down his last narcotic-cushioned hours. Entry into the room was gained after the coded knock; the door opened only after cold-eyed scrutiny from within. Inside, Bill rose from the trolley and saw the room had been transformed into a covert mini operations base. Digital screen images showed the car park, the corridor and Bill noted with sudden attention, the dying Tom, curled on the bed in peaceful foetal fold.

Over hot tea two senior covert officers bought them up to speed with developments. It was now 7pm and the last visitor had left. Joe Tama again. Tama one of the Te Kuri's top-tier lieutenants, the man who had worked most closely with Tom over the time of the operation. Tama, who truly felt as a brother to Tom, had been with him since early afternoon. He visited on behalf of the gang. It was a duty as a representative of the criminal family to which he believed that Tom also belonged and an acknowledgment of Tom's apparent loyalty to the gang over the last two years. Tama had visited every day for the two weeks Tom had lain awaiting death in the hospice. And yet ironically it was Tama who had unwittingly, unknowingly contributed most over the two years to the gradual building of that brick wall around the future freedom of the gang. This night Tom had finally told Joe Tama to go. He needed rest. Tama left with the relief that the healthy instinctively feel when allowed with grace to escape the proximity of the damned. After the bro shakes and promises to return the next day, Tama was watched by video and live surveillance out of the hospice. The gang car was watched from the carpark and away through suburban streets by vehicle-based agents, supported by police chopper in the overcast darkening sky.

Now, as Bill watched, Tom stirred in the bed and waved impatiently but weakly at the CCTV lens that he knew was watching. "Let's go," said Kingi, and the door between the two rooms was unlocked and opened. Bill heard from behind him the commands to the agents outside by coded and scrambled two-way as they were placed on extra high vigilance. All agents knew that the briefing was underway and that no interference would be permitted.

So, Agent Peters met Agent Burns. Kingi sat Bill down near the head of the dying man's bed. He saw the deathly pallor and veiny parchment skin of this once powerful man's face, etched now in the agony known only to those who had suffered this most aggressive of cancers. Kingi spoke softly to his agent who clearly was under floating on waves of opiate relief. "Tom, mate," he leaned down close to the sick man's ear, "Mate, we don't have to do this. I think we have enough. Young Bill, he's been a quick learner." But they watched the painful, visible struggle as Tom surfaced and focused through his mist. Tom, impatient now, signalled to the medic behind Kingi with a harsh, cracked, throaty, "Ok, let's do it." The medic moved forward and with immaculate care found a vein under the yellowing skin and injected the supine man with almost immediate and, to Bill, startling, effect.

Tom appeared to physically convulse, to tighten and grunt as the pain, now unblunted by chemical buffer, attacked. "Naltrextone," Kingi explained to Bill, "Tom's idea, reckoned he needed a clear head to brief you." Tom appeared to gather himself, almost to relax, although with a beaded sweat breaking out across weathered brow. "What was that?" Bill asked, perplexed. Kingi explained, "A drug called Naltrextone, Bill. It's an anti-opiate used to save junkies from overdoses. It has a chemically negating effect in the body. Wipes the effects of the opiate from the system. Amazing stuff. Tom insisted on it."

Then in a whispered aside he said, "He's going to pay for it, Bill, make it worth it." And then Tom talked talked to Bill. He saw him, smiled at him, and awkwardly reached to shake his hand.

He motioned the young man to sit closer. Kingi stayed, hovering, worried in the background, bringing tea. It was drunk by Bill, not offered to nor wanted by Tom, his thirst being sated by intravenous saline drip. Bill listened as Tom fought the waves of the razor wire of his senses. He told his story. It was the story of his last two years. He was desperate that his time, his effort, should not be wasted by his death. Death itself did not frighten him, he had seen death. He had learned, however, that pain frightened him. Not the pain of an injury, not the pain of a wound, because that was a living healing pain. No, it was the unrelenting killing pain created by his own traitorous cells that he now felt. And he knew that he could never escape. That pain frightened him. But despite his fear and the deadly fatigue the pain caused, now, by choice, he deliberately released that raw pain again. And as Tom told of his two years, Bill recognised that this session was invaluable. Straight from the horse's mouth, he thought, and immediately and with every neuron of attention, he concentrated on the nuances of the tale. Tom spoke of each of the main players, the three brothers, and the sister who was seldom seen, protected from the lifestyle, cosseted, treasured. He spoke of his analysis of the structure, the tiers, and the lines of command all leading invisibly up to the three Whetu Brothers. In a strained précis, he took Bill through the two years of the operation, how he had gained trust, respect, and then friendship of the mid- to higher-level lieutenants, but was never allowed to really connect to the Whetu brothers due to the systems set in place by them. He spoke of his first induction, when he was taken to the island and had to fight a selected challenger, Joe Tama. After that, although apparently accepted by the gang, his contact with the brothers had been restricted. Tom told how, slowly, from the trust and contact with the lower tiers of command, he had got a handle on how the gang operated.

He knew of the drug factories from careless usually alcohol or drug-affected comment from trusting confidants. He knew well of the burglary teams as he had provided the conduit for the ill-gotten gains that had so consistently and richly rewarded the gang over the two years.

He talked for five hours softly, steadily weaker. Strangely, in the telling, he appeared to relax, become more contented. At midnight he finished. They stood to leave him. Bill suddenly realised how weary he was, how physically stiff, how mentally fatigued, from the concentration that he had awarded Tom. And urgently then, Kingi called for the nurse to again dispense the powerful pain-killers to Tom. They walked away to leave him, but Tom, with voice suddenly intensely strong, called from the bed, "Kingi! Bill!" They went quickly back, one each side of the bed, and Tom took them each by a hand with powerful claw. And he died.

Chapter 19

Since My Baby Left Me

What was to be the last six months of Bill's sojourn in Kalgoorlie passed slowly. Without the company of Maria, brief though that time had been, his was a solitary world on the busy mine site. Stan tried his best but his natural way was gruff and short and his interest was soccer not "zat blardy ossy rules shet, or zat crazy rukbee," and so sport was out as a topic of conversation. Bill made subtle enquiries after Maria and received, he felt sure, deliberately vague responses from Stan. He found Talia, Maria's mother, more than proudly happy to fill him in on news about her "special flower" when he occasionally joined his benefactor for a heavy Slav meal.

All he did was work solo, train solo and sleep solo for those 24 weeks. As a result he was lonely, hard as nails and frustrated to hell. The only positive consequence, apart from the fact that he had so far touch-wood evaded capture by the police, was the money. After nine months he had nearly $30,000 in cash stashed away in his secret cache in the unit walls. He could not believe his unexpected wealth, and when possible he had Stan swap the smaller notes for $100 denominations to cut down the bulk. He then spent days clumsily sewing a sturdy money belt that fitted snugly around his waist, just in case that day arrived where flight may be the only option.

He worried how Stan could hide $30,000 as petty cash, but his worry was relieved when Stan explained that one tyre for a Haulpak retailed for more than that, and that in the scheme of things his petty cash was easily hidden in the financial tapestry of the huge mine's operation.

Through this time, when he could, he checked into Kingi's listening post. In the early hours he would use the orange pay-phone supplied on site by the mining company. With so few men living in the camp, Bill had found that he could easily avoid contact with the other camp dwellers and they, similarly, appeared to be the rogue bulls of their species, chased from human herds and happy to avoid him also. So when Bill, with stacks of coins to feed the voracious machine, called Great Aunt Ruby in faraway and fast asleep New Zealand, he was secure in his privacy.

And so he received a message from the old woman one cold star-splashed night that focused his mind and flooded his emotions again with the raw hurt of those horrific events of his past.

Kingi was on the trail. The old boys' network had sniffed the stale footprints of the beast, the tiny piles of the cold excrement of rumour left behind. Recent tracks: East Timor. A retired British commando, now a security adviser to an international construction company working to rebuild the tiny newly sovereign nation, had heard of the man Kingi sought. The story was that he and his men were slinking about the region on a ship. Informants spoke of the wheeling and dealing in the misery of the human cargo. Asylum seekers; that flood of refugees from sad and dangerous places toward Australia. And on the desperate journey, criminal dealers in blood-money and misery offered varying modes of transport to those peoples.

The word was he was in that region. Kingi spoke cryptically to Bill through the old lady. "Wait. I have activated other means of finding him. It looks like Asia, but maybe the top end of Australia. He may sail from home ports." From this, Bill gained hope. He now had a focus, and a need to consider leaving this red dust that had hidden him so well. Somehow he had to get north, high up on the continent, closer to Asia if the definitive word came of his target's whereabouts. But Great Aunt Ruby finished with Kingi's instruction: "Stay put, son. Stay put, stay safe and check in again. In one month." And so Bill waited, restless now. Hungry also for human companionship or even just the sight of others and despite himself he began to include the town in his training runs, the fringes at first, late at night ducking into bush or behind fences at the sound of vehicles. He soon found that in a town full of men he was not alone in his early-morning or late-evening runs. Sometimes dozens of like-minded joggers would be cris-crossing the wide streets of the old town's urban blocks like disturbed bull ants.

He ran with track-suited hood disguising head and face but even the brief panted "giddays" to the other joggers provided some measure of contact at least. He increasingly considered a nocturnal visit to the houses of sin along the town's Hay Street. In fact over the months, his runs began to almost magnetically include a voyeuristic jog past the stables, but always out of sight on the opposite, darkened side of the wide street. He even began to carry a couple of hundred dollars in the pockets of his jogging shorts, or tucked sweatily down a sock, just in case physical necessity overcame caution. Who knows? he reasoned, one dark night his sex-starved body might just jog him straight into the mysterious perfumed enclaves despite his discipline of mind and survival instincts. He laughed at this picture of himself. Jogging body suddenly and dangerously veering out of the dark like an athletic John Cleese. A mad huge step march across the road toward the musky maidens lounging in flimsy negligee as his frightened but captive head attempted by fruitless leaning and sideway jerking to veer that determined physicality away from the promise of flesh, away from the danger of discovery.

But it was that danger of discovery that stopped him.

And then everything changed.

It was the fourteenth day of the shift cycle, a Saturday night. The month was June. It was mid-winter in the desert town and the cold pierced through the clear black sky. Six hundred kilometres inland from the west coast and 400 from the south coast it took a determined and significant cloud band to force its warming fluffy blanket protection over the Goldfields. Bill was on a run, body on auto-pilot, mind ticking over. His thoughts were general: what to do tomorrow, get up, read, into the bush for a tae kwon do work out, another run, some sprint work, alternate against tonight's gentle distance work, eat, read, wank, sleep. He was comfortable now running in the town, more so in town because, as he had learnt from experience, he was less conspicuous. A solo runner at night out on the fringes of town was more likely to attract the territorial attentions of the town's dog population, both tame ones in backyards and the feral dingo types hanging on the fringes. He was less likely to come suddenly on the camping human fringe-dwellers from desert-dwelling tribes or white fellas struggling to find work and dreaming of better times to come, jobs, wages, food, and housing. For months he had become just another jogger through the suburban streets, the very least of the local constabulary's problems. They were drawn more to the commercial cluster of the twin town centres to patrol the constant detritus from the pubs, some of which even opened for breakfast. At that waking hour, incredulously skimpily-clad waitresses served plates of bacon and eggs greasily washed down with cold bitter Swan middies to hordes of dirt-encrusted miners coming off night shifts.

This evening Bill was heading out along Piccadilly Street, the name of which always reminded him of the tart cumin condiment he so enjoyed on a sandwich. He became vaguely aware, as he approached the football square, of a group of people near a bus parked against the verge. He cursed himself softly for not being aware earlier and being able to make the necessary diversion away from the group but realised he was committed to pass quite close. And so he put his head down in exaggerated concentration of his pursuit to trundle past the noisy gathering.

As he drew close, trotting softly on the reticulated verge, he suddenly identified threat as a small but obviously determined figure broke away from the mass and arrowed across the short grassy distance toward him. Instinctively his martial art training kicked in. His two arms moved to adopt a side attack block and his body adjusted for the side axe-kick blow that he would follow with a spinning back kick to smash the falling body of his assailant. Luckily, so luckily, just before the self-defence and counter-attack moves were activated, his finely tuned senses picked up and in that split second recognised the banshee cry of his assailant. That recognition halted those almost automatic reactions as his little mate, Maria, launched herself at him and up onto his back with an affectionate, "Boof-head you big wanker." He wore the lithe figure first on back and left shoulder before expertly flipping her up and over with casual adjustment using her momentum to then catch her into his arms like a child, both laughing at the moment. He dropped his little friend softly to the grass. It was then she told him in that first gush of hello that her dad, Stan, had told her that he had moved on with no message and no known destination. They both realised suddenly that Stan's concern was misplaced, although they had connected in more than just friendship. "It's so good to see you, Fred," Maria said with a wink, using the pet name she had for him during their work together. Then, taking him by the hand she started to move toward the group by the big blue bus. "Time to meet my man," she said, and he was introduced as "Fred" by Maria to TJ, her boyfriend.

The two men shook hands. The bubbly Maria and the half-pissed and welcoming TJ told Bill that he was in the midst of the rugby team Maria had told him about. It appeared the team was in Kalgoorlie to battle in a social game against the town's own mighty Bushwhackers team.

TJ looked hard then at Bill in a somewhat judgmental way. Bill felt a twinge of concern that Maria might have confessed to him about their activities, but that worry was allayed as TJ asked, "Mate, have you ever played rugby?"

"Yea, I did some years ago," Bill admitted and without further ado a large bearded figure, who introduced himself as "The Animal", threw a royal blue rugby jumper at him with a hearty, "Welcome to the Mighty Nedlands Nomads, petal!" "But I've got no gear," Bill laughed as the rest of the motley crew surrounded him with cheers and back slaps. Noisily they introduced themselves with hearty handshakes: Bulldog, Whale, Panos, Muzza, ET, Crusher,

Moon, Maddog, Brownie, Hurricane, Oppie and five or six other assorted characters welcomed, or, more accurately, press-ganged Bill into filling in the missing front row prop. Soon, from a kit-bag taken from the bus, Bill was provided the off-white shorts, blue and yellow socks and size 11 aluminium-studded boots. Maria explained that this gear, unwashed since some long-past game the season before, was the property of the team's missing prop "Aussie-Bob", lost in action somewhere in the town overnight. He had been last seen tumbling roly-poly down the steep carpeted steps of Sylvester's night club in the early hours of the morning, much to the hilarious delight of those others who could actually focus enough to see The Animal commit the trip. Bill changed quickly in the bus and then joined Maria again outside. While he put on the smelly boots and laced them up she brought him up to date with her life, laughing at her father's uncharacteristic deceit and asking how he had been. Surrounded by the other players putting on boots, strapping ankle, wrist and shoulder injuries and rubbing liniment into thighs and calves, their conversation was necessarily cautious. Bill cheekily told her, "I did miss your helping hand," and then rubbed the pinch mark on his midriff, to which she responded with a mischievous grin.

The shrill of a whistle from the paddock centre changed the dynamics of the group. Bulldog, a feisty muscular half-back and obviously the captain, brought the team to attention. There followed a brief stretching and warm-up session that had the larger forwards in particular groaning from the previous night's excesses. The lager farts and beer belches that exploded in the practice scrum as the forwards put down against the backs, and the resultant volatile gaseous mix, caused the backs to complain bitterly and the wingers to dry-retch. Bill found himself laughing quietly in warm recognition that he was again in the brotherhood of the team, that spirit applicable to most team sports but with the special traits and characteristics of the social rugby team.

He was reminded happily of his time with the New York University Ungulates, the same inane, crude humour, and the same sense of common competitive purpose but with an alertness for the ridiculous. He soon found out that the fugitive Aussie Bob had been the tight head prop. With left arm wrapped around the body and hand tucked into the shorts band of the hooker Hurricane Hamilton, he was soon crunching against the practice front row put down by the backs and he at once felt comfortable. Another shrill blast on the ref's whistle had Bulldog rounding them up like a human version of his namesake with, "come on you fucken guys, focus, fucken focus!" The team was moved in a messy flock toward the centre of the oval where Bill saw the locals, the Bushwhackers, standing in line, waiting. After handshakes and the Riot Act read by the referee, the coin was tossed. The Bulldog won and with Maria's solo cheer-squad efforts from the sideline, the battle began.

For Bill the next 80 minutes were heaven. The tensions and frustration of the past nine months were relieved in the joy of sporting battle. He loved the pounding sprints of team-members in the pursuit of the common purpose. Top teamwork and skills were required to obtain and to retain possession of the ball and to move it forward over the square of the paddock by pass, by kick, and by chase. The ballet and science of the set plays, the line-outs, the scrums, the rucks and mauls provided to Bill a physical and almost spiritual release.

At the first of many scrums Bill found his front-row opponent a solid mountain of bearded Australian manhood. There is a camaraderie peculiar to front-row rugby forwards the world over. After the two had tested each other's strength, by look and nod only they entered that special unspoken agreement that they would compete fairly with each other as equals in what front-rowers know is the toughest arena of the chess-battle of the game of rugby the scrum. They squared off shoulder to shoulder as bulwarks against which the second-rowers and loose forwards strained for the combined weight and strength advantage of the forward pack. They avoided the old illegal tricks of twist and dip and lift that each would have employed mercilessly against a less strong or experienced pretender to the elite ranks. By half-time the scores were even, ten-all, two tries each with conversions missed. As they trudged back to the sideline, Maria busied herself, tending to the wounds, the muscle pulls, the bruises and grazes, fussing around the pack. The players rested in the cool evening taking in copious amounts of water with steam rising from athletic effort into the crisp black sky. As she bent over, attending TJ, who had played a blinder as a crash-tackling try-saving loose forward, Bill sidled up behind her in the crush of bodies and rewarded himself with a sneaky soft pinch of track-suited right buttock. He then received in casual reply a reverse flick backward and upward of her foot to his groin to suffer his first significant injury of the game.

Half-time over and ruefully rubbing the ache in his right testicle, the team returned to the centre to resume the battle. After 38 minutes there was no change in the score. With Maria yelling herself hoarse from the sideline and Bulldog exhorting them with verbal lashings of, "come on you fucken guys, fucken push, fucken jump, fucken run, fucken ruck, fucken pass, winners are fucken grinners, a good loser is still a fucken loser," and other such jewels, the Nomads found themselves on attack two metres from the Bushies' try line with a line-out awarded after a desperate clearing kick from the besieged Bushies' full-back. Bill took up his position at the front of the line, hands on knees, pleasantly pooped. Meanwhile, Bulldog at half-back barked out a string of nonsensical names and numbers, "Blue 21, Kal 69, TJ 10, orange orange 7," which, when decoded, was an instruction to the hooker to throw the ball to TJ at the far end of the lineout. The Bushies, having heard such coded instructions all game were now calling TJ by name and readied themselves for the ball to come floating down the twin lines of forwards to his approximate position. It was then that everyone's attention was diverted to the road verge as a police paddy wagon pulled up.

It was Aussie Bob. He let himself out of the passenger's door with a cheery and suspiciously familiar wave goodbye to the sturdy, middle-aged female constable driving. The wagon pulled away from the park with toot-toot of farewell to Bob who yelled toward the teams, "Am I late?" Bill, with quick and cunning raise of eyebrow to Hurricane Hamilton, was delivered the ball at the front of the line.

With the benefit and advantage of surprise, Bill brushed past the late and despairing hands of the man-mountain and trotted otherwise untouched over the try line and under the posts to score the first try of his brief but so far brilliant career. With the referee rewarding the sly initiative of the act with raised hand and shrill confirmation of the score, the place erupted with bitter complaint from the Bushies and the Nomads mobbed Bill with cheers and hearty back slaps. They hoisted their new-found hero high on shoulders in a triumphant parade back to the centre while Brownie, the team's kicker, coolly slotted the ball over the posts for the numerical icing of the conversion and the referee blew time for the end of the game. With Maria screaming hysterically and jumping joyfully onto his back, Bill enjoyed the hilarity of the situation as the entire team fell into a messy pile on top of him. He grinned with face mushed into the red soil of the park and felt the soft body of Maria squashing against his back by the sweaty heavy bodies of his new found best friends. And he could only wish that he had fallen the other way.

Chapter 20

Leaving on a Jet Plane

With Tom's passing, Bill was immediately on his way. In the humid
evening air of the Auckland night, Bill and Kingi were hustled out
the rear of the hospice and into the back of a plain sedan which sped
away rapidly on the highway back toward the airforce base. Upon
arrival, the sedan was waved through the guard-house checkpoint
without delay and out onto the runway beside the pride of the Royal
New Zealand Airforce VIP fleet. This was a Boeing 727 purchased
as a second-hand bargain from another nation's failed airline to
fly the country's politicians around the country and the world in
a manner befitting their status. Not in any way approaching the
excesses of the American President's Airforce One 747, the smaller
jet had proved eminently suitable for its task.

Now the Captain and crew, on 24-hour call for this very
possibility, had the modern craft warmed and ready for a quick
trans-Tasman flight from Auckland to Sydney.

On the black pitch of the tarmac, Kingi farewelled his charge.
On the journey to the base he had briefed Bill on this next phase of
the operation. And he made his last offer that Bill could simply walk
away from the operation. Bill looked at his mentor in the darkened
car, "I'm in, sir," he spoke clear and strong. "I am sure that I just
met the bravest man I will ever meet." Kingi smiled and nodded

in appreciation of the emotion he had also felt at Tom's bedside. A respect for that quality of courage, for the man gone, and now for this young untried man. "Ok, mate. We will have the hospice tell the gang of Tom's passing."

Bill knew that over the past two weeks since he entered the training unit, Tom had casually managed to introduce by story and reminiscence to his contacts within the gang particularly Joe Tama stories that suddenly included his nephew. Young Bill George, the son of Tom's deceased brother, living in New York, USA. Tom's story told in ever more detailed piecemeal over the last weeks, had been that before his own return to New Zealand three years earlier, he had worked with and trained young Bill in the same trade in New York. He told Tama that he had sent for young Bill as his only living relative to tidy up his concerns in the homeland.

The cover story seemed good enough. They had quickly, with the cooperation of Interpol, implemented some traces of actual fact in relation to Bill's time at NYU. And with the full cooperation of the US authorities in New York, they had neatly produced false but apparently faultless documentation detailing a minor criminal past of one Bill George. This documentation, held now as a public record in the States, showed that Bill George held both USA residency and New Zealand citizenship from his parents: his father previously employed in the New Zealand diplomatic corps, his mother a lecturer at NYU, both some years deceased. The public record showed that young Bill had gone off the tracks somewhat, but had only ever been convicted of minor misdemeanours. However, the records clearly suggested that he was suspected of more significant drug and property-related crimes.

A cursory search in the US by corrupt contacts of the Te Kuri would hopefully satisfy that organisation that Bill George was both the nephew of Tom and that he was probably of a criminal persuasion. Trigger mechanisms within the data collection and storage systems of law enforcement and within the justice, taxation and customs services of the USA would alert the FBI, and by that organisation, Kingi Potiki of the New Zealand Police, as to any nefarious inquiry as to the bona-fides of Bill George.

156

The dying man had shown his closest contact in the Te Kuri, Joe Tama, old family photos. Photos included shots of Tom and Bill together, cleverly created by photographic experts in the NZ Police covert operations section. The aged photos showed Bill and Tom in various settings apparently over several years, including in sombre dark-suited pose at the funerals of his parents. The most recent photo had been left with Joe. And Tom had told Joe the day before he died that young Bill was now en route to Auckland.

The basic cover story was in place. Once Tama had been advised of his compadre's death he was to e-mail the sad news to an electronic address that was in fact sourced to a New York Police safe house in the village. This innocuous flat was apparently the contact address for one Bill George. Tom had told Joe that his instructions to his nephew were to check his e-mails as he skipped his way south across the various sovereign nations toward New Zealand. Tom told Joe that Bill would reply to the e-mail with his flight details and arrival time.

In the meantime, Agent Bill Peters was on his way to Sydney to meet the Air New Zealand Flight out of LA on its way back to Auckland. A search of the passenger manifest would falsely show that a Bill George had boarded LAX 5 from Los Angeles after a connecting flight from New York. Tama had been asked by Tom to arrange for Phil and Bo to pick his nephew up from the airport. Phil and Bo were the two undercover operatives who had worked the two years past with Tom at the warehouse.

So with that last briefing and with a strong handshake from Kingi, Bill boarded the 727 and the jet taxied out for take-off toward Sydney. Three hours later the jet touched down at Mascot Airport, the international avionic gateway to the state of New South Wales. By prior arrangement, NZ Consular Security personnel met the aircraft at the far end of the taxi runway and, using the motorised stairs, took off one only passenger. As the airforce jet took off again and tracked south-east back toward Auckland, Bill George, dressed casually in blue jeans, black Armani shirt and reflective wrap-around shades, looking suitably New York white-trash sinister, was escorted up and into the international terminal. Inside he mixed in with jet-lagged passengers out of LA, and fresh passengers out of Sydney before boarding the cleaned and refuelled plane for take-off back to Auckland, New Zealand.

Chapter 21

Fun and Games

"It's beer-a-fuckin-clock!" was Maria's rallying cry as she dragged the largest custom-built cold box Bill had ever seen from the big old blue bus. Both teams straggled in small groups across the paddock to where the bus was parked. Maria opened the lid of the box and from the icy depths began lying a mortar pattern of the state's finest 'Swan' lager cans, caught and cracked thirstily by the returning combatants. Then followed the typical re-living and re-telling of the game, a humorous disassembling and reassembling process whereby although each man had been there, his opponent or team-mate had seen things differently.

The antics and mistakes of the characters of the teams were aired before the gathering through a process of hilarious debate. Then, if by the democratic weight of evidence no matter how passionate his own defence a man was found guilty of whatever foul or incompetent deed he had been accused of, his immediate punishment or reward was to skoal a shaken can of beer. The skoal an antipodean version of an ancient Scandinavian toast translating as 'may you prosper' had evolved to what was now an Australian sporting ritual with the modern intent of the victim's peers far removed from the original good wishes. In Nomads' lore, the battlecry involved an accompanying act of aggravation whereby the can is punctured, the victim encouraged to place his mouth over the hole, and then the tear-top pulled, the effect being the forceful flushing of the can's icy contents down the throat of the accused, like a flash-flood into a rabbit hole.

Aussie Bob, Bill, or Fred, as they were calling him, and the referee, Noel, (a local deli-owner in his non-sporting life) were being particularly harshly judged by their beer peers.

Bill found to his delight that he was being fined on a regular basis, accused in the main of being a "fuckin hero" and then a "fuckin bold opportunist" by the Bushies. The Bushwhackers had started it. Each time one of them rose from the lush grass to eloquently insult the general honesty and suspected parental integrity of Fred and then to punish him summarily with another can to skoal his own team felt compelled to protect his honour, and did so with gradually less eloquent replies. The trouble with the system was, Bill discovered, that he was then expected to celebrate the defence presented, by the skoal of yet another can to the insistent chant of his new mates with a, "down-down-down". By the time the group had exhausted the supply of beer, a state of affairs met with panic by the likes of Aussie Bob, Bill thought he had drunk about eight to ten cans.

As Maria again herded her messy, sweaty, and pissed flock toward the nearby Piccadilly Pub, where the Bushies had their clubrooms, Bill could certainly recognise the flush of alcohol into his previously dehydrated body. He thought he might slow down a bit, and was determined to enjoy the night in the company of this mad bunch. As the men crunched over the road, aluminium studs against gravel, he hugged Maria's petite form in a surge of affection and kissed the top of her head as they laughed together at the unexpected pleasure of the reunion.

The clubroom offered no respite from the alcoholic intake. With the 30 or so men standing naked in the steamy confines of the shower room, waiting in patient turn for one of the showers, Moon, the Nomads' manager, came across Aussie Bob's lost wallet. Fatefully, for reasons only of misplaced solidarity, since he hadn't played in the game, Aussie Bob was showering. Moon then used

160

Bob's credit card to purchase several cartons of beer for the boys, signing the credit slip with a scrawled notation that the Perth Fraud Squad subsequently deciphered to read "Dark side of the…" And as Moon delivered the beer into the steam, Aussie Bob called for "three cheers for Moon!" in unsuspecting glee at the sight of more beer.

With showers over, the teams gathered in the garden bar and, under the clear night sky, were fed a sumptuous BBQ prepared by the Bushies' support crew. These fine local women were assisted by Maria as the sole other-gender representative of the Nomads, a somewhat feral herd who had not been able to convince any other friends or acquaintances of the opposite sex to accompany 18 blokes on a pissy rugby bus trip from Perth to Kalgoorlie. Bill ensured that he ate heartily of the greasy sausages, the thick hunks of white bread, and the hearty but suspiciously chewy steak. He was determined to recover some control from the beer and then to carefully top up, come down, top up, and so on and so forth through the night, which he suspected was to be long and eventful. Then followed the compulsory speeches. Bill laughed quietly at the speech, which was the same one he had heard all his rugby life. In halls and clubrooms, captains chosen for their courage rather then their eloquence would stand awkwardly and in clichéd repetition talk of, "the game played in the right spirit…thank the ladies for the spread …thank the ref for his control although we didn't always agree with the interpretation… and am particularly proud of my boys…"

With the formal part of the evening over the Polynesian members of the Bushies, far from their Maori, Rarotonga and Samoan homelands, took to guitars in circled harmony. Bill sat beside Maria in the garden bar to reminisce over stories of Nobody's Child, Delta Dawn and Devilish Women as the meal settled and the mood mellowed. Then at midnight, as the party slowed, the Bushies fondly farewelled their wives, girlfriends, sisters and mothers with slurred promises to be home soon and safely. And from the fragmented flashbacks of his previous night's meandering, Aussie Bob suddenly recalled the tattoo show on at the Exchange Pub in the centre of town. With over-excited recollection, Bob told of bar-girls in little or no clothing erotically exhibiting the inked art on the canvas of succulent young bodies. Within minutes of his promise to the women-folk to wind down the night with just a few more quieties, the entire Bushies team followed the Nomads into the big blue bus for the short trip to the 'tat and tit' show at the Exchange. A raucous ten minutes later, the bearded Animal manoeuvred the gasping old bus into a spot close to the pub. The hydraulic door shushed open and disgorged the Nomads, the Bushies, and various hangers-on into the swinging saloon doors of the noisy, smoky bar. The Animal then backed the bus whiningly away from the intersection to a safer haven back from the pub. With Moon directing by frantic drunken shout and energetic but unseen hand signal, the old bus crawled backward alongside a line of gleaming Harley Davidson motorcycles parked up on the footpath. Beasts whose burdens, with uniform ZZ Top beards and outlaw leathered emblems, were already in the bar in a menacing feral grouping.

In these early hours of Sunday morning, the old mining town was alive. With the tattoo show as the drawcard, the corner bar of the century-old Exchange was packed and cooking. Unfortunately, however, the human ingredients, that diverse mix of the sociological types within the bar, was set to be explosive. The occupants of the old bus, high in spirits from the earlier athletic combat and high also in mood, entered as a phalanx, forcing by number and physical presence a hole within the mainly male mass and filling that vacuum with their own happy humanity. Bill, deliberately not as intoxicated as most of the others, instinctively and immediately picked up the territorial vibes from the bikies through the wrap-around reflective visors and he succeeded in steering the rugby gang toward the opposite wall of the wide bar. The smoky room was set around the central island of the horseshoe bar, where scantily clad young beauties served a generally glazed clientele and was overwhelmingly enveloped in raw noise as voice competed with the thump-thump from the over-sized sound system. Bill stayed close to Maria, subtly steering her beside him. He found a position with his back against the wall that allowed a view across the room as the group eased into the atmosphere of the new surroundings, with bulk purchases of beer from team funds to maintain the fluid intake. Although remaining aware of the potential threat from the pack in the dirty black leathers on the fringe, Bill slowly began to relax. His newfound friends almost imperceptibly began to merge first as a distinct physical grouping and then into the emotional or even spiritual mood of the bar.

And what a mood.

Bill and Maria tried to chat, her soft lips tickling his ear as she was forced to shout queries and responses, and, when he spoke, he cheekily trying to bite her soft lobes. Bill delighted at his friend's clear enjoyment of the night, holding hands with her man TJ on her left side and flirting outrageously with him on her right as she punished his mischief with her small but sharply booted kicks to his shins under the bar. At 1am the tattoo show fired up again on the small stage, with the bulk of the rugby boys joining the testosterone-fuelled throng milling closer. Although few of the boys would profess to a true appreciation or fascination of the art of the tattoo it was the appreciation and fascination of the canvas that held the lustful focus of the crowd. As the young lush female bodies were teasingly revealed by coy removal of bikini, or by hitching of g-string between swell of buttock, the groan of primitive male desire underscored the compère's description of the work.

It was amid this hormonal angst that Maria decided to visit the ladies room, on the far side of the bar. Bill watched her as she skirted the rear of the tattoo appreciation crowd and then the fringe of the bikie pack camped near the toilet doors. As the tattoo show finished and the sexually-charged, frustrated men stumbled back to their pre-show gatherings, Maria came back out of the ladies' and headed towards Bill. He saw his petite friend scooped up without invitation by a big, hairy, tattooed arm, and placed into the circle of men.

Bill sprung to immediate action. He pulled TJ close and said, "The bikies have just grabbed Maria, tell the bouncers then get the boys together."

"Right."

"Do it now, TJ," Bill tried to impress him through his slightly glazed concern. "I'll try to get her out without starting anything."

TJ nodded, focusing, and headed off toward the white-shirt security staff while on the way signalling an urgent "follow me" to Aussie Bob and several other of the Nomads. Bill quietly, and without telegraphing threat, approached the feral mass as if on his way to the toilets, but then as if by sudden drunken and smiling recognition spotted Maria, desperate inside the ugly circle, battling the groping touches of her assailants. Bill saw that her t-shirt had knife slits down it and had also been ripped. Now she fought off the circle of grasping hands from the soft flesh of her exposed breast, while her jeans belt was being ripped through the denim loops. Bill sly-crashed into the circle by shoulder with a slurred, "Babe, where have you been?" and encircled the intended prize of the mob. Before they were really aware of the loss Bill forced again through the messy circle. He propelled his frightened catch toward the advancing cavalry of the two security staff barking into collar-based walkie-talkie. Behind them were gathering the larger, more animated combined forces of the Nomads and the Bushies. The bikies, suddenly deprived of their sexual game, immediately welcomed the challenge of the fight. The spark of the initial combat ignited the tension-laden atmosphere as Bill ducked a heavy bar-stool thrown at his head. His peripheral vision told him that the two security men took that stool full on at chest height and they crashed back into the crowd as the bar exploded into violence. Bill ran from the fighting, protecting and propelling the distraught but furious Maria and forcing TJ also away until the three of them tipped out onto the pavement. "You guys get the bus, I'll get the boys," Bill commanded and all three heard the first distant wails of police sirens as Kalgoorlie's finest headed toward the trouble. With that, Bill ducked back inside behind a group of heavily muscled security men who had come from nearby pubs and nightclubs in answer to the call for assistance.

Bill then began a process of plucking the Nomads from the fray. He was able to separate the team from the maelstrom of the brawl one by one, as if sorting sheep, progressively flicking each familiar

164

figure outside to TJ. With Animal at the wheel gunning the old girl, TJ and Maria pushed each retrieval kicking and complaining onto the idling bus. Meanwhile, in the bar, the increasingly courageous general local bar population took advantage of the rare opportunity of numerical superiority combined with common intent over the bike gang to pummel them into the blood- and beer-soaked floorboards of the old hotel. With the police sirens getting closer, the few dazed and desperate outlaws still standing made a concerted rush to escape the trap of the bar and by force of numbers crashed out the swinging doors just as Bill and Maria were forcing Aussie Bob up the stairwell of the old blue bus. Bill shoved Maria up the stairs and barked at Animal, "Go, go, go!" just as the bikies got to the door. He met the surge with a rear swinging axe-kick that immediately dropped the lead man onto his arse with sickening crunch.

As the bus jerked away from the pub with the Nomads' faces pressed to the windows, the bikies, the Bushies and the locals who had gathered were then witness to Bill Peters tae kwon do black belt, seventh dan in a full contact, bone-crunching, soft tissue-tearing display of the discipline.

Watching as well was a silent technological witness the covert, closed-circuit video security system installed by the owner of the Exchange to provide evidence to the police of incidents. Later, Bill had to admit that he did enjoy the fight. Not tested since those dark days in New Zealand, but hardened physically with the last year's solo training, he enjoyed the opportunity to implement the full range of his skills in defence, but more particularly in rare outright offence, against the five bravely half-pissed bikies who clumsily engaged him in the warm air of that Kalgoorlie morning.

As he despatched the last bearded rebel to bloodied unconsciousness and to the cheers of the spectators, Bill started to consider running as the sirens were now audibly accompanied by tyre screeching some short blocks distant. And then he saw out of the corner of his eye, a big blue bus at full throttle leaning around the corner to head back up toward the fracas. As Bill watched to a chorus of anguished yells from several damaged but still conscious bikies, the big blue bus rose heavily up onto the sidewalk. With the Animal singing the Nomads' battle-song at the steering wheel as he chopped graunchingly through the gears, the huge rubber wheel clipped the first of the line of the Harley Davidson motorcycles down onto the pavement. In a slow-motion domino of destruction, the bus crunched over the 20 bikes, leaving only a mangled mess of metal, chrome, rubber and a spreading pool of petrol.

The bus squealed to a halt alongside Bill and with one arm Maria pulled him up inside. Belching diesel fumes, the bus farted away and Moon casually flicked a glowing cigarette butt out the window towards the wreckage. With a tired 'toot-toot' of farewell to the admiring applause of the locals, the bus rumbled away into the darkness with lights off. And as the bikies gathered in a distraught, cursing audience in front of the mess, Moon's glowing cigarette butt rolled gently along the pavement between black-denimed legs into the pool of petrol. And with a *boom*! and hot-blue flash of ignition, the bikes and the pub verandah went up in a whoosh of spectacular pyrotechnic destruction.

Chapter 22

Welcome to my World

Bill's arrival at Auckland International Airport in the humid early evening was low-key but watched intently from the sidelines by friend and foe alike. The late Tom's assistants, two elderly agents, Phil and Bo, met him in the arrivals hall with genuinely warm hugs and hearty handshakes. The Te Kuri's Joe Tama and heavily-muscled, leather-clad sidekick watched from the vantage point of the mezzanine floor above. The operational support agents in various guises and disguises in turn watched the Te Kuri. Male and female agents were sprinkled about the busy terminal dressed as customs officers, airport cleaners and backpackers. Kingi Potiki, although tempted to reassure his young charge by casual contact in the terminal, watched through the two-way mirror of the airport's police office. Kingi had first watched him enter the luggage collection area from one end of the long darkened office, and then saw him into the arrivals area from the other, as he anxiously followed Bill's progress into the reality of the operation.

As group followed group in a disjointed conga, Phil led the way to the scruffy brown Ford Transit van parked in the bustle of the public carpark. With bags swung into the dusty blackness of the rear cargo bay, squeaky doors were slammed shut. The three then loaded themselves into the van's front bench-seat and Bo eased the old girl into the shuffling line of vehicles as the newly landed impatiently sought to escape the airport grid-lock.

Under the watchful eye of agents, Tama and his man joined another heavy male figure in a dark Ford LTD waiting unchallenged in the pick up-put down bay. With passengers inside, the gang car slid forward to wait near the mouth of the carpark exit for the van. The van finally lurched out through the boom gates and into the heavy flow of traffic. Then down the busy multi-lane artery from the airport to the city and then through tiki-tack suburban housing sprawl and toward the operations base, a building known affectionately by the agents as "The Factory".

Kingi had carefully selected the warehouse for their operations base three years before. It was a tatty, old, corrugated iron-sheeted structure with the first-floor internal office converted in order to incorporate Tom's home. The building was set on a large commercial block off a dark cul-de-sac within a lush South Auckland paddock. Twenty years before, prime dairy cows had mooched and fattened on what had been some of the best farmland in the nation before progress claimed it for one of the city's ugly commercial satellite suburbs. The Factory was a short 10-minute drive east from the airport, half an hour from the city centre to the north and 20 minutes from the Te Kuri island fortress.

A near-feral, ever-angry pack of Dobermans roamed the Factory grounds behind a 12-foot high security fence. The fence was topped with six-strand razor wire and aggressively boasted electrification. The security, although serious and intimidating, was outwardly no different from that of surrounding premises, as honest merchants had responded over time to the local youths' nefarious incursions to damage and steal.

High above the traffic and just below the low cloud in the Auckland sky, the Pol-air 1 police chopper tracked the van, both visually through ghostly green glow of night vision and also from electronic signal emitted from a Sat-Nav device secreted into the vehicle. Bo weaved casually off the main thoroughfare with the gang car shadowing each move a hundred metres or so back. And, as briefed, the three agents in the van were immediately into character. The Te Kuri's surveillance abilities including audio capture capabilities were known. The technology owned by the gang was sophisticated. The conversation was exactly as would have been expected by the most suspicious observer, the most cynical or analytical of listeners: a saddened nephew seeking comfort from his uncle's two most trusted friends. Information was sought and provided about the funeral, the cremation, last words, last wishes. The discussion then casually turned to Bill's intentions for the factory, and the business left to him by his uncle. Bill, seeking time to sort things out, reassured both men that he would consult and advise them once he'd had a chance to assess the situation.

Bo steered the van into the cul-de-sac and as the steel gates whirred open, Bo whistled for the dogs, which came alongside in a yapping pack to escort the vehicle to the factory's steel roller-door. The door clanked open, again by remote electronic pulse, and they entered the factory, disappearing from public view. Joe Tama watched from the front seat of the gang car as, with lights off, it circled sinisterly around the cul-de-sac. Then, with a grunted command, he ordered his driver away as the roller door descended. The car prowled off back toward the Island fortress, tracked from above by the police chopper.

Bill stepped onto the cold concrete floor of the factory, as Bo began to click on the large fluorescent banks of lights. As the overhead illumination flickered more strongly, Bill was hit by an icy jolt of reality. The consequences of the decision he had made had arrived.

He was in. No honourable retreat was now possible.

Chapter 23

Run, Run, Runaway

"Holy shiiiiiiiiit!!" was the shout from the battle-bloodied Nomads
as the Animal gunned the old bus away down Hannan Street toward
the outskirts of town. With the bus lights off, the interior was back-
lit by the pyrotechnics behind them at the pub. Moon sat, beer in
hand, smiling innocently in quiet satisfaction in the flickering lights,
while Maria decided the group's immediate future. With a calm,
"turn right here" and "turn left there," she directed the Animal off
the main roads in a twisting escape until, after 15 minutes, they
rolled off the tarseal and crunched quietly up the soft gravel of the
mine road. At Maria's order, near the turn-off to the single men's
camp, the bus stopped and she sent Bill off to pack his gear and
meet them back at the heavy machinery workshop. Bill hurried to
the unit that had been his refrigerated haven for the last 12 months.
He was still buzzing with the mix of action and alcohol but coldly
aware that his cover was, in all probability, totally blown. He didn't
know that video footage had been obtained by the CCTV camera
above the pub door and had been fed back to the manager's office at
the Exchange. He had no way of knowing that, even as he bustled
around the unit packing and wiping surfaces clean of the evidence
of his existence, the animated publican sat with several of the local
constabulary and reviewed the action in living colour.

Despite themselves, the younger policeman enjoyed watching the events that had so bloodily damaged the members of their local outlaw annoyance. Meanwhile, outside the pub in heavy fire-proofed jackets, the men of the Kalgoorlie Volunteer Bush Fire Brigade hosed down the last steaming remnants of the carnage. The inferno had melded the Harleys into a long line of molten mess but, happily, the high jarrah balcony and the weathered granite walls of the old building had only suffered superficial scorching.

Back in the unit, Bill began to assess and analyse the probabilities. He accepted the possibility that his actions may result in his identification. He also knew that the significant and immediate result of the night's excitement was that each of the opposing local forces of good and evil being the police and the bikie gang (listed in order of merit) now had a very real interest in the bus-load of maniacs whose company he had shared. He quickly folded and packed his meagre belongings into the kit-bag provided those months before by Rangi of The House of Lash. He pulled the bed away from the wall and unscrewed the panel that hid his cash. Stripping away his tracksuit, he changed into blue jeans, the black RM Williams boots he treasured, and a warm polo shirt. Into the canvas money belt he carefully packed the crisp denominations he had saved through the year. Just over $30,000, mainly in $100 notes. Strapping the belt against his skin he put on the mine windbreaker and zipped it shut. With one last look and mental checklist run through from the doorway he pulled the door shut and trotted through the scraggly bush towards the workshop.

With the sudden startled rustles of snake or lizard, and strange thump of fleeing roo preceding him, he quickly adjusted to the darkness and picked his way through the familiar landscape in the light of the half moon. When he got to the workshop he could then appreciate Maria's cunning genius. She had the bus backed into the heavy machinery paint shop. The 18 tired and emotional Nomads were all busy around their bulky chariot, some with mechanical sanders whirring dustily on faded steel skin, others with hand-held sandpaper quickly and brutally scoring the chalky old paint surface. Meanwhile, others on mobile scaffolds or unsteady ladders used masking tape around lights, wheels and windows in messy protection.

Maria smiled her welcome to Bill, still appreciative of his protection of her in the pub, and slung his bag into the underbelly baggage compartment of the bus. With the old girl scraped, buffed and masked, Maria ordered the main bunch out of the way into the workshop's smoko donga for coffees and microwave-heated pies. Then, at Maria's direction, TJ and Bill manned the pneumatic spray guns on each side of the bus in the cavernous paint shed. With rainbow-paint encrusted coveralls and enclosed helmets in place, the two clumsy Van Goghs soon transformed the bus into a bright orange creation. In appearance, the bus now melded with the hundreds of mining vehicles that worked the pits diggers, excavators and haulpaks and also those that cruised the streets, such as utes, four-wheel drives and buses to transport the mine workers. With the orange painted sides still sticky wet, Maria then stencilled the company logo on in black while Bill shook his head in appreciation of his friend's lateral thinking.

And as the hours moved toward daylight from various depots, garages, mine sites and homes in and around the town, yawning employees and employers fired up hundreds of diesel engines. With forward gears engaged, the diverse convoy rolled out. Orange-coloured vehicles trundled towards various rendezvous. And a big orange bus pulled out of a mine road and coughed smokily towards the Kalgoorlie township. The bus, driven now by a newly shaven Animal, with beard and hair sacrificed to the cause, apparently carried only four or five safety-helmeted occupants sprinkled along its length. A closer inspection would have revealed a bumpy carpet of adult men and one woman lying on the floor in anxious concealment as the bus growled past the blackened Exchange Hotel. The bus attracted only a cursory inspection by gathered bikies and weary police and fire officers.

And so the Nomads escaped Kalgoorlie with Bill on board as their very best new-found friend. The bus trundled slowly the 600 kilometres westward out through the arid desert toward the wheatbelt and the region's big service town, Merredin. Much later, the road would rise up into the hills of the Darling Range, fringing the river valley of first the Avon and then the Swan Rivers and then twist down to the coastal surf-splashed plains of Perth. And on the long journey through the day as tension eased and the team slept, Bill and Maria sat together and talked.

It was at a fuel stop about halfway that Maria saw the news coverage of the previous night's events on the roadhouse's small snow-screened television. With sudden shock she saw the Kalgoorlie Police Inspector identify "the suspect" as "believed to be Bill Peters, the dangerous NSW fugitive". As he spoke, the coverage cut away to excerpts of the video footage of the battle with the bikies. The tae kwon do had given him away. The Police Inspector, with the shot of the still-smoking wreckage of the Harleys, smugly compared the frozen video footage with the photo of Bill from his New Zealand days the same photo that had graced the cover of the *Bulletin*.

And as he earnestly sought the cooperation of the public and warned of "the danger of approaching Peters," Maria nervously paid the oblivious attendant and, as casually as she could, wandered back to the bus with a carton of greasy replenishment for the hungry Nomads. When once again the sated mob fell off into sleep, Maria, in quiet conversation under the chugging drone of the bus, told Bill of his discovery, and confirmed his nervous expectation since the night before. They discussed the possibility of either the police or the bikies' Perth associates watching for a bus coming into the city from the main arterial route, the Great Eastern Highway. It was agreed that as soon as it was possible, the Animal would divert off the main road and track into the big city along lonely rural back roads, avoiding the larger towns such as Northam. With the bus zigzagging away from the direct approach to the city, Bill and Maria then talked of his options once within the bustle of the metropolis.

Maria offered Bill shelter, refuge, in her small flat or with her friends. But Bill declined, touched by her loyalty, determined not to affect her life, her glowing future, both professional and personal as an integral aspect of that future muttered and farted wetly in his sleep beside them.

No, he would make his own way somehow, hide in the city until escape somewhere, somehow, was possible. He would check in with Kingi when or if they got safely into the city. Contact the listening post for an update. Kingi may have pinpointed a location by now and then he would know where he had to be. When he knew that he could go there and do what he had to do. He had the money to sustain him for a long time. He just had to avoid the renewed police interest and efforts to track him until it died off again.

Maria relayed what she had heard and they analysed the country cop's media responses as best they could.

Yes, the police thought that Peters was probably hiding somewhere in the Goldfields area and may have worked may still be working locally.

Yes, it was possible that he may now run east, west, north or south.

Yes, the NSW Police still wanted him on the drug charges, but more so for the near fatal assault on the NSW police inspector.

And yes, Sydney Major Crime Detectives were on their way to Kalgoorlie.

Yes: the State's vast network of police districts, divisions and stations had been alerted, print, television and radio media advised, the public appealed to.

No, there was no actual proof of a connection to a local rugby game. Members of the Bushwhacker team had been shown the pub video and denied that Peters had either played the game or was with the teams at the pub. The police believed that their man had just happened to be in the pub at the same time. A coincidence. Peters had not been dressed in the team uniform, but enquires were being made to interview the team from Perth once it could be located. But that was mainly in regard to a brawl with a local bike gang for which the publican and numerous witnesses had blamed the bikies.

Police were looking for a blue bus.

It was early evening when an orange bus crawled down the hill from the bush suburbs of Perth, and the passengers were treated to the sprawling patchwork vista of the city's suburbs. Bill saw the city

174

skyline off to the west, with tall office buildings lit like welcoming beacons, as the bus joined the heavier stopstart traffic heading into the heart of the city.

Maria had told Bill of the suburb of Northbridge. This late-night restaurant and nightclub strip was where locals and tourists mixed in a bustle of fun and activity most days and nights. It was an area of inner-city apartments and backpacker hostels where the city's suburban young and not-so young congregated and mixed with the national and international equivalent generally in mutual tolerance and goodwill. At Maria's direction, Animal steered the bus into the nightspot along busy Aberdeen Street and Bill said his farewells. There was a quiet handshake with TJ who had recognised that there was a special bond between his girl and the man he knew as Fred. And a heartfelt hug with Maria, awkward on the bus seat. With tears in her eyes, and nearly in his, the strength of their hug was a confirmation of the affection and friendship forged by circumstance, tested by shared experience and, although brief, found to be true. While most of the Nomads still slept, Bill, with hearty shake from the Animal at the wheel, waved a last goodbye. With the old bus wheezing at a red light he rescued his kit-bag from the baggage hold. Then, Bill watched as the faces of Maria and TJ, looking back through the grimy window, diminished and disappeared as the bus swung wide into Lake Street and away.

Chapter 24

Wasted days and wasted nights

For five months nothing happened. Twenty weeks. One hundred and fiftyish days. Bill, and indeed the operations command and control, the intell section, even Kingi, started to think that they had been blown somehow the gang had got a sniff that all was not as it was supposed to be. It hadn't come from Bill. That much was clear as the gang stayed away. The only time Bill had personally been even near the gang was the day after he arrived at the Factory. At Tom's cremation.

After a sleepless first night, jet-lagged and trying to sleep in a dead man's bed, Bill had finally given up. He clicked on the TV in the bedroom and drifted fitfully into a semi-daze in the wakening hours to the low buzz of the infomercials. Earlier, Bo and Phil had said goodnight after showing him around, silently indicating the duress alarms covertly secreted about the place and particularly in the living quarters. Bill had already been briefed about the secure coms room. The tiny, hidden, cramped alcove, big enough for one man only, ran off the vehicle service pit set in the back of the warehouse. The pit itself was not obviously in use and was accessed through a maze of shelving that rose near to roof height and onto which the ill-gotten gains from the fence operation were stacked for cataloguing, packing and removal.

The warehouse paraded as a removalist business. This allowed superficial explanation for the movement in and out of covered trucks. In fact, Bo and Phil from time to time engaged in genuine, contracted removalist work, shifting transferred public servants around the region as part of the total cover.

The coms room was where a video recorded de-brief statement was done each time contact was made with the gang. The statement was recorded remotely from the operation's headquarters, at leased premises in the town centre. The room contained a totally secure, single-use, dedicated optic cable connection that allowed Bill not only the video connection but also direct voice access to Kingi. From this room over the two years of Tom's phase of the operation, thousands of hours of recorded evidence had been compiled for that time when arrests would be made, cases built, prosecutions proved and the deconstruction of the gang achieved. Now, with the passing of Tom, they had lost that vital human witness and effectively had to do it all again.

This was now Bill's job.

Bill knew that to enter the room he followed an unmarked path under the shelving. He then must climb down a rusted steel ladder set into the concrete pit wall. By exerting pressure at a given point against the innocuous, grease-stained wall, the false door swung open and allowed cramped entry.

The first morning Bill somewhat gratefully arose when Bo and Phil returned to the warehouse at 6am. Both were retired navy men, both divorced with grown families. No ties. The operation had set them up in a suburb where each had in fact grown up, and in which they were basically part of the furniture to neighbours, shopkeepers, and publicans or to any party that may choose to inquire. The jobs they had at the removalist warehouse drew no suspicion from the gang. They had been treated as Tom's labourers and added street-cred to the total appearance of the web of deceit spun by the operation.

In the early afternoon of that first day of operational reality, Bill was driven in Tom's sedan an ageing beige Holden Commodore to the Catholic Church of The Mother Saint Mary in Mangere. Only the three of them sat in the cool beauty of the church for the service. From the church, Bo followed the gleaming black hearse in stunted convoy to the crematorium. There, the funeral directors' assistants, with that practised exaggerated respect and fake solemn demeanour for a man they had never known, slid the pine coffin from the hearse onto the silver trolley and into the chapel. From there the body of a much-crashed crash-test dummy appropriated from the Department of Transport was then to be consigned to the conflagration. As the three men stood in sad repose in the small chapel, the Te Kuri representatives Joe Tama and his two men from the airport entered the chapel to pay their final respects. Respects for the passing of a man who they knew as a brother over the last two years. In actual fact, Tom's body had been solemnly buried in the presence of Kingi Potiki and an honour guard of some 50 police and army mourners the previous day in a quiet ceremony on the north shore of Auckland. He had been laid to final secret rest in the nation's Naval and Military Cemetery.

But now as the coffin silently slid from view through purple satin curtains, Bill was struck by the sudden incongruous beauty of Tama's melodious voice as, in the tongue and with the inherent harmony of his ancestors, he sang a farewell Waiata. With shivers from the chant, Bill turned to greet the three who, with cultural correctness, took the hand of the un-met relative of the departed, and touched noses with Bill and then with Bo and Phil as a mark of their respect for the deceased. No words passed. The three then turned and walked from the chapel. And then nothing happened for one hundred and fiftyish wasted days and wasted nights.

Chapter 25

In the Navy

Northbridge on a Sunday night. The place was packed, the pavements a flood of multi-coloured, multi-ethnic humanity flowing in either direction, shoulders brushing in mid current. The suburb's boast was that the commercial strip held more restaurants per square mile than anywhere else in the nation, and those eateries catered to palates from Albanian to Zulu and most points in between.

Bill, with kit-bag slung on shoulder, cut across the main tidal flow seeking quieter back streets. Following the mud-map directions provided by Maria, he walked away from the bright lights and toward a series of old-style hotels converted by local entrepreneurs into international backpacker hostels. These attractive buildings had been renovated to cater to the lucrative market of the industrialised world's youth. These young travellers sought safe adventure in safe nations before settling down in their own generally safe lives. It was Maria who had suggested that such a hostel with the disguising conglomerate of nationalities would be the best place for Bill to hide out for the short term.

As he made his way up Beaufort Street he noted the proliferation of the white naval uniforms and green marine cloth of the US Navy's finest amongst the civilian crowds. The hulking and bulky carrier, USS Enterprise, was in town, anchored square off the coast near the Fremantle port. Most of the smaller but still powerfully intimidating escort ships of the battle fleet the nuclear-powered and armed strike force of destroyers, cruisers and the fleet's supply vessels had parked within the harbour itself. Bill knew that Fremantle Harbour was only a short dash by road or by river to Perth. The small, busy harbour was the drain where the dark tannin-stained waters of the ancient Swan River eddied out on tidal flows to mingle with the salted blueness of the Indian Ocean. And from the steel grey platforms of war, the mix of men who crewed the awesome military tools of the world's last remaining superpower, weary from duties in the Middle East, flowed into the city's night-life seeking recharge and discharge.

The city and the people generally welcomed these visitors for their injection of cash and generosity of spirit. Local suppliers of food, alcohol and sweet female flesh girded their collective loins as the fleet disgorged a small town's population over 5000 fit, hungry, young and not quite so young men. In train, taxi, by bus or keenly on foot, the varying shapes, sizes, colours, and variations of accent of the American melting pot of ethnicity raced from the port in their pursuit of relief, emotional and physical, from the masculine military constraints of a ship-board existence.

Moving away from the busy streets of the restaurant heart, Bill found himself with a choice of several backpacker hostels. After some deliberation he chose the scruffiest one. The *Do-Drop-Inn International Backpackers* offered rooms at $20 a night or shared accommodation at reduced rates depending on access to amenities. Bill booked in at the dingy and darkened lobby adjacent to the broad jarrah hardwood stairway that led upward in a regal curve that hinted of past glory. He paid the disinterested and somewhat chemically distracted male clerk seated behind a mesh cage for ten nights in a single occupancy room with en-suite toilet and shower. Bill insisted quietly that the room be on the ground floor and near to the rear access. The unshaven, pony-tailed clerk found nothing unusual in that request due to recent multi-fatality fires in backpacker hostels that had attracted significant interest from the media. With the key received and a hand-scrawled receipt for $200 there was no request for identification, just a bored acceptance that he was indeed Fred Smith from London, a fact that was duly recorded into the guest register against his room number.

Bill hoisted the kit-bag back onto his shoulder and wearily creaked along the threadbare carpet of the dark corridor to the room. He entered the musty box and locked the heavy, paint-coated door behind him. Thankful for the shelter and at least the perception of security within the four walls, he set the kit-bag on the wood-grain formica surface of the table and stripped off his clothes. He stood on the cracked, mouldy tiles of the shower cubicle and luxuriated under the weak warm pulse of the water. He then dried himself with a clean t-shirt, pulled back a somewhat patched and suspiciously stained off-white sheet and collapsed onto the sagging mattress of the rickety single bed.

Within minutes he was asleep.

And that next week he lay low. Apart from one late night when he dared a nervous walk to a nearby 24-hour market and stocked up with consumables, Bill stayed put in the room. Religiously, on the hour, he scanned the radio waves from newscast to newscast to get a handle on the degree of interest in the Kalgoorlie story. But within three days it had disappeared as a news item. He didn't risk the common TV room at the hostel, unwilling to needlessly expose himself to the scrutiny of those he could hear through the walls, living, laughing, and occasionally loving, in the holiday atmosphere.

By the early hours of the next Saturday morning he was stir crazy. Physically and mentally he needed to get out from the four-by-four room. All day he had alternated between push-ups, sit-ups and shadow boxing. He worked through the pattern of the tae kwon do offensive and defensive tables until, in the summer heat of the room, despite the best efforts of the old air-conditioner and the weak squirt of the tiny shower, he was stale and sweaty.

There was the irresistible, driving need to check in with Kingi, to make that call from a public phone box in some dark street. Bill convinced himself that with all due care he should be able to mix anonymously into the mass of people moving through the area. He needed to replenish food and drink but, more urgently, to fill the desperate need for information and stimulation by getting his hands on as many local and national newspapers as he could source. He dressed in black jeans, runners and a dark blue, long-sleeved shirt and tucked a black wool beanie into the pocket of his jeans. With money-belt strapped securely against his belly, Bill slipped from his room, locking the door.

He went casually out of the rear exit, under a weak exposed bulb into a small guest parking area at the rear of the old double-storeyed hostel. In the carpark he noted the fleet of tourist-owned VW vans and the surfers' classic old Holden stationwagons resting and rusting. Down the broad concrete steps he slunk away around the side of the hostel into a dark alleyway. After a quick rubber-neck out of the alley both ways, Bill strode into the flow of nightlife away from the hostel and down toward the buzzing hub.

Yanks still in town, he confirmed to himself as groups of US navy personnel, dressed in the various civilian youth pop-culture or athletic trend brands, wandered the streets. They were now only a day away from sailing again from the shores of this friendly nation back toward the uncertain tension of unfriendly waters. This late at night, after hours or, in some cases, days of seriously seeking the distractions this town had on offer, some of these stragglers radiated a more desperate vibe. Most of the shipmates, sated from a week on shore, had returned to the ship, money spent, urges catered to. But these guys were still prowling.

Bill felt, as he had supposed he would, invisible amongst the crowds. The atmosphere was relaxed and happy as people either headed home after a pleasant evening full of good cheer and great food, or moved on to favourite nightclub, still generally in command of intent and inhibition. Bill found all he needed in the 24/7 market in Lake Street. Shift workers were stocking up, ladies of the night replenishing smokes, KY jelly, chewing gum and condoms. Bill bought one of each available newspaper and current affairs magazine, and a couple of cheap crime novels for some light relief. Then he moved into the food area and hungrily selected fresh produce from dew-glistening trays.

Crisp green Granny Smith and red Fuji apples from the state's orchards in the south-west at Donnybrook; sweet, wrinkled-skinned mandarins and grapes from the lush vines of the Swan Valley; Lady Finger bananas from the tropical coastal town of Carnarvon in the north. He selected thick-crusted, flour-dusted rolls of Italian olive bread and fat, white, soft cheeses. He chose a small pot of salted butter from the Margaret River region in the south-west, red Roma tomatoes, a cucumber and purple-fleshed sweet salad onion from the market gardens that had been established by the sons and daughters of Italian, Chinese, and later, Vietnamese, immigrants. With supplies replenished and beginning to feel refreshed again in spirit, Bill headed back toward the hostel. Just one last week of exile, he assured himself, during which time he could plot a course of action and a way of escape to a safer, more pleasant, hideaway.

Then he saw a phone box. It was set dark against the edge of a small park, interior lights previously conveniently smashed by some drunken vandal. Bill had changed a twenty at the store for ten shiny two-dollar coins and quickly fed the telephone slot with all of them. He tapped out the international codes and Ruby's phone number and again, through the genius of unknown telecommunication heroes the electronic buzz buzz was answered in the gently rounded vowels of the old woman.

"Kiaora."

"Kiaora, Aunty, this is Bill."

"How are you, son?" she enquired, always genuinely interested.

"Fine thank you, Aunty, and you?"

"Can't complain son, can't complain."

"Any message, Aunty?"

"Yes dear, hold on." The old lady softly clunked the handpiece down and Bill could hear her searching. "There, son?"

"Yes Aunty, I'm here."

"OK, he says: information points to top-end, a trawler, name not known, maybe Darwin. Check back in four weeks. Give Ruby day and time and call then. Stay put until then. Take care son. … That's all Bill."

Then Bill passed his news, illogically compelled by his circumstance to use a clumsy code. "Aunty, tell him gone from the red dust. Now where the black swans swim. Will call four weeks Tuesday midnight."

"I have got that, my dear," Ruby softly confirmed.

"Thank you so much, Aunty."

"It is my pleasure boy." And they said goodbye.

Kingi was getting closer to finding him. He could feel it through the words. And Kingi must want to talk to him in person that would be why he wanted a day and a time for his next call. Yes! Great, there was movement at the station, Bill thought as he collected three of his coins from the retrieval slot.

These were his thoughts as he again left the pulse of the busy streets and tramped soft-soled along Beaufort Street toward the dingy haven of the Do-Drop-Inn and his musty sanctuary. As he stepped off the roadway and down into the darkness of the alley alongside the hostel his mind ranged over the possibilities of escape. A ship out of Fremantle port? A coastal trader or maybe a foreign flagged vessel? Or, with his cash reserves he could buy a car and head up north along the coast or inland, via mining towns in the Pilbara. Then he could disappear into the Kimberley region his old mate Jack had told him tales of. All he really had to do was keep low for another few weeks, keep to himself and out of trouble. Meanwhile, hopefully the interest of the local law enforcement, media and the public again would completely wane and die.

And then he stumbled into trouble.

The muffled shrill desperation of trapped prey. Human, female prey.

Halfway down the pitch-blackness of the alley with the dim-lit carpark 20 metres further on he found them. Two young women, clearly tourists, and no doubt backpackers they had that look. One was blonde, long flaxen hair tied back, the other one brunette, with short spiky hair. They were both pretty, foreign and in their twenties. The blonde wore faded blue denim cut-off shorts with frayed fringes, had shapely, tanned, muscular legs and had topped the look with a little midriff boob-tube. The brunette was in three-quarter

length dark pants and a white singlet. Both wore the trademark
Euro tourists' tramping boots and the compulsory bum-pack around
each shapely waist. Both were in big trouble. Two very big men,
one black, one white, hugged each fair maiden from behind as if to
drag them further into the darkness of the hostel where the stinking
garbage bins hulked.

"Fuck!"

"You right, guys?" he thought it was a nice icebreaker under the
circumstances.

"Fuck off!" came the response in American-accented unison,
and, "Help, pleeze" in what he guessed may be Swiss, German or
perhaps Dutch-accented feminine pleading. It was obvious that the
two steroidal muscular monsters were mighty pissed off that Bill had
interrupted their game of finders-keepers.

But what to do? Can't get involved, he told himself. But Bill
couldn't walk away, and he slowly shifted the food-filled kit-bag off
his shoulder.

"Hey, just fuck off buddy!" said alpha male one, white, 28 years,
six foot tall, 110kg, crew-cut so short the square head appeared to
be modelled on the flight deck of the huge carrier he had no doubt
disembarked from earlier.

"On you way, ass-hole," barked alpha male two, black native
of New York's hard-knocks school of life, six foot two, 120kg, 25
years. His thick Bronx accent was slurred from the alcohol they
had drunk. The drinking had also modified the men's personalities,
mixing potently with the steroids both men probably regularly
injected into their bulging glutes in their macho pursuit of size and
power.

"Well, you see guys, that's the problem. I can't. The girls are
with me, you see." Bill was calm, quiet, friendly.

"Fuck you, man." The big white arm squashed down across petite
breasts. As he staggered backwards, the brunette appeared terrified
both of her predicament and the possibility this stranger might take
the brutal advice and leave.

"No, come on fellas, fair suck of the sav, the girls are with me."

Quick look-up and down the alley with peripheral vision for some distraction, some help.

Nothing moved at either end. The quiet alley was perfect for the yanks' ambush of the girls. In the black they had awaited the girls' soft footsteps and happy lilting conversation as the two went to pass the dark maw of the alley. Then, two big bodies trained in combat, striking quick out and back dragged the two off the road and down into the blackness, determined to take what the local female population had politely declined their drunken clumsy requests for through a frustrating week on shore. Bill slipped his kit onto the garbage-littered tarseal of the driveway.

"Hold this," said white alpha, passing his catch to black alpha. With consummate ease black alpha held both wriggling girls against his bulk in a groping bear hug. Bill readied, turning side-on to white alpha as he also took a stance, crouching at the hip, huge paws of hands now outstretched. Bill considered his choices.

"Hey, man, I'm a lover, not a fighter," he joked and turned as if to finally accept the inevitable and walk away. Then white alpha took a step into the zone. And Bill acted with a surprise attack that all self-defence disciplines encourage when out-sized, out-muscled, and out-numbered.

All he did was flick back-handed.

Fingers splayed across white alpha's eyes. The big man grunted in surprise and searing pain, involuntarily lifting both hands to his eyes. And Bill, with toes stressed downward in his flexible runners, kicked full-legged, connecting the weapon of his foot to the flaccid weapon of intent the big man's genitals with disabling splat and that most primal agony.

"Fuuuuck!" a whoosh of beer-stench breath came at Bill as white alpha sank despairingly backward, furiously angry at proceedings and the promise of murder in his pig eyes. Black alpha pushed away the girls in the realisation that this threat had to be dealt with seriously and set himself to avenge his friend's suffering.

"Fuck you, man, you fuckin dead," he promised, as Bill waved the two girls away toward the carpark. The two ran together but stopped three metres away, screaming out into the night for help.

186

Both girls turned back, unwilling, despite their raw fear, to abandon their unknown knight.

"Run, run!" they screamed to Bill.

"You run," he implored, but they didn't. Instead, with their own indignation building, both bent and picked up broken bricks and empty soft drink cans that lay amongst the debris and threw them hard but misguidedly at the alphas. And with the distraction of the girls Bill made a mistake.

He underestimated the agility, the speed and determination of black alpha, collecting the swift charge of the gridiron line backer as a huge bone-hard cranium smashed into his belly and the two went down. Bill under, the big man drove with the muscle of his massive thigh and turned his shoulder into Bill to lift and power down, to hurt and disable. In this proximity and with a bigger, stronger foe, the tae kwon do was ineffective. Writhing in back-scraping desperation on the rough alleyway, Bill realised he was in trouble. In fact, he was in deep, deep shit as the black alpha freed one huge fist from the tangle of limbs and began to smash the lighter man again and again. Bill blocked most of the blows, taking the bone-knuckling force on his forearms and elbows, but also in his ribs, the side of his head and his face. And then the black alpha manoeuvred himself upright to sit across Bill's chest in the classic schoolyard-bully move enabling him to pummel his pinned victim to a messy pulp.

Meanwhile, through all the excitement of being bashed by one of America's baddest, Bill saw looming behind the hulking limping figure of the slightly recovered white alpha, with what appeared to be a very satisfied and expectant smile.

There is no doubt about it, Bill thought remarkably clearly to himself. If I don't get this big bastard off me quickly, I'm dead. Dead.

And then, with poetic justice, his opportunity arose.

From his right side, white alpha lined up a very big kick indeed which was intended, Bill decided, to remove his head from his body. As the heavy combat boot arrived, Bill, with almost all remaining energy, timed a sudden violently executed shift using bent legs to prop and back to curve his chest, and then his face, under the sweaty yeasty arch of the crotch of black alpha. The result was that white alpha kicked black alpha right off the prize. Free Bill flipped back onto his feet and he used that momentum to flow into a twisting reverse kick. With the pendulum force concentrated from his rotation, the side of his foot crushed white alpha's Adam's apple in collision of rubber sole to throat. This blow caused sudden and immediate breathing difficulties for the big man. But as white alpha fell back again to the tarseal with panic in dulling eyes, black alpha pride really the only hurt from his friend's kick had rolled up onto his feet and with a primal roar of outrage was heading back in an attempt to duplicate his earlier attack. But this time he met an enemy ready and waiting.

As the big body speared towards him, head down, Bill spun from his path and worked his way along the passing carcass with kick, elbow, and hand strike in a flurry of retribution.

With his heavy momentum failing to meet the human resistance that he had intended, black alpha continued on his path, head still bent in the charge. And with a final spurt of acceleration thanks to a kick between his massive bent buttocks, black alpha's lowered head then met the solid limestone block of the alley wall with a sickly crunch and the lights of consciousness went out.

And just then the cavalry arrived, late as usual. In fact two police officers of the mounted police section respectively atop a fine grey and an equally impressive tan example of equine being, clip-clopped past the alley entrance on their grid patrol of the suburb. The officers wore helmets with inset torch and, as they trotted along the darker streets of their patrol, that light illuminated along the sweep of head as the officers checked down driveways and darkened alleys. It was that weak light that threw up the scene in the alley beside the Do-Drop-Inn. What the constabulary thought they saw down the alley was two large US serviceman laying prone as several smaller darkness-disguised persons kicked the shit out of them in brutal attack. What in fact they saw were two young respectable female Swiss tourists, recently saved from certain defilement, kicking two very dazed US servicemen in brutal reprisal as Bill ran around in circles trying to shoo the girls away. Fortunately for Bill and his two new friends, a big horse needs a big turning circle. Alerted by the shouts of the officers to desist and the sight of the big animals twisting around to get the sharp end moving into the alley, Bill quickly moved the girls away. Scooping up his bag and pulling the blonde by the arm, the brunette instinctively followed and the three ran out and out of sight across the dimly lit carpark.

Quick decisions needed to be made.

He didn't want to abandon the girls, but may have to, he thought. Into the hostel? No a trap, surely. The carpark was bordered on three sides by the walls of surrounding buildings. The only escape was back up the alley where the police horses had now stopped by the prone Americans. Bill could hear the barked request for "back up and ambulance to the Do-Drop-Inn." Shit, he thought, might have to go through the hostel and back out onto the road. But already they heard sirens as nearby mobile patrols reacted to the plea from the mounted officers. A cordon of the thin blue line, coordinated from the communications room at police headquarters, had already begun to take rough circular form and was closing in like a lasso on the central hub of the Do-Drop-Inn. Then the blonde took the initiative. "You come!" she commanded, and she led Bill and the brunette into the mix of vehicles in the carpark. They ran diagonally away from the alley towards the back wall and there in the dim light she unlocked and opened the sliding side door of a very yellow 1982 VW Kombi van. Bill had no intention of trapping himself in the van but then a big grey horse burst out of the alley mouth clattering steel-shod hooves on brick paving and suddenly there was no choice. Against all instinct, Bill and the two girls scrambled inside in an awkward jumble of limbs onto the softness of mattress in the curtained rear of the van. They could hear the mounted officer barking rapid observations and suggestions into his radio and it was obvious that he had not seen them. The blonde gently slid the door shut on oiled runner and locked it. Silently, the three politely shifted bodies apart to rest against the van sides. As eyes slowly adapted to the dark interior, each tried to calm rapid breath and thumping heart as they settled down to await their immediate destiny.

Chapter 26

Treat me nice

Bill mulled on it. In all honesty, the time that had passed since Tom's death was not totally wasted. He used the time to be educated and trained by Bo and Phil in the practical workings of a stolen property fencing operation. For the last two years the Te Kuri had used Tom exclusively to dispose of the proceeds of burglaries, armed robberies and freight hijacking operations. The gang, in practical effect, acted as a business. It sub-contracted the criminal juveniles from the coal-face the suburbs. The senior gang members selected and trained, and disciplined and rewarded local groups of misguided youths who otherwise would have been doing break-and-enters anyway. The strict rule was that those young recruits were not immediately connected to the Te Kuri except by controlled and distant association. Joe Tama was the manager of the hot goods operation. He dealt at a local suburban level with men and woman who acted as foremen, or leading hands, and who set up the groups. Where necessary, they provided heavy-muscled protection and retribution to any opposing criminal interest foolish enough to interfere.

The kids themselves were rewarded for their efforts with shelter, food, and guidance by the expendable but well-paid Fagins. These gang members lived with or near the juveniles supplying shelter, money and drugs, and then ran them as an effective burglary business. The child teams didn't even really know about the line of command. They could never connect the authorities to the Te Kuri. Despite the occasional Fagin being caught and prosecuted over the years, the system had worked to the huge financial benefit of the gang. Over time, the gang had perfected the systems, selecting kids under the age of 14 and training them in the methods of break-and-enter and providing shopping lists of desired property.

If apprehended by the police the young thieves were guided into the juvenile justice system and if they became too well known to authorities they were simply discarded by the gang's system. Star recruits and solid performers were eventually transferred to higher duties, moving into the full daily life of the organisation including living on the island. The system bred loyalty and dependence.

The Te Kuri had based its initial growth and financial strength on the funds raised from the burglary teams. With that money, the knowledge, equipment and raw materials of the infrastructure of the evil network had been established so that now the manufacture and distribution of drugs by the gang was its primary income source. The steady flow of dollars from the burglary teams, however, was still required by the Whetu brothers. But with the death of Tom and the arrival of the unknown nephew the gang was prepared to sit back, watch, and wait.

When Kingi Potiki had targeted this aspect of the gang's operation as a potential Achilles' heel, and after the TKs had accepted Tom as the point of sale for the stolen goods, the police operation itself had developed systems for handling the massive quantity of stolen goods. It was recognised as vital that the conduct of the police operation could not be attacked in the future judicial proceedings in regard to either encouraging or entrapping the gang.

The mechanics of simply handling the goods had been carefully devised. From receipt at the factory, to the details of payment, labelling, photographing, videotaping and subsequent disposal there were formal procedures for each step in the process. Obviously a variety of parties retained an interest in the property. Those interests included the owners from whom the goods had been stolen, insurers of those goods, and the aspect that the police, or more properly the government through that agency, having paid for the goods, also had significant legal interests in the property.

The general rule of thumb was that a criminal receiver or 'fence' paid a thief about 10 to 20 percent of the item's resale value. Tom, via the police operation, had paid the Te Kuri a negotiated 30 percent of agreed value to reward exclusivity on behalf of both the parties. In truth though, in the early days of the operation, determined and targeted policing had systematically eliminated competing avenues of stolen good disposal.

During Tom's time with the operation, the government had paid out from a secret budgetary allowance over two million dollars to provide the cash to buy the goods from the gang. This money had been paid in the operational expectation, and with the acceptance by the government, of a philosophy. The philosophy was that to pay good money to halt forever the criminal activity of the gang that had cost society a multiple more, was worth it. The hope was that the dubious means would justify the conclusive end.

So, after the evidence of the receipt of the property had been properly collated to the highest evidential standard, the operation quietly returned items, where possible, to those whose homes had been burgled. Bill learnt this and also learnt the valuation system. From the evidential ledgers maintained over the operation, he spent long days and nights studying the massive sequence of dealings with the gang, the details of each purchase. Over time the gang had recognised that jewellery was the easiest and most portable of loot and Bill familiarised himself with grades and weights of gold and quality of precious stones. He also had Bo and Phil test him until he felt confident that, if given the opportunity, he could accurately quote on a Sony DVD player or a Panasonic wide-screen digital TV as well as a gold box-link bracelet or diamond ring.

Time passed and Bill began to consider that it might not happen. He started to think about what he might do if it all folded. If it did, he would be free. He thought about how happy his dad would be, how he would visit his mother again in the States. But then it happened. He heard them coming, in the early hours of a cold wet South Auckland Sunday morning. Rain slashed down outside against the corrugations of the thin iron sides of the building. He heard the gate forced open in the quiet morning, a screech of metal. The dogs barking. Going crazy. Then yelps of pain and terror as the pack avoided whatever deterrent the gang had cruelly presented. He heard the unmistakeable growl of a V8 engine as a heavy sedan crunched up the driveway. Bill lay quiet in the bed and waited. A solid thump signalled the door below splintering with heavy kicks against the lock. Muffled steps approached, up the steel mezzanine stairwell. And Bill rose from the blankets arranging a deliberate startled countenance as first a strong torch beam found him, and then the bedroom light flickered on. Four heavy-set, black-clothed male figures, each sinister in a black balaclava, pushed into his room.

"Dress!" came the wool-muffled command, and he quickly clambered out, pulled on jeans, t- shirt and runners.

"Turn!"

Bill turned away. Wide grey gaffer-tape stickily unwound behind him. They pinned together his wrists in front of him, and taped over his quickly closed eyes. Then, with a big man either side, he was moved awkwardly out and down the stairs, and into the cold night air. With a guiding hand, not unkind on his head, he bent into the rear seat and was pushed across to the middle as his abductors sat either side. Yes! he silently rejoiced, clenching fists in triumphant relief. Finally it had begun.

Chapter 27

Dancing Queens

It was their victims who saved them.

As the two big marines lay groaning in the filth of the alley, police vehicles and personnel moved into the cordon that centred on the Do-Drop-Inn. The eerie aural pulsations of the ambulance heralded its arrival by degrees until it growled up the alley to join the two dismounted officers in the headlamp-lit alleyway. The horses, saddles empty and shifting heavily, let out snorts of sweet breath. The dying rotations of the ambulance's red hazard lights flashed around the car park and all the chinks between curtain and window-frame of the kombi van.

The soft redness played across the Bill's anxious features. In the tension, the two girls still had not spoken. And Bill's body was tightening and bruising where black alpha had damaged by force of fist. Senior officers joined the two horsemen in the alley and quick situation reports were taken. Meanwhile the ambulance staff tended to the two fallen heroes. And as they came to, black alpha groggily first and then white alpha, they described a gang of male assailants. Painfully, in hoarse whispers, they spoke of an unprovoked attack, bravely defended. With false description electronically broadcast by across the various airways, a search began radiating out from the Do-Drop-Inn.

"Search for five to seven adult male Caucasians dressed in dark clothing and bearing weapons believed to be baseball bats over."

The ambulance was soon away with both men to be treated initially at the city's large teaching hospital, the Royal Perth. It was later the next day that, with the sympathy of the city's media and gifts from its people flowing to them, the two were returned to the battle group by Sea King chopper. With sleek-hulled destroyers splitting the waters they steamed to join the massive carrier in escort. In the shipping lanes off the port, the big ship hauled huge chain anchors from the sandy bottom and set course off to the north-west and away into the Indian Ocean.

But before that, in the dingy car park of the Do-Drop-Inn, the officer-in-charge of the scene coordinated his investigative team, tasking his officers to the variety of roles based on their experience and capabilities. As the various pieces of the investigative jigsaw fell into place, the grizzled sergeant tasked the local beat patrol to a careful patrol of the carpark and vehicles within. With quiet authority he instructed careful examination and recording of the details of each vehicle including torchlight attempts to look inside and underneath each.

The kombi was about the last vehicle to be examined. As the two young and inexperienced constables impatiently completed cursory torchlight sweep under and into the interior of the kombi with eye to window, Bill and his two newest friends huddled together under the complete camouflage of a soft doona.

Keen to join the chase for the violent gang who had cruelly assailed the two men, the beat cops trotted away from the kombi to report completion of task and current availability to the veteran sergeant. And then, senior officers moved on to other pockets of excitement as testosterone and alcohol flared up the busy nightspot and the night slowly lightened into day. Forensic officers took final photos and scene searches were recorded; final door knocks were completed. The bleary-eyed and startled occupants of the hostel answered the heavy knocks of inquiry officers in those early hours to provide their personal details and any knowledge of the events, or of the heavy-scented smoke lingering in the rooms.

In the van, in the coolness of the morning, the three desperados relaxed and spoke in quiet whisper.

The two girls confirmed they were Swiss.

"Ah yes, I know that country ABBA, Dancing Queens, etcetera," Bill teased.

"No, no. Not Sveedish, vee are Sviss," the two countered with annoyed looks, unimpressed by Bill's deliberately erroneous cultural references. Inga, the flaxen-haired blonde, was 25, a medical graduate, having just completed her degree at Zurich University. She was travelling with her childhood friend the brunette Hana, same age, a banking and business graduate with dark Italian good looks. The Roman influence inherited from some long-past randy male relative who had skipped across the border from northern Italy, seeking the Nordic feminine delights of southern Switzerland, just a short journey over the alpine range. Hana was, she explained to Bill in attractively cute halting English, soon to start a job with her nation's premier financial institution, the Zur-Bank. Soon she would be dealing with the secret movement of funds from good and not-so-good international citizens who for one reason or another chose the anonymity of the tiny nation's unique banking structures. Both girls were on a post-study, pre-career, pre-marriage, pre-kids, big overseas adventure that had started in Sydney where they had bought the kombi from a French tourist for $2000. They had now been in Australia for a month. They had headed out of Sydney virtually straight away and had puttered trouble-free along the continent's bottom through Melbourne, "lovely city, ya," Adelaide, "ya, very pretty," and then along the long, lonely, fascinating stretches of the Nullarbor Plain. A gorgeous couple of 'ya-yas' in all, Bill thought to himself.

While they chatted in the darkness, Bill pulled his kit-bag to him and from it offered the girls the orange and apple juices. They all drank thirstily. He was enjoying the getting-to-know-you session and asked, "How long are you intending to stay in Perth?" Inga explained that they had allowed two more months to travel the 2500km haul up the west coast to the tropical warmth of Broome. The girls laughed at the idea of that trip, 2500km! In Switzerland, a trip from the southern Italian border to the northern German border was only 150km.

Hana continued, "Ven vee have enough of Broome then vee go on to Darvin. After Darvin zen Queensland before back to Sydney in March. Then Svissair and back home."

Bill carefully peeked out the kombi window and saw that the sun was rising to the east. It was quiet outside and it appeared that the Police had finally left. The three talked more freely, relaxing in each other's company as they stretched out, careful not to touch, and reclined in the still-dark interior. Soon the air-vent on the roof began a lazy squeaking rotation as an early breeze swirled around the buildings, bringing the scent of the Swan River, which lazily eddied past the cityscape.

The girls then told him that it had been their plan to leave this morning anyway on the next leg of their journey, north to Broome and the tropical sunshine. As the interior lightened with the day the girls gasped in consternation seeing the dark shadows of deep bruising across Bill's face and body from the fight. Doctor-in-waiting, Inga, keenly began to fuss over the cuts and bruises, finding the kombi's first-aid kit stacked neatly in the impeccably-ordered interior of the van. The neatness seemed to be in accordance both with the girls' nationality and their gender. Inga ordered Bill to take off his shirt and money belt and lie flat while the girls eased to either side of him kneeling on the soft mattress base. At their joint instruction he rolled first onto his belly and then on his back while both cleaned and bandaged the cuts and grazes, painting him a patchwork brown with copious daubings of iodine. Despite the mild discomfort of the wound cleaning he delighted in the gentle touches and ministrations.

The girls asked Bill about himself.

Who was he? Where was he from? And he told them. Lied, of course.

Also a tourist, from the east of the country. "The name is Bill," he said. "I'm looking for work but intending to travel, maybe south to the fruit-growing areas to pick apples, maybe north to the mines."

As he laid on his back, arms raised above his head with a final check for tears and bruising, the three discussed the events that had thrown them together and Doctor Inga worried about the white alpha. She had seen him go down from the throat strike and felt that with the fragility of that structure and the force of Bill's kick that the yank was "maybe not so good." The girls packed away the first-aid kit and engaged together in gentle staccato conversation in their native tongue while Bill sat and gingerly shrugged back on the blood- and dirt-soiled shirt over the sweat-darkened money belt. As the girls finalised their discussion, Hana quietly conveyed the joint agreement to Bill.

"Beel, you vant to come to Broome?"

Immediately he saw the sense of it, away from trouble. North in the disguise of the company of the two pretty girls, tourists. North to where, from what Great Aunt Ruby had told him, it appeared that Kingi's search was narrowing.

Also, he knew from the overheard conversations and reporting of the Police earlier that there was no mention of and no search for the two girls. If the marines were seriously hurt, if that throat strike had crushed or fractured rather than bruised, then the hunt would really be on. He knew that if either man spoke of the assailant's martial arts skills then an astute investigator may make the link to the events in Kalgoorlie, and then the link back to Sydney, and to New Zealand and straight to one Bill Peters. Yes, they would know. Bill Peters, the fugitive, was now in Perth. The tae kwon do would be the identifying tag.

Anyway what other choice readily presented itself? Sweet f-all, Bill thought. So he agreed. He was grateful. "Ok. Yes, please. That would be very good."

And the girls nodded in unison. So it was decided.

"Ok," Inga determined, "now vat vee do?"

Bill didn't really have much in his hostel room, only his clothes. But if he left the gear there, surely a thorough police investigation would wonder at the guest who hadn't returned? So Inga and Hana, surprised to find that he too was a guest at the salubrious Do-Drop-Inn, took his key and quietly slipped out the side door. Bill locked it from the inside and rearranged the curtain but peeked through a sliver to watch the girls. They looked around anxiously and then zigzagged through the rows of cars before going up the old concrete steps into the hostel. Inside, they made their apparently casual way first to their own room. They met with other guests in the dusty corridors, animated and chattering gatherings in variously accented English. The polite and petite Japanese, boisterous and cheeky kids from the UK, the occasional twang of a Canadian and their brasher southern neighbours from the US. The girls joined in the flow of conversation about the events that had disrupted the hostel in the early hours, and learnt that the police were after a savage gang of violent anti-American, anti-war, local males.

The girls relaxed a little and went then to their room and packed their sparse possessions into brightly coloured backpacks. They then made their way together down the stairs, signing out with the same tired clerk Bill had met on his arrival. Then, with cheery farewells to the other travellers, they made their determinedly casual way towards Bill's room, the nearest to the hostel's rear exit.

With no-one in sight, Inga turned the key in lock and both girls were quickly into the stale room that reeked of man. Hana, button nose wrinkling, bravely gathered the small quantity of assorted drying undies, found the t-shirts, shorts and remembered, at Bill's insistence, the dusty RM Williams boots, rolling them all into a ball. Inga also under instruction, courageously stripped a stale bed sheet and wiped each of the surfaces clear of fingerprints and any DNA that Bill may have sweated, smeared or leaked during his short stay. Within five minutes the girls creaked open the door and after a check both exited the room and the Do-Drop-Inn for the last time.

It would be a week before the clerk bothered to check the room.

The girls made their way back across the carpark to the Kombi. They jumped into the front seat, lifting the backpacks through the black curtain into the back of the van, with Bill helping from the darkness. Inga fired the classic, aircooled engine bring-ding-dinging into life and reversed the old girl, coughing oily smoke, out from that far corner of the carpark. It's surely too good to be true, Bill thought, crouched up against the front seats and peeking through the curtain. With graunch of Germanic engineering, Inga lurched the yellow van slowly forward and Bill took a big breath as they approached the alley mouth.

But all was well. The police had finished their scene examination and were elsewhere, crashing with the judicial authority of search warrants through the doors of well-known, inner-city troublemakers. They headed out onto Beaufort Street and toward the freeway, and were soon tracking north through the radiations of the city's suburbia. Like rings of a tree trunk, the further they got from the central business district, the newer the housing estates.

In one hour they were on the Great Northern Highway that lead straight to the tropics. The girls started, first in surprise but then in enjoyment, as their new friend burst into his rendition of Glen Campbell's "Country Roads". It was a choice of musical artist and genre that would have made his old mate Jack sigh in appreciation. And the old yellow Kombi chugged smokily away from, and yet toward, trouble.

Chapter 28

Jailhouse Rock

And so began the self-destruction of the Te Kuri Gang, with a somewhat theatrical but still threatening early morning abduction. The Whetu brothers, with Joe Tama's encouragement, had decided that it was time to meet this nephew of a proven faithful. Ironically, the six-month wait-and-watch after Tom's death had reassured Joe Tama, and the Whetus. With patience and careful surveillance and after many discussions, they felt that they could now move on. The gang had the itch and if this Bill George could scratch it, if he could provide the same service that his uncle had provided in cold hard cash, then why not try him out?

"Thuck! If it don't work, I could always waste him," lisped Pedro, the younger Whetu, eerily serious in his grunted offer to the meeting. So, via criminal networks that led through old Portuguese family bloodlines to more recent Puerto Rican connections, the relevant enquiries were made. Favours were called in, rewards offered, and debts satisfied. In a dusty brownstone police station in downtown Greenwich Village, a fat, corrupt precinct cop, in exchange for a grimy $100 green-back, single-finger tapped into that state's law enforcement database to find the falsely inserted but apparently genuine NY Police files on one Bill George. That data was then transmitted by email from New York City to tkenterprises@nz.co. Within an hour, alerted by electronic trip-wires, the confirmation that the unauthorised inquiry had been made was recognised and emailed from the New York office of the FBI direct to Kingi Potiki's office at Operation Te Kuri, Auckland.

The gang now felt that they had some comfort; that young Billy was not a person of particularly good character and therefore may just fit in with their organisation and its ideals. Further, as the brothers took turns reading the print-out, the extensive file notes recorded in that typical international police-talk shorthand impressed them. These notes had been creatively composed by Kingi himself and drew colourful pictures of Bill's alleged activities in that precinct. The suggestion was that he was much more of a criminal than local law enforcement had been able to prove. The Whetus liked that in a person. Now they wanted to meet the man.

But as was their instinctive manner they wanted their guest to be at a disadvantage, hence the early morning abduction. From the factory to the Island was a short 20 minutes. There was no talk, and Bill with tape over eyes recognised the method behind the gang's madness. To disorientate, to terrorise. Despite his training, his eager expectation of this moment, and despite his relief that finally things were happening, Bill did, in the heavy masculine crush and stale body odour stench of that car ride, admit to a thrill of uncertainty. Even a bowel-tingling fear. But he had no time really to sweat as the big car revved and decelerated through the sleeping suburbs. He imagined then from the sounds and sensations of the ride the car's progress down the long, exposed dirt road above the sewerage ponds, slowing and stopping only momentarily at the two gates in sequence and then crunching into the fortress of the gang compound.

Still no words were said but big hands guided him roughly out of the car and across soft gravel ground. In his blackness he had an awareness of a man ahead, a man behind, and a flight of wooden stairs. The night's gentle noises dulled. He was inside a building, his senses told him. A grunted "steps" in his right ear, so he knew to lift feet up with clumsy cooperation, then he was pushed onto a landing. And pushed again down onto a seat. The tape was cut and unwound from wrists. And hard-nailed fingers searched for the tape edge as he braced and winced when the heavy grey strip was ripped away, taking with it a selection of eyebrow, eyelash, and side-burn hair. Bill blinked into a musty dimness. Shadowy figures were seated a few yards in front. He was aware of heavy maleness grouped to each side and behind.

He was in that same clubroom, the gang bar really, where Tom had been initiated those two-and-a-half years before. Bill wondered whether this night would require him to fight as Tom had when the man Tom had damaged and broken was in fact Joe Tama. Tama: the man who had become both Tom's friend and unwittingly his primary source of information about the gang. The information came in, piecemeal, over the two years and had been faithfully and forensically collected, analysed and recorded to establish the basis of the evidential proof intended to destroy the gang.

With eyes now adapting to the dim light, Bill recognised the three brothers from Kingi's videos and photo sessions with a shiver of excitement. The eldest Matu, the leader: purportedly the criminal brains of the evil triad. More his grandfather's progeny, his mother's son than the laidback Maori father he had only known as a very young child. Now aged 30, solid and muscular but clean cut, handsome even. Cold black eyes were set in an impassive countenance that looked beyond Bill. Matu, Bill noticed, was dressed casually but impeccably in an expensive Italian-cut black shirt and tailored black trousers. Shit! Bill thought, this dude could be a businessman waiting for a cappuccino at a café.

To Matu's left sat Louis, the middle brother. Louis was the drug man. He had taken the early risks, had travelled the world at his brothers' behest learning and copying the nefarious techniques and chemical equations necessary to manufacture the drugs that had built the gang's fortunes. Lou Whetu was now 29. Slim built, his glossy black mane reached his shoulders. Tied in a ponytail, the look seemed to characterise hoods throughout western society like a badge of dishonour. Lou was the ladies' man, Bill knew from the briefings. A good-looking pants man who trawled the trendy bars of the city. Lou bedded models, actresses, and society's beautiful people either sex he apparently didn't particularly care. He fucked

203

physically the same people whose lives he fucked in innumerable other ways.

Then Bill looked to Matu's right and immediately wished he hadn't. Pedro. He was the youngest, and was obviously the mad one. In complete contrast to his siblings, Pedro Whetu was dressed rough and dirty and looked genuinely mean. The hint of black, quasi-tribal tattoos edged out from the collar of a dirty black t-shirt and ringed the heavy surely steroid-induced bulge of biceps. Pedro, 27, glared at Bill with considerable menace. This guy was, Bill knew from Kingi's sombre warning, the psychotic intimidator and the suspected exterminator for the triad. It was not even the case that in more recent years Pedro had to personally involve himself in the dirty work. With the financial strength of the TK organisation, the brothers could, and did at any time, employ any amount of muscle when required. No, it was just that Pedro enjoyed human terror. He revelled in the sound, smell, sight, and unbelievably sometimes even the taste, of fear and blood. With the coldness of the true psychopath, Pedro in fact lived for that special, final moment. When in dark and lonely places it was just he and his terrified victim, and he would watch closely as the mystery of life faded away.

Pedro had missed out. Not only on his share of the family brains and personality but he had to be one of the most butt-ugly men Bill had ever seen. Fuck me, Bill breathed under the heat of Pedro's 1000 yard stare, and he chose to look at big brother.

With eloquent intonation Matu welcomed Bill and then flowed into an explanation and near apology as to the means by which Bill was brought to the gang fortress.

"No hard feelings," Bill said. "In fact, I am very pleased to be here as my uncle had spoken of you."

Pedro growled low like a chained pit-bull in response. Matu, with sideways glance, continued with the ease of the natural speech-maker genetically gifted from his father. The oldest brother lectured Bill through a history, from his perspective at least, of the gang's evolution to its current place in society. The gang had, against all the odds, succeeded through a journey of struggle, hardship, and prejudice. In fact, if Bill did not know better, the brothers and their followers should be elevated to minor sainthood for protecting those who could not defend themselves against the evils of mainstream society. Matu Whetu concluded with: "Your Uncle Tom provided us with a valuable service, and we are prepared to trial you in his place." He then spoke warmly of Tom, and commented with sincere regret that, "It was with sadness that I and my brothers could not attend the funeral." This was perhaps the eulogy he might have given if he had felt the freedom to attend Tom's funeral.

Again, like a full-stop, the Pedro gave a muted grunt of disagreement. Again he attracted a warning glance from his older brother.

Bill spoke only to Matu. "I understand why you could not attend my uncle's funeral, and thank you for your kind words. I would only say to you that I am now in a position to trade at any time you are ready."

"Yes. You will deal with Joe Tama," Matu ordered. "You have met Joe?" Matu indicated with a nod of his head to behind Bill, and Joe stepped forward. Bill stood up. He turned to Joe and took the bro-shake and Joe patted the younger man's shoulder with his free hand. "Alright, that's done." The gang leader stood and, followed by the middleman Lou, welcomed their newest sub-contractor with a formal bro-shake. And as the group of about 30 men perceptibly relaxed with talk and laughter between them, the younger brother, Pedro, approached Bill.

He came within the boundary that is personal space. *Too fucking close*, Bill thought, and then, *Fuck, you are ugly!* Pedro's facial features were out of proportion to the size of his head. He had broad, flat, flared open nostrils, and heavy purple lips that were almost obscenely sensuous. And those mad, wide-spaced, slightly unfocused eyes. Which one did you look at? He had just a simple greeting, grunted, thick-lipped with a weird, incongruous effeminate lisp: "You thuck up cunt, I kill you." And then he walked away, his shoulder clipping Bill's, to join his brothers.

That was it; he was in. No fight, although he had been ready.

"Drinks!" Matu ordered and the place relaxed another notch with the staunch and true Te Kuri inner-circle beginning a rising murmur of conversations. Joe Tama, like an old mother-hen, took Bill into his care and made polite introductions as beers were distributed in celebration of Bill's successful job interview.

Bill recognised the faces and nicknames thanks to Kingi's training. He felt relieved by events but he couldn't relax even as he tipped the familiar sweet bitterness down his throat. At no time had Pedro Whetu taken that lunatic grin-stare from Bill's face.

That first meeting with his new employer was a long one. Once the beer started it continued to flow through those early hours well into the next day as the men enjoyed the company of their fellows. The brothers did not stay long before quietly slipping away. And Bill breathed a quiet sigh of relief. He had felt Pedro seeking him out from beside the doorway where he waited like a faithful guard-dog for his brothers. Seeking out the new man with that dangerous feral stare that Bill studiously ignored. He was determined to avoid any possible locking on of evil eyes that would surely end in tears. Then, finally, with the bosses gone, the Polynesian amongst the gang located guitars and song began to fill the increasingly hazy atmosphere. Bill joined in, able to hold a tune to the immediate appreciation of his hosts, particularly when he could negotiate past the first two lines. He had in fact been well-schooled in singing. He was familiar and experienced through his attendance at the army and diplomatic corps parties of his childhood, and then the rugby parties of his youth, in those perennial sing-along verses that always pleased. When the sun rose to the dying verses of a Freddy Fender classic, the gang's women brought them happiness with trays of salty bacon and oven-warmed plates of eggs fried in rich butter soaking into thick hunks of home-baked toast. Bill was slurringly introduced by his protector, Joe, to the various mammas of the gang's inner circle. These tattooed matrons giggled their way around the room, busily feeding their men and then leaving them again to the business. In this gang the women took a decidedly inferior position. Not only in the actual organisation but also within male-female relationships. These were men who were in some way damaged from either harsh, deprived upbringing, or from mental or physiological disorder. Amongst the men was a strict pecking order based either on physical strength, fighting prowess or, in some cases, charisma, intelligence and cunning. But as with these types of gangs worldwide, no woman had the status of even the weakest man, and any dissent by a woman was slapped down brutally. There was one exception to this. But Bill would meet her much later.

It was very late that next evening when Joe Tama took Bill back to the factory. Drinking bros now, they sat comfortably together in the V8 as a sober driver steered the big sedan up the gravel drive. There was an affection between the two men. Joe was feeling protective of the younger man, in the same way that he had genuinely liked and trusted Tom, and Bill was taking full cynical advantage of this early connection. As Bill tiredly lurched from the car and waved his farewell, a relieved Kingi Potiki took the call from an agent secreted in a surveillance van parked in the neighbouring factory lot. "The lamb is back and all seems well." Bill staggered up the steps through the newly repaired door where he was met by Bo and Phil and the three celebrated laughingly with messy high-fives in appreciation of progress made.

In the following weeks, vans and trucks began to arrive again at the factory. This was always pre-arranged by calls from Joe Tama to Bill. The dishonest commerce had recommenced.

When Tom died the gang had at first tried other avenues of disposal of their plunder but had found varying difficulties with each. As a result, Bill and his men dealt initially with a backlog of stolen goods as the burglary and robbery teams had not rested during that time. Using the expertise of Bo and Phil and the detailed information of Tom's journal, at each delivery Bill assessed each item of jewellery, each load of truck-jacked cigarettes, electrical goods, liquor and even container-loads of new tyres. He gave fair price in the stacks of used currency supplied covertly by the treasury. Each note, with serial number recorded, each transaction filmed by the covert closed-circuit tele-video system installed in the factory's steel beams above. All transactions were visually transmitted to the operation's headquarters. Each evening, late as planned, with gates and factory locked, Bill slipped around behind and under the shelving and into the pit to access the tiny coms room.

There, in lead-lined silence, he connected to his handler Kingi and provided the sworn declaration as to the day's dealings.

Kingi and Bill talked privately after each evidential de-brief and, as is always the case in long-term deep-cover operations, the agent and handler grew close. Kingi often confirmed conversations he had had with Bill's dad, passing kind thoughts and warm wishes of paternal and by that proxy maternal love from father to son and back. Kingi was soon very happy both with the way that Bill was conducting himself and also with the increasing flood of evidence that would ultimately damn the Te Kuri.

Bill was also happy at the initial progress but soon he wanted more. He wanted to better Tom's results. He wanted to break through and reach and directly implicate the Whetu brothers. Although he knew the operation would cripple the gang, he wanted the triad's head to be lopped.

The trouble was the systems in place kept him from the island. The gang came to him through Joe Tama. Bill had no reason to go to the island. No invitation would be extended. And although he hinted to Tama about a return to the bar, Tama actually preferred to drink with Bill and his men at the factory. There, he could relax away from the critical scrutiny of the brothers. Bill soon found that the naturally gregarious Tama could be loosened up by beer and rum. When the giggle juice hit the grey cells, that was when Tama would slyly boast and hint to his young mate about the gang's power and its various activities. Tama did not like the drugs element of the gang's operation. He was a somewhat old-fashioned crook and wanted to stick to the more honest dishonest trades. In his view, burglary, theft and robbery were activities without the stigma that hung like foul smog over the gang's drug manufacturing and distribution operations. Tama felt that over time his efforts had diminished in importance in the Whetus' eyes. He was somewhat aggrieved that the hard-earned rewards of the teams he controlled and which had provided the early financial muscle to the gang were now well overtaken by the huge and almost immediate profits generated from the gang's drug labs. So, as Joe grew to trust Bill, he talked. And all was recorded, logged and filed.

Then, after eight months, came the breakthrough. It was a warm Auckland summer afternoon. Tama and two of his offsiders had delivered and unloaded another van full of suburbia's loot to the factory. While Bo and Phil stacked and sorted the booty onto the shelving in classifications for valuing later by Bill, Tama and his two henchmen relaxed into the sofas next to the big old Kelvinator beer fridge in the dusty warehouse. The three men cracked cold beers and watched as Bill finished off a tae kwon do training session. Bill was dealing to a big red punching bag, pouncing and prancing on a soft black section of carpet underlay. Tama and his gang members were soon suitably impressed by this unknown martial talent of their new friend, and especially by the heavy black belt he wore around his waist. In their world, physical prowess actually mattered, and Bill's skills created animated discussion amongst the group. As Bill kicked and chopped, punched and blocked, it was Tama who developed a bright idea. "Hey, little bro," he called as Bill completed the discipline of the set routines, "reckon you could teach that shit?"

So it was arranged. Tama spoke to Matu Whetu. Bill was summoned to attend the island that next Saturday and demonstrate his skills to the brothers. Tama hinted that if he passed muster he might then be invited to teach the martial art to the community's young men. He had found a way in.

Chapter 29

Flip, Flop and Fly

They made good time that first day. Once away from the stops and starts of the city traffic and the outer suburban streets, the old Kombi chugged north at a steady 100kph. By 10am they were half-way to the coastal port of Geraldton. They had stopped occasionally at isolated roadhouses where the girls trotted off to dank, graffitied outhouse toilets, swatting the voracious flies from their faces, and then stocked up on cold drinks and mysteriously concocted fast food. Bill stayed in the van while the young petrol attendants clumsily and desperately flirted with the exotic foreign girls. He got his toilet stops on isolated stretches of lonely road. Much to the delight of his two companions he would duck off cautiously into the scrubby bush, hard red ground stinging his bare feet, furiously flicking the moisture-seeking bush flies from his eyes and mouth, while nervously expecting at any moment deadly ambush by a snake.

On the long stretches of the journey Bill slept in the warm steel cavern of the Kombi on the girls' mattress while they chatted happily through the curtain and swapped driving duties at roadhouses.

Once at Geraldton, the girls suggested that they should continue the run north, and Bill agreed it would be wise to keep up the pace while the going was good. They had picked up the news story about the Americans on the radio. Clearly, from the tone of the broadcasts, the police were earnest in their intent to track down the perpetrators of this unprovoked, violent attack. The police spokesman talked of "promising leads" and "breakthroughs expected in the near future," with "several persons assisting with inquiries", which somewhat comforted Bill and the girls as obviously the coppers had no idea. The important thing was that no connection seemed to have been made to them. So it was in Geraldton that the girls turned Bill into Lars. It was Hana's bright idea, just in case there was a description of Bill, especially as he would be wearing the bruising and grazes for a few days yet. They stopped in the city centre and Hana ducked into a chemist, returning with blonde hair dye. Once out of town, when only the occasional road-train disturbed the increasingly heaviness of the warm air, they pulled over and parked amongst thin silver gums.

Bill sat uncomplainingly on the camp chair whilst the girls delighted in first cropping his brown locks into a trendy Swiss tourist cut with the small scissors from the first-aid kit. They then dyed the remaining hair the whitest shade of white possible. Bill could not but laugh with his two giggling companions as they did his eyebrows to match. Once finished, he checked himself out in the side mirror of the Kombi. When he thanked them in an exaggerated Swiss accent with lots of "ya yas", the girls collapsed in hysterical celebration, as much from relief as the sight of their companion.

By 2.00pm they were running for the small picturesque town of Carnarvon, five hours north on the Gascoyne River. This lovely little coastal fishing village also grew the state's bananas and other succulent fresh fruit and vegetables in the rich red soil of the flood plains of the upside-down river so called because, except for a short period in the wet season, it ran hidden along a subterranean course under the broad sandy river bed.

They decided that to be safe Bill should not drive. Even on the long, lonely stretches between towns they had seen police highway patrols lying in wait for the unwary motorist. They could not risk being stopped while he was driving. So both girls took turn about at the wheel. And while the other rested in the back, Bill kept the other chit-chatting about life in general. Occasionally, to the continued amusement of the girls, Bill took time out to admire his new look, leaning out exaggeratedly from the van to preen himself in the warm wind-rush behind the wing mirror and muttering a "ya, ya" of approval.

They were tired when they wandered into Carnarvon at 8.00pm that first night.

In the heat of the sub-tropical evening banana plantations surrounded their approach to the town, open windows capturing a chorus of birds and insects. At the fluoro-bright roadhouse on the outskirts Inga refuelled while Hana resupplied the van's gas-powered fridge with cool drinks and bought greasy fast food, and as a special treat three frozen chocolate-dipped bananas. "Ze local delicacy," Hana explained as they enjoyed the cool sweet treat. The owner also provided directions to the least popular of the town's caravan parks and they headed off to book in for the night.

With the van parked and tucked away on the fringe of the park they tracked across to the concrete ablution block. In the men's, Bill luxuriated in the cool splash of the shower finding no need to trouble with the hot tap as he lathered furiously with the very feminine scented soap Inga had provided him. With teeth brushed glowingly clean of the detritus of the day's consumption, he towelled off and put on clean shorts and a light cotton t-shirt. He sat outside, refreshed, under the night sky on wooden bench near the showers and waited for the two girls.

He could hear them sing-song chattering and giggling in the echoing of the concrete shower block. It was then he wondered about the sleeping arrangements. Really, he believed, there was only comfortable room for two side-by-side in the back cabin. Maybe he could bed down across the Kombi's front seat? That should be ok. He wondered briefly about sleeping outside but the mozzies were already starting to feast. They would suck him dry without a net.

Oh well, he thought, let's see if the girls have any solutions.

Finally, out they came, much later than him but he was so comfortable with the two of them and so grateful for their help and

212

lovely company that he only gently teased them, herding them with a flicked wet towel as they squealed and giggled their way back to the van. While the girls hung their towels off the side of the van, and arranged the doona, Bill suggested that he should sleep in the front. "No, Lars," Inga giggled. "Vee all fit in ze back, I think. Ok?"

"Ya, ya. Ok," he submitted. Shit, who was he to disagree?

First Hana clambered in, across to the far side. Slipping her petite little t-shirt-covered self under the doona, she coyly turned onto her right side as Lars obeyed Inga and took the middle spot. Shit, it's a dream come true! Bill only teased himself at the thought of sleeping between two such attractive young women. In fact he was becoming somewhat uncomfortable just thinking about the pure practicality of the situation. He felt that they were all getting on marvellously well becoming friends. Although, to be totally honest, he thought to himself with some understatement, perhaps I am sort of attracted to them.

Probably Inga the blonde a tiny bit more than Hana, the brunette or maybe it was the other way around.

But he hadn't felt any return vibes from either girl, other than simple niceness and politeness. Also, serious thoughts of romance were really far from his mind, given the past 24 hours. His biggest worry was not to offend the girls in any way. Snoring, bad morning breath, involuntary gaseous emissions after a day of fast food consumption topped with a frozen fucking banana.

Bill clambered awkwardly into the van and on bended knees duck-walked, quacking stupidly to hilarious laughter from the girls, into the middle of the bed. He tried to gently lay six feet, two inches and 95kgs of clumsy male down without tearing anything. His size-10 feet poked out the end of the doona and touched the cooler skin of the Kombi door. Hana kindly tucked a pillow under his new blonde head in a comforting fashion, while Inga slipped gracefully into the van on his right side and pulled shut the sliding door with total darkness descending.

"Goodnatchet mine fraulines, ya, ya and ya, " Bill cooed. And both his companions exploded again in hilarity. And he settled down and relaxed into the situation. Shit, I suppose the Swiss might be more comfortable with this type of thing … there's nothing to be taken from it, he reasoned to himself, as on either side the girls adjusted into better position for sleep.

Fuck, this is great really, Bill thought and a big smile creased his face in the blackness with the breathing either side and gentle feminine snuffles getting softer and more regular. The close company of two other human beings the bonus that they are both beautiful young women was sublime, he thought, as sleep started to ease him off.

He didn't even feel the first touches. Took a few seconds, two soft hands. One either side, on sensitive belly. Stroking so softly under cotton of t-shirt, small circles each hand. But he was wide awake when he felt the hands meet each other, and cross each other, and then return and stay in unspoken territorial agreement on either side of his now very tight stomach muscles. Both soft warm little hands up under his shirt, across the expanse of his chest, his breath suddenly impossible to draw in, pure heart-thump of excitement. "Ooooh, fuck!" almost audible, his breathing louder. He stretched in an almost involuntary reaction to the sensations. Cautious, like a cat-stretch in enjoyment of the touch but not wanting to assume, or presume, or startle, or goddamn it! stop them.

Then again in unison, a small head snuggling either side into the crook of his neck, exquisitely sensitive, almost beyond bearing. Soft lips and gentle suction against the erogenous zones of his neck. Then the inevitability of what was happening as both hands tracked down again onto his muscle-twitching belly. Together, almost in perfect timing, under the loose elastic of his shorts, the trespassing hands bumped agonisingly each side against the throbbing hardness of his erection, down further a gentle Swiss roll over his sac and along his inner thigh, legs parting like a Swiss boy-slut. "Ohhhhh," he moaned long and low, quietened only when lovely Hana covered his mouth with hers and with a shuffle of doona, lovely Inga covered the ache of his glans with her equally hot soft wet and sensuous mouth. For the next hour or three he would never know how long his world was a sensual swirl of moistness and appreciation. In the same confusion he would find his turgid flesh deep into a third party, with impatient hands seeking soft adventure of nipple tipped breast, and glorious silky orb of buttock in a smorgasbord of sexual exploration and climatic release. That first night he came quickly once, twice, three times in a lady. Which lady? He didn't know, didn't care. And once again, in the worrying pattern of his life, he went from the stress of battle to the escape the release of the flesh.

Sometime late, or was it early? they finally let him be. No more aggressive suction of hungry mouth against his bruised lip or around his deflated masculinity in demanding head bob. No more desperate press of soft-fuzz, musky-scented crotch against his mouth. And both girls sated, he prayed in hope to some un-met god of lust, they fell finally asleep, while he pondered the events, nursing a weary tongue and sore and sorry prick. Shit! This ménage-a-trois stuff's not all it's cracked up to be, he thought, as now, totally drained in all respects he quickly followed the girls into the oblivion of sleep.

He woke, "Way too fuckin early!" in the half-light of the early hours to the unexpected irritation of Hana's mouth again on his traitorous member. Which, despite himself, had selfishly risen to her soft ministrations while the rest of his tired body attempted recovery. Meanwhile, Inga snoozed softly beside him. Topsy-turvy. Her tiny feet were only a few inches from his head. She lay, legs apart in an unconscious pornographic genital display. Finally, Hana, with a triumphant grin, rose up and sat herself roughly onto the quite useful tool that she had created from a few tired inches of floppiness just a few short minutes before. And when Hana arrived sweating at her destination some 15 tedious minutes later, she was then quickly replaced by Inga who had awoken to her little friend's increasingly ferocious grunts and then had warmed herself up with languid hand rotations until it was her turn to take the stand.

Fuck, Bill thought, I know I should be enjoying this but it would be nice to actually be involved. Here he was the porno-Nureyev of the Kombi van stage the principal dancer in every man's supposed dream ballet. And yet it was not quite working for him. Strangely, that morning, he found that ejaculation wasn't a risk or a problem, as he was simply a physical tool for the girls. I'm being used, he whined pathetically to himself. Finally, the gentle rocking and suspension squeak of the old van was eased by Inga's little yelp of physical relief and she fell off him backward onto the doona. Both girls then, much to Bill's relief, seemed happy enough to leave good enough alone, at least for the moment. Both momentarily regained his affection with a nice cuddle from either side. And all three sweat-slicked bodies fell asleep again for that last hour when the sleep seems to be the deepest, and dreams the most vivid.

All was not well, however.

Bill, or the Lars that he had become, quickly found that he was to be the vital component in the two Swiss misses great Australian sexual adventure. Both from conservative Calvinist families, the girls had been celibate tourists so far on the trip of a lifetime. Apart from the occasional harmless clothed grope of male backpacker on the various dance floors of the cities they had visited, and apart from the one or two teasing kisses goodnight from randy but denied English, French, and American youths who had walked the girls home to their various hostels, their sex life had been deliberately zero.

But now they held captive in the Kombi what they both agreed was an apparently safe, nice, polite, gentle, physically acceptable, and very much trapped, grateful, dependent male specimen. With the anonymity and the safety of the situation and the constant availability of the male body, the girls decided that they would catch up with the barren deprivation that they had imposed upon themselves. And catch up with a vengeance. And so, as over the next two weeks a yellow Kombi van meandered up the west coast of the continent, Bill found himself a sexual slave to two very attractive, polite, but virtually insatiable young Nordic goddesses. "I'm just a piece of ya-ya meat, a blond Swiss sex slave," he sometimes huffed, desperately joking with himself for comic relief in rare quiet moments. While one girl drove them up and along the vast expanses of lonely highway the other would be pounding him mercilessly in the back of the van. At night stops a tag-team of perfumed assailants would keep themselves entertained, manoeuvring their compliant but increasingly jaded captive into an experiment of positional

216

changes in which Bill participated physically but somewhat mechanically.

Since that first night at Carnarvon, he had found the key to his sexual survival in this intense contest. The little-known and much less practised art of the faked male orgasm.

In his past experience he had always felt strong attraction to, and, in fact, usually an intense love for almost all of his sexual partners. In those cases, taking into account youth and inexperience, he had found that release was inevitable, and that its timing relied upon discipline of emotion as well as control of the inevitable, rising physical sensations. Now Inga and Hana well, they were nice girls but when he realised that he was a sexual prisoner for their wanton needs and deeds, Bill soon assessed that their happiness depended simply on the maintenance and duration of a certain rigidity. He was willing to provide the means to their ends, or his end to their means, so that he could travel with them. He hoped that eventually he would escape from the honey trap of the van at some appropriate northern location.

And so, quite by accident, it came to him that first morning when Hana and then Inga had so rudely awakened him he faked his orgasm.

He found that if timed to clinical, cynical perfection with some theatrical moans and groans and accompanied by a false frantic thrust and orgasmic seizure, his apparent passion actually drove the girls to their peak. Strangely, his body appeared to adapt. Deflation was not an issue without the actual release. The girls never caught on to his deceit. They just concluded on a limited history of prior experience that all men must be capable of the multiple orgasm. When, in years to come in cold Zurich flats, that proved not to be the case, the girls dreamt of their Aussie Lars and sighed at their disappointment with the Nordic male.

And so they journeyed on slowly north, the girls in no hurry to reach Broome. They stayed for nights at isolated but amazingly beautiful coastal stops. The girls delightedly patted the dolphins at Monkey Mia with ohhs and ahhs, and Bill made similar noises for different reasons as he lowered his bruised member into the healing sting of the blood warm Indian Ocean.

At the Ningaloo Reef near the old USA base of Exmouth, they witnessed sea life from the never-ending stretch of painfully white beach. Bill witnessed the tanned girls' excited, naked, jiggling rush to the water's edge. He joined them as whales and turtles surfaced just off the beach. A mass of tiny, gorgeously painted tropical fish darted in the shallows where the girls gently savaged him again in dual attack in the pristine waters. And Bill felt a strange, intense love not for his two hungry companions, but for the moment in the enveloping heat; the intensity of the pure natural environment, of the deep blue cloudless sky, the splash of gentle water around the soft female buttocks and breasts as, on grunted command he thrust and tongued and fingered and caressed and thrust and thrust and thrust some more.

Over two long weeks the girls did not leave their prize alone, and so Bill took advantage of the time to train himself in the pure mechanics of the business of sex. "Applied Sexual Techniques and Deceit 101," he laughed.

Bill trialed and, depending upon the response, either adopted or discarded his many variations of the sexual act. From the depth and variation of thrust, to the strength of application of rotated touch, to the gentle force and technique of tongue and mouth, to an almost infinite number of positions. He twisted and turned his appreciative captors to ever-increasingly bizarre contortions. Bill suffered, not in silence, but with increasingly theatrical faked orgasms, amusing himself as he took more and more artistic licence.

The negative orgasm went something like this: *No! no! no! no! Oh nonononononoooooooooooooooooooooooo!!*

And the positive: *Yes! Yes! Oh yes! Yeah! Yes yes yes fuck yeahyeahyeah!!*

The religious: *Oh God! Oh Mother Mary! Oh Christ! Sweet Jesus! Ohhhhhhhhhh my Goooooooood!!*

And his own combination of all three, which he titled "The Swiss Roll" and for which Hana and Inga punished him when his idiocy broke their concentration. Then they laughed until they fell off him,

218

softly kicking, hitting, and pinching in retribution. The Swiss Roll, which he sprung one night parked in a truck stop near Port Hedland, went something like: *Aw Ya! Ya! Ya! Ya! Unt nine! Nine! Nine! Nine! Oh mine got! Mine got! Ah ya yaaaaaaaaa!!!* and was pulled out of the bag when he really had had enough.

Then, finally, late one warm afternoon they trundled into the beautiful tropical township of Broome.

Chapter 30

Always On My Mind

Bill drove himself to the island at 9.00am on that first day of training. It was a humid South Auckland Saturday morning. For reasons of image or criminal cred for the new young hood around the town, Kingi had arranged a few months before to buy him a 1964 convertible notch-back Ford Mustang coupe in the appropriate sinister black. To Bill's delight, it was Kingi who had suggested the classic V8 muscle car, one of many thousands lovingly restored and exported from the USA around the western world. Kingi knew that the coupe would be admired by the ilk of the gang much more so than Tom's old fawn Commodore.

So on that first Saturday morning he made his grand entrance sweeping dustily down the access road to the island. That two-kilometre gap from the mainland to the island was traversed by the dirt road that was really the bevelled top of the dam wall between ponds. Before the construction of the sewage plant in the seventies this expanse between the mainland and the island had been the tidal flats of the Manukau harbour. Bill was surprised to realise, particularly with the top down on the convertible, that only a slight mustiness rose from the ponds. He surmised that the heavy action to treat the city's waste no doubt took place in the massive cluster of plant and buildings off to the north boundary. That was where subterranean pipes rose like huge black serpents from the swamps and fed into a conglomeration of tanks and massive cylinders. The dark, still waters were the final stages of the treatment by biological agents and apparently the water was clean enough to drink if anyone was desperate enough to consider it.

He reached the first gatehouse. An imposing gate topped with razor-wire and signage warned visitors not to attempt entry without prior authority. As he crunched to a halt, the electronically-altered voice of the welcoming Joe Tama boomed from a speaker, with a cheery, "Kiaora, little bro." The huge gate silently eased across on rails, and he purred the classic V8 through and down the last 50 metres to the fortress's main gate. This was a solid sheet-steel, 12-foot high barrier above which sat a watchtower. As approached, that gate also slid open and Joe waved him into the compound to a parking area beside a broad grassed courtyard. Beyond the courtyard were the clusters of buildings of the imposing gang headquarters, and the various structures that housed the gang. In the light of day Bill was impressed by the clean orderliness and the affluence of the gang, evident in the buildings and possessions, including the vehicle compound where rows of gleaming Harley Davidson motorcycles and modern modified sedans and panel vans sat under a broad expanse of corrugated roof.

Through a row of mature pines, Bill could see the shape of a black chopper on a helipad with the wide sweep of rotors tied down. Tama greeted his protégé with a hearty bro-shake and paternal pat on the back. Bill grabbed his kit-bag from the back seat of the 'Stang and followed Joe across to the buildings. He recognised the same double-storey, rammed-earth building he had been brought to for his job interview. Joe showed Bill to a shower and change room, where he donned the full tae kwon do training uniform of coarse white linen. He knotted the thick black belt with the embossed 7-dan ranking securely around his waist and then followed the chatting Tama back outside onto the lush grass of the courtyard.

By this time, the gang's young men had gathered in a curious grouping of some 30 assorted kids, ages varied from about six to 16. Clearly, from the variety of physiques, features and skins, the grouping was representative of the greater New Zealand gene pool. Bill noticed a gathering of curious parents around the boundary of the courtyard. The men sat or lay in casual repose around the several outdoor tables. The mums, aunties and sisters gathered on the wide steps of what looked like a communal food hall on the eastern edge of the grass. Tama's usual sidekicks and some who had relaxed with Bill that first night called out and waved greetings, fists raised with pointed thumb and small finger in the gang's dog's-head salute. Joe Tama fussed around and gathered the messy flock

"Ok, youse kids, now shut up! This here is Bill, he's gunna teach youse Kung Fu. Pay attention, do what he fuckin says or I'll show you some bum fu!" Joe teased, with a boot raised, and the kids laughed. And then, with his natural teaching skills that had been honed in Korea and New York as a tae kwon do instructor, Bill soon brought structure to the lesson. He formed lines of kids, roughly dependent upon size; smallest at the front to the biggest kids at the rear. Bill ran the enthralled and, he noted, very disciplined kids, through a short, colourful history of the martial art, and then concreted their respect forever with a one-man display of skill, completing a complicated training table. That was all it took. For the next hour he schooled the fascinated boys in a simple set of blocks, punches and kicks. When the lesson was completed, he knew that he had captured the imagination not only of the class, but also of the adult members of the gang who clapped when he bowed at the kids and the lines bowed back at their master.

After he had showered and changed Joe took him into the food-hall for lunch. Bill took his seat beside Tama and found the younger trainees shyly trying to sit as close as possible to him. The gang mammas served up bowls of succulent, steaming, flesh-packed pork-bones with fat, green vines of watercress and purple-stained kumara. Bill appreciated the home-cooked food, wiping his plate of the mixed juices with slabs of oven-baked Rewena bread.

At the completion of the meal a representative of the gang's young Turks approached the table. Bill had seen this group watching earlier. They were the 16 to 25 year-olds, a group of muscular young men in jeans and cut off Ts. As the second generation, they were the future of the gang. The leader, Kahu, a fine-looking 18 year-old and, Bill found out subsequently, the son of Matu Whetu, spoke to Joe quietly and Joe then passed on his request to Bill. He asked if they could also join the training. And so it was organised.

Each Saturday, the older youth would train after the kids. Before long, in the weeks that followed, the gang's assorted age groupings of young men became increasingly proficient under Bill's expert tutelage. He found himself at the fortress most of the day, and then due to an increase in class size, and as mothers pushed their daughters into the classes, he was invited to schedule an additional two, then three, nights a week. Bill was pleased to report to Kingi that he was becoming part of the furniture.

Since contact with the gang had resumed and with the trust that had grown from the business-as-usual approach to the fencing of goods, they were now some 18 months into Bill's part of the operation. Kingi began to talk about how they would conclude the operation. Late night discussions in the coms room revolved around the timing and strategy of raids raids designed to result in the arrest of most of the adults of the gang. Kingi proudly advised him that the best legal minds available to the Crown were very satisfied with the evidence obtained so far. Further, advice was that the weight of the criminal conspiracy against the gang would drag all key members of the organisation through the courts for many years to come.

Bill sought Kingi's consent to pursue the matter of the drug labs further with Joe. Tama gave a little more each time he and Bill had a session on the rum. Bill now knew that Lou Whetu had established and managed the labs. Bill roughly knew the identities of those who undertook rostered duties in the lab, which was hidden deep in bush a two-hour night-flight by chopper from the fortress. He knew how the gang avoided detection and pursuit, by contour hugging, flying low and fast.

Tama told him of a visit he had made to the lab in the chopper. In a rum-slurred late-night tale captured on video at the factory, the faithful servant of the Te Kuri told how Grizzly, the gang's Vietnam vet pilot, had dropped the chopper violently down out of the sky in a pitch black night to a torch-lit landing zone. He told how the chopper was fitted with on-board radar that confirmed there were no other aircraft in the area.

"Fuckin near shit myself," Tama shook his head, remembering the chopper's terrifying near-autorotation, a manoeuvre the pilot had practised decades before in the jungles of Vietnam. Joe recounted how the chopper was fitted with night vision and infra-red detectors. Using these modern scanners, Grizzly had ensured that the surroundings and approaches to the labs were clear of any unwelcome human presence. Bill knew from Kingi that when, in the past, the police had tried to follow the distinctive gang chopper with the dogs head logo, the pilot had led them on a wild goose chase for many frustrating and expensive hours. The police did not have the time or money to track the chopper every time it rose from the fortress.

So after much discussion between agent and handler and following consultation between Kingi and his superiors and with the legal advisers, a decision was made that the operation, although already considered a success, may as well take advantage of Bill's inroads into the Te Kuri structure. But, as originally planned, it would only run for six months more.

Bill received that news by phone late one night and silently pumped his fist in triumph while keeping his voice as calm as possible to his mentor. Six months! He had to find a way to get past Tama to the brothers.

And then he discovered their sister.

Born Mere Whetu, she had changed her name by deed poll at her mother's instruction when she was 18 years old. She was at the beginning of her law degree at Auckland University. Her brothers had already gained notoriety and the attention of police and national media as the pre-eminent criminal gang in the isles. That attention had finally resulted in a concerted official approach to destroy their organisation. Mere's mother and grandfather, however, had planned a different path for their princess, and it was decided that the Whetu tag may detract from the academic future toward which they guided her.

So she had taken her maternal grandmother's maiden surname of Lopes. By the time Bill Peters was part of the furniture at the gang fortress she was in the final year of the degree. The lecturers' expectations were that they had an honours student on their hands. A vision of youthful firmness, with hourglass figure and luxuriant black hair that fell to her mid-back in glossy waterfall, Mere Lopes was the belle of the campus, the erotic fantasy of the pimply young men and mature bearded lecturers alike. But although friendly and companionable on campus, her honour had been impeccably maintained through the four years of academia. During that time, no-one could recall a boyfriend, although many had applied in testosterone-inspired enthusiasm.

Mere herself was bemused that these presentable young men, although shyly encouraged by her to pursue at least her company, never sought a second date. She didn't realise the life-altering effect of a late night visit from Pedro Whetu upon those innocents.

They were terrorised in the sanctity of their own bedrooms with a butterfly knife at their throat and a rough callused hand cradling their family jewels under the covers, the agony of the biological modifications that Pedro promised them, in his girlish lisp, if they dared to even "thucken talk" to his sister again.

Mere lived with her mother in luxury in a harbourside apartment that the brothers had bought for them, paid for through the security business the gang ran. This business employed the sons and daughters of the older inaugural members and acted as a laundering mechanism for the burglary and drug money.

Mere, however, was no fool. She had learnt that her brothers were one of the primary criminal organisations in the country. She knew also from research in the uni newspaper libraries, and from subtle questioning of her morose and Prozac-ed mother, that her maternal grandfather had laid that criminal foundation for the boys. Mere also learned from her mother that dear old Grandad had disposed of her father. This changed forever her perception of the frail old Portuguese gentleman she thought she knew and had loved.

To all appearances Mere Lopes was a beautiful young woman without a care in world and an impressive future ahead of her.

Underneath, however, she was a troubled young woman. She instinctively loved her brothers but for the last five years had lived separately from them. She lived off their dirty money she knew that. She drove the latest Honda CRV, wore designer clothes and had access to bank and credit accounts that never dried up, though she had never worked a day in her life.

With final exams in sight and six months to graduation, Mere chose one sunny Saturday morning in June to visit the island. She wanted to catch up with her three brothers and her nieces and nephews whom she loved and who absolutely adored the beautiful Aunty Mere. It was on that fateful morning that Mere met Bill. She arrived in her trendy, red four-wheel drive just after 10.00am. With the gatekeeper forewarned of her arrival, the gates at the outer and inner boundary swung open before her and Mere wheeled her little ute to a park beside Bill's Mustang. Mere had not heard about the martial art training, but as the kids called out greetings to her from the parade ground she watched in giggling amazement as the ranks moved in near perfect choreography, shadowing the white uniformed young man who stood before them. Bill did not miss her as she wandered around the boundary, calling greetings to assorted friends and relatives. And it was clear to him both who she was, and that she was adored.

The day's first lesson ended shortly after she arrived and the class warmed down in a variety of stretches. Students were dismissed after bowing to Bill in unison. Then, as soon as they were released, the smaller kids sprinted to Mere for hugs and kisses, the older kids more casual but still heading that way. Bill felt the same urge but as the older class took up position in their lines before him he could only surreptitiously admire the form of this attractive young woman. Mere was dressed casually in tight blue jeans which, cut at the hip, revealed a milky, athletic belly. As she turned, he saw in silhouette the perfect swell of shapely buttock and long denim encased legs. Great arse, he breathed.

She was an all-round healthy, beautiful young specimen of breeding-age, he decided. Not overly buxom but the swell of breast against the top hinted at near-perfect symmetry of the feminine form. "Jesus," Bill whimpered in mock anguish under his breath and then thankfully for his concentration, she was dragged away by the kids and the womenfolk. Although … he was near certain she gave a backward glance his way as the troupe disappeared into the hall.

Later that day, during lunch, eye contact was secretly sought and maintained daringly by both of them for that nanosecond longer that confirmed that the interest on the basis of pure physical attraction was mutual. In the bustle of the food serving and the cacophony of the meal, Bill felt a surge of hormonal excitement and heart-thump of instinctive interest in this woman. As luck would have it, Mere felt the same. As she ate the hearty lunch at the long pine tables and chatted and listened to the island folk, she would on occasion peek up through the activity of the arms and heads of the massed diners along the table to the unmet young man. She liked what she saw and had admired the athleticism of his martial art display. And so it was with planning and care, and yet without conversation in those early weeks, that each manoeuvred to initiate the inevitable.

Mere joined the women's class. Cunningly, or so she thought, she got the approval of Matu, her eldest brother (and nominally the head of the family). Matu was aware of the possibility of attraction between the two young people, but felt that in the community of the island and under the feral glare of Pedro all should be well. Secretly, Matu considered that if his sister was attracted to this Bill then maybe that was all right. Bill seemed, by Matu's standards, to be a pretty good bad bloke in any event, and he was certainly proving to be an asset to the organisation. Pedro? Well he was not so convinced. Louis didn't care. Being a pants man he knew that his sister was an attractive and desirable woman. Lou knew no reason why Mere shouldn't follow the same type of urge that ruled his life. But Pedro had decided that sooner rather than later he would have one of those chats with Bill. Such discussions he considered to be effective contraception as far as his lovely sister was concerned.

Meanwhile, Bill kept Kingi up-to-date with developments but neglected to tell his mentor of both his growing attraction to Mere and her apparent return of that interest.

Mere not only joined the Saturday lesson, but also two of the week-night sessions. Here she soon proved that her athleticism and physical grace quickly translated into a natural talent for the flowing structure of the discipline. Her progress in those first weeks both surprised and delighted Bill. He found that he could focus on her in the training without drawing undue attention as it was clear to everyone that her natural talent had her leap-frogging even most of the men. They still kept a distance under the watchful eye of the gang elders and the brothers who would come sometimes to proudly watch their little sister. But in the training they found that they could touch through the heavy white linen of their uniforms in the variety of grips, chops, blocks, and throws, and they both enjoyed and sought the vicarious physical sensations.

The kids especially could pick up the vibes between the two and so both Bill and Mere kept a deliberate coolness and distance between them by a mutual and unspoken understanding. Both were waiting for some future opportunity to explore the signals of the instinct.

Finally, an opportunity arose in late September. Bill copped an invitation to a Hangi to be held at the island to celebrate Matu Whetu's birthday. By this time, Bill was considered part of the community. He had, under the authority of his international qualifications in tae kwon do, organised for a Master from the certifying Dojo in Auckland to visit the fortress. The Master, an imposing Korean who the young people of the gang considered in awed silence, witnessed the regimes of the structured exercises with grunts of appreciation at the standard. At the completion of the displays, certificates and the coloured belts of rankings were formally presented amid much bowing, a gesture that the gang kids had decided was "choice". That night, the gang kids and the adults participants and spectators alike were bursting with a rare legitimate communal pride.

So, when the time came for the Hangi feast and party, Joe Tama sought from Matu and was quickly granted the authority to invite Bill. When Bill told Kingi, they discussed the opportunities that the invitation may present. One much-desired outcome was for Bill to place a magnetic Sat-Nav tracking device on the gang's chopper. It was agreed: the opportunity was too good to miss. He would attend the Hangi.

The Hangi is a traditional Maori method of communal cooking. The method allows for big quantities of meats, sweet potatoes and other tubers and green vegetables to be fragrantly steamed in an earthen pit to culinary perfection. Traditionally, men did the cooking. Bill volunteered to help and was heartily welcomed that early misty morning. He was dressed in clothing supplied by Tama in compulsory shorts, black t-shirt and gumboots. With the good humour and camaraderie of the workers, a square, shallow hole was dug in the heavy black earth and a sterilising fire lit, where a substantial pyre of untreated pine logs was set aflame. On the cool morning, with a gentle breeze off the sea, the men interspersed the precious Hangi rocks amongst the warming conflagration. These river rocks had been handed down through generations as heirlooms. The wood flame would glowingly soak into the granite, which had been created from magna-heat in centuries past. The rocks would radiate the heat back out under a wet sack and a heavy layer of soil to pressure-cook the feast slowly, over several hours. As with recent tradition, although it was early, the workers stood round the fire leaning on shovels in semi-circle away from the smoky side and drank from a dark quart of ale.

When finally the flames died to ember, Bill followed barked instructions from the Hangi master, Tama. With the others he repeatedly approached the scorching heat of the pit to shovel out all wood ash and ember remnants. They then assembled the glowing rocks on the clean earthen floor of the pit. When the rocks were all that remained, the men carefully lifted the wire cages that held the muslin-protected feast. The bulky meats fat legs of pork, bloody rumps of beef were placed on the bottom of the cage. The smaller lamb cuts, and seasoned, stuffed and trussed chickens were layered in succulent delight in the middle. Above, sat the jigsaw of potatoes and kumara, carrot, pumpkin and cabbage. Finally, well wrapped against the scents of the lower layers, were the heavy steamed puddings, to be eaten afterwards with dollops of cream and thick sweet custard.

It was with exquisite care that the food cage was lowered onto the rocks. Tama quickly covered the hissing mass with heavy wet sacks and a layer of soil. He then wet down the hump of soil further with water from a barely flowing hose, and the process of steam cooking that had been learnt over centuries and used in times past to cook human meat to perfection, began.

During the long afternoon the men set up a marquee on the parade ground. Finally, their bit done, they sat in agreeable companionship and drank beer and rum and sang to tunes strummed on guitars. Meanwhile, the women prepared the inside of the marquee with tables and chairs for the feast. Bill was delighted to see Mere arrive in the late afternoon. From his bench by the Hangi pit, he watched her walk to the tent with her mother. The three brothers met them, each greeting the elderly, dumpy, black-frocked figure with clear respect. Mere was looking particularly gorgeous, Bill decided, and he tried not to stare as she approached the gathering of the faithful, who called to her in warm greeting, which she returned with hugs and kisses. She wore silky black trousers that hugged and accentuated the lines of her thigh and buttock, a pink wool top and an expensive black leather jacket against the slight chill of autumn. As people gathered they sang in harmonious chorus with the domination of Polynesian vocals and the community slowly moved into the marquee. Inside, they sat around a brazier of glowing pine logs, crackling and spitting as sap periodically exploded. Mere sat opposite Bill across the wide circle. They engaged in the game of body language across the space of the circle. Both were excited by the flow of sexual energy. The flirtation, Bill soon found, was fuelled further by his consumption of beer and by Mere's more modest intake of rum. The party gathered momentum and in the early evening the feast was dug out from the steaming earth pit. The men proudly carried the heavy cage into the tent to the "oohhs!" and "ahhs!" of the kids.

The matronly gaggle of women-folk gregariously took over the dishing up of the perfectly cooked meal. As they worked, laughing and chatting, bossing, arguing and giggling, the smoky Hangi scent filled the room. Each woman delivered a plate to her man while crooners sang sweet Maori melodies in the native tongue. Big enamel tin plates were covered in steaming assorted protein and starch. Bill's heart leapt when Mere tapped his arm and boldly gave him his meal, to his stuttered, "hey thanks", to which she giggled and returned a cheeky grin. He noted with approval the sensual soft thickness of her lips, the white evenness of her teeth, and the sparkle in those mud brown eyes.

With the satisfaction of the meal, the party really gained momentum and children disappeared off to bed progressively through the evening. Bill took time in the buzz of the alcohol to reflect on how he had come to be where he was this night. He was amazed that he felt totally comfortable, not even always consciously aware of his role as the Judas to the gang's future. He had found that once accepted, he had quite quickly and naturally fitted into the Te Kuri community. He knew of course that in some near future he would be the agent of the gang's destruction. He knew that each of the families and the individuals he now sat with, sang and feasted with in companionable atmosphere, he would damage, and in some cases, destroy. Bill knew that his actions had already and would further provide the conduit of the evidence that would prove their complicity in the criminality on which the gang was built. He knew that the men he now drank and joked with would be arrested, charged, and prosecuted, and in most cases, jailed.

He also knew from Kingi that he would identify with the members of the gang. It was ok, he was told, that he liked some of them most of them, in fact. Really, he found that despite knowing they were bad per se, that this organisation was criminal and therefore evil, his deliberate, total immersion in their lifestyle had made him almost one of them. This syndrome was well-known in psychology. Similar to the hostage scenario, the emotional experience of the victim or, in this case, the agent was known as the Stockholm syndrome. People taken hostage often grew to sympathise and identify with, and, eventually, against all logic, attempt to protect their criminal abductors. Bill knew all this but still found that he had to periodically remind himself of the pretence of the situation, whilst accepting that immersion in the character he was playing was integral to the credibility of the deep cover.

The night passed comfortably and in a noisy haze of music, marijuana and alcohol. Bill lost track of Mere, as from time to time she left the tent in the company of her brothers or her mother. By the early hours he hadn't seen her for some time and thought that she may have gone to bed. He decided to try his luck placing the small, flat tracking device onto the chopper. No-one particularly noted his exit from the tent. All night the men had wandered in and out to relieve full bladders from the copious intake of beer. Bill wandered out and away into the dark, toward the line of mature pines separating the parade ground from the helipad, and then the sea on the harbour side of the island.

Off to the right, Mere saw him from the dark doorway of the rammed earth accommodation block. Earlier, she had put her tired mother to bed with a hot-water bottle and a powerful sleeping pill. She quickly scanned the area. No-one else was out and about. Mere made a quick decision based on emotion and desire, inhibitions blunted by the rum. She quietly began to track her prey in the darkness on soft-soled shoes. Bill reached the chopper, unaware that he was being followed. When he reached it, he crouched down and attached the magnetic tracker onto the far underside of the skid mount. As he stood, he saw a figure behind him, reflected in the black glass convex of the passenger window. His heart just about stopped dead in his chest, his bowels nearly bursting open in pure terror. Luckily, the combination of the alcohol in his blood and the discipline of his martial art allowed him to analyse and relax, rather than react, and he pretended to be admiring the machine by cupping his hands onto the window. She came towards him and placed both hands onto his hips. And as he turned, she slipped right up against him in a warm embrace and he felt her soft form press into his back and her arms envelop him across his chest. "I surrender," he breathed. He twisted gently around in her arms, and slid his around her. Their mouths met, urgently hungrily, with a mutual moan of the suppressed desire of their instinct. And while they tasted each

232

other that first time he marvelled at the softness and fullness of her lips, and the firmness of her pressed body, which he pulled towards him, with hands on her buttocks, into the male contours of his body. He stroked up through her mass of lush black hair and down to the rise of her buttock. Her slender, long-fingered hands tugged his shirt loose from his jeans and touched his warm skin, sweeping up from his waist to the broadness of his shoulders.

Meanwhile, 100 metres away in the carpark, one Pedro Whetu was at the Mustang. In a strange coincidence, Pedro was fitting a magnetic Sat-Nav tracking device to Bill's car. The tracker was attuned to the gang's base tracking screen, which sat in the office at the island, and another had been fitted to the chopper. Pedro had decided unilaterally that he might need to know where Bill was at any given moment. He had seen Mere feed the stranger at the Hangi, he was suspicious, he was pissed off, he was protective of his baby sister in the sense that she was precious gang property, and one of only two women in the world he tolerated. Now, at any time, Pedro could locate the Mustang, and if he could find the car, he could find Bill.

Pedro returned to the tent. Mere and Bill weren't to be seen. Pedro found Tama dopey and bleary-eyed. He whispered into Tama's ear and when Joe shook his head in the negative Pedro left the tent and checked his mother's room. Still no Mere. Pedro became seriously concerned.

Meanwhile, Lou Whetu had just orgasmed into the hot young mouth of the teenage daughter of one of the lowly-ranked gang members. Lou was standing, joint in mouth, beer in hand, the bottle resting cynically on the girl's eager head and leaning back against the rough bark of one of the pines in the windbreak. Lou had seen Mere follow Bill and in turn had watched his little sister, from the cover of the trees. Whilst his young partner enthusiastically cleaned up his mess, Lou was enjoying watching the passion of the two young lovers by the chopper. It was Lou who saw Pedro explode from the tent. It was Lou who rudely dismissed his young and very temporary partner and called quietly in warning to Mere and Bill. Lou waved for the startled duo to join him on the walk back to the tent. He put one arm around Mere and the other around Bill and when Pedro met them in the parade ground it was Lou who explained that he was showing off his toy, the chopper, to his guests.

Pedro could not but accept that that was the case. In a soft lisp he offered to walk Bill to the Mustang but Lou insisted on accompanying them as Mere wished all an innocent goodnight and turned to join her trumpet-snoring mother in the guest room of the main block. Once there, with her heart thumping from both recent encounters, Mere watched through the curtains as Lou and Pedro farewelled Bill. Even from this distance, Mere identified a different vibe from each sibling toward the young man she knew that she had fallen irretrievably in love with. She watched as the red tail-lights of the Mustang faded away down the long driveway.

Chapter 31

Unchained Melody

Bill believed in love at first sight.

After all, he had fallen in love with the beautiful Mere so long ago at first sight. Now it had happened again. A second time in one man's life. Except this time it was not a woman, it was a place, a town, a perfect beach, the tropical sky, the turquoise sea everything. He fell in love with Broome, that tropical coastal hamlet in the north-west of Western Australia. The tiny town set back from the coastal mangroves was founded by the early pioneers of the wild pearling trade. They were the fearless sons of Indonesia and Malaysia; the early free divers. Shamefully, local Aboriginal pregnant women were also forced to free dive in the preposterous belief of the times that, with more oxygen in their blood, they could stay deep longer. Later, young Japanese men in heavy, bronze-helmeted suits died in the pure turquoise waters in their hunger for the shell.

Death came in many guises.

They died from the huge destructive seas and immense winds of seasonal cyclones; from the crippling curse of the bends; from invisible viruses borne by tiny, irritant mosquitoes; they were wounded and poisoned by the fatal attentions of marine predators that fed on the flesh of man or fish. Huge, rapacious sharks, box jellyfish, stonefish and sea serpents all took their deadly toll.

The prize was a wild and native treasure the silver-lip oyster, *Pinctada Maxima* the bivalve that produces the silver-white lustre of the South Sea Pearl. The trade had boomed over the decades with the early interest in the mother of pearl. It went bust with the advent of synthetic materials for buttons and inlays. At that time, any pearl found in the succulent flesh of the oyster was a bonus and not the main game. In the 1950s the town boomed again as aquacultural ingenuity perfected the seeding of the harvested wild oyster shell. And slowly began the farming of cultured pearls in remote sheltered bays along that north-western coast.

From the first seeding at three years of age to the first pearl harvest at five years, each oyster could be reseeded and produce several progressively larger pearls, growing fat in the plankton-rich, blood-warm waters. After harvest, the pearls were sold to the jewellery markets of Japan, USA, Hong Kong, and Europe to be fashioned into necklaces, earrings and rings. They graced and decorated the varying hued skins of the women of those distant nations. The industry evolved over time to become the nation's second most valued natural resource after WA's rock lobster industry.

By the time Bill and the two Swiss Misses meandered into town, Broome had again boomed from the tourist trade. This trade had first been opened up by the English-born entrepreneur, Lord Robert McAlpine, in the eighties. The eccentric Englishman had fallen in love with the tropical mysteries of Broome and with the vision of a true adventurer he had risked all to build a luxurious resort on Cable Beach, which was in the middle of nowhere. By force of personality he harassed the politicians and bureaucrats of the State Government sitting in Perth, 2500kms south, to share his vision. That government built an international standard airport to receive the heavy jets that brought in national and international cash-rich tourists for a taste of the tropics.

Despite that boom in tourism and the resultant increase in the services and facilities that changed the look of the old town, the essential natural physical beauty of the locality remained and Bill felt an immediate affinity for the place.

This will do me, he breathed, as the Kombi trundled away from the tiny commercial centre, following the signposts toward Cable Beach. The girls were happy. They told Bill they had enjoyed the last two weeks of their holiday the most so far. Both girls were glowing with good health and relaxed satisfaction.

Bill, on the other hand, had lost condition. Muscle had wasted and he had started to develop the haunted gauntness of the stressed, the strained, the well-drained.

The girls had discussed "maybe a veek in Broome," and "then off to Darvin" before embarking on the long trek around the north-east coast and heading back to Sydney. Bill noted a certain presumption that he was part of their plans. It appeared they had no intention of letting him go before then and had made vague promises to leave him the Kombi when he dropped them at the airport. They were even subtly hinting that perhaps "Beel" should start making plans to join them in Switzerland as soon as he was able. Bill made his decision as they stopped the Kombi in the carpark on the cliff over Cable Beach.

He would leave the girls in this place. He was far enough away from Perth, close enough to south-east Asia, but also close enough to Darwin to wait until Kingi found his man. Yes, it was time and this was the place.

As they walked from the carpark up to the grassed area above the beach, the huge red globe of the sun was setting spectacularly, awesomely sinking down below the western horizon into the waters of the Indian Ocean. Bill and the girls were so moved by the sight that in the red glow they stood together, Hana one side, Inga the other, arms around each other and again despite himself he felt a surge of what might have been deep affection for his two companions.

That feeling did not last. Again, that night, trapped in the van, they feasted on his disinterested but traitorously compliant body. The following morning the three decided to hit the world-famous Cable Beach and from the caravan park they crossed the narrow road and climbed down the stairs of the beach cliff and onto the soft white sand.

Although it was relatively early there were already a few dozen people spread along the broad expanse of pristine beach and they walked through the small bustle of commercial activity that operated just out from the steps. There were two caravans and one large marquee set semi-permanently in position, all the better to tap into the beach-goers' needs the comfort-hungry tourists who fed disposable income into the tiny town's economy. One caravan hired out lounge chairs and candy-striped beach umbrellas for the lazier, more mature visitor. Another provided boogie boards and surfboards to the more adventurous. The large white tent, Bill saw from the artistically painted poster, offered "Massage by Gypsy," catering for the seekers of the sensual experience.

Bill glanced into the murkiness of the massage tent as he passed in the secure grip of the girls and was an appreciative witness to the finest female rear-end he had ever, or would ever see again. Although the owner of the perfectly proportioned and sun-browned muscularity was facing away from him, Bill noted a lime green thong bikini that tended to disappear and reappear between the lovely globes as the masseuse leant into her work.

Her customer, who groaned gutturally in appreciation of her attention, appeared to be the very white, obese carcass of a German tourist. Although he had unconsciously stopped in his tracks in appreciation of the view, the two Swiss misses soon hurried him away from the tent toward the gentle bash of the ocean waves against the sand.

That sun-filled day passed slowly. After that initial dip into the water the girls walked Bill down the beach and then up into the dunes. In the privacy of the small sandy auditorium bounded by the dunes they spread their towels, and over that afternoon in the warmth of the day the girls sunbathed in their petite and beautiful nakedness. That day they made no demands on Bill who lay with them, except when they had him rub sun cream over their lovely bodies, a task he rather enjoyed. Late in the day with both girls asleep beside him, he made the mistake of remembering that tanned figure he had seen in the masseuse tent. His mental recollection had immediate physical effect, and Hana was pleasantly surprised when Beel woke her with a passionate kiss and increasingly targeted caresses, and the two made love for the first time. Although his subsequent orgasm was by proxy, Bill's actual and total release caused by the fantasy image of Gypsy, pushed Hana too over into that ultimate flood of sensation. When he gently rolled off her, Hana felt well satisfied that based on his intensity Lars truly was hers, more so than Inga's.

Then, at the end of that day, the tired trio wandered up toward the massage tent to climb the stairs. Bill, somewhat jaded, head down, the limp meat again in a Swiss sandwich, noticed two small sun-browned feet just inside the tent opening. He allowed his gaze to follow the shapely calves up past the muscular thighs to the petite trunk and gorgeous face belonging to the butt that he had fallen so deeply and sincerely in love with that morning.

Gypsy, he breathed.

She smiled at him with wide grin and startling green eyes and his heart flipped as the Swiss army wives pulled at his arms and away up the steps.

The week passed slowly. Each morning the girls led him down the cliff path to the beach, one or the other would stay with him while one or the other walked back to the beach kiosk to replenish liquid and food. During the day the girls would leave him alone, but each afternoon they would escort him back to the van where during the night one or the other would again selfishly gorge upon him.

During his week of exquisite torture, Gypsy would smile at him when he passed the tent and wonder at the dynamics of this strange trio.

Chapter 32

He ain't Heavy, He's my Brother

The very next night, after the thrills and near spills of the Hangi, with Bill having cruised dreamily through the day, distracted and excited by the memories and fading recall of the physical titillation of his brief encounter with Ms Lopes, her brothers came a-calling.

With wary canine chorus, the dogs heralded the arrival of the gang's sedan up the winding entrance. Alerted, Bill stood outside by the wide, graffiti-tagged roller door and met the familiar vehicle in the comfortable anticipation that Joe Tama had dropped in for a rum or ten. But when the dark tinted driver's window whirred smoothly down it revealed in sequential frames the handsome smiling countenance of Lou Whetu, with a broad-grinned, "Kiaora, bro." Bill stooped to look inside the shiny car and his view went from one extreme to the other as went from Lou's handsome good looks over to his younger sibling, monster-mask complete with silent, foul-toothed snarl. "Gidday, Pedro," he offered, but was unrewarded for his effort. "Jump in, bro," Lou ordered, with reverse nod of pony-tailed head to indicate the back seat of the LTD, and Bill dead-locked the factory entrance door and climbed into the white leather interior of the car.

"Good piss up last night, eh?" Lou said, as he spun the big auto smoothly around on the gravel and Bill settled back with a,

"Shit, yea, Lou," and recognised that there was subtle change in Lou's demeanour toward him that was relaxed and promisingly familiar. He gave the silent, covert fist-pump he was wont to do when progress was made in his endeavours with the TKs. That fist was then filled with a can of rum and coke passed back over Lou's shoulder from a carton in front. Meanwhile, Pedro sat alone in his demented world, not avoiding but not hearing the polite to and fro as he swigged sweet, black rum directly from the bottle. Bill tipped his own drink back and he enjoyed the hair-of-the-dog recharge from the previous night's exertions.

"We're off to do some collect and deposit, bro," Lou chuckled in response to Bill's unasked query. The joke was appreciated by Pedro who was half-way through a gurgle of rum and exploded it in a sticky mist all over the inside of the windscreen. "Funny cunt, Lou," Pedro coughed, and caught his breath though those loose purple fat flaps of flesh that were his lips. Lou cracked up with the effect of his brilliant wit upon his not-so brilliant brother and Bill very carefully joined in with a polite but cautious giggle, ready to shut it down should Pedro think for a moment that he was laughing at him. With periodic bad jokes interspersed with offerings of casual bullshit and several more cans, Lou aimed the car through the heart of Mangere township. They skirted around the South Auckland commercial hub of Otahuhu and then into the suburb of Otara one of the local breeding grounds of Te Kuri burglary recruits.

As midnight approached, the car turned off the main road into a ghetto, thanks to 1960s-designed state housing. The bulky, two-storey flats were known locally as 'multies'. The buildings stood like drab sentinels guarding scruffy, handkerchief-sized front yards dotted with car wrecks. The obsolete, rusting beasts housed half-feral guard dogs that snarled at passing vehicles. Lou snapped from the casual, hospitable drinking companion and brought the sedan to a smooth halt. Half-pissed, he relayed instructions to his two equally inebriated passengers.

"Billy, what I need from you, bro, is just to watch our backs, eh? What this is here man, is us just collecting what belongs to us, ok?"

Bill nodded somewhat unnecessarily as he was behind Lou and the car interior was pitch black.

"I am going into that corner multi," he pointed. "Shouldn't have a hassle, man, just picking up some monies owed. One of our boys fucked with us last year, took what was not his. Funny thing is, he not around no more."

A snort of evil laughter erupted from Pedro

Lou continued, "Well, tell a lie, he's around — all around — all around his own back garden, eh Pedro?'

Bigger, snot-assisted series of bubbly snorts shot from Pedro.

"Anyways, bro, his lovely Pakeha missus is now paying back what her man owed. Shifting some gears for us eh," explained Lou, "but she's a bit behind, soos I may have a bit of her behind, eh Pedro?"

The comedian's loyal sibling audience was now in rum-assisted paroxysms of moronic mirth, and he moaned, "You funny cunt, Lou."

"OK boys," Lou took charge, "Pedro, you come with me and stand guard outside. Bill, you drive this baby and sit her back just down the road on the other side so you can scope the joint."

Bill nodded again.

"I will do the bizz inside. If anything happens, bro, give us one blast on the air-horns, eh. I will be, say, half an hour I reckons, don't stress. If you need to, bro, don't be shy to use this," and Lou reached under his seat and passed him a sawn-off, double-barrelled shotgun, gleaming in well-oiled preparedness. "There's ten in the mag, bro. Shouldn't need it but we are close to some old boyhood enemies out this far from home."

Lou and Pedro got out. The interior light had long been removed, and with the car lights off, Bill climbed into the driver's seat. Lou leaned down by the open door to take a small blue tablet from a leather pouch and pop it into his mouth, "Ekkie, bro, to increase the sensations I am about to sensate. Give you one later, eh," and the two dark beings slunk off along the black street toward the dim light emanating through the floral curtains of the flat.

Bill waited. He was in a quandary. Could he should he do something to stop what sounded to him like an attack on a defenceless woman? *What the fuck should I do, what the fuck can I do?* It was, he recognised, a classic moment in an undercover agent's operational life. But that recognition, along with Kingi's counselling, his training at UTU, and his time with the psychs, reminded him through his own little rum-induced mist that he must simply await the outcome of what was unrolling before him. Don't second-guess, just wait, record, remember, and recall the aim, the bigger picture.

And so he moved the car in to the spot directed by Lou, quietly and without attracting particular interest. He noted that the target multi was somewhat isolated anyway, at the end of the dead-end, with swamp land to the front and side and an empty lot behind. He parked, reversing back under the blanketing cover of some mature willows on the edge of the swamp, turned off the car, and watched. As his night-sight improved he saw Lou and Pedro arrive at the flat's white picket fence. There were no car wrecks or feral dogs patrolling this proudly tidy dwelling. He saw Lou wait, crouched by the leafy Fijoa tree on the front boundary, as Pedro scouted around the back and side to ensure his commander would not be sprung. In the dim light of the back porch Bill could see that Pedro was still taking the occasional swig from the rum bottle he had nearly emptied in the car. With the thumbs up, he took his crouched position. Lou politely knocked on the front door, and then he entered after apparent invitation.

Bill sighed in relief, Lou's entry had appeared, from his distance of some 30 meters, to be non-confrontational. Maybe the talk in the car was just the booze, maybe the poor woman did have the dollars made from the drugs? Maybe?

But then he heard it, with the cars window down, a thin desperate scream of feminine terror and pain, clear in the black and silent night. Fuck! Fuck, what to do, what to fucken do? And even as he moved to leave the car, to go toward the event, instinctively unable to just sit and leave whatever the fuck was happening to happen, he knew that the operation was over. There was no way he could just sit back and watch this.

Then he saw a dark figure, a young slim teenage male coming from down the dark lane at the back of the flat running furiously toward the sound from the flat. And even before he could call in warning from beneath the canopy of trees where he now stood, shotgun in hand, he saw Pedro move and trap the young man. He tackled him, rolling over the top of him like a lion with a young springbok and, like a lion having made the kill, he saw Pedro drag his struggling victim by the head around to the rear of the flat.

Ok, no questions now. He was going to act even if it did fuck the entire operation up. His warrior instincts kicked in. The most obvious and vital danger was the mad cunt Pedro him first. And he ran silently, soft-soled shoes kissing through the lush grass. Approaching the rear edge of the flat he slowed to see, determined not to blunder in in rage-fed impatience. And it was his speed that saved the boy, for he was a boy, the 15 year-old son of Lou's victim. And even in that moment he could hear the woman of the house in a rhythmic sad-sob as Lou perpetrated some grunting, unseen primal savagery on her. Pedro, meanwhile, was playing with his kill. He straddled the wriggling, terrified boy who was hoarsely crying, gasping for life's-breath after being choked near to death. Pedro was distracted. He had his back toward Bill and was cutting the young man's clothes from his pubescent body with his razor-sharp knife in preparation of some unknown horror. That twisted violation would remain unknown because although it had formulated in Pedro's rotten psyche, the effect of a sawn-off shotgun's oaken barrel smashing against his temple effectively negated it, and all other conscious thought. Bill smashed Pedro from the struggling boy who rolled and sobbed in his own renewed terror at the dark figure now standing over him. "Keep still, keep quiet, mate, I am helping you, ok?" and the boy nodded hopefully, tears pulsing from his oxygen-starved, blood-reddened eyes. Pedro moaned, but his animal instincts fought to awake only to be dulled again by Bill's chopping kick to the back of his ugly head. The boy gasped, "My Mum, my Mum!" and Bill quickly stooped and said, "Listen to me, ok?" He nodded, realising that this man was on his side. "This is what I need you to do." The boy nodded again, standing now.

"Take this shottie and when I say, you fire it and keep firing it, ok?"

"Yea, but "

"Just listen, son. Fire it in the air. I am going to get these two pricks out of your life, but you have to help me."

"Yea, but Mum …"

"Son, listen" Bill whispered urgently. "I'm on your side, ok? We've got to do this my way ok?"

The boy nodded.

"I need you to shout like fuck, in fact like ten people, and fire that gun off and don't stop, make heaps of noise, ok, when I say."

"Ok." He nodded again. The young man took the gun.

Bill thought fast as adrenalin flooded him and overcome the alcohol, allowing decisions and actions to be formulated. "Ok, boy, well done. Your mum will be proud of you. It's going to be fine, son. Now quickly help me kick the shit out of this freak." And a short but happy shit-kicking party occurred on the multi's back lawn with Bill and the young bloke kicking the living crap out of Pedro Whetu, baddest mother-brother number three of the infamous Te Kuri gang. Then, as the kid started to enjoy rearranging Pedro's face, Bill spoiled the fun by picking Pedro up like a bag of manure and dumping him heavily face down by the side of the flat.

"Right, son, I'm going in to help Mum. Do not come in. Ok? Go back by the shed and start firing that shottie and start yelling and banging stuff, ok?"

The young man held out his slender paw. "Thanks, bro," he said, in scared bravado, and the two shared a quick bro shake.

Then the carnival began. "Boom!! Boom!!" The first two 12-gauge shotgun shells erupted into the quiet night in vicious, ear-smashing explosions, and neighbours cringed and turned off lights, lying with the kids down on the floor.

Bill pulled the old fashioned ceramic fuses from the fuse box on the back porch. The multi went black. Bill heard Lou call out from inside in high-pitched incoherent fear, unwittingly pin-pointing his exact location. In the dark, a silent invader with unimpaired night-vision entered the tiny lounge of the flat just as the ecstasy-fuelled rapist was pulling himself out of the bent body, brutally forced face-down over the back of the patched lounge chair. Lou had no night-vision, no awareness of his surroundings or the imminent danger. Lou's world exploded. Bill's side-swinging axe-kick whistled over the body of the bruised, weeping woman, and smashed Lou's nose flat against his cheek-bones in a star-burst of agony. Meanwhile, it sounded from the shotgun shots, and the banging and shouting outside, that an entire regiment of opposing forces was on the attack. As Lou fell yelping to the floor, blood spurting, Bill scooped up the woman. He carried her outside to her son like a bride across the threshold, and she modestly attempted to cover her ravaged nakedness by pulling her torn nightdress down over her legs. "Mum, Mum," the young man called, dropping the shotgun, cordite-scented smoke lazily curling from the twin stunted barrels. Mother and son embraced.

As she sobbed against her child in frantic relief, Bill spoke to her with desperation in his voice, "Ma'am, I am sorry I can't explain this now, I will one day just go now to the police station, tell them to call Superintendent Kingi Potiki, ok? Tell Mr Potiki that Frank's son sent you, ok? Kingi Potiki, got that? And Frank's son sent you."

She looked up at him with a confused and emotion-mottled face curtained by unkempt long dark hair. "Thank you, thank you, thank you."

"Just go now."

But before they could move a near-naked man exploded noisily into view out from the tiny front porch of the flat. It was Lou, pantless, bleeding and grunting. "Bro, bro, where the fuck are youse?" And before Bill could react the young boy did. He picked up the shotgun and fired it.

Now a sawn-off shotgun is a terrifying weapon. But being sawn-off, it does lose accuracy over several metres with the buckshot spreading wider and wider as the hot pellets hurtle out to bury themselves in the target. With the young bloke's excitement combining with the physics of the weapon, Lou Whetu was hit only with a dozen or so lead slugs. By that time he was some 20 metres away, hurtling in bowel-loosening fear toward the hopeful sanctuary of the black swamp. The fact that the white-hot rotating slugs buried themselves into Lou's fleshy arse saved his life and provided some poetic justice to mother and son.

As Lou slushed away through the dark swamp, Bill sent the victims on their way toward witness protection down the dark alleys of the housing estate.

Bill then picked up a loose white picket from the fence and proceeded to smack it forcefully against the soft tissue of his eyebrow and lip until rewarded with a trickle of blood. He bent to the faeces-scented, raggedly breathing body of Pedro and lifted him in a fireman's sling, awkward with the shotgun, and headed back to the car. He flung Pedro down on the rear seat, then quickly started it and moved darkly away before any brave local, or less likely in this no-go zone, a police car, came looking to see what the fuss was all about. Using the boundary roads he was able to skirt around the few acres to the rear of the swamp. Well away from the scene of the crime, Bill started a single periodic beacon-blast of air-horns to draw Lou back to the car. Sure enough, after half an hour, a stinking, half-naked, bleeding Lou crawled from the toxic mysteries of the swamp into the car's headlights.

Lou was a sobbing wreck, for although the ecstasy had increased the physical sense of perverted pleasure with the woman, the chemical reaction also exaggerated the sensory perception of pain. Bill ran down the flax and toi-toi-studded bank to the edge of the swamp in mock frantic relief.

"Thank fuck, Lou! Thank fuck, bro, you're OK. We was ambushed, mate, a whole fucken gang of them, shotties, fucken cunts, I smashed a few but they were too many, man."

Lou fell forward into Bill's arms, shattered, gasping. Drug-, exertion-, and injury-fucked, he croaked, "Billy, where's Pedro, bro?"

"He's ok, Lou, he's in the car, I managed to get him out, they jumped him first, mate. I think I got a couple with the shottie, man," Bill offered, as both staggered up the grassy knoll. Bill supported Lou as he struggled to the car, pulled the back door open and finally saw his little brother sleeping soundly, if somewhat messily, on the seat.

Lou Whetu sighed in relief. He stood up straight, staunch now, even with blood dripping off his peppered arse, and swamp juice dripping from his body. He turned to embrace Bill. Te Pakeha had proven that he was staunch also. And even as Bill shyly held his lower body away from Lou's shrivelled filthy nakedness, in the intimate moment, Lou said, "Billy, my bro, we the Te Kuri will never forget what you did for us tonight. Bro, consider yourself blood."

Chapter 33

For the life of me

On the last day in Broome Bill was ready.

He had surreptitiously recovered his money belt, wads of cash still enclosed, from beneath the mattress in the van. The girls discussed one last swim in the late afternoon before heading east toward the Northern Territory. They were to travel by night to avoid the shimmering heat of the day.

Bill had no intention of leaving with them. He had written the girls an affectionate, apologetic farewell during the week when alone in the shower block and now, as the girls happily fussed with the packing, he tucked the note into the glovebox of the old van. They left the caravan park an hour before sunset and drove the 100 metres to the beach. Bill, Inga, and Hana wandered down for a swim just as the sun began its slow descent below the distant, western horizon. They stood together in the tidal surge, thigh deep, and Bill, suddenly sad and affectionate, put both arms around their shoulders.

When the huge red globe had finally sunk he told the girls he needed to, "viseet ze leetle boys room, coo coo," and gestured back to the toilet block. The girls giggled at the idiocy of what he called his pigeon-Swiss. Bill kissed each of them on the cheek. They suspected nothing and stood together, relaxed, looking out to sea, two petite tanned figures in bikinis, while he innocently strolled back in the gathering darkness whistling low the old standard, "Now is the Hour."

As he reached the massage tent he saw it was closed and secured by rope knot. In the failing light he darted off the pathway, behind the tent and rolled under the back flap into the dark, jasmine-scented interior. His meagre possessions were in the van but with his Kalgoorlie cash strapped securely around his belly he had no real concerns about that loss, although he decided he would miss his boots. As he lay in the blackness, he reached a tentative hand back out under the flap and smoothed the sand disturbance his clumsy entry had caused.

Soon, people began to make their way back up the steps to the cliff-top. Finally, he heard the chattering Swiss misses pass by the tent, their lilting accent fading with their ascent up the stairs. Bill quietly gathered sheets and pillows from the massage tables and curled up on the floor in a comfortable bed. He heard the girls calling for him from the cliff-top for an hour or so after they discovered him gone. "Beell, Beell," they called into the night and his heart was momentarily sad but his body was glad. Finally, they either accepted his escape or perhaps had found the note because he heard the familiar chug of the Kombi fire up and then slowly fade away, east toward Derby, Kununurra, Katherine, Darwin, Switzerland and out of his life forever.

He slept then and dreamed of soaring above Cable Beach. He was free.

Chapter 34

Heartbreak Hotel

And so Bill was blood.

The events of that fateful night entered the folklore of the Te Kuri and, like dogs, loyalty was respected and reciprocated; although not so much from Pedro, who, if given the choice would have refused to be embarrassingly saved by Bill death before dishonour.

But Matu, the elder, the brother Bill had the least to do with, summoned him to the Island. There, in the bar and in front of the staunch and true, Bill was taken into Matu's embrace and welcomed as a true brother.

And, against all the rules of engagement for a deep-cover agent, Bill fell in love with Mere. There was just no avoiding the increasing mutual attraction between the two. After the kiss at the helicopter the taste and sensation and promise of those soft Polynesian lips he was caught; no way out.

He kept it from Kingi, knowing that even hinting at a burgeoning relationship with the sister of the operation's primary targets, and even perhaps a target herself, would attract disapproval to say the least! No way, he reasoned, late at night, trying and failing to sleep in the factory's dark, loft bedroom. In fact, Kingi might even pull him out. Yeah, he would. He would conclude the op immediately.

Bill convinced himself that he needed a bit of time to sort things out. He wanted to work through what was happening to him and whether there was perhaps some way out for him and his Portuguese Maori princess. Not that they had even consummated their intense draw to each other. Mere Lopes was Catholic. The guilt-based discipline had been ingrained by her mother as a young girl, and was enforced by the omnipresence of her fisherman grandfather, until his death of old age when she was thirteen. But aside from Mere's religious strictures, they had the problem of just being alone together. Theirs was a cautious, fearful romance played out under the watchfulness of Mere's family. Not only the close-knit, dangerous immediate family, but also the dozens of members of the extended family, as well as the gang minions.

For a while after the Hangi, their only contact was at tae kwon do. In the sessions, each found a reason to practise the closer, body-to-body holds. Hearts pumping, sly physical connections, a hand brushing here, a thigh pushing gently there, Mere as much a tease as Bill. He was often glad of the loose uniform as his masculine tension threatened to reveal all to lookers-on.

While he was distracted by the promise and risks brought by his feelings for Mere, the sat-nav device he had secreted onto the gang chopper had paid dividends. In the month that had passed since the Hangi, the chopper had made two late-night flights to the drug labs. On each of those flights, high above the earth in the black quiet of space, the telecommunication satellite silently tracked the tiny black bird from lift-off to landing. As quick as those descents were, in the wooded valley landing-zone near the hidden drug laboratory, Grizzly's violent manoeuvres did not confuse the mathematical accuracy of the technology. Kingi now had the coordinates of the gang's chemical wealth creation. The last piece of the jigsaw was in place; it was time to bring the operation to its conclusion.

Kingi described these recent advances to Bill late one night when sat in the tiny coms dungeon. He warmly congratulated his protégé, hinting at the expectation of huge success for the operation. "Two weeks," he told Bill. "Only two more weeks while resources are put in place, final plans drawn, logistics and communications prepared, movements and tactics rehearsed."

Kingi had permission from the highest levels of government, police and military to bring the fatal skills of the crack SAS squadron to the final mop-up. These cammed-up special-forces commandos would focus on the drug labs. Flown in close by Blackhawks, they would rappel under the darkness of night to the lab. They would then shift into violent action mode to quell any dissent from the ragged bunch that worked their foul shifts for the Te Kuri.

Meanwhile, back in Auckland, the long-desired attack on the island fortress was being planned to immaculate precision. It was to be by air, by sea and by land. The specialist squads of the New Zealand police had been tasked to execute the intended total dissembling of what had been for too long the nation's law enforcement's nemesis.

In the two-year operation, the young, untried agent had excelled all expectations except, perhaps, those of Kingi and Frank Peters.

And so Bill started to wonder if he could simply walk away from this woman. He agonised with the romantic certainty of his youth that surely she was his destiny. With an unrealistic, but testosterone-fuelled optimistic confidence, Bill decided that he must try to keep her. He sensed that if he did not, he would forever suffer the regret that he didn't try.

Then Mere's mother left for Portugal. Her uncle had passed away. He died of old age in a tiny, picturesque stone-walled village near the coastal town of Oporto, the home of the liquid velvet port wine. Mere could not accompany her as she was in the last week of exams. These exams were the culmination of four years' work, and would hopefully result in the delivery of the crisp parchment of her Bachelor of Laws (Honours) degree. Mere saw her mother off at the airport late that afternoon and then drove directly to the island.

There, radiant, she joined Bill and 30 or so other young people in a spirited and increasingly skilful work-out through the patterns of the martial art. As usual, Mere showered, changed and left before her tutor, since the bachelor would usually take advantage of the gang mummas' home cooking in the communal food hall.

But this time, soon after crossing the black waters of the ponds in the darkening evening, Mere switched off the lights and parked her little Jeep in the quiet of a side road. And she waited.

After 30 impatient minutes she saw the twin burn of the Mustang's headlamps come prowling across the dirt causeway and turn slowly onto the seal of the exit road. His thoughts totally on Mere, Bill saw the little Jeep's lights flick on and the CRV cruise out behind him with a cheeky double flash of high beam. His heart jumped. A sudden thrill of sexual expectation buzzed down his spine. He drove carefully off the main road and down a quiet cul-de-sac. Mere followed and pulled up behind him, lights off. He watched in the rear vision mirror; she got out; she was alone. She walked to the passenger door of the Mustang and Bill leaned over, flicking the lock up and pushing the heavy door ajar. And then she was in. Hair slick from the shower, musky perfume scenting the cabin, giggling happily at her own cunning, she was onto him like a cat. And the two young lovers met across the seat in a kiss with soft kisses and sighs. They kissed and caressed, increasingly hungrily, passionately, as Bill pulled her gently down with him on the red leather bench seat. The car radio accompanied the moment with the rhythms of black American soul. When finally, unwillingly, Mere pushed him away, and they lay, eyes only inches apart, they spoke quietly of their feelings; each surprised by the depth of emotion of that first true love. It was Bill who finally spoke the words almost involuntarily, questioningly: "I love you." Mere responded in feminine echo. And that was that. They agreed that night, lying together as the precious hours passed too quickly in the increasingly glass-misted car, and as a pale half-moon rose in its circumnavigation of the black night sky above, that they were to be together.

Mere spoke of her increasing unhappiness with her circumstances. She explained to Bill her origins. It was as if she needed to reveal all so that there would be no surprises for him. She spoke of her love for her brothers but her awareness of their

254

criminality. She spoke of her broken mother and the reason for the old woman's overbearing grief. Spoke of the tragic romance of the events that had robbed her of her gentle father. She spoke of her ruthless grandfather, and the mirroring now of those worst family traits, exposed in varying degrees of sophistication, in her three brothers. Bill let her talk. He let her cry, held her and comforted her, kissed her for long intense periods between the chapters of her life. She told all. And it was from that telling that he gladly realised that she knew little of him nothing.

Just that here he was. Training the gang's youth in tae kwon do; on the fringes of the gang but with no obvious, direct involvement. Now she sought to know about him. And that first night he chose caution, confirming only what she knew. Yes, he was training the kids, doing his bit. He had been introduced by Joe Tama. He told her nothing more. She was clearly relieved.

Mere was bluntly honest. She warned him that if he had been part of the fabric of her brothers' business their illegal activity then she would not, could not, have anything more to do with him. Bill could not be quite so honest. Not yet. And so when she pushed too hard, too close, he quietened her with kisses to distract her and change her focus.

In the early hours she suddenly remembered her date with the university examiner that day. The two of them made quick plans. "You must meet me tonight, Sweet," she said. She gave him the address of the harbourside mansion at Devonport where she and her mother had lived for ten years. Across the water from the old, lovingly restored, turn-of-the-century dwelling perched on the cliff-face, rose the steel-and-glass skyscrapers of the CBD. Devonport was the base for the nation's naval forces. The incongruous sight of massive, sleek-grey, slab-sided frigates sliding past the house on the blue waters of the city's famous harbour provided fabulous contrast to the thousands of yachts and power craft that skittered over that playground.

"Down the hill about 200 meters from the intersection is a small block of shops, you will see them on your left as you drive up. Park your big macho Stang behind them." He grinned his response. "You must walk up the hill until you are near the top. On the right there is an alley. It's dark and narrow, but a big boy like you should be alright," she giggled. "About 50 meters down our gate is on the harbour side, it's a wrought-iron side gate almost hidden by a big passionfruit vine. I will meet you there at ten tonight, Sweet, and don't be late or even your black belt won't save you," she teased.

They shared a long kiss and then she went gracefully back to the CRV. Bill sat in the dark car and waited until she purred away. Then, as the engine grunted into life, Bill shook his head in pleasure-clouded amazement at the turn of events and slowly made his way back to the factory.

Ten days left. That first night as he drove across the harbour bridge toward Devonport he found that he was nervous, tensing, with the multiple stresses. He had not yet lied to Kingi. But he was acutely aware and of his deception by omission. A man who trusted him implicitly; a man he respected enormously and from whom he was now keeping, suddenly, this immensely significant change of circumstance in the tapestry of the operational quilt. Earlier that night he had sat ensconced in the coms room during what were becoming increasingly intense briefings from Kingi as to how the operation would conclude. Day, date, and time, what he was to do and where he was to be, down to the exact minute. The impending closure of the operation now lent urgency to the rendezvous with his newfound love and forced his decision.

As he purred the old V8 off the interchange, down the gentle curving slope on the Northshore side, he knew that he must tell her who he was. He must explain to her what he had done, and why. He had to make clear the real consequences of his actions for her brothers and their gang. He had to lay it all on the line and trust his instincts about this woman. Not tonight though. He needed to know her better needed to time things right.

That night Mere greeted him again at the gate as promised. She was excited, so happy to see him. She led him quietly up into the old house and to her darkened room, candle-lit. Until midnight they lay together, enfolded around each other on her soft bed. And with conversation and kisses the two bonded intellectually, emotionally and physically.

It was that night that Mere made clear to him that he would need to wait for another time, and a better place, to engage with her in total physical connection. He concurred, of course, solemn and responsible, the best of honourable intentions. However, lacking total self-discipline in the closeness of the body-to-body caress, his hands irresistibly found their way under the warmth of her top and soon enjoyed, unrestricted, a sensual sojourn as they wandered around the curves of her femininity. As they talked, he stroked her back and shoulders and later, eventually cupped and nipple-rolled firm, bra-less breasts to her almost involuntary, semi-orgasmic moaned responses. But that was as far as they went that night and for many nights to follow.

During that endless week Mere effortlessly completed her final exams, having studied long and hard in the preceding months. Bill would meet her each evening at ten at the gate. The two would then lie together until the early hours of the morning when Bill would scurry away to the hidden Mustang and head back to the factory.

And finally then there was only one week, only seven days left. The forces of society's good had been gathered, briefed, and were ready. The Blackhawks had practised with the SAS troopers in night-vision goggles and light combat kit. They had rehearsed the rappel from hovering choppers in the bush at night. Four dark men at once in a rapid, vertical, flying-fox descent from the choppers on invisible ropes, like huge spiders dropping from the nest at night to the prey below. It would be a deadly delivery of the nation's elite military strike-force directly into the combat zone.

The police special units were also ready. The anti-terrorist squad had been formed decades before, at first in response to the perceived threat of international, fanatic terrorists. Ironically, the units were first tested when the French Army clumsily provided terror by bombing the Greenpeace vessel *Rainbow Warrior* in Auckland harbour.

The operational plan had been drawn, checked and rechecked. All was ready. Kingi briefed him. "Phase one, Bill, is to execute the entry. The first armed officers will land on the island's helipad at 0500 hours on Sunday morning. Two minutes from the Go, two troop-carrying hovercraft, which we have seconded from the airport's rescue service, will make their way across to the island, up its banks and it will crash through the boundary fence, delivering our men." Bill nodded, entranced, impressed by the scope of the effort. "Meanwhile, my boy, a converted, ex-army Bedford ten-tonne truck, fitted with a massive bull bar will be charging well, let's say crawling down the causeway. This truck will crash the two causeway perimeter gates. From the rear of the truck 20 armed officers of our elite Armed Offenders Squad and the squad's five alsatians will be let loose as a roving reserve.

"Phase two is the securing of the scene," Kingi continued. "With all the troops on the ground, the anti-terror boys will secure the headquarters, and the team-police will hit the village." Kingi used the police's colloquial name to describe the sprawl of accommodation for the gang minions. The 'village' included a jumble of cabins, caravans, tents and trucks. "Our team-police will round up all adults, barring nursing mothers, and march them off to the parade square. At the same time, the armed offenders squad officers and the dogs will float as trouble-shooters, so to speak." Kingi paused and Bill nodded his understanding of the structure of the raid. "Once the island is seized and all persons within controlled, we move into phase three, the processing.

"This will bring a convoy of ten police buses down the causeway with 100 fully-briefed, uniformed inquiry officers aboard. Each adult member of the gang will be processed on site by our mobile unit. All adults will be handcuffed with plastic bonds, photographed, fingerprinted and identified by name. He or she will then be removed from the scene by the assigned officer, sat on the bus with that officer and taken back to the major police stations in the district for interview and arrest.

"That's basically it, my boy," the old warrior concluded with a tired smile. Clearly, Bill thought to himself, the culmination of the two years was to be a massive, incisive operation. The qualified but confident expectation was for total success. Kingi was happy, "It's all come together beautifully, son. And that's thanks to you."

Nothing could go wrong now.

Bill had made his decision. For eight nights now they had met, talked, kissed, loved and bonded. He knew it was right and she told him it was right. It had been Mere who had suggested that they simply disappear, elope. "Sort of history repeating itself," she said, "just as my mother and father did so many years ago." They talked about where they could go, what they would do. She spoke of finding legal work. With the confidence of an A student she knew that she had passed — easily passed — her exams. "And you have no ties, my sweet, right?" He had only fed her snippets over the time of a father still alive and living "up north" and a mother "working in the States".

And so it was Mere who made it not easy, but possible. She set it up for him to tell her. And he left it to the Friday night, 30 hours out from the *go!* the command from Kingi that would mark the beginning of the end of the operation.

Again they lay close on her soft bed in the darkened bedroom, close now to his midnight departure. And he reluctantly pulled back from her soft, full-lipped kiss and was suddenly serious, and tense. "Babe, I need to tell you about me. All about me," he said, and she knew that this was to be a revelation. Mere had, she must admit, become a little concerned by Bill's vagueness when she had sought to firmly establish his story, his origins, over the last week or so of increasing and comfortable intimacy. She had put his apparent reluctance to open up down to shyness or male reserve, but was mildly disappointed that she had told him all and so far he had given back very little. She had determined to keep working on him as a life's project. And she had decided that they must run away together. She had to get away from this life in which she was so very unhappy. Mere now saw only a future with Bill. "I have been waiting for this moment, my sweet," she teased.

"Mere, what I am going to say is going to shock you. It may upset you," he paused, a quiver in his voice. "Please don't make any immediate decisions. Please believe that I truly do love you. And I want to be with you forever."

She stiffened in anticipation. "Tell me," she breathed, wondering at his secret.

"Mere, I will be as honest now as you have been with me. Totally honest with you."

She nodded and stared deep into him.

"Babe," he said softly, holding her eyes with his, "I am a cop, an undercover agent."

There was a very pregnant pause then.

"I have been working on the gang, on your brothers, for two years now."

She inhaled sharply.

"It's all about to finish and your brothers and the gang are finished, they're over. And I have done that."

She went rigid, breathless. He held her still but was uncertain, waiting as she pulled back from him but only minutely so she could again read his face. "Remember what I said. I truly love you and want us to be together." He pleaded, worried now.

Mere Lopes was an intelligent woman. After the shock of the meaning of the words, her analytically-trained mind very quickly dissembled and examined the nuances, consequences, and possibilities brought with this information. She considered her own beliefs and expectations. And Bill, that moment frozen forever in time, misinterpreted her reaction with an immense gut-sinking realisation that he, and perhaps the entire operation, was now in trouble.

Then Mere leaned forward on the bed and kissed him.

"Thank you, Bill — now, is it Bill?"

He nodded.

She continued. "I also love you, and I want to be with you." She pulled him in closer and for ever it seemed, they didn't talk. Only entwined themselves desperately closer against each other's body. And even with the emotion of the moment he was aware of the feminine shape and feel of her body against his. It was Bill this time who pulled away though only to talk seriously.

"Sunday morning, Mere, the curtain comes down. The entire gang, most of the adults anyway, will be taken away, interviewed, and most of them charged. Your brothers will all be locked up. For a long, long time." He paused. "I want to get you out of here."

"What do you want me to do?" she asked, trusting and accepting him to his amazement and joy. "I want you to take the Mustang on Saturday shit, that's today," he realised, as the clock had ticked over midnight. "Take it and drive to my father's house at Opononi up north." She nodded. "I want you to stay with him until I am finished down here. I will get up there as soon as I can."

"How long will that be, do you think?" she asked softly.

"Well, they'll use me to front all the key gang guys in the interviews, including your bros," he said. "That will take a day or two. After that I will get away and join you and Dad." He kissed her. "Will you do it, babe?" He didn't wait for her answer. "Then as soon as we can, we will go. I will have a ton of money from the op, we can go anywhere in the world you want, together." Then, with some emotion, he said, "Mere, I am asking you to marry me."

With a tear rolling softly down her cheek, she said, "Yes. I accept, first to be your wife and also to do as you ask."

With that, the minor details were arranged. Bill gave Mere the car keys and wrote down the exact detail of his father's address in a scrawled mud-map.

"I have thought about it over the last few days, and I reckon the Mustang is the best car for you to take. If your CRV is still at the house they might just think you're at uni. They probably won't miss you for a little while. What do you think?"

"I'm in your hands, Bill" she said, smiling now with anticipation of the adventure. They organised that Mere would pack, leaving a letter for her mother's return, although that was not for some weeks. They agreed that Mere would leave for Opononi, three hours north, early that Saturday morning before any hint of action at the gang headquarters. Bill would catch a taxi back to the factory. If he had to explain to Kingi where the Mustang was he would say he had it in for a service. That would be the very least of Kingi's concerns at this time and Bill knew he would accept his explanation, no questions asked.

So, in the early hours of Saturday morning, Bill left the house. He kissed Mere farewell, murmuring, "until we meet at Dad's house in a few days". He savoured the taste of her lips, her mouth. Then in the dark coolness of the early hours he trotted cautiously down the hill into the trendy village of Devonport. He went to a phone box and from memory rang the series of numbers that connected him to the curious, sleepy voice of his father.

"Dad, it's me," he said. "Dad, just listen please," he interrupted as his father responded with joy and surprise to hear from his son after two long years of third-hand messages. "The operation is finishing tomorrow, Sunday, it's all ok, I'm ok, but I need you to do some things."

His father became immediately serious, concerned. He knew that something was wrong, something was up; the agent didn't break cover just before the operation concluded. "Ok, tell me, boy."

"Dad, I know it sounds crazy but I've fallen in love, I need her to — her name's Mere — I need her to come up and stay with you until I can get up there. Is that ok?"

"Yes. Of course, Bill."

"I can't say too much more just now Dad. Please don't tell Kingi about this. Everything's ok, it's just that I need to get Mere out of the way. I will clear it all with Kingi myself."

"Ok, boy, you sure it's all ok?"

"Yes, Dad, don't worry, she will be up probably about midday today, driving a black Mustang, my car, her name's Mere, we are going to get married, Dad. Please look after her for me will you and I will be up probably about Tuesday, maybe Wednesday."

"Ok Bill, are you sure you're ok?"

"Yeah, Dad, couldn't be better, just need you to look after my girl and I will explain it all when I see you."

"Love you boy."

"Love you, Dad. See you soon."

Chapter 35

Gypsy Woman

Bill woke with a smile on his face. He had had a deep, satisfying sleep, comfortable on the soft Persian carpet in the massage tent on the beach. He sighed and then rolled over, and it was then that he realised that the constant state of alertness had deserted him. Because, as he rolled over his face met those two perfect, leather sandal-ensconced, sun-tanned feet.

He slowly raised his eyes up along the shapely calves to the hem of the purple sarong and finally up to the amused features of Gypsy, the masseuse. She sat in a fold-up canvas chair obviously having patiently awaited his return from nod.

"Morning," he offered guiltily and she smiled a broad grin of delight and replied, "And good morning to you, sleeping beasty. To what do I owe this pleasure?"

"So sorry, Ma'am. I am a poor but honest traveller who was lost in the cold night and sought shelter from the cruel elements. I do hope you don't mind?"

"So have you lost your two pretty companions?" she asked and giggled at the look on his face.

"My two warders, you mean. That's a long story."

"Never mind, you do have an honest face although not an honest colour of hair," she laughed.

"That's a brief chapter in the long story," he advised and then rose and tidied the sheets and pillows while she set about opening the tent for the day's trade. She offered him tea from the large vacuum flask she had brought with her, to last the day he supposed, and he accepted thankfully with the dry mouth of the heavy sleeper. She wouldn't expect a customer this early, they usually arrived late morning after sleeping in at the luxury resort nearby.

So over the sweet tang of the chamomile tea, "good for PMT," she educated, Bill spoke to the gorgeous woman he had admired from afar each day as she plied her trade to the tourists on the beach.

He had been attracted to her petite but muscular, tanned body a cross between a power lifter and a ballerina, he had decided. Each day she displayed upon that body a variety of minute thong bikinis that had him captivated and, he was certain, ensured a regular flow of middle-aged male clients into the mystery of the massage tent. Bill found that she was relaxed with him, having observed the unusual threesome over the past week.

"I am a masseuse," she told him. "I trained in sports massage, but I fell for a Broome boy, a pearl farmer a few years back." Tommy worked away at sea on a seasonal basis, either harvesting the wild pearl shell along the coast or tending to the aquatic farming of the captured and seeded shell.

Gypsy had chosen not to be with him at sea although that had been their original idea.

It was not until the first season after she had moved from Perth, when they had set out from Broome port's long wharf, provisioned for a three-month stay at the farm 50km north, that she discovered a rude truth. She suffered chronic seasickness even in conditions of dead calm. Tommy had kindly although under threat of painful death turned the tender around after only half an hour steaming and had dropped his pale bride-to-be back onto terra firma at Broome.

Since then, while he was at sea, Gypsy ("no really, it is my real name hippy parents") spent her days rubbing and kneading bodies that needed rubbing. Her clients were both tourists and locals who chose to avail themselves of the sensual, healing treat.

Then she asked his story, and he was colourful but grossly dishonest in a tale that took him from Perth with the two Swiss girls on a working holiday around Australia as their English language translator, paid for by their rich parents. She sought no detail or explanation anyway, as the town of Broome traditionally welcomed such itinerant travellers.

When the big German Bill had seen the previous day stumped down the cliff-side steps, Gypsy shuddered and breathed an, "Oh, no." Bill quickly inquired as to that reaction. She told him of the obese man's suggestions and obvious physical response to her work. As the week went on he grew bolder and more forceful in his broken English requests for her to provide a helping hand with a small but growing problem. She told Bill that it was an occupational hazard and she had ignored the man's uninvited attentions but clearly she was not relishing his return.

That is when Bill made himself if not indispensable, certainly handy, to Gypsy. He volunteered to stay while the big kraut was being tenderised and she gladly agreed. The German was clearly not happy that Bill was about but apart from an occasional mutter of bad temper he behaved during Gypsy's work. It was while Gypsy was hammering away in an attempt to reach nerve and muscle through the German's impressive layer of blubber that another piece in the jigsaw of coincidence fell into place for Bill.

As he sat peacefully in the canvas chair, one eye on the German, the other out on the water, an elderly local female client of Gypsy's wandered in from the nudist beach for her weekly treat. Old Mavis had lived on-and-off in Broome for five years now after a late-life divorce from a cranky, old, retired public servant husband. Mavis had joined the march of the grey nomads. These were older, retired people who were a feature of the north-west and the tropical areas as they wandered the continent in 4WDs, campervans and sometimes, renovated buses. Mavis had sold her unit in Sydney and to the horror of her grown children and renewed conviction of her ex-husband that "the old bitch is mad", had bought a converted bus. Now for the last five happy years Mavis had roamed the nation, always returning in the dry season to her favourite spot Broome. One of her favourite people was Gypsy and once a week she treated herself to the young woman's healing touch as they chatted on the mysteries of life and the bastardry of men.

Bill quickly stood for Mavis and she gratefully lowered her wiry, 70 year-old frame onto the canvas chair. Then, with a glint of mischief in her eye, Gypsy introduced Bill as her trainee masseur and to his horror, arranged Mavis on a table and flipped a dark blue bottle of sandalwood-scented oil into his hands.

Mavis lay there, face down, modestly dressed in an old-fashioned bikini, the bottoms of which she was carefully rolling down and tucking between her withered buttocks, awaiting his attention. Bill realised that any further delay would only exacerbate his embarrassment. He could see Gypsy's delight at his predicament out of the corner of his eye as she flipped Mr Berlin over for attack on a beer belly that spoke of many Octoberfests. Nervously, Bill smeared the first thin coat of oil onto Mavis's leg.

It was strange, he thought, but he quickly found the exercise of massaging this wonderful elderly woman to be an absolute pleasure. She chatted away to him and across to Gypsy as she finished up with the German who, by now, was relaxed if not relieved. Bill found that although he had no real idea what he was doing the natural instinct of touch was guided by Mavis's responses as to how hard, how soft, how brisk or how slow he should rub her aged but fit chassis, and this allowed him to stumble through. Gypsy watched with a professional interest from the chair and then from time to time stood and showed him a technique, a stretch, a manipulation, while Mavis basically fell asleep into a fog of sensual enjoyment and relaxation. They left her sleeping when Bill finished and Gypsy tenderly covered her in a warm towel.

"I think you've got it, Mister; the touch," she teased, but with an impressed undertone. Then Mavis awoke and insisted on paying although Bill and Gypsy tried to refuse as the apprentice completed the lube. It was when Mavis told her that she was off to tell the girls at the caravan park about her new young masseur, and then booked an appointment for herself at the same time the next morning "with Bill please" that Gypsy offered him training and a job.

When he suggested that she not pay him but allow him to sleep nights in the tent, they sealed it with a hand-shake, her tiny hand disappearing into his. Bill's new career was born.

Chapter 36

Ring of Fire

"Alpha leader to all units: Operation Neuter is Go! Go! Go!"

Detective Superintendent Kingi Potiki's deep voice crackled across the airwaves in a scrambled code on restricted frequency at 4.50am, Sunday 13th December. Located at various positions, the message was acknowledged by operational team leaders in turn.

"Bravo leader copies, 10-2."

This response came from the inspector in charge of the anti-terrorist squad aboard the Pol-Air 1 chopper. The chopper had lifted off from its base at Ardmore aerodrome in South Auckland with its specialist five-man, armed squad half an hour earlier, and was now circling at 3000 feet above the island. With thumbs up to the pilot and then to his squad seated back-to-back on the canvas, combat slings behind him in the green-lit cabin, the Inspector pointed down. And the pilot slipped her sideways and down in a gentle arc toward the gang fortress's helipad.

"Charlie leader copies, 10-2."

This from the armed offenders squad inspector, a sinister figure in dark blue coveralls and kevlar body armour, and black balaclava under riot helmet. He was in charge of a squad of 20, and the five canine weapons of peace. The O/C grunted his "Go!" to the driver of the Bedford. The diesel turbo roared into gruff life and growled out from its hiding place in a disused factory off the access road. The big machine lurched away on oversized tyres up toward the island.

"Delta leader copies, 10-2."

This response was barked back by the chief inspector in charge of the tactical response group. His team, drawn from the district's highly-trained crowd-control unit, comprised 50 super-fit police officers of both sexes. The anonymous, helmeted officers were now incongruously seated in the luxury, air-conditioned cabins of the two hovercraft. The rescue crafts' fan engines had been warming on a concrete ramp a short five-minute fan-propelled hover from the island. At the signal, the big machines lurched upward lifting their heavy rubber skirts and air cushions and powering heavily over the water towards their destination.

"Zulu leader copies, 10-2."

This came from 200 kilometres south at 3000 feet. In two Blackhawk choppers sat the army's elite SAS troopers in eager anticipation of some rare peacetime action. Amongst them were those who prayed for an armed response from their quarry, and with the sudden dip of the chopper and acceleration into the dive, the special forces men as one smiled a deadly grin under their night vision hoods.

"Alpha leader to good shepherd: collect the lamb, over."

And with that order, the factory suddenly filled with the sights and sounds of a major, organised raid, with police cars, lights and relentless, piercing sirens announcing the end of the status quo. With gates crashed and doors kicked in, one Bill Peters, a.k.a. Bill George, emerged, handcuffed and escorted somewhat roughly into a police van to be whisked away.

And so the day of reckoning began.

As gang members slumbered in their warm beds, a seagull's view of the island would have shown a coordinated gate-crashing of the compound. As the chopper sank to the tarmac the two huge hovercraft breasted the bank. The behemoths simply barrelled through the mesh fencing like whales through a herring net, disgorging determinedly organised blue-clad figures. Meanwhile, at full revs the Bedford van noisily smashed down the two front gates.

The early morning peace was well and truly shattered. The resistance of the gang was brief and stupid. The two men on the gate, distracted by the descent of the alien chopper and blinded by the white heat of its spotlight, were then totally confused by the sight and sound of the hovercraft attacking from the rear, and the monster truck from the front, its massive headlights blinding them from the causeway when the big outer gate suddenly fractured and disappeared before their eyes. Up in their guardhouse, high on the inner gate, they did two things. One of them hit the kennel release switch and the gang's pit-bulls were freed as a pack into the no-man's land between the two boundary fences. And the other man fired his shotgun at the huge white beast that was surging forward over the shambles of the outer gate. If he had lived, his defence to the firearm charges would have been that in the darkness and confusion, with noise in front, behind, and above, he had no idea who the fuck the invaders were. His problem was that the truck kept coming. The lead shot only kissed the armour plate of the windscreen as the vehicle's massive bull-bar connected to the main gate, catapulting the guardhouse backward from a height of 20 feet as that gate responded to the laws of physics and deconstructed. Now, if a person falls properly he can survive a fall from that height. But both guards arrived at ground level at about the same time as 12 salivating, snarling American pit-bull terriers. These hungry, territorial beasts, suitably excited, came bounding toward the commotion. The dogs did what attack dogs do. They attacked. And their targets lay stunned and broken from the fall. A pit-bull is bred to fight; bred to kill. The men were easy pickings. Three of them fought over the throat of the shotgun man, tearing and ripping through flesh and cartilage in a fatal efficiency. The second man lived, but would never dance again. He wisely stayed in the crashed structure of the small guardhouse where it lay shattered. He screamed and kicked at the tearing pack as they tried to help him out of the sanctuary. And by the time 20 precisely aimed police gunshots cracked out into the night, the dogs had removed most of the muscle mass from his flailing lower legs. The armed offenders squad knew of the feral dog pack kept by the gang. So with that barrage of lead they set back the Te Kuri's breeding programme forever. The shocked gang members offered no other serious resistance. Only scattered attempts to fight, and foolish attempts to run difficult against highly trained, motivated, fit and well-equipped members of the special forces. For a few minutes these isolated struggles provided hysterical activity with coldly intent police officers and snarling, determined police dogs. Effectively and efficiently the combined forces quickly and, where necessary, brutally, took control of the dazed occupants of the village.

Within 30 action-packed minutes, phases one and two of the police operation were concluded. Then, with the scene commander on site and his men in total control, down the causeway came the convoy of bus-loads of inquiry officers. These investigators removed the sullen male adults from the island as a priority, and then the protesting, cranky women. The children of arrested gang members screamed for their mothers and fathers, but were gently diverted, tear-streaked and snotty-nosed, to another fleet of buses by soft-spoken social workers.

Each police investigator had been assigned a gang member as a suspect. A suspect file, detailing identification, allegiances, and evidence of crimes committed, had been painstakingly prepared. Senior and experienced investigators had been assigned the senior and experienced criminals. Virtually each and every adult male and many of the womenfolk of the gang had, through the evidence gathered by the operation, been identified as being party to major criminal conspiracies. These crimes had then been converted into charges by the operation's Queen's Counsels.

Each adult was formally identified at the scene, then photographed in-situ, tagged, handcuffed and finally led away to the buses by the assigned investigator. Each bus, with its ill-matched pairs aboard, then headed off for a formal, video-taped interview. The questions and more importantly the answers had been thoroughly prepared by the best legal minds available to prevent any of the rotten fish slipping the net.

Throughout that morning the island's population emptied out as if so many turds gurgling down a toilet bowl. The most senior of the gang, Matu and Louis Whetu, alternated from furiously silent to loudly demanding lawyers. Joe Tama and other highly-placed personnel stayed in the clutches of small specialist investigative teams and witnessed the initial search. This search included the sniff work of the force's dogs. The dogs methodically worked a grid of the entire property in a search of drugs, firearms, explosives and concealed property. The processing of the human elements of the gang was to take several days. The physical search included a court-authorised deconstruction, brick-by-brick, of the island's entire collection of buildings, and the digging up of selected areas of top-soil, and took ten days.

There was no way that Kingi meant to miss this opportunity, and their endeavours produced major finds that added to the success of the undercover agents' results. Secreted goodies including many hundreds of thousands of dollars of black money, caches of cannabis plant and oil, bricks of heroin and cocaine, and plastic-wrapped bundles of amphetamines and other drugs were located in what would have been otherwise undetectable hiding places. Police officers crawled into century-old underground cesspits to find hidden shotguns, automatic rifles, pistols, explosives, and ammunition tucked away deep in the shit. By surveyors' measurement and mathematical analysis it was found that the huge limestone blocks of the headquarter building were found to contain false walls. These, when torn apart, revealed vaults. The vaults had provided storage areas for vast collections of illegal drugs and cases of money violently obtained.

That first morning Kingi finally came down to the scene around midday, crunching into the carpark through the shattered remains of the main gate. He got out of the car with two of his intelligence agents and surveyed the bustle of activity. Kingi was happy, very happy. Word had come in from the coromandel earlier that the SAS incursion was a total and faultless success. The gang personnel at the bush lab had, as usual, sampled their own chemical products that night before. They avoided being wasted by being wasted when the troopers woke them by pressure of serrated daggers against dry and terrified throats. The suspects at that lab were quickly taken into custody, and even as he strode about the island compound now, Kingi knew that the forensic and investigative team were on the ground recording and gathering evidence.

Kingi's late arrival at the fortress was not only due to his coordinating role at the HQ, he had also taken the time to spend an hour with his young agent and friend. When Bill had been 'arrested' earlier that morning, he had been taken directly to a police safe-house outside the city, temporarily tenanted by several armed and dangerous officers. Kingi greeted him affectionately at the luxurious, secluded property where he would be housed, fed and pandered to for as long as both he and Kingi decided was necessary. They sat in the spacious lounge-room and drank a celebratory coffee while Kingi briefed Bill on what was about to take place.

"Ok, son, first thing is that you will undergo a debrief with the intel guys and the psychs. That's scheduled to begin here later today, ok?"

Bill nodded in response, enjoying the filtered coffee and the realisation of impending freedom.

"We need you to be available for the next two days at least to make a few sudden guest appearances at interviews, etcetera, particularly those of the major players," Kingi said. Bill knew from earlier briefings that the introduction of the undercover agent into an interview at a crucial time was a technique sparingly used, but often with devastating effect. When denying a line of questioning about nefarious historical circumstances that only the offender and a select few could know about, Kingi had found the revealing of the police agent could simply destroy a suspect's ego and confidence. This was particularly so when the more confident and determined major players were involved. And as the two men finished the first of innumerable cups of coffee to be drunk on that day of victory, Bill knew that in cold, intimidating, windowless rooms in South Auckland police stations, specialist teams of detectives would be starting the clinical work of interviewing the Whetu brothers. There was only one small problem with the operation.

One brother had gone AWOL.

"It had to be the mad one," Kingi muttered to Bill. And not only was Pedro Whetu missing, but the gang's chopper and old Grizzly the pilot had not yet been found. The sat-nav tracker had done its job by pinpointing the bush drug lab, but for some unknown reason had stopped broadcasting its signal a week ago. This was not unknown with such devices and did not necessarily mean that it had been detected. In fact, with no change of behaviour by the gang, Kingi was satisfied that they had not found the device. More likely was that it had fallen off due to the constant vibration of flight, or that the tiny battery had faded. The immediate concern, however, was where the fuck was Pedro?

A nationwide APB alert had gone to police and customs and Kingi felt confident that the chopper would be found soon. Already the police media relations personnel had been on morning television explaining the necessity for and the success of the operation. They spoke with a certain air of professional satisfaction about this fine example of the effectiveness of the local law enforcement. It didn't seem necessary to mention the fact that on many previous occasions they had been left red-faced by the legal victories of the gang in the civil and criminal courts. News broadcasts that morning flashed up photographs and descriptions of Pedro and of the chopper and all over the country the eyes of good citizens were looking up.

They never found Pedro, Grizzly, or the chopper. What had happened was that on that Saturday morning Pedro had decided to replenish the gang's wild pork stores.

Pedro in particular enjoyed the dark tang and fibrous texture of the meat of the wild pig. But he also enjoyed, more than most mortals, the stench and sounds of the close-in kill. And Pedro had always thought, "what's the use of owning a fuckin chopper if you don't use it?" So every now and then he would rustle up Grizzly, load his pit-bulls into the chopper's cabin, much to his brothers' subsequent disgust, and they would head deep into pig country.

Grizzly, after the blood and guts of Vietnam, was not one for hunting. But he was happy to be a servant of the gang. He had found security and worth in the gang after the damage caused by his time in south-east Asia.

So that Saturday, very early, Pedro had dragged Grizzly away from his hugely obese but cuddly and warm Polynesian wife and the two headed off without telling anyone else where they were off to or for how long. This was not unusual for Pedro and if he had been needed the chopper carried all the latest communication gear. On this occasion they went north up into the pine forests of the Kaikohe. They travelled past Auckland then tracked up the west coast toward the northern tip of the island, putting down eventually in an isolated bush valley where Pedro had hunted successfully for some years now.

Grizzly knew that Pedro needed this release. He was one of the few people who almost understood Pedro, having seen men like him in Nam, men with a lust for blood.

After landing in a tiny, grassed clearing, Grizzly set up the bivouac. He threw a camouflage net over the chopper's rotors to avoid attention from the local police cannabis-plantation detection flights, but also to pin down the rotors and the chopper in case of inclement weather. While Pedro hunted with his dogs, carrying only his lethal, razor-sharp boning knife, Grizzly relaxed in the camp in quiet contemplation, reading and writing poetry. From time to time Pedro would grunt back into camp, increasingly fouled by sweat, guts and blood, humping on bent shoulders the still-steaming gutted carcasses of young wild pigs. Grizzly noted that Pedro silently revelled in his destruction of the life force. He suspected that this was Pedro's substitute to ending human life. That night they feasted on butter-fried pig heart and onion, and char-grilled fillet and beans, and later slept, warm in sleeping bags under the clear, star-filled sky.

It was on the Sunday, with Pedro again wandering the valleys in murderous search, that Grizzly heard the news about the island on the chopper's radio. Impatient and anxious, he waited until Pedro returned with the day's first victim. He was repelled by Pedro's feral stench as the gore-encrusted maniac had not bathed since his bloody endeavours the day before. As Grizzly relayed the news, he saw a furious and frightening rage grow in Pedro. Pedro was rat-cunning though, and for the next few hours he tried to establish what had happened back at the island. They relied on news broadcasts on the commercial radio stations. The two men listened impatiently to the official police version of events and analysis by journalists as the massive operation was dissected. Pedro learnt that the raid had resulted from the successful implant of an undercover police agent into the gang. Increasingly furious, Pedro quizzed the now very nervous Grizzly about any suspicions he may have had as to who that agent could have been. In the meantime they decided to stay put.

Pedro considered trying to contact his brothers using the chopper's communication equipment but Grizzly warned him that if he broadcast they may be tracked.

From time to time Pedro lost his calm and poise. He strutted about the tiny bush camp shouting precise, anatomically-related obscenities, kicking and knocking over what few possessions they had. He stabbed and slashed the pig carcasses in his blind rage. And even the pit-bulls, which instinctively recognised a dominant and more dangerous creature, whined and cringed out of his way.

By the time they listened to the news the next day it was clear that the gang's life as an organisation was over. There were gloating reports and interviews with the nation's top police and legal fraternity explaining the years of planning, and boasting vaguely as to the scope of the evidence gathered. Although the matter was sub-judice the opinion was that the investigation had been able to uncover a conspiracy of such depth and breadth that the gang was to be no more.

The other matter of direct interest was that a healthy cash reward was offered to anyone who could help locate one Pedro Whetu and the black Bells Ranger helicopter, registration "Tango Kilo 666".

Late that night, seated in the chopper in the pitch black, Pedro finally worked it out. A police spokesman carelessly alluded to the Te Kuri's Achilles' heel "the fencing of stolen property" and even though the hint was vague Pedro knew immediately that the rogue agent was Bill. In the cold fury of his insanity he swore that night that he would avenge his family. He would destroy Bill, as long as it took.

Meanwhile, the target of Pedro's murderous intent was going about his business. All that Monday and Tuesday Bill was kept busy with command performances. As an investigative team reached a vital point in an interview, Bill would be invited into the room to front the gang member who believed they had known this Judas as a friend, even as a 'bro'. Due to his training and the psychological support at the operation's close, Bill found, quite to his surprise at first, that somehow he had maintained his perception of his place in these events. He had grown close to some of the gang, particularly to some of the young people he had trained in tae kwon do. The people he had been closest to were the most devastated when he revealed his true identity to them. Most of these gang members were particularly destroyed by his cold, professional manner. His unwavering gaze conveyed his equally unwavering belief that he had done right, and that they had done wrong.

Joe Tama in particular was shocked beyond belief. Joe was so shamed by his close association with Bill, that he became clinically depressed in the maximum-security prison that was to be his home for life. He was aggressively shunned by all his old friends who also shared the close confines of Her Majesty's cold complex. One year later, Joe was an easy and almost receptive target for the primitive shiv that was pushed deep into his liver from behind in the steam of the communal shower block. As the never-to-be-identified assailant slipped quietly away from his pooling blood, Joe died.

Bill, though, was happy. He did his job over those two days, and Kingi stayed with him at all times as the operation moved through the arrest phase and into the prosecution phase. Kingi stayed at the safe-house. And the two talked into the early hours as he deliberately de-briefed and repeatedly congratulated and thanked his young charge. It was during this time that Bill discovered that the Whetu mother and sister had not been considered targets. He found this out from Kingi himself late on Tuesday night after sly, surreptitious digs for information as the two dissected the events of the past two years.

When Bill's heart leapt in his chest at that snippet he plucked up the courage to tell Kingi all.

"Sir, I have a confession that I need to make to you that I don't think you are going to be too pleased about."

"Now that wouldn't be about young Mere Lopes, would it, son?" Kingi asked, po-faced.

Bill was speechless. "Wha " he stuttered.

"Young man, I appreciate your belated confession. But I have known for some time what was going on there."

"Shit! you knew?"

"Yes, son," Kingi smiled, enjoying Bill's discomfort. "The reason we discounted the mother and the sister from the gang's unlawful activities is that for several years we have had the ladies' house bugged."

Sudden dawning. "So you knew I was with her there?"

"Yes, son and I decided that we would run with it. In fact the time you spent with that young lady further cleared her and her mother from suspicion and involvement."

And Bill remembered the long, honest and emotional discussions about her brothers' criminal activity. "And the Mustang?" Bill queried.

"Of course son, an audio bug and a sat-nav tracker were there just in case for your own safety, of course."

Bill felt foolish, caught out. Apart from his love talk being heard and recorded, Kingi must have heard him exposing the entire operation to Mere that last night. What must he have thought? "Sir, I am so sorry, it was just suddenly out of control," he began.

"Don't worry, son, I trusted you. I knew that the two of you did have something going. And I made the decision to watch and listen. And look, it's worked out! So tomorrow you and I can take that drive north. You to see Miss Lopes and me to catch up with your Dad."

"Jesus, Sir, I'm lost for words."

"Good. Let's sleep on that, boy, and hopefully we can get away by midday."

278

Although mortified by his realisation that his verbal lovemaking to Mere had been listened to, recorded and dissected by Kingi and probably others in the operation, he was also massively relieved by the turn of events. Mere was in the clear, he was in the clear and he would be on his way to see her that next day. Eventually, sleep took him away.

The following day, late in the afternoon, Kingi and Bill extricated themselves from the operation and with Kingi at the wheel of the plain police Commodore, they headed north.

Bill was three short hours away from two of the people closest to him. He hadn't telephoned his father yet. Initially, that was because he hadn't known that Kingi knew of his relationship with Mere. And then it was because Kingi told him that he had spoken to his father and that the message was, "not to worry, Mere was there, she had arrived safely and his father could see why his son was so besotted".

They were to be three endless hours of pure, joyful anticipation.

Meanwhile, Pedro had been busy.

With no future in New Zealand and no intention of surrendering to the authorities, Pedro had finally broken radio silence and on short-wave had made contact with old family ties in the fishing industry. By threat and promise Pedro made his arrangements. Later that night, a deep-sea trawler skippered by a distant cousin would be waiting 30kms off the west coast in the Tasman Sea. Using the radar, voice communication, and light signals, the chopper would land on the rear deck of the big long-line trawler and disembark Grizzly and Pedro. The chopper would then be lifted by the ship's crane and sacrificed to the murky depths. Such was Pedro's plan. The trawler skipper, having been promised substantial economic reward, would then set the compass nor-west to take the two passengers to a rendezvous off the west Australian coast. With other family members involved in prawn fishing off Western Australia Pedro felt sure he could while away a few years avoiding the fate that had befallen his brothers.

So, at sunset the Bell Jet Ranger, Tango Kilo 666, lifted heavily from the valley to a yapping, howling farewell from the anxious pack of abandoned pig-dogs below. The machine spiralled up in noisy darkness, then closely and skilfully followed the contours of the coast north.

It was the cold and random hand of fate that intervened that night. Bill and Kingi at that same time were 50kms from Opononi, closing in on their own rendezvous with much gentler thoughts. As the chopper coincidentally crossed the coast south of Opononi to track north, Pedro suddenly noticed the flash of the sat-nav receiver in the cockpit. The technology had picked up a coded signal from a small transmitting disc on its exclusive frequency. It had found in the ether, the small disc that Pedro had hidden under the rear bumper of a black Mustang coupé those weeks before.

"Thuck, I've got the cunt!" Pedro suddenly screamed into the microphone of the headset, and Grizzly, concentrating on his instruments, near jumped from his seat. "Follow that signal!" Pedro ordered. Grizzly set the device to home in on the data that flicked up onto the screen. He banked the chopper to follow the signal down, like a smart bomb to its target.

Ten minutes later, Kingi and Bill topped the last rise of the coastal range before the road turned down towards the Hokianga harbour. At that moment, Grizzly was flaring the chopper down onto the front paddock of Frank Peters's home and haven, near the classic shape of the Mustang parked in front of the house. Startled by the noise, Peters Senior and his beautiful young houseguest, Mere Lopes, looked at each other in amazement. "Ha! That's my boy, Frank laughed, elated. "He couldn't wait, they've come by chopper," and excitedly the two jumped up from the table. Frank took her hand spontaneously, and they dashed to the front door to greet the figure that was trotting towards the house. Frank flung open the solid kauri door. He and Mere stood under the bright light of the front verandah, Mere waving in eager greeting to the running arrival. Too late, the old soldier recognised the gleam of the shotgun's twin barrel. Too late, Mere saw that the figure carried a jerry can in his other hand. It was then that the enraged, insane Pedro Whetu pulled the trigger of the semi-automatic shotgun, whooping with a maniacal war-cry of brutal excitement. In that nanosecond, the heavy-bore pig-shot exploded in fatal spread across the closing distance and into Frank Peters and Pedro's own little sister, Mere Lopes. Mere died immediately. She took the impact of the fatal load deep in her torso, and she folded in half. Even as she crumpled, the sawn-off shotgun spat again, in a cordite stink of destruction, as Pedro fired from his hip at her falling form. This time, Mere took the load in her beautiful face, and the classic, fine construction of her features was no more.

Frank did not die immediately. He fell, wounded and confused. "Why would my son do this?" Then his assailant came closer, and he saw with strange acceptance and relief that this ugly Satan was not his son. And then Frank died.

Pedro did not know who he had killed, did not see the people, just the death. He simply assumed he had killed Bill. He ran bounding up onto the porch firing again and again, spent, smoking, red plastic cartridges spitting out the side of the weapon, as the rotating ten-shot clip auto-loaded the gun. Stepping over the bodies he was certain the male was Bill. Same build. Too damaged to confirm, but confirmation didn't even occur to him. The Mustang was enough. The other kill was a female, he knew that at least. "Fucken bonus!" he yelped.

It was dark now. The shots had taken out the front porch light, and the scene of bloody carnage was only faintly back-lit from the kitchen light. He heard the chopper's engine suddenly rise in pitch as Grizzly readied for urgent take-off. Pedro quickly splashed the Avgas from the jerry can onto the bodies, onto the porch, and then he hoisted it heavily through the open door, the can gurgling out its contents. He backed away, running backwards toward the chopper. He fired the shotgun into the doorway, sparking the shot against the quarried granite tiles of the entry, and the house exploded into fire. Turning, he dived in the chopper as it lifted away, laughing wide-mouthed in crazed triumph. Grizzly had the machine screaming at full revs, rising and sliding away from a vehicle that was skidding and swerving at the point of loss of control, up the gravel driveway to get to the house.

The two men in the car could only watch as if in slow-motion as TK 666 pulled rapidly up and away into the dark night. Bill screamed, "Fuck! fuck! fuck!" foot pumping non-existent passenger's side accelerator. He flung himself out of the broad-sliding Commodore before Kingi could bring it to a skidding stop. By the time he got up from the ground, grunting throat-raw breaths, and hurtled in a crazy, knee-pumping sprint toward the front porch, the house was entirely and furiously ablaze. And so too were the huddled, obviously human forms, on the front porch.

Kingi, almost as distraught as Bill, was forced to tackle and wrestle the younger man away from the flames that threatened to engulf them both. Still Bill fought against him to get to the two bodies. "It's too late, son. It's too late," Kingi cried quietly, over and over. And Bill finally heard those words and understood the profundity of their meaning.

Kingi held him, cradled him backward from the incredible skin-scorching heat of the destruction, until his legs crumpled, knees-weak, down onto the lush grass near the car.

Bills eyes stayed fixed, intensely focused, never leaving the cruel theatre of horrible conflagration on the stage of his father's porch, as the two lumps of humanity were cremated. He felt a sudden, intense pain of loss in his chest. His young heart, his soul, his very being, was torn apart. In that agony of despair and helplessness, he witnessed his past and his future depart from his life.

He became terrified, frightened beyond comfort, helpless, hopeless. He wrapped his arms tight around his bent legs and wept. He fought against the soothing numbness of shock that his body was attempting to impose on his mind. He wanted he knew that he needed to suffer this pain, to understand what he had lost. Lost forever.

Bill heard it first, a rhythmical *slap, slap, slap,* but only when Kingi's voice, rising in emotion and cadence, forced his attention, did he look away from the fire to the man who stood in a half squat, both palms slapping time on his bent thighs. Bill saw then, in the red fire-glow, the naked, slab-muscled torso, marked by traditional tattoo, and by welt and scar long healed that spoke of many battles.

Kingi spoke to the tortured spirits of the departed in the ancient beauty of his tongue. He farewelled his spiritual brother and the lovely young Mere in a traditional and haunting Waiata.

As Kingi chanted, Bill heard him mutter amongst the soft Maori vowels the words "Frank", "Mere" and "Wiremu" the Maori version of his name. He stood, not really knowing why, and tears spilt from his eyes, tracking down his ash-stained face, and trance-like he joined Kingi in the ceremony. The young pakeha stood slightly behind and to one side of the Maori warrior chief, joining the slap of thighs as the two men faced the pyre and said goodbye.

And as they heard the lonely, futile wail of the small town's volunteer fire brigade, Kingi turned from the fire to face the coast. An anaemic moon had begun its journey through the cloud-scudded blackness. High on the hill with the burning house behind him, Kingi stood, eerie amongst the gusts of grey smoke and embers, and began the battle challenge. He issued his ancestors' formal promise of fatal revenge for deeds done. With heavy slap of palm on thigh, thud of clenched fist on chest, smack of feet into the soil, Bill joined him in the actions, vaguely learnt from a lifetime of watching the All Blacks. He too tore off his shirt, and found an unexpected distraction from his pain, and again and again he smashed his fists against his own reddening chest in brutal time with Kingi, as the elder led him in the Haka.

"Ka Mate! Ka Mate!"

Chapter 37

Lay All Your Love on Me

Bill fell into the easy comfort of the lifestyle known as 'Broome-time' as if he had been born to it. In the all-enveloping warmth of the tropical paradise it was if the stress and pain of the past four years shed from him physically, like an old lizard shedding skin to reveal a new shiny creature.

The spiritual influence of his new friend came with a perception of his place in the world that he had never before experienced. From the army life of his childhood to the intellectual discipline of his academic endeavours and through the rough and tumble of his sporting life he had not known this exploration of self. Even after the harsh consequences of his brief and tragic career as an undercover police agent, he had never allowed himself to consider life's greater mysteries. In the company of this woman, a genuine free spirit, Bill was exposed to a fine intellect that sought to explore those abstract notions of what it was all about. She was not religious, but her aura of healing spirituality enveloped him and he began to consider other aspects of his mind and ego that he had not known existed.

Gypsy instinctively knew that Bill was damaged goods and soon realised that he would not easily reveal to her the events that had so scarred him. She was aware of the evasive armour of humour that he wore and while enjoying that quirk of character she determinedly applied her natural skills to healing this man.

Bill enjoyed this beautiful woman's attention. He decided that, in a purely physical sense, she was a total spunk, and only 26 years old. Although he knew she was not single, simply working with her in the tent and occasionally mixing with her after hours was a real pleasure. Gypsy trained her willing student each day as Mavis, and increasingly the matriarchal population of Broome's caravan parks, lined up through the increasingly busy days to be massaged by Gypsy's 'new boy'.

As they had agreed, Bill slept in the tent. Cautiously, not to attract any official attention, he would use the public shower and toilets further up the coast.

One month after his last phone call to Great Aunt Ruby he made another midnight call from a phone box situated near the Cable Beach Resort.

Disappointingly for Bill, Kingi was not there. But he had passed on the advice that the trail had gone cold. Ruby told Bill that he was to call again, "Same time, each 30 days."

"Tell Kingi I am now top-end," he asked her, and then rang off. He could only wait. And while he waited out those long, lazy, sensual Broome days, Bill trained. He did this to distract from his dark thoughts and also to prepare himself for the time when the quarry was finally cornered. He ran along the beautiful, golden, convex stretch of Cable Beach and found a distant sand-hill where he sprinted in thigh- and gut-tearing bursts up and down the shifting sand. At the point of exhaustion his body would enter the endurance zone, releasing opiates into the bloodstream and offering renewed vigour. Bill would then force his body through the exercise and discipline regime of the black belt as the red sun set into the sea.

He grew lean and strong and tanned by the sun and as the dry season passed he and Gypsy formed a strong friendship. Their bond was cemented by a daily massage for the other. Bill quickly discovered that he had a discipline that surprised even him as, alone in the darkened tent, he would lovingly oil and caress almost every inch of her lovely surface. Except for the tiny bikini bottom, Gypsy bared her golden tanned body to him with an uninhibited naturalness that relaxed him and took away any sexual tension. He found the self-discipline of thought and focus was vital during these sessions, since he wore only Speedos, which hid little as long as it stayed little. It was only when he mastered a visualisation technique that it was in fact Mavis and not Gypsy who lay below him, sighing on the massage table that he was able to prevent embarrassing uprisings. In any case, Gypsy was in love with and was, in every sense, loyal to her pearl farmer Tommy. Bill knew that they would soon meet, since the farm tenders and trawlers headed home for rest and repair during the cyclone months.

With the approaching wet season, the tent was removed from the beach and stored. Each afternoon, roiling grey clouds formed massive thunder-heads. Gypsy took Bill to her studio in the resort opposite the beach. Then, through those humid months, the two massaged international corporate executives as big firms took advantage of the resort's convention facilities and the bargains of the off-season.

Bill met Tommy during this time and found that he was a deep-thinking and gentle man. Tommy had no difficulty with Bill taking up residence in the sleep-out of their tropical bungalow on the outskirts of the old Chinese section of the town. He also introduced Bill to the gentle science of fishing in the area's bountiful aquatic surrounds. Tommy was happy to find a mate with whom he could share the occasional early morning journey out onto the warm waters in his tinny. Once floating on the gentle swell at shallow anchor, or drifting on tidal surges over reefs and knobs below, Bill discovered the waters were home to amazing varieties and quantities of fish that couldn't wait to fling themselves in shuddering suicide onto cruel hooks. Unlike his pig hunting experiences, Bill found he had no real empathy with his cold-blooded prey and he greedily pulled that beautifully decorated and highly prized eating fish, the coral trout, into the boat in repetitive triumph. After an education from Tommy he soon was catching, kissing and releasing the less fancied varieties, enjoying the sport of the catch without taking unnecessary life.

286

Thanks to their generosity, Bill could have used Gypsy and Tommy's phone anytime to make calls. The only call he had to make was to Great Aunt Ruby. But he had decided that he would not create any trail that may then lead any person or agency to that peaceful dwelling. Therefore, it was while standing in the tiny shelter of the public call box one midnight with sheets of tropical rain cascading down around the plastic dome that he finally spoke to Kingi.

"Hello, son," came the unmistakable deep timbre on the line. And the connection between the two men was immediate, due to the bond forged in the heat of terrible sorrow and loss.

"Sir," his voice quavered from the strength of sudden emotion. It had been a long time since he heard the man himself and not just his words through the old lady.

"We have him!"

Bill could barely believe it. "Where?"

"He was in Darwin two weeks ago. He is on a ship. It's small, an old tub. Maybe a trawler. It's called the *Princess* or something. My source has not seen it. On good advice it is heading west from Darwin. Apparently it works the top-end, fishing and moving refugees out of Asia. They're dropped on atolls right on the territorial boundary."

"What do you suggest, boss? How do I get him?"

"This man can help you, Bill. If you can get to Darwin he will put you up. Listen, son, if you can't if you don't want to it doesn't matter. We can report it through the official channels, I can do that from this end. He will get taken out that way."

"Too good for him, Sir. No, I need to do it. I reckon I can get off to Darwin and wait for him. I owe it to them. To both of them."

And so it was decided. Bill would get to Darwin, meet Kingi's man, and wait.

He had time to play with. Kingi said the trawler had left its home port of Darwin and would be out for weeks, maybe months yet. Bill wanted to go now. With the remaining, healthy balance of his Kalgoorlie cash Bill decided to find the right vehicle and buy it, somehow source a firearm, and buy that. Then, by night and with stealth, he would travel through the top of the state and cross over into the Northern Territory, making his way towards the beautiful port city of Darwin.

He knew that he would say a sad farewell to Gypsy, to Tommy and to Broome. With the nature of his mission in Darwin there was no guarantee he would ever be back. And so he began to plan and prepare for the farewell. Gypsy watched his sudden withdrawal; a seriousness come over him. She found it hard to believe this was the same Bill she had spent time with relaxing and unwinding. She tried to find out what was troubling her friend, but he was reticent, silent, moody.

It was one Saturday night in that April with Bill close now to departure that Tommy and Gypsy insisted he come with them to the sprawling, happy and riotous garden bar of the town's Roebuck Bay Inn. This big old pub was where locals and young backpackers gathered to enjoy the rock-and-roll of a local outfit, the Pigrum Brothers Band. The band members were that unique Broome mix of the proud dark bloods. A fascinating product based on the genealogical foundations of the indigenous aboriginal owners of the land, combined later with suggestions of the various nationalities and related hues that each trend or quirk of the town's commercial history over the last one hundred years had brought. There may have been some influence of Afghan, Timorese, and Indonesian, or a twist of Japanese, a smidgen of Chinese and a hint of Irish in the members of this family who played melodic, home-grown tales of growing up in the paradise of Broome.

Bill and his friends arrived after dark with Tommy parking the ancient jeep near the mangrove shore. They went through the garden bar gate, past the usual huge security guards and into the cacophony of sound and immediately Bill was glad he had come. As the locals called out in greeting to Tommy, Gypsy, and, to his delight, to him, the trio made their way over to a jarrah table under the perfume of a frangipani tree in the farthest corner of the garden. Tommy took orders and friends soon surrounded Gypsy, chatting happily, while Bill, comfortable and at ease in the scented tropical warmth, sat in the dark under the fragrant, leafy canopy and took in the view. The

288

band fired up with a lilting story of young love in the tropics and Bill relaxed and enjoyed the balmy night. Out to sea, silent flashes of lightning from a far-off electrical storm danced across the dark heavens.

And then his blood froze.

Coming through the pub entry gate was Pedro fucking Whetu!

He immediately recognised the ugly head, and then the greying hair tied back now in long plait down his back. He was older but was still all sinewy biceps and black tattoos. Bill felt a cold murderous rage as his body went rigid, readying for combat. Blood pumped to his extremities, his heart raced in anticipation, and adrenalin surged into his bloodstream to enable instant reaction to his brain's commands. But even as he moved to rise, Gypsy saw him and was shocked by the change in his face, which was now a mask of focused hate. He rose, breathing hard as if he had run, but Gypsy lunged along the seat and held him around his middle.

She didn't know what was wrong but knew something was.

"Bill, what is it?" she implored and he snapped out it for a moment at her genuine concern. Eyes not leaving his quarry, Bill stood still. His brain clicked through possibilities, and he watched as Pedro, in company with several sun-scarred, swarthy fellows, clearly trawler men, bought cartons of rum from the bar. An aura of evil rose from the group, causing even the alcohol-dulled, young backpackers to instinctively swerve away as they made their way back outside. There were too many of them, his quick analysis told him. An immediate, instinctive attack, taking into account all factors including the number of them, may not succeed. His training allowed him to see past the act to the consequences.

The odds at this place, in these circumstances, could mean too many things.

Including the possibility of failure.

That failure could include Pedro's escape, harm to Bill, and his own capture by the police who were based a block away from the Roebuck Inn. No, he needed time to survey and to choose the ground of battle.

He must follow them and find out where they were staying, and then plan an effective revenge against Pedro an act from which he himself could escape.

After so much pain, life had again become worth living and he would not allow the filth that was Pedro Whetu to take that away from him again.

Bill looked at Gypsy who still held him and he tried to pull back from the raw emotion that the sight of Pedro had exposed. An unconcerned Tommy arrived back at the table, a beer-filled jug in one hand, a glass of mango punch in his other.

"The banditos are in port," Tommy commented with clear distaste.

"Who are they?" Bill asked, sinking back down in the realisation that these men were known to Tommy. He needed to know more before deciding his course of action.

"Ahh, just a bunch of thieving, cheating bastards," the gentle Tommy advised, pouring the cold amber liquor into the two middie glasses. "A mixed lot of bad mongrels. They've got a trawler called *The Portuguese Princess*. It's a stinking old black thing, saw it tied up in the port today."

Tommy sipped his beer. "They sail out of Darwin, supposedly prawners, but from what I've heard they aren't welcome in the Territory either. The suspicion is they run drugs and people illegal immigrants from south-east Asia. Bad news, really. They're suspected of all sorts of devious acts, but nothing's ever proved. It's just that they are always about when things go pear-shaped."

"I know one of them," Bill said quietly, as Gypsy almost unconsciously rubbed his forearm. "From a long time ago," he breathed. "So are they in port now?"

"Oh yeah, mate," Tommy replied. "They will be in for a few days now there's a cyclone warning off the coast." He took a long gulp of his beer. "And I know from a mate that their tub is in for some engine work over the next couple of days. They're going no-where fast."

He had time.

He would take that time to plan and act.

290

Chapter 38

Last Farewell

It was over. With Mere and his father gone, life, his future the vital core of his existence withered and died before him. He was empty. Just empty.

There was the sad beauty of the funeral at the desecrated home-site. Bill and Kingi had stayed in the tiny hamlet for that. Bill rang his mother, barely able to speak, she, frantic with her concern, devastated by the shock death of the father of her son, uncertain at the emotion she felt for the unknown young woman her son had loved and had lost. He found himself comforting her as she sobbed for him on the line thousands of miles away. They decided she should not come. He would come to her again when he was ready.

So, on a misty morning on the Hokianga harbour, as the heavens wept gentle, cleansing tears for the departed, the townspeople gathered in respect and affection for Frank, and for the son's unknown love. The ceremony of farewell was incongruously, unbearably beautiful amid the soft vocal symphony of the Maori dirges. Respecting each other's culture and beliefs, the priest and the local tribal elders shared the form and the etiquette of the ceremony. Their flesh and blood had not withstood the heated destruction. A minute forensic search had not found even enough to bury. And so it was symbolic that as the service concluded, the dust of the ruins rose in a misty spiral on a sudden freshening breeze, as if to lift the two freed sprits away. And the grieving Maori recognised those forces and sang.

The death of Mere Lopes had other effects. Mere's elderly mother, still in Portugal, did not survive the telling. A police officer from Lisbon in a dusty Renault had hand-delivered the sad news on consular letterhead. Despite the instant, wailing support of her many relatives, the distraught old woman died that very night. The brothers Matu and Louis, incarcerated and awaiting trial on a multitude of charges, were each devastated beyond sanity by the news. Although sympathetically delivered by the prison governor, the situation was further aggravated by the news that the key suspect was their brother Pedro.

Without a doubt, the gang was finished. Bill and Kingi returned to the city and with fierce purpose Bill entered the arena of criminal prosecution. This involved proving on a spiritual oath, and beyond a reasonable doubt, that the facts as alleged are true. And that standard must then withstand vigorous and searching attack against its witnesses. Time and time again, Bill faced that attack by his opponent's expensive and talented legal representative in the country's highest court. He won, and won again with his emotionless certainty and transparent honesty. Finally, the foe wisely chose not to fight his credibility in the courts. Instead, the major players attempted to bargain for lesser sentences, for mercy. But Kingi's careful control and meticulous running of the operation meant that the cases were tightly constructed and supported by the covertly-gained evidence. Then came the domino effect of the gang's minions and lesser lights, with all to lose and nothing to gain, rushing to bargain, and to provide damning inside evidence. The Crown could afford to show no mercy.

Matu and Louis Whetu: life sentences at Her Majesty's Pleasure, no parole.

Joe Tama, and the other lieutenants: 20 years maximum-security, no parole.

All the gang assets, the island, vehicles, and proceeds of bank accounts on- and off-shore, were seized under proceeds of crime legislation and then forfeited upon the owner's convictions to the Crown.

Pedro Whetu: warrants to arrest on suspicion of murder of Frank Peters and Mere Lopes. Further warrants to arrest on the numerous criminal conspiracy, drugs and weapons charges. International Interpol alert.

At a sombre meeting with his friend, the Commissioner of Police, Detective Superintendent Kingi Potiki was offered the stark choice of resigning or being charged. The charge would allege that he had neglected his lawful duty when he made the operational decision to allow the Agent Peters' relationship with an operational target to exist, and then to develop.

Kingi chose to resign. Sickened anyway by the tragic consequences, he was allowed to retire, but only after all cases had been dealt with, and when he was certain Bill was at least in good hands. Then Kingi was thought to have disappeared into the tribal mountainous bushland of his Tuhoe ancestors. Although the man himself was gone, in police lore, Kingi the legend lived on.

And Bill Peters, while impatiently waiting out appeal attempts by those convicted on his evidence, was transferred on secondment at the Commissioner's personal request to Sydney, NSW, to while away his time on guard duty. Bill had received two full years' salary and allowances from the NZ government. He had received from his father's will the land and all remaining assets. He was now financially comfortable, even wealthy. But that knowledge was no comfort to him. Before he left Auckland for Sydney, he gave full power of attorney to his father's trusted lawyer. He would invest the sudden wealth Bill had never wanted to acquire in fact, it was almost immediately forgotten about.

With an acting rank and salary of detective sergeant, Bill was then transferred to Sydney to take up his sweet connection with Mrs Italiano.

Chapter 39

Got a Lot of Living to Do

It was 2.00am and Bill was under the heavy timbers of the wharf in the Port of Broome.

It was pitch-black and the wind had come up as a baby tropical cyclone was beginning to ruffle the air. There was a developing eye 200kms to the north-east in the Arafura Sea. The forecasters at the Bureau of Meteorology in Perth watched the foetal beast carefully from the fluoro-lit offices. Experience and data gathered over decades, combined with the bells and whistles of technology, told them that that the massive movement of air would either continue its deadly rotations until nature's momentum drove it spinning wildly south toward the continent, or dependant upon temperature, pressure, and other variables it may just fade away as a lesser category of storm.

Bill was on an intelligence-gathering mission. After seeing Pedro at the Roey, his mood had sunk to a point where he excused himself with apologies and reassurances to Gypsy that he was off to bed and would tell her all in the morning. He checked with Tommy that he could take the old pushbike from where it hung on the back of the Jeep and quietly snuck away from the increasingly boisterous crowd in the garden bar. It was a 7km cycle away from the tiny town centre up along Port Road past the gentle mooing of the half-feral

Brahman-cross cattle moving uneasily in the cattle yards. The dark herd of the strangely hump-necked dusty beasts gathered close to the port for their live export across to the hungry mouths and markets of south-east Asia. The smelly live-carrier ship sat waiting, anchored off the wharf, to load the beasts after they had grown fat grazing on the tropical grasses of the huge cattle stations of the Kimberley.

Under the wharf, wooden beams and pylons supported a broad walkway and vehicle access out 1000m before the wharf dog-legged south for another 500m. Fifty metres back from the wharf, Bill tucked the creaky old bike away by the dark, obsolete hulk of the grain silo. Even at this hour, Bill could see along the wharf the bent, seated figures of local fishermen taking advantage of the turn of the tide from the low at midnight. In this port and this region the tidal flows were massive, with the rise and fall variable to several metres.

Bill climbed quietly and carefully down to the beach and came up under the wharf structure, climbing up the thick, galvanised steel bolts set into one of the beach-end pylons, and then walked along several metres of beams. The heavy bolted jigsaw of beams were a one-metre by one-metre square of rough-hewn jarrah, milled decades before from old growth forests in the state's south-west and shipped up to Broome on coastal traders. Bill was in his soft rubber-soled runners and dressed in black. He had cammed out his tanned features with tiger stripes from the red dirt at the wharf.

He made easy progress up to the catwalk that had been built to allow tradesmen and engineers access to the water and sewerage pipes and the electrical and telecommunication wires, which ran along under the timbers and on the catwalk. Bill was up to the dog-leg within five minutes. One hundred metres up, the services rose up through the wharf floor and into the Port Authority buildings where they were then periodically mated with the male connections from the various ships that tied up to load or discharge.

Bill had seen the black bulk of *The Portuguese Princess* from the shore. It was tied up to the last section of the dog-leg, lying well below the wharf on the beach-side and on the ebb tide.

She was an old K-class trawler. It was a steel-plated, wide-beamed vessel designed and constructed for local waters and conditions.

Bill now quietly made his way up along the mid-level and mid-section beams, every three metres clambering through the v of the intersecting supports until he was within ten metres of the fly deck of the trawler. On the low tide the 50-metre long ship was a good five metres below the level of the wharf decking and on the high tide she would rise up alongside so that a man could step on and off. It was now one hour past the midnight tidal low and the heavy vessel was rising perceptibly on the incoming tide.

Bill had seen from the shore that the cabin and deck lights were still on. As he clambered closer he could hear the muffled commotion of voices and occasional harsh laughter from a group of men down on the rear deck. He moved to the seaward side of the wharf so that he was directly opposite the trawler. Bill then cautiously crossed over the width of the wharf using the rounded pylons to mask his approach.

He was close. Three metres from the harbourside edge.

He was just starting to be able to pick out individual voices, sentences, and words, when harsh barking erupted from the trawler. *Fuck, a dog!*

It was the last thing he would have suspected. The mutt went ballistic, obviously picking up his scent on the freshening sea breeze.

He froze in his tracks, pressed himself like a lover into the tar stink of the pylon behind which he had been leaning out to scan the activity below him. *Fuck fuck fuckin dog.* He heard the unmistakable grunt of Pedro Whetu from the trawler, "Fuck up, dog!" and the dog stopped as if its throat was cut and whimpered from the dark of the top cabin. Bill didn't dare breathe, let alone look out from behind the pylon.

A minute passed.

Then another.

And there was no obvious action from the trawler, which continued to rise slowly upward on the tide. He needed to get a little bit closer, as he could only hear snatches of conversation. By the sound of it, the men were well into a rum-drinking session.

The talk was loud and rough. Slowly, slowly he crept around the circular pylon, and tiptoed over to the harbour-side edge, back and above the stern of the trawler by only two metres.

The dog exploded again, its territorial instinct overcoming its fear of its owner. It leapt on a clank of heavy chain on the deck above the men, claws scratching against steel, snout pointing like a setter in a grim snarl. It barked directly at the man it heard, smelt, and saw in grey outline ducking behind the pylon. This time, Pedro, although dulled by the alcohol, trusted his dog. His bulky figure rose and staggered across to the fixed spotlight on the rear transom flicking it into bright life. He aimed it high to the wharf decking four metres above and then played it through the wharf to the other side.

Bill cringed against the pylon as the beam illuminated his entire world.

"Get him boy, sic him," Pedro growled drunkenly as the dog, now with his pack leader's permission, erupted in savage staccato. Bill knew he had to choose action.

Run back along the beams?

Drop into the water and swim?

Two very poor options, he decided. Or he could tough it out and see how far Pedro would persist in uncovering what was bothering his dog. And then, as luck would have it, one of Pedro's relatives intervened and saved Bill's arse.

A pink-snouted, fat, male *ratus ratus*, king of the Broome wharf rat pack, rudely interrupted from a session of squeaky love-making, emerged from his lady-friend's nest to see what all the fuss was about. Just then, Pedro swung the hot beam of the spotlight right onto it.

Transfixed by the light, pink eyes glowing, the rat then took the full force of a perfectly-aimed empty rum bottle, swung with awful precision by Pedro Whetu. The blow bounced the stunned rat off the beam the momentum threw it out to fall, unfortunately for the rat, but fortunately for Bill, onto the upper deck and right into the snapping jaws of the blue heeler-bull terrier cross. Pedro, satisfied by the cause of the dog's interest and especially by his expert aim, switched off the spotlight and returned to his circle of drinking companions.

Meanwhile, fatal squeaking, crunching and satisfied growling from above confirmed the fate of the rat.

With the return of the blackness Bill could then listen and watch his quarry.

Pedro sat with his back to Bill and talked with the six or so other men lounging around in a semi-circle. Bill took it all in. He caught snippets like "out by Wednesday", "Joy's Creek" and "the farm".

He heard "midnight", "no lights" and "international waters". Pedro laughed at the "cyclone warning keeping the local soft-cocks in port" and with a thrill of excitement, Bill realised that this unsavoury lot was again up to something.

Over the next hour, as the trawler men drank and talked and argued and drank themselves increasingly into a stupor, Bill had worked out that the crew of *The Portuguese Princess* were planning to raid a pearl farm at a location he had already heard about, called Joy's Creek.

Joy's Creek was about 100km north of Broome. Bill knew the farm would be set on floating rafts and long lines in the pristine waters of a tiny offshore atoll, 10km from the coast. During cyclone alerts, all personnel were usually retrieved and returned to port. The cyclones on this coast had a cruel history of death and destruction as the Broome graveyard could attest to and local wisdom insisted that when one was in the brewing, all human life was safer on land.

Finally, as Pedro and the others slipped into a snoring slumber and the faintest hint of the morning began to lighten the eastern sky, Bill made his escape back down the underneath of the wharf and onto the beach. With one last look back toward the sinister black-hulled trawler, now only a few metres off the top of the wharf, he remounted the creaking old bicycle and began a tired ride back into town and to his soft bed.

Bill awoke around nine to find Gypsy smelling like sandalwood oil, long hair still wet, sitting demurely at the end of his bed. Her lithe, tanned body was modestly wrapped in a golden, patterned sarong tied in a knot above her breasts. He lunged cheekily at her and she easily slipped his attempt to pull her down onto his bed, giggling at his cave-man antics.

"Me, Gypsy," she retorted. "Now, Tarzan to tell me what happened last night."

"Or what?" he asked.

"Or Gypsy kick Tarzan's arse," she laughed.

And so Bill told her.

She sat transfixed by the enormity of his story and he told her absolutely everything. This time, the telling was different from when he had told Maria, so long ago at the Kalgoorlie billabong. The emotion was different. Then, he had needed to unburden himself of the sheer pain. This time, vengeance was foremost in his mind. He needed and wanted to share his story with this woman who had become his confidante, his friend.

He needed to seek, in some measure, her opinion of his approach to this opportunity. He almost needed her to agree with him, to qualify his desire for that revenge although he did not spell out the extent to which he intended to wreak that revenge.

Gypsy saw the opportunity differently and her perspective helped him to formulate a better plan. "You know, you have two choices here," she analysed. "One, you can report the fact that Pedro Whetu is here to the local police. From what you say he is wanted at least in New Zealand. Or, two, if what you overheard is right, then we can work with Tommy and the local police and set them up."

"Be waiting at Joy's Creek," Bill breathed.

"Yes," she agreed, nodding sagely. "Which will mean they will be arrested here in Broome just to make sure this Pedro does not get away this time."

"You know," Bill joked, "Tommy's quite wrong you are good for something." Then he had to protect himself as Gypsy launched at him and, giggling, they wrestled in exaggerated soft combat on the bed. Bill became uncomfortably aware of his nakedness under the sheets and the sensations and consequences of wrestling his gorgeous assailant. So, to hide the increasingly obvious, he surrendered and curled away from her in foetal defence under the sheet while Gypsy hammered up and down his prone form with a pillow. Finally Tommy called from the kitchen, "Come on children, break it up, brekkie's on." Wafting into the sleep-out came the irresistible smells of garlicky, butter-fried coral trout fillets sizzling in the pan and the yeasty sweetness of fresh-baked pumpkin bread. Gypsy called finally for his unconditional surrender and from under the bed he found and waved a white flag his Calvin Kleins and offered her those.

The three then sat down to the feast and, with a little prompting, Bill repeated a précis of his life story for Tommy. They then discussed at length, and over mugs of hot black filter coffee, the options that now presented. Bill chose not to reveal the fact that the main outcome of whatever course was eventually decided on would be the painful, tortured death of Pedro.

Tommy and Gypsy understood the difficulty of involving the Police. Bill was still considered a criminal on the run and he could not afford for his identity to become known. He had decided while under the wharf, before the timely rescue by the rat, that he wanted to live. He wanted to live in Broome, and he wanted to be free.

They discussed the possibilities that a voluntary surrender may present. They concurred that the fact that he had been set up would be impossible to prove. Particularly against the evidence of the NSW Police Commissioner and the resources he would have at his disposal. Bill knew that if they got him to court he faced a long time in prison.

There was no avenue in the NZ police or government that Bill could think of that could help him.

Kingi Potiki was *persona non grata*.

Kingi could not help with the New South Wales problem and Bill chose not to tell Gypsy and Tommy of his long-distance assistance in planning the revenge for Mere's and his father's death.

It was Tommy who came up with a scenario that might just work. "Listen, folks, I know the owners of the Joy's Creek lease," he announced. "One of the Darren brothers."

"Yes, and so?" Gypsy prompted.

"Well, at the pearl lease, set up on the tiny atoll, there is an underground cyclone-proof concrete bunker. It was built in the 1940s by the government as a lookout for visiting Japanese ships and subs. It is set into the small mound of the limestone hump of the island and is available these days as an emergency shelter."

"Go on." The prompt was from Bill this time.

"I've been there, the shelter is hidden in scrubby bush and is virtually invisible from the bay". Tommy went on to explain that the isolated bay held the anchored long-lines and drop-lines that slung the precious living shells into the waters, with solar-powered flashing lights set high on orange buoys marking the lease boundaries. "With your permission, Bill, I could speak to the leaseholder, tell him of the problem". And so it was agreed. Tommy would suggest that if the lease-owner was willing, then Bill would be taken out by fast tender and dropped with supplies and a satellite phone for communication on the tiny island to act as a lookout. If Bill's suspicions about the rotten old hulk and its roughneck crew were proved right he could await the arrival of the raider and alert Tommy by phone when he saw the trawler approaching. It would take a fast boat just under three hours at 35 knots to get to the lease from Broome. They worked on the plan as Gypsy refreshed the coffee. If the raid happened, the local police twin-engine Beechcraft could be in the sky within the hour to track *The Portuguese Princess* until the boats could intercept.

Gypsy analysed the known facts.

"If the trawler does raid the pearl farm then this Pedro fellow will be caught in the act." She ticked off a second finger. "Pedro and his crew will be arrested and charged with serious crimes. Bill, you can stay hidden. Tommy, you can take Bill off later with the tender, never to be seen by the police." By this time they were all nodding in unison. "If the trawler does not raid the farm nothing is lost," Gypsy said, "cause through Tommy's network in the north-west fishery, we can track the vessel away from Broome. Then we can feed information anonymously to the local police who would then have time to arrange arrest warrants from their New Zealand counterparts." She finished and looked from Tommy to Bill. "Well?" she enquired of her housemates.

"Bloody genius," was Bill's response. In his mind, however, Bill silently deduced that if the second scenario happened he would be waiting at that next port of call to ambush his old nemesis under circumstances of his choosing. "Yes, it might just work," he murmured.

The only other consideration and complication was the cyclone warning. They could hear outside the rising winds off the ocean. The point was, though, that Bill should be safe if the cyclone struck, and that was by no means definite anyway as the swirling beast faded and then grew, faded and grew and was now about 150km north off the coast.

Tommy left to speak to Ben Darren of the pearl farm. He returned within the hour with Ben's blessing and thanks, both for the information and the offer of the lookout. Bill packed, helped by Gypsy who apologised that she could not go in the boat with them due to her propensity for seasickness. Tommy dusted off the camping gear and the provisions that he had brought ashore from his own lease to the south. He packed them into two large diving bags.

To fill in time on the island, if that became an issue, Tommy also packed for Bill a collapsible fishing rod with hooks and lures, and a pair of old black dive flippers, goggles and snorkel. He warned Bill, though, that to venture too deep at the lease might attract the attention of the area's rapacious shark population. Or even, he warned soberly, a saltie.

Tommy explained to a suddenly very interested pupil that the huge reptilian dinosaurs of that coast were incredible swimmers and undertook amazing offshore journeys of discovery. They were well capable of venturing out to the Joy's Creek lease for a look-see. Bill quickly decided that shore-based fishing might be the more sensible option during his surveillance.

That night as darkness fell Bill kissed Gypsy farewell at the house with heartfelt thanks. She pressed on him a bag of her bread, cut into thick sandwiches with aromatic brie cheese and sliced purple onion, in accordance with her vegetarian principles. Tommy had his sleek fibreglass 15-metre lease tender loaded on the boat trailer. They putted down to the Cable Beach ramp and launched the boat into the water to avoid being seen at the port. During that day, Tommy had confirmed that the black-hulled trawler was going nowhere for at least two days, since the diesel engine was in a hundred greasy pieces on the engine-room floor. They set off. Tommy soon had the twin 200 horsepower Mercs throttled up and the deep v hull of the tender carving northward at 30 knots into the slap of the white-caps. Seated back in the plush comfort of the padded and shock-absorbing cockpit seats, Bill and Tommy looked warily away to the north-west at the black cloudbank on the horizon that foretold of weather on the way.

Three hours later, Bill was stepping ashore at the atoll.

Tommy had cruised the boat into the half-moon of the bay over a submerged reef and slid her close alongside the coral-crushed beach. Bill slung his gear up above the tide line with two quick trips in the darkness of the unsettled night. Tommy pointed up the hill, which rose only ten metres from the tiny beach. "Right on top, you can't miss it, there's a hinged hatch. Ben said to look out for snakes. See you mate!" Tommy yelled, as he hit the throttle and the boat roared off into the gloom.

"Fuck me! Snakes, crocs, sharks, and Pedro Whetu, what the fuck have I let myself in for?" Bill laughed to himself as he waved Tommy away. He hitched the two kit bags onto his back and headed up the hill.

He felt exhilarated by the prospect of ambushing his enemy. 'Yes, sir, this just might work out,' he announced to the atoll and the unseen snakes. He found the bunker after a brief search in the dark, finally digging the waterproof torch out while jumping nervously this way and that from suspicious rustlings that marked his progress through the scraggly bush. The bunker was insect-proof and ventilated and once he lifted the hatch he found that creature comforts had been allowed for by its builder. Inside was a small but well-planned room. He lit the kero lantern that hung in the middle and saw two bunk beds, linen, a small library with dusty books, and board and card games. He checked the book collection. "Oh great! Chopper Reid's entire collection!" He slung his gear down and slowly unpacked, placing his things in tidy, practical piles on the top bunk. He took the satellite phone from its waterproof case. As arranged, he rang Gypsy and had a two-minute flirt with her at Tommy's expense until she realised the cost of the call and told him off, giggling as she hung up.

He went back out into the night and checked that the soft lantern light inside could not be seen from the bay. Then, after some adjustment of towels and sheets across the solid shatterproof slit windows, he was satisfied. He chewed thoughtfully on one of Gypsy's pumpkin bread sandwiches and, in the soft lantern glow, lying in the lower bunk, caught up on Chopper's latest bullshit and then settled down to a restless, dream-filled first night.

When Bill awoke the next morning he could not at first work out the noise. When he eased open the hatch, he found the wind whipping up around him. It appeared that the cyclone was real and getting closer. Through that first day and the next, the weather fluctuated as the cyclone teased the forecasters. Bill was forced to stay in the vault and each night made his quick phone call to Gypsy and Tommy. On the second evening he received the news that *The Portuguese Princess* had steamed out of the port at 6pm that night. With Tommy watching through binoculars from the shore, the old tub turned north. The other good news was that the cyclone had been downgraded to a tropical storm, well within the capabilities of the K-class trawler to cope with.

Bill got ready.

Chapter 40

S.O.S.

Deep in the heart of the Maori tribal-lands of the gentle Tuhoe, standing alone in a tiny, grassed clearing, was a small, rough-cut timber hut. White wood-smoke curled out of its red, tin-plate chimney. The hut was a two-day trek from the nearest gravel road through thick bush, over high ridges and through steep valleys.

That misty morning came a rude clattering as the New Zealand police chopper shattered the morning calm and descended, lurching, to settle on the bracken and silver fern carpet. A dark, bearded figure emerged warily from the doorway of the hut and watched as the country's most senior law officer, the Police Commissioner, disembarked alone from the machine and waved to the pilot to close it down. With head bent under the whoop of the slowing rotors, he made his way under that circling to meet with Kingi Potiki who waited impassively at the hut door. The two men shook hands and after a short discourse went into the hut and closed the door.

Half an hour later, both men emerged. Kingi was carrying a battered pack and climbed into the chopper with his ex-employer. The pilot fired up the turbine and again the pristine peace of the valley was disturbed. The white chopper dipped forward and slid into the air as the pilot revved her up in a tight spiral out of the clearing and away north, toward Auckland.

Chapter 41

Waterloo

At 1am he finally saw her.

The storm was in its dying phase as it tumbled down to the south and the dissipating tail only ruffled the calming waters at the Joy's Creek pearl farm.

Bill was dressed for the night all in black. He had been scanning the horizon when the small, dark shape first appeared and the excitement kicked in. The old trawler slowly but inevitably closed the distance as the moon broke through for the first time in the three nights to bathe the atoll in soft, lunar reflection.

Bill made the call. They kept it brief, as agreed.

"Gypsy 1, the storm is with us."

"Gypsy copy."

They were necessarily circumspect, uncertain as they were about the electronic scanning capability on board the *Princess*. As he ended the satellite connection, he knew that Tommy would be on the line to the Broome police. The officers were known to him and they would trust his information. Tommy would then make a brief phone call to Ben Darren. He would then get into the Jeep and collect Darren and four of his deckies, armed with two shotguns and two old .303 Lee Enfield rifles. A dash through the quiet town to the beach, down the ramp and on board the two lease tenders and they would be away from Cable Beach within 20 minutes of the alert.

Within the hour, the police twin-engine Beechcraft was warming on the tarmac of Broome airport. The police pilot talked by radio to the Royal Australian Naval patrol craft, *HMAS Perth*, currently steaming at 20 knots, ten kilometres south-west of Broome. Even as the captain spoke to the police on the ship's radio she turned her graceful steel bow and headed full-speed ahead, both engines, toward the Joy's Creek coordinates. The hunt was on; the hunters en route.

Ninety minutes later, the trawler was in the bay, anchored just off the shoreline. Strategically placed sacking muffled the chain's rusty clang, as a heavy pick splashed into the water. Bill could see the men on the after-deck busy lowering the two rubber duckies off the transom. He saw his canine mate prowling the upper fly-deck and thanked the wind gods that the breeze was onshore. The raiders were slick. Bill grudgingly admired the speed with which the duckies were launched and prowled off to either far boundary. There were three men in each. Pedro was obviously in charge, coordinating on the trawler deck. Seven men, he noted.

And then it was a matter of waiting.

Pedro waited also as his men hauled up the lines that held the mesh cages enclosing the heavy, mature oysters. The mesh was cut open by wire cutters and the oysters tipped into the duckies until each boat sank down with the load. The crew then chugged quietly back to the trawler. It was a quick transfer. A lift-net hooked to the small hydraulic crane on the aft-deck. The precious shells were then lifted and swung onto a stainless steel table. The rubber duckies unburdened, purred back to steal more bounty from the warm ocean. On the trawler, Pedro Whetu, with brutal, skilled precision cut, open the sinewy muscle at the oyster's hinge. Once the armour of the protective shell was open, Pedro dug into the labial softness of the warm salty flesh, and popped out the cultured treasure, clinking each pearl into his overall pocket. Gradually, progressively, the rape continued and Bill grew impatient, waiting.

Jeez, these guys are fucking slick.

He checked his time in the cover of the bush. Two hours had passed since his alert.

All I can do is wait.

He knew they were on their way and that the weather would not slow them. He had experienced the lease tender boats. He knew that they would be flying across the wave tops to make their initial contact. Bill suspected that if it was not already circling high above, then the police aircraft would be close and probably already had *The Portuguese Princess* on her radar.

While he waited he began to consider the what-ifs.

What if the baddies heard or saw on their radar the approach of the cavalry?

What if they simply dumped the booty and made tracks quickly away? Sure, the aircraft would have them at the scene of the crime but would the crime be provable to a judge and jury without the pearls? They could easily be lost forever, dropped into the sea.

Fuck the what-ifs, he decided.

It was time to act.

He wanted the trawler right where it was when the good guys arrived. He crawled cautiously back to the vault. It was all in darkness, as scudding clouds covered the moon. He slipped inside and found the flippers, mask and snorkel.

From the equipment stacked along the far wall, Bill took a length of braided steel rope, a loop five metres long held in a tight circle by plastic ties.

He slunk back out of the vault and checked the scene in the bay. Still, the two rubber boats quietly and industriously progressed along the grid pattern of drop-lines, working closer and closer to the trawler. Pedro was still in sight, busy at the table.

Bill could hear the repetitive splash of the pillaged shell as Pedro flipped the gaping bivalve back into the water for the final indignity: reef fish feasting on the usually impregnable treat. Satisfied that all was well, Bill climbed carefully down the other side of the small hill and then dropped onto its jagged, weathered shore. Ever so cautiously he made his way the 50 metres to the end of the small island and then crept on his belly around that far corner and back to face the lee-side of the trawler swinging at anchor 100 metres away. From this side, Pedro was out of view and the scabby bulk of the trawler hid Bill from the action. He could not see the dog but again the wind was blowing scent and noise, he hoped, off the trawler toward him. Bill slipped into the warmth of the water until he stood at shoulder depth. He eased on the fins and the mask, and pushed the snorkel around the back of his head. He wouldn't use it. The hiss and blow of a snorkel would be too loud. With the steel rope light around his shoulder in its loop, Bill began a gentle breast-stroke just below the surface towards the heavy hull. With the fins, his progress was swift and sure and apart from a phosphoric wake that spread out behind him in the moonlight there was no other sign of his passage. As he reached the stern and cuddled against the bulbous side of the trawler, he could still hear the crunch and splash of Pedro's endeavour.

He needed to gather his senses. He was exhilarated by the fact that he was so close.

Determined to finish this job, he needed to control his shallow, pinched breathing and find a more relaxed, deeper rhythm. He was going to dive under the hull to wrap the steel rope around the trawler's heavy bronze propeller. Bill waited until he heard both duckies chugging quietly back to the other side of the trawler to unload. When both were alongside and there was the hydraulic hiss of the crane and quiet talk between the men, he dived under.

In the blackness he marvelled at the silence. There were only pings of noise, a whine of the rubber duckies' idling motors. As he came down alongside the props, he was distracted by the incredible fluorescent maze and commotion of the feeding reef fish.

Bill had the steel rope unlooped and trailing behind and then quickly, as his lungs began to complain, he wrapped the rope in a clumsy knot around the single large screw, wound it up and pulled it tight.

He had done it.

With lungs bursting, he eased himself back up the convex curve of the scaly hull until just his face, upturned, broke the water on the far side. But as he silently gulped in the warm tropical air he heard the shrill electronic squeal of an alarm.

Suddenly there was commotion.

No shouting. Just rapid, urgent movement.

Pedro called to his men: "Get on, get back on, boats are coming!"

And then as the men clambered on board and the crane squealed with the lift of first one and then the other rubber duckie, Bill pushed off the hull and began to slink backward toward the shore.

Pedro pushed the ignition button to start the diesel engine.

Newly serviced, the motor sparked into a noisy chug of life. And if Pedro had kept her in neutral, her mechanical existence would have continued. But of course, he was keen to get away from the scene of his crime. And with the men at the bow operating the anchor winch and the old trawler swinging now with the gentle currents, Pedro threw the gears into forward to take the boat's weight off the anchor. With that, the steel rope twisted, tightened, strangled, and froze the old screw solid.

With the drive shaft still trying to rotate, the superheating, fracturing and mangled destruction worked its way up that shaft to the gearbox and then to the engine. With the varied forces having nowhere to go the engine basically imploded with a fantastic noise of metallic death. "What the fuck?" was the anguished scream from the cabin. Pedro ran to the stern, soon followed by his men to look over into the water. "Lights, thucking lights," he cursed, increasingly desperate. Bill was not far enough away.

With the million-candlepower spotlight flicked on by a crewman, an area with a 30-metre radius became daylight. Pedro and his men were confronted by the incongruous sight of an unknown snorkeller casually paddling away from their suddenly very inoperative trawler.

Two things happened.

The crewman instinctively focused the beam on the swimmer.

And Pedro Whetu recognised him.

Although a flawed specimen, Pedro Whetu was a man of action, an evil warrior. Within seconds he was armed with a gas-powered

311

spear-gun and was lowering the second rubber duckie back into the water. Two of his men jumped into the boat with him at his command and one tugged the outboard into life. Just as the small boat settled and was released off the crane hook it gunned around the stern and powered towards the now much more urgently swimming figure.

Pedro was screaming. A blood-curdling, lisping dirge of curse and obscenity from the boat.

"Thuckin cunt! thuck you! You're a dead cunt!"

As they closed in on the new Joy's Creek Australian crawl champion, Bill glanced backward in desperate head-twist of fear and saw that Pedro was leaning over the bow toward him, spear-gun aimed. Bill timed his dive and desperately ducked down, kicking furiously as he felt the bow wave surge approaching. But he was still a distant 15 metres from the shore, and from any chance of escape or of life.

Pedro fired the hissing spear at the disappearing man and the cruel shaft unreeled its nylon line toward the bubbles and then sprung to a shivering halt as the razor-sharp arrow head buried itself into the back of Bill's thigh. Even as he screamed bubbles in pain and terror, Bill felt the blade slide off his femur and set itself in his flesh. Spluttering at the searing pain, Bill rose for a desperate breath and dived again. He saw above him a dark shape block the moonlight. The rubber boat was virtually upon him. Bill could not see, but his assailant was grinning with hatred. Pedro began to reel in his human fish. As the cruel spearhead talons opened in his flesh against the backward pressure, Bill fought his body's urge to close down from the shock. To fall into unconsciousness now would be fatal.

Bill lay under the surface, spread like a huge starfish. He looked up at the silky surface toward which he was being hauled to what must be his death.

No fuckin way, Pedro. You will not win.

Bill's fitness, his discipline, his anger and his will to live pulled together and kicked in. Taking the nylon cord with both hands, he curled his body like a crayfish. Then, with Pedro eagerly leaning over the side of the boat, with his last ounce of effort, Bill flicked his body open and pulled down. Suddenly he was no longer alone in the water. His hunter had tipped in on top. In his awkward, cursing fall, Pedro dropped the spear gun and it fell below Bill onto the sandy bottom, tugging with its weight unbearably down on the shaft.

He must get away. Bill kicked toward the shallows with the big fins pulsing against the trapping water, his clumsy one-legged kick dragging the spear-gun along the bottom and winding out the heavy nylon from the reel. He was almost at the shore. But Pedro had dived under the boat. He had found the spear-gun skipping along the sand and grabbed it again. Pedro was happy now, laughing, standing waist-deep in the water, the boat circling behind. Pedro reeled Bill in toward him.

Bill was now too weak to resist, he was desperately fading from the pain, from the loss of blood that clouded pinkly out from his leg and enveloped Pedro and the rubber boat in a macabre mist. Bill realised that he was floating gently toward his death. He was floating on his back and being wound in again by the only person he truly feared and hated on this earth. Pedro now walked in shallower waters and with the increased stability was enjoying his game, playing his prey with exaggerated jerks for the benefit of his motley audience.

Bill knew it was over.

In the fading of his consciousness he saw Mere and then Gypsy and he farewelled them.

And then Pedro reached out and grabbed and twisted the spear. Bill's agony was a surreal white heat of disbelief. As Pedro then produced a gleaming knife, out deep in the warm currents a dark and dreadful torpedo shape turned towards them a massive tiger shark. A scavenging, opportunistic, aquatic death machine. Attracted first by the frenzy of the feeding reef fish, the shark had made its inevitable, silent, gliding way from the black depths of the coastal currents toward the atoll. With the tide high, the curious hunter easily passed over the reef toward the excitement. And now, this predator of the depths picked up a bigger prey than the surging reef fish. A more vigorous struggle. The big shark tasted the blood of a mammal. Immediately, the inherent ruthlessness that had seen its breed succeed over the hundreds of thousands of years of evolution clicked into motion. This killer of immense power and fatal beauty accelerated effortlessly with a muscular flick of its tail. The huge, classic dorsal fin now broke the shallow surface as it aimed its streamlined bulk toward the centre of the action. And at that pink-hued epicentre stood Pedro Whetu, ecstatic, even sexually excited. He was transfixed in anticipation of the torture that would precede the slow kill. He had floated his near-comatose enemy up close for best access. Pedro was in no particular hurry. He meant to ensure that Bill was awake as he slowly pushed the razor blade of his knife into the soft, giving skin of the lower belly to disembowel, to empty, him. This was one kill he would savour even more than the others in his cruel past. This one he planned to gut totally, clinically in the buoyant brine and then, before the Judas died, he meant to taste the living heart of his nemesis, even before the dreadful visions faded from Bill's eyes.

As Pedro cut the black cotton top down from the collar with the immaculately sharp blade, the shark reached full attack speed. Pedro saw nothing. Bill was confused he felt the rush of an aquatic express train underneath his body. A surge of displaced mass lifted him up on its wake. At that moment, Bill looked up into the ugly face of his killer. Curiously, he saw his tormentor's leering face suddenly, mightily, shunted sideways. Pedro was lifted up, torso out of the water, and was inexplicably moved away like a morbid synchronised swimmer. He was shunted out of the circle of light thrown down from the trawler and the shark took its screaming victim out exit left, and into the terrifying, lonely dark of the deep water. Pedro cries were heard from the black but faded quickly, with a last, sad, "Mumma," as the shark's back-swept razor teeth tore the man to shreds. And so it was Pedro's and not Bill's guts that spilt milkily into the sea and which the big shark feasted upon in gulping bites.

And finally, the cavalry arrived. The two fast tenders hurtled into the bay, Tommy at one wheel, Darren at the other. They were just in time to witness the final death throes of the shark's victim. It was Tommy who saw Bill in the shallows, pin-pointed by the spear shaft sticking grotesquely upwards. He dived in and held him. He pulled him to shore and wrapped a tourniquet around his thigh to stop the bleeding. Bill remembered nothing more. He had no memory of the RAN warship *Perth* which steamed impressively into the bay an hour later, while the crew from *The Portuguese Princess* sat shivering on the shoreline in withdrawn horror, hands and ankles tied and with Darren's men unnecessarily training shotguns on them. Bill was not aware until later of the navy's careful forensic grid search for the shark victim in the crystal clear waters. Only torn clothing was found. The legs of blue overalls were collected with the gleaming pearls still secure in the pocket. Bill was unaware of his transfer to the sleek grey ship or of the tender, expert care of the trained medical staff on board. He was oblivious to the trip back to Broome, the steel shaft of the spear still jutting from his thigh, packed and strapped to avoid any movement.

He did remember Gypsy waiting at the wharf. He remembered her holding his hand as the ambulance tore through the small town to the regional hospital. But in the chemical fog of morphine, all this was dreamlike. He thought later, but never knew for sure, that he had told her he loved her.

He was, however, clearly aware of one thing as they prepped him for the operation.

It felt great to be alive.

Chapter 42

The Winner Takes it All

She was there when he awoke. Seated beside his bed in the heavy, old woven-rattan hospital chair, her legs tucked up under herself, with that cheeky grin to greet his return from the land of nod.

"Hi, gorgeous," he croaked. He was still groggy, thick-voiced, from the drugs that had allowed the surgeon to cut down to the steel spear deep in his thigh, and then push forcefully on the long shaft until it eased right through his leg and was free.

"Hello, old friend." Gypsy unwound herself and leant forward to kiss him on the cheek.

"Where's my good man, Tommy?" he queried, suddenly recalling all that he had done for him the night before. Just in time Jesus, yes!

She was suddenly serious. "A few things to tell you, young Bill," and she held his hand, making him feel very concerned. "First of all, I have good news and not-so-good news."

"Good news first, please ma'am," he said.

"Well, you are now my tenant. You have the big house to yourself; you finally get to sleep in my bed."

"Huh? Please explain?"

"Ok, my boy, Tommy and I have taken up the lease of a resort down the coast," she said. "It's an opportunity we have been after now for a long time. Tommy's been working on the deal and he's just had the word, while you were bludging on the operating table. It's ours and at our price." She seemed enthusiastic and excited. "It's a retreat for beautiful people. It's for the spiritually aware, the alternative life-stylers my fellow ferals, as you so rudely call them but the wealthy ones. The concept is for an environmentally sensitive holiday retreat; eco-tourism at its best. It's at a beautiful isolated bay. It's a paradise, Bill. I'll run the massage and healing studio and Tommy will run the management side and the accommodation. And he will operate fishing trips and camel trekking. It means that he and I can be together for a change. It's time for us. I have promised my man a baby, Bill. It's time to breed." Gypsy was on a roll, eyes sparkling. "We've sold the pearl lease to the Darren brothers. Tommy and Ben got talking on the way back from Joy's Creek, so after all these years of hard work we finally have our dream."

"Gypsy, that's fantastic for you," he offered with a genuine acceptance of her good fortune. "Shit for me, great for you," he teased. And she laughed at his exaggerated sad face.

"Tommy's waiting outside," she said and giggled again at Bill's bemused expression. "You do know that he sees the feelings between us," she said, and with the first mention of the so-far unspoken, Bill grew more serious himself. "Bill, I can tell you now that I'm going. We are such different people, but I want you to know that if I wasn't with Tommy, then there is a slight possibility that I would hunt you down like vegan after a seaweed sandwich," she laughed. Bill was touched, but also somehow relieved. He leaned out to her, and she half stood from the chair to accept the hug and his "ditto", whispered into her ear. Then, while she was vulnerable, trusting, he attacked. In one scoop, his right arm under her shapely buttocks, the other around her upper back, he flipped her up onto the bed and chewed at her ear, making wild-animal growling and snuffling noises. "Carnivore bastard!" she squealed. And then he dropped her softly back next to the bed as the pain in his leg shocked him white. She smoothed the voluminous, pleated gypsy dress she wore as he writhed quietly on the bed. "Tarzan's an idiot," she giggled.

"Now, my friend, there is one other thing." Bill waited for the hot streak of pain to subside from his thigh. "You must trust me now," she said, standing, holding his hand, and then when Bill nodded, confused by her actions, Gypsy gently let go of his hand and walked across the small hospital room to the door. She opened the door and beckoned to an unseen person in the hallway.

Bill near jumped from the bed in total surprise.

It was Kingi Potiki and the New Zealand Police Commissioner in his tiny hospital room in Broome, Western Australia! "At ease, son," Kingi laughed, moving quickly over to his bed. The two men held each other in an awkward bear hug that had Bill suddenly tearful, immediately homesick, and deeply missing his father, and Mere.

When finally they separated, the Commissioner approached. Bill had always respected him in the brief dealings he had with him after his father's and Mere's death. Bill took his hand in greeting.

"Well, young Peters it's very good to see that you are all in one piece."

At the end of his bed, Gypsy was crying, emotional at the clear strength of the bond and the feeling between the old Maori warrior and his protégé.

"OK," Bill said. "I'm ready what's happening?" A variety of possibilities flicked through his mind. Had Gypsy betrayed him? Had Kingi been brought over to bring his rogue in? Was this it? His days of freedom over?

"Relax, boy," Kingi said, sensitive to Bill's apprehension. "Everything is ok, very much so, in fact. And you have this young lady to thank."

Then the Commissioner spoke at length. He told a tale of sex-drugs-lies-corruption-and-video-tape. It appeared that when Bill's brief but tragic tryst with Mrs Italiano had occurred (Gypsy snorted that detail had been omitted from the story of his life), Inspector Barney Hill, the handcuff wizard, had been the target of a royal commission into police corruption. Italiano had been, up to that point, a respected police commissioner, and was not made aware of the covert inquiry into one of his senior command officers.

318

Italiano had not previously been linked to criminal corruption. Commissioner Italiano was not a target of the inquiry.

The royal commission investigators finally pounced on Hill. He was caught red-handed on yards of grainy video footage in dirty dealings with undercover agents, over many months of painstaking investigative work. Hill had then rolled totally, as corrupt coppers often do, confirming the defect of character that had allowed the corruption in the first place. Hill knew that with his past, a prison sentence would mean death, or at least a constant fear of tough love from tattooed room-mates. He sought desperately to do a deal with the Royal Commissioner. He gave up dozens of colleagues and contacts from both of his worlds, criminal and police. But when he needed more to seal it, Hill gave up the incident that had changed Bill's life those two years before.

With a subsequent early morning raid upon a very surprised NSW Police Commissioner, carried out by federal investigators supported by the Commissioner's own blue-uniformed employees, his fate was finally settled with the evidence of Mrs Italiano. A sad, angry woman, she had waited a long time for the opportunity. And now, Frank Italiano was himself sitting gingerly in a dark cell at Long Bay Prison in Sydney.

The trouble was, no-one knew where Bill Peters was. Hill had sworn that he had escaped and was not suppurating somewhere in a shallow grave. The police liaised desperately with their New Zealand counterparts, but in the end they could do nothing but hope that Bill would resurface somewhere, sometime. Of course, Kingi Potiki was no longer in the high command information loop and no-one thought to ask if he might know where his young protégé may be. But in the meantime, all negative records and alerts for Bill Peters on police files throughout the Commonwealth, as well as Interpol's international records, had been expunged. There were no warrants for his arrest. There was, however, remaining on the various databases, an alert throughout the region that if Peters was located, the New Zealand Police Commissioner's office should be urgently contacted.

And then, after a long anxious wait, out of the blue came a phone call from Broome, Western Australia, to the Commissioner's office in Wellington, New Zealand. The insistent young woman would speak only to the boss himself. Gypsy had believed her friend's tale of his past. She had decided that she must speak to Kingi Potiki and the only way she could envisage finding him was through the Commissioner. With impeccable timing, her call came when all had been revealed in Sydney. The result of her intervention was that Kingi and the boss were now seated in a room of the Broome Regional Hospital as bearers of good news. The Commissioner also had with him a bank draft for the equivalent of Bill's last two year's full pay, as well as a generous ex-gratia offer by the Australian government to cover severance, superannuation and compensation. "If that is what you want, Bill? Because I can also offer you your old job back. Well, not that exact job. But a new position in Police HQ involved in ongoing undercover operations. One thing though," he joked. "With your past history you're not coming anywhere near my wife," and his three visitors laughed at Bill's wincing embarrassment.

No-one in that room was surprised when Bill politely declined the offer of re-employment. "Thanks boss," he said, admiring the numbers on the cheques, "but I think I'll just buy me a boat and go fishing," and he sighed and leant back on the pillow, sore in body but relaxed in spirit for the first time in almost five years.

The Commissioner shook Bill's hand and said goodbye. Kingi saw that Gypsy was restless now, needing to get away, and so he excused himself. "I'll just show the Commissioner to his car," he said. "Back soon, son." But before he went from the room Kingi went to Gypsy. She was red-eyed but radiant, smiling. He took her tiny hands in his paws to her obvious delight, held her gently and looked into her eyes. Before he could speak he was pulled into her natural affinity for the hug, much to his delight. Then he said, "I want to thank you so much for looking after my boy." And again she cried. Kingi smiled and kissed her cheek, and then he finally had to walk away to break her grip on his hands as she instinctively was drawn to the charismatic Maori elder. This was a man who, in past times, would have been a wise and powerful warrior chief of a warrior race.

And then they were alone. The weary warble toot of the old jeep came up from the road, showing that even the gentle Tommy had grown impatient to be away on their next adventure. "We must say our farewells," she spoke softly, "for now." She made him promise that he would visit them at their resort as soon as he could. With emotion he thanked her for what she had done and eventually she turned to leave. "Don't worry, my friend, our paths are intertwined. They are destined to cross and cross again," she promised mysteriously from the door.

"I'll be seeing you tonight, my Gypsy girl. In my dreams," he teased, as she tried to leave, only her head poking through the door.

"You know," she said cheekily, "With all these adventures, maybe you should write the book of the film."

He laughed. "Yeah, maybe I will. But who would I get to play me in the film? Johnny Weissmuller's long dead."

"Tarzan's an idiot," she laughed and was gone.

Bill was alone. Shit, what a day! What a last few hundred days.

And then Kingi was back, and he walked across the room to the small balcony to look out across the lush grounds of the hospital. It was late afternoon and the clouds and thunderheads that had built up throughout the day began the theatre of the tropical afternoon. Startling *craaaacks* resounded through the room, warning of the intense white light that would moments later flash into the room in an awesome display of nature's might across the rain-dark sky. Soon, rolling choruses of thunder *crump-crumped* overhead and then huge, heavy droplets of blood-warm rain cannoned down upon the township.

Bill felt that this was a long-awaited cleansing and wished he were outside, naked in the downpour.

Kingi said, "Well, son, it is done. And it was best, the way he died. I know that you and I would have taken that evil life to pay for the two he took from us. But he was taken by a creature of whatever God does exist. And that was better." Bill was moved by his mentor's words and nodded as Kingi continued. "Son, I am not a religious man, but gifted to me from my ancestors, and from the experiences of my own life, I am a spiritual man. It is my belief that the beast that took the beast was sent." Kingi's deep voice resonated in the room, with the dramatic backdrop of the weather outside. "I believe, Bill, that your father, and my brother, closer to me than a biological brother, was watching over you that night." Bill nodded, almost prepared to accept the idea of his father's influence extending beyond mortality. Then Kingi said, "But now, boy, that part of your life is over never forgotten, but completed. Your father and Mere have now been avenged by your intervention. The circle of fate is now complete. Both you, and also I, must now move on."

Bill shuddered with a flush of emotion at his words. And in that moment, with the lightning cracking and joined by thunder and slashing rain, Bill finally recognised what the old man was saying. He felt the completion, a renewing spirit, and a forgotten, joyful anticipation of times to come, of new freedoms, new journeys, and he stood awkwardly to embrace his old friend in farewell.

About the author

Born an army brat in New Zealand, Peter "Magnum" Williams now lives in Perth, Western Australia, from where he creates his rollicking crime adventure series following the life of his fictional son Bill Peters.

All authors talk the talk, but Magnum, as he is known by his Nedlands Rugby mates, has also walked the walk. He has been a pig, a demon, a screw and a private dick.

Magnum joined the NZ police force at 18, and was a police officer and a detective on the busy streets of South Auckland for ten years. He has since worked as a private investigator, except for a few years when he went to prison (as an officer!), when he had to get real job for a while. He has seen it, experienced it, tasted it — and now he writes about it.

Part proceeds donated to the battle against youth suicide.